Loans are up to 28 days. Fines are charged if items are not returned by the due date. Items can be renewed at the Library, via the internet or by telephone up to 3 times. Items in demand will not be renewed.
Please use a bookmark

Date for return		

Check out our online catalogue to see what's in stock, or to renew or reserve books.

www.birmingham.gov.uk/libcat

www.birmingham.bov.uk/libraries

Q45612r1

PENGUIN BOOKS

The Dead Room

Chris Mooney is the author of five previous thrillers, of which Remembering Sarah was nominated for the prestigious Edgar Award for Best Novel. The Missing and The Dead Room, the first two outings for CSI Darby McCormick, are both available as Penguin paperbacks. Chris lives in Boston with his wife and son.

The Dead Room

CHRIS MOONEY

Set in 11.25/14 pt Monotype Garamond
Typeset by Jouve (UK), Milton Keynes, Buckinghamshire
Printed in Great Britain by Clays Ltd, St Ives plc

A CIP catalogue record for this book is available from the British Library

PENGUIN BOOKS

PENGUIN BOOKS

Published by the Penguin Group
Penguin Books Ltd, 80 Strand, London WC2R ORL, England
Penguin Group (USA) Inc., 375 Hudson Street, New York, New York 10014, USA
Penguin Group (Canada), 90 Eglinton Avenue East, Suite 700, Toronto, Ontario, Canada MP4 2Y3
(a division of Pearson Penguin Canada Inc.)
Penguin Ireland, 25 St Stephen's Green, Dublin 2, Ireland (a division of Penguin Books Ltd)
Penguin Group (Australia), 250 Camberwell Road,
Camberwell, Victoria 3124, Australia (a division of Pearson Australia Group Pty Ltd)
Penguin Books India Pvt Ltd, 11 Community Centre,
Panchsheel Park, New Delhi – 110 017, India
Penguin Group (NZ), 67 Apollo Drive, Rosedale, North Shore 0632, New Zealand
(a division of Pearson New Zealand Ltd)
Penguin Books (South Africa) (Pty) Ltd, 24 Sturdee Avenue,
Rosebank, Johannesburg 2196, South Africa

Penguin Books Ltd, Registered Offices: 80 Strand, London WC2R ORL, England

www.penguin.com

First published 2009
2

Copyright © Chris Mooney, 2009

ISBN: 978-0-141-03987-9

www.greenpenguin.co.uk

For John Connolly and Gregg Hurwitz

Day 1

I

Darby McCormick stepped over the dead bodyguard as she ejected the two empty thirty-round magazine cartridges from her Heckler & Koch sub-machine gun. By the time the cartridges hit the floor she had loaded two fresh clips.

Sweat running down her face and back, she moved to the side of a door and tried listening for movement underneath the low and steady *thump-thump-thump* of the helicopter blades coming from the roof.

She couldn't hear anything but knew Chris Flynn would be heading this way any moment. Downstairs in the main bay, crouched behind a stack of wooden crates as Flynn's two bodyguards fired rounds from their automatic weapons, she had caught sight of Flynn rushing up the set of stairs just before her SWAT partner had cut the power to the warehouse. She ran up the opposite rickety balcony stairs to the first floor to intercept Flynn before he could make his way to the stairwell, his only means of escape.

Darby felt confident he hadn't reached it yet. She swung around the corner, looking down her weapon sight at the long hallway lit by dim light bleeding

3

through the windows. Still too dark. She flipped the night-vision goggles down across her eyes.

The darkness inside the warehouse room disappeared in a green ambient glow of light. She moved down the corridor, making her way to the stairwell.

A door slammed open and then she saw Flynn standing behind a frightened woman with his forearm wrapped around her throat, the muzzle of a Glock digging against the side of her head. A single eye peeked above the woman's shoulder. No single body part was exposed.

Shit. No way to get off a clean shot. She didn't want to kill him, just wound him before he could reach the copter. Her orders were explicit: capture Flynn alive. Dead, he was worthless.

'*I know what you assholes want me to do,*' Flynn screamed, his voice echoing through the stifling hot air. '*I'm not going to say shit.*'

Darby inched her way down the hall. 'I'm here to protect you, Mr Flynn. The cartel –'

'*Stop right there and drop your weapon.*'

Darby stopped but didn't lower her weapon. 'The cartel will kill you, Chris. You know too much. They can't afford to keep you alive. We can offer you protection in exchange for –'

'*I'm not playing around here. Drop your weapon right now or I swear to Christ I'll kill her.*'

Darby had no doubt the 38-year-old American

banker would do it. He had strangled his girlfriend of twelve years to death when he found out she had talked to the Boston police about Flynn using his cheque-cashing company to launder nearly half a billion dollars in cocaine profits for the Mendula family, a Columbian drug cartel.

Flynn lurched forward, using the woman's body as a shield. The woman stumbled, the heels of her shoes scraping across the floor as she clutched Flynn's arm. Her long black hair covered most of her face. She wasn't dressed like any of the warehouse employees. She wore rhinestone T-strap pumps and a white business suit professionally tailored for her tall, curvy frame.

SWAT can track the copter, Darby thought. *They might be able to move people into place by the time it touches down.*

'Please do what he say,' the woman cried in broken English. 'Two babies at home. I want to go home and see babies.'

Darby spoke in a loud, clear voice. 'Okay, Chris, you're in charge. I'm backing away from the stairs.'

'Now drop the gun.'

Darby still hesitated.

'Let the hostage go and you have my word.'

The woman yelped, a harsh, choking sound.

'*I'll do it, I swear to Christ –*'

'Okay, Chris.' Darby lowered her weapon, then released the clip for the shoulder strap.

Flynn inched towards the stairs. The FLIR night

vision provided excellent clarity and contrast. She could make out the tiny, worm-like scars on Flynn's bald head, could see the woman's diamond rings and the intricate details of her bracelet.

Darby dropped the HK and kicked it down the corridor to her right. If Flynn decided to fire, she might be able to duck down there. She wore a bullet-proof vest underneath the camouflage, metal armour plates on her shins and legs. *You better hope he doesn't try for a headshot.*

'Your turn,' Darby said.

'I still don't trust you.' Flynn stepped closer. 'Get on your knees – and no sudden movements.'

'I'll do whatever you want as long as you promise not to harm the hostage.'

'Then *do* it, nice and slow. You pull any shit and I'll kill her, understand?'

'I understand.' Darby knelt and slowly moved her hands up by her face.

'Stay right there,' Flynn said. 'Stay right where you are and I'll let her go.'

Flynn stopped near the bottom steps of the stair-well. The corridor's hot, musty odour mixed with the unmistakable scent of the woman's Chanel No. 5.

He released the hostage. Darby heard the woman run up the steps, tripping in her ridiculous shoes.

Flynn didn't follow. He stepped forward, his hand-gun raised.

Fear flooded her body, turning her skin slick and

cold. Darby didn't see her life flash before her eyes and all that bullshit; she did what she'd been trained to do.

She jerked her head to the side as Flynn fired. The shot hit the wall. Her hands came up lightning quick. One hand clutched his wrist, the other wrapped itself around the Glock's muzzle and twisted it back so that it pointed at his stomach.

She yanked him towards her. Flynn stumbled, caught by surprise. He couldn't gain his footing.

Darby pulled the nine from his grasp. She turned it around in her hands and shot him in the thigh.

Flynn fell to the floor, screaming. She spun the nine to the hostage standing on the stairwell landing. The woman was holding a sub-compact Beretta pistol with a laser sight.

Darby fired twice, hitting the woman in the stomach. The woman stumbled back against the wall and Darby fired two more shots.

Flynn was scrambling across the floor. Darby threw him down on his stomach, dug her knee into his spine and yanked his arms behind his back. She grabbed a pair of Flexicuffs from her tactical belt as the lights came back on.

Darby flipped up her night-vision goggles, blinking sweat away from her eyes.

'God*damn*,' the hostage said, staring at the dark red splotches on her white suit jacket. 'These paintballs really do sting.'

The man playing Chris Flynn groaned. 'Quit your bitching, Tina. I've been killed three times over the past two days.' He rolled on to his back. 'Christ, McCormick, I think you bruised my spine.'

A fireplug of a man with a brown crew cut and a worn sun-blasted face stepped into the hall – John Haug, the SWAT instructor for the Boston Police Department. He snapped his fingers and pointed to the doorway.

'McCormick, with me.'

Darby trailed a few inches behind Haug, as the adrenalin rush of the training exercise – the first part of her final SWAT exam – started to evaporate and give way to a bone-crushing exhaustion. For the past three days she had grabbed fistfuls of sleep while conducting round-the-clock surveillance on the warehouse.

The first week of her SWAT training, she had started each morning with a ten-mile run under a blistering August sun on Moon Island. There were eight other recruits. All men. For the rest of the morning she carried out close-quarter combat exercises and firearms training. Late afternoons were spent crawling through old sewer tunnels wearing blacked-out goggles to test the limits of her claustrophobia. She completed night-time diving exercises in Boston Harbor and abseiled from a Black Hawk helicopter. One recruit broke his foot. Two other men suffered physical injuries and dropped out. The five remaining members graduated to 'The Yellow Brick Road', a punishing gauntlet designed to crush the human body.

Dressed in a military flak jacket and combat boots, wearing a backpack loaded with thirty pounds of sand

and with an assault rifle strapped across her chest or held above her head, she ran in the sweltering heat until her legs buckled. She picked herself up and ran some more. She crawled through mud. Climbed ropes and nets and scaffolding. She trod water dressed in her SWAT clothing and tactical gear. When she removed herself from the stream, the sand-filled backpack now twice as heavy from the water, she ran until she collapsed. When the fun ended, she was treated to a boxed lunch – two bottles of water, bread and an apple – and ate it along the way to the firing range, where she shot at targets until the muscles in her forearms cramped. The training ended at 10 p.m. After a quick shower, she slumped into her cot at the all-male bunker and woke at 4 a.m. to start the process all over again.

The second phase of training, Darby knew, was also designed to break one's mental spirit. Without proper sleep, the body couldn't heal. The physical toll tore down the mind's protective walls and lead to frustration, anger and, in some cases, dementia. Two more men dropped out. They couldn't hack it. The final three made it to the live training exercise.

Haug walked quickly down the final set of stairs. Her SWAT partner lay on his back smoking a cigar, his chest and one shoulder covered with blood-red paint. He saw her and waved. The members of Haug's SWAT team who had been brought in to play the roles of Chris Flynn's bodyguards smoked cigarettes and cigars and talked among the crates and shelves. They didn't look at Haug; they were looking at her. She felt their glares drilling into her skin.

They're pissed I killed them. She grinned.

Haug stepped into the car park. Sweat had soaked through his grey T-shirt. He fitted a thick wad of chewing tobacco in the pocket of his cheek. As usual, it was impossible to read his face. The man lived behind an emotionless mask carefully crafted from his years as a marine.

He walked briskly around the side of the warehouse, his tactical boots crunching against the gravel. The hot air throbbed with crickets.

'The woman you killed,' he said after a long moment. He looked straight ahead into the darkness surrounding the woods. 'What made you think she wasn't an actual hostage? What tipped you off?'

Darby had anticipated the question. 'I wondered what a well-dressed woman would be doing working at the warehouse at such a late hour.'

'You didn't think she was the owner? During the planning sessions, I told you the owner's wife saw to the day-to-day operations of the warehouse and often worked late hours.'

'You also said that Ortiz was a frugal son of a bitch.'

'Your point?'

'That woman was wearing a Cartier love bracelet.'

Haug's head whipped around, eyes wide and brow furrowed. 'You recognized her goddamn *bracelet*?'

'And her Christian Louboutin pumps,' Darby said. 'Those shoes cost about eight hundred bucks. The bracelet, around three grand. I don't know about the suit she was wearing but it looked expensive. What is it? Gucci? Armani?'

'I strike you as a guy who knows shit about clothes?'

'The way you dress? No, sir.'

Haug jogged up the road leading to the restricted site for bomb disposal.

'The intel you gave on the cartel didn't state whether the ringleader was a man or a woman,' Darby said. 'After Flynn released her, she didn't run into another room. She didn't scream for help. She ran up the stairs leading to the roof – same destination as Flynn. I thought that was odd, so, after I shot Flynn, I turned to the stairs and there she was holding a Beretta. I take it she was the head of the cartel.'

'She was.'

'So the plan was for her to play the hostage role and, once Flynn released her, if he hadn't killed me then she would when I went to cuff Flynn.'

'That was the plan.'

'How many of the recruits got shot?'

'You're the only one who pulled it off.'

'That's what happens when you send in a woman to do a man's job.'

Haug spat a dark blob of tobacco juice and turned left on to a new road.

In the distance Darby saw the small ranch building

where she had lived for the past two weeks. She could see the glowing lights coming from the locker room and bunker.

'Why are we heading there?'

'Some guy is here to escort you back to the city on the orders of the police commissioner,' Haug said. 'Don't ask; I don't know the details.'

Darby had an idea. She was the head of Boston Police Commissioner Chadzynski's Crime Scene Unit, a specialized group comprised of the department's top investigators and forensic specialists. CSU was assigned to violent crimes and missing persons.

Haug spat again. 'I know you fought like hell to earn a spot on this programme. Your shooting skills qualified you – you're the best in the group, no question. And I'll admit to having a lot of reservations about accepting you. In my experience women don't have what it takes to be SWAT officers.'

'Glad I proved you wrong.'

'You're the second woman I've ever trained. The first broad was a world-class cunt.'

Haug didn't look to see if he'd insulted her. He didn't care if he had. The man spoke his mind and didn't give two shits whom he offended. She found his attitude refreshing.

'This broad demanded her own locker room,' Haug said. 'Kept bitching about the workouts, that she wasn't as strong as a man and didn't have the same endurance and stamina. All that happy horse-shit. The truth was she couldn't hack it. That didn't stop her from trying to file a discrimination lawsuit, which the court rightfully shoved up her ass.

'You, on the other hand, didn't request anything special. You slept, ate, showered and dressed with the boys. You worked out the logistics on your own. You didn't burden me with whatever feminine problems you had, and on top of that you survived pretty much everything I threw at you. And not once did you bitch or buckle. You kept your yap shut and your ears open. You worked your ass off.'

Haug spat again. 'Heard you're a doctor. Got a degree from Harvard in criminal psychology.'

Darby nodded.

'Never had a doctor – or a forensics fellow, for that matter – do what you did back there. They teach you to shoot like that at Harvard?'

'I've put in a lot of practice at the firing range.'

'It shows. You took down all of the bodyguards, you prevented Flynn from reaching the chopper and the way you took him down was pretty goddamn impressive. You remember what I told you about fir-ing your weapon?'

'Every bullet has a lawyer's name on it.'

'Right. Now if what happened here tonight had been an actual hostage situation, you'd breeze right through Internal Affairs like shit through a goose, but that doesn't mean some lawyer won't come after you. Lawyers don't give a crap about what's right, or that you risked your life. When blood is spilled there's money, and these lawyers will crawl up your ass and hibernate there until they've leeched every last penny. You're quick on the trigger, so you best keep that fact forefront in that thick Irish head of yours, understand?'

'Understood.'

Haug held open the door to the front office. 'You can watch my back any day of the week, McCormick.'

3

Darby dropped off her field gear and weapons at the vacant front desk and walked rubber-legged into the locker room.

Her lab partner, Jackson Cooper, sat on one of the benches bolted to the floor between rows of steel-grey lockers. The hard, knotted muscles in his back and shoulders moved underneath the dark blue fabric of his short-sleeved polo shirt as he thumbed through a wrinkled issue of *Playboy*.

'You always hang out in men's locker rooms?' Darby asked, unbuttoning her flak jacket.

Coop didn't look up from the magazine. 'Your instructor, GI Joe, told me to wait here. Fortunately I found this on the floor to keep me entertained. Did you drop it?'

'What's going on?'

'Some sort of home invasion in your old home-town, Belham. Marshall Street. Woman and a teenage boy tied up to kitchen chairs. Woman's dead, kid's at the hospital.'

'What are their names?'

'Amy Hallcox. I don't know the boy's name.'

Darby didn't know the family but she had grown

up less than two miles away from Marshall Street. She remembered the neighbourhood as an area of big old New England-style Colonial homes with ample land and wooded backdrops with trails leading to Salmon Brook Pond. Doctors and lawyers had once lived there. It was – at least when she was growing up – considered one of Belham's safer places to live.

Darby sat on a bench and began unlacing her boots. 'Who's the lead?'

'Guy named Pine.'

'Artie Pine?'

'That's the man in charge.' Coop looked up and stared at her, one eye blue, the other a deep green. 'How do you know him?'

'Artie started off as a patrolman along with my father. Then he became a detective and was shipped off to . . . Boston, I think.'

'Christ, you stink.'

'I've been living outside in this heat for three days.'

'Most women I know spend their vacation relaxing on a beach – take Samantha, for example.'

Darby tossed her boots into the locker. 'Who's Samantha?'

'Samantha James, Miss September.' He held up the centrefold. 'After spending her day rescuing puppies and kittens from kill shelters in her hometown of San Diego, she unwinds at the beach with a beer and a good book. I bet she enjoys reading the fine literary novels of Jane Austen.'

Darby laughed. 'How do you know about Jane Austen?'

'This woman I'm dating, Cheryl? She's really into Jane Austen.'

'Every woman is.'

'No, I mean she's *really* into it. We do a little, ah, role-playing, and she makes me dress up in a suit and pretend to be this Darcy guy from that awful *Pride and Prejudice* movie.'

Darby smiled, thinking about Colin Firth as Mr Darcy.

'You've got that same dreamy look Cheryl gets,' Coop said. 'What am I missing?'

'You wouldn't understand. Go back to your picture book.'

Darby stood and tossed her balled-up socks into the hamper.

'Nice shot. How are things going with the yuppie investment banker?'

'Tim and I are no longer seeing each other,' she said, working the wet T-shirt over her head.

'And why is that?'

'Typical excuses. I'm really into my career. I'm not ready to commit. I'm –'

'Gay.'

'It's just as well.'

'That you found out he's gay?'

'He's not gay, you dink. Tim's a nice guy, but we really didn't click. Check this out.' Darby grabbed her belt buckle with one hand and removed a compact knife. 'There's also a razor wire, compartments to hide things and —'

'I can't wait until you get married. Your wedding list's going to be *real* interesting.'

'No need to buy this. I get to take the belt home with me.'

'Congratulations,' Coop said, his gaze dropping back down to the magazine.

Darby slid out of her trousers and stood in front of him dressed in a black jogging bra and a pair of training shorts. She didn't feel self-conscious. Coop had seen her plenty of times dressed like this. They worked out together at the gym and often went running through the Public Garden after work.

And for the past two weeks she had refused to use the women's locker room. She'd dressed here, in this quiet corner, while men stood in the other aisles. They sat and walked naked to the showers. These alpha men had barely given her a glance or nod. Any sexual energy they'd had at the start had quickly been channelled into surviving 'The Yellow Brick Road' and whatever other physical tortures Haug threw at them.

She slung a clean towel over her shoulder and carried the ball of sweaty clothes over to the hamper near the sink. She undid the rubber band holding her hair together and caught her reflection in the mirror. Her gaze shifted to a thin but hard white scar peeking out from the greasepaint above her fake cheekbone.

The implant had replaced the bone shattered by Traveler's axe.

Darby wet the towel and began to scrub the grease-paint from her face. Coop stared at her. Their eyes locked in the mirror.

'Nice six pack,' he said.

Darby looked at the sink, felt her throat close up. Not from the compliment but from this awkward feeling she'd been experiencing lately – the way Coop's voice hung inside her chest at the end of the day. Sometimes she caught herself thinking about him when she was alone in her condo. Coop was the closest thing she had to family – the only thing, really, since her mother had died. Darby wondered if this newfound feeling she had for him had something to do with the fact he was being headhunted for a new job. Coop had been approached by a London forensics company that was making new technological advances with fingerprints – his area of expertise.

'What's the latest from London?' she asked.

'They increased their offer.'

'Are you going to accept?'

'Say it.'

'Say what?'

'Say you'll miss me.'

'Everyone will miss you.'

'You especially, though. I'll leave and you'll lock yourself inside that fancy Beacon Hill condo of yours and listen to John Mayer while drowning your sorrows in Irish whiskey.'

'Don't every say that again.'

'That you're going to miss me?'

'No, that I listen to John Mayer.' Darby grabbed a clean towel from her locker. 'I need to take a quick shower. Give me five minutes.'

'Take your time, Dirty Harry.'

4

Darby wanted to get a handle on the crime scene before she reached Belham. She called Artie Pine half a dozen times while driving out of Boston and each time she got his voicemail. On the last call she left a message.

WBZ, Boston's twenty-four-hour all-news radio station, had the 'breaking story'. The twenty-second pre-recorded audio spot, courtesy of an on-scene reporter, offered up only vague details: 'A Belham woman and her son were victims in what police are calling a botched home invasion. The woman was pronounced dead at the scene, and the son is listed in critical condition at a Boston hospital. Belham police won't release the names of the victims, but a source close to the investigation called it "grisly and horrific, the worst I've ever seen".'

The story ended and switched to the local weather report. More rain and more oppressive humidity. People were running their air-conditioners day and night, putting a drain on the state's electric grid. A spokesman told people to expect more blackouts.

Half an hour later Darby pulled the crime scene vehicle, a navy-blue Ford Explorer, on to Marshall Street. Residents crowded the pavements around the cul-de-sac, flashing blue and white lights flickering on their faces as they stared across the roofs of three cruisers parked at the end of a driveway leading up to a massive white Colonial home with a wraparound farmer's porch and an attached three-car garage. Only the middle door was open.

An antique-style lantern light was mounted on each side of the home's front door. The same lights had been installed on the garage. A wooden fence at least seven feet high separated the driveway and a basketball court from the backyard.

The driveway had been taped off. Darby parked against the kerb, got out and lifted her kit out of the back. All the shades had been drawn on windows facing the street.

Coop moved across the trimmed front lawn, lugging his kit. Michael Banville from the Photography Unit, a big bear of a man who had a permanent case of five o'clock shadow, stood on the porch near the front door, dressed head to toe in a heavy-duty white Tyvek coverall.

Darby turned on her flashlight and made her way to the edge of the lawn to examine the driveway. Bloody footprints gleamed in the bright beam of light. She placed evidence cones next to one.

'Don't bother,' Banville called from the porch. 'The EMTs left them on the driveway, the walkway and the front steps.'

Must be a hell of a lot of blood in there, Darby thought.

She placed her kit on the grass and, watching where she stepped, made her way to the garage.

No cars inside, just mountain bikes and a John Deere ride-on mower. Dark stains on the floor. *Motor oil*, she thought, until she moved the beam of her light and saw bloody footprints. A single set made by a narrow shoe – a sneaker or running shoe, judging by the shape of the tread marks.

In the back of the garage she found blood smeared against a set of wooden steps leading up to a door.

'When the queen shows up,' a man said from behind the fence, 'are we supposed to bow down and kiss her ass?'

'When you get a good look at her you'll want to do more than kiss her ass,' a different male voice replied. 'You'll want to bury your face between her thighs and not come up for air. You ever see her up close?'

'I've seen her on the news a few times,' the first man said. 'Looks like that English actress that always makes my pecker stand up at full attention and bark – the one from those *Underworld* movies, Christ, what's her name?'

'Kate Beckinsale.'

A snap of fingers. 'That's the one,' the first man said. 'The McCormick broad is the spitting image of her but has that nice dark red hair. Wouldn't mind running my fingers through *that* while she's on her knees giving me a blow-e.'

Laughter all around.

Darby shrugged off the comments. She had learned early on that a good majority of men viewed women as nothing more than sexual objects – receptacles solely designed to satisfy a biological urge and nothing more. *Pump em and dump em* was the phrase she'd overheard around the station, when her male counterparts thought she was safely out of earshot.

'Listen up, boyos.'

Artie Pine's voice sounding older, deeper and raspy – a voice ragged from too many cigars, too many late nights and booze. Hearing it brought her back to the long Saturday afternoon barbecues her father had thrown every other weekend right up until he was shot a few months shy of her thirteenth birthday. Pine, a big bowling ball with feet, would sit in a lawn chair and smoke what her father called 'fives-and-tens' – cheap dime-store cigars rolled into thin wrappers the size of a pencil, the odour so bitter and pungent it scared away the mosquitoes after the sun went down. Pine would sit in the chair all day, smoking and drinking and telling stories to an audience that always ended with wild eruptions of knee-slapping laughter. He'd ask kids to fetch him another beer from the cooler and always gave them a folded dollar bill.

'That's Big Red's little girl you're talking about,' Pine said. 'When she gets here, make sure you show her the proper respect.'

Darby shut off the flashlight. She made her way back to the front and saw bright camera lights from far across the street. Belham police had corralled the small media crowd behind sawhorses.

Coop stood on the porch talking to Banville. Darby examined the bloody footwear impressions on the blue-stone walkway. Two different sets of footprints. They matched the ones on the driveway.

She joined them and said, 'The footprints on the walkway and driveway are different from the single set I found inside the garage.'

'I'll get to work on it,' Banville said, picking up his camera equipment. 'I've already photographed the foyer and kitchen. Before you two head in, you're going to need to change into one of these fabulous bunny suits.'

'Awesome,' Coop said. 'It's not like I'm sweating my balls off already.'

'One other thing,' Banville said. 'The front windows facing the street? The shades and blinds were drawn when I got here. The windows facing the back-yard, and the sliding glass door in the living room – none of those shades were drawn. That's what we call a clue, Coop.'

'Good to know.'

Darby grabbed the suits from the hatchback. They slipped into them while flashbulbs popped over her shoulder. She put on a pair of clear glasses, walked back up the lawn and eased open the front door.

The foyer looked as if it had been hit by an earth-quake. All the pictures had been removed from the walls and smashed. An old wooden secretarial desk lay on its side, its drawers pulled out. Papers, family pictures and shards of glass covered nearly every inch of the tiled floor. Bloody footprints stretched across the foyer and back into the kitchen. Broken plates and glasses covered the brown-granite worktops. The cupboards – at least the ones she could see – had been opened, each shelf emptied.

Darby looked at Coop. 'Did Pine tell you about this?'

Coop shook his head. 'If he had, I would've called the Wonder Twins and asked them to meet us here. We can't process this by ourselves – not unless we want to be working around the clock for the next week.'

Darby unzipped her suit, took out her phone and dialled the Operations Department in order to request the services of Mark Alves and Randy Scott. The dining room, she saw, was right off the foyer. What looked like a china cabinet and sideboard had been overturned. All the drawers had been pulled out, the contents dumped on an oriental rug covered with shattered glass.

'Let's go through the dining room,' she said after hanging up. 'Looks like the easiest route.'

Carefully navigating her way through the dining room, she smelled cordite and, lurking underneath it, blood – a strong, coppery odour that always made her eyes water.

An archway led into the kitchen; to her left was the living room, where she went first. A flat-screen TV and console had been thrown against the floor. Muddy footprints on the beige carpet led away from a sliding glass door of shattered glass. She spotted a few of the same muddy prints on a redwood-stained deck and wondered if one of the responding officers had left them.

When she reached the archway, she turned the corner.

Darby saw the woman's fingers first. The ones still attached had been broken backwards and were now splayed at odd angles. Thick duct tape bound the woman's wrists and forearms to the armrests of a kitchen chair. More tape, strips and strips of it, had pinned her ankles against the chair legs. Her throat had been slashed from ear to ear, the cut so deep it had nearly decapitated her. Her eyes were taped shut and her severed fingers – three of them – had been stuffed inside her mouth.

'Jesus,' Coop said behind her.

Darby broke out in a cold sweat despite the A/C. Pools of blood had collected underneath the chair and stretched like fingers across the white tiles. A second chair covered with cut strips of duct tape lay sideways. One of the cut strips fluttered from the cold air rushing through a vent.

Bloody footprints covered the floor. Two bright red trails of blood stretched across the floor and down the hall leading to the door for the garage. A black handbag lay on its side, its contents scattered across the tiles.

Every inch of the long, wide kitchen had been ransacked. Every drawer had been pulled out. The refrigerator door hung open; the shelves had been wiped clean. The oven and dishwasher doors were open; the grills had been pulled out. The kitchen island had been unbolted and overturned. The bloody footwear impressions in the hall led back and forth. Someone had made several trips between the garage and kitchen.

Coop swiped the back of his arm across his forehead, his face as white as a sheet.

'Go outside and get some air,' Darby said, making her way to the living room. 'I'll go talk to Pine.'

Darby's gaze swept across the bare white walls covered with an arterial spray of blood. She forced her attention back to the chairs and wondered if they had been arranged so that the woman faced her son.

5

The living room had a high cathedral ceiling and two spinning fans. Someone had taken a knife to the black leather sectional sofa and two matching armchairs. The cut fabric had been pulled aside, exposing springs and wood. Each cushion had been gutted. White cotton filling and foam covered the overturned furniture and smashed pictures in a fine blanket, like snow.

Drops of blood on the beige carpet. Drip lines and smears on the shards of glass shaped like shark's teeth sticking out from the bottom and sides of the door that led to the redwood-stained deck.

Darby found the switch for the backyard lights.

She looked again at the muddy footprints that lined the redwood-stained deck and stairs. The handrail to her right had a bloody smear running down it as though someone had gripped it.

Darby pulled the handle of the sliding door. Locked. She found a security bar placed along the bottom railing to prevent intrusion. The only way to get through the door was to break the glass.

There was plenty of glass on the carpet but very little on the deck. She looked at the other side of the living room. On the bare white walls, two holes in the plaster – the kind left by bullets.

Someone had stood on the deck and fired at the door; that explained the glass blowback on the carpet. Then the shooter had moved inside the house and . . . what? Tied up the victims? No. Someone had reported hearing gunshots. A single shooter couldn't have fired, moved inside, subdued two victims and tortured the woman. Too much time.

For the next twenty minutes Darby searched the living room for a spent shell casing. She didn't find one. She checked the kitchen floor. No luck. Had the shooter taken the time to pick up the brass?

She removed the security bar, unlocked the sliding glass door and stepped on to the deck. The shades on the back windows hadn't been drawn. No reason to, as there were no homes back here, just a big backyard with an in-ground pool and shed and, beyond the fence, the woods leading to Salmon Brook Pond.

Pine stood with two patrolmen near the fence separating the backyard from the driveway. He seemed taller than she remembered, but his body still carried that odd mixture of fat and muscle, like a football player who'd gone to seed. Bald on top now, the remaining black hair on the sides shaved close to the scalp.

They all had phones pressed up against their ears. Pine didn't see her. The tall, pale patrolman with the crew cut did. He stared at her while she searched the deck.

Darby made her way down the steps, sticking close to the clean railing on her left, away from the blood and muddy footwear impressions, pausing to drop evidence markers. When she reached the backyard, she turned the corner and ran the beam of her flashlight on the crushed rock underneath the deck.

A wink of metal in the light. She ducked underneath the deck and saw an evidence cone next to an expended round; Banville had already photographed it. Using a pen, she picked up the shell casing. The words '44 REM MAG' were stamped on the round metal 'spark plug'.

.44 Remington Magnum ammo. A single shot could put down a bear.

Darby eased the casing back on the crushed rocks and searched the area around the deck. She didn't find any other casings.

She moved back to the steps and ran the beam of her flashlight across grass yellowed by the sun, bald patches full of muddy rainwater.

There, fifteen feet away from the stairs – blood on blades of grass.

Out of the corner of her eye she saw Pine and the two patrolmen heading her way.

'Boyos,' Pine said. 'Let me introduce you to –'

'Stay where you are,' Darby said. She dropped an evidence marker and continued her search, thinking back to the drag marks in the kitchen hallway. Two straight parallel lines, the kind made by dragging a body. A bloody smear leading down the garage steps and across the garage floor and then no more blood. Had a body been hauled inside a vehicle?

The teenager had been transported to the hospital and the mother was inside the house. Was there a third victim?

The blood drops on the grass stopped at a gate. It was unlocked. She eased it open, found a bloody handprint on the wood.

Inside the woods, footwear impressions moving up a steep incline blanketed with dead leaves and pine needles.

'Put on a pair of furry ears and you'd look like the Easter Bunny,' Pine said.

She turned and saw him standing just a few feet away, the underarms of his white shirt dark with sweat. He reeked of cigar smoke.

'It's been, what, three years since I last saw you?'

'My mother's funeral,' Darby said. 'What's going on with the teenager? I heard he's at a hospital.'

'Physically he's fine. He's in some sort of shock. One of the ER docs tried to give him a sedative and he freaked. We're giving him some space to calm down. I've got people guarding his room at St Joe's, so there'll be someone there when he's ready to talk.'

St Joseph's was Belham's main hospital. 'The news said he was at Mass. General.'

Pine's hound-dog eyes twinkled with delight. 'Yeah,

that's what I told the press. Figured we'd get the vultures to head to Boston. Most of them did. Some of them, as I'm sure you saw on your way in, are still camped out front.'

Nice move, Artie. 'What's the kid's name?'

'John Hallcox. Mother's name is Amy Hallcox – we found her Vermont licence in the handbag. Neighbours say she and her kid came here about a week or so ago. They don't know his name. They pretty much kept to themselves. Some of the neighbours saw them flitting about the house but mostly they stayed inside. Woman drove a red Honda Accord. Got the plate number all over the radios but so far nobody's seen a damn thing. You see the drag marks in the kitchen hall?'

Darby nodded.

'My guess is someone dragged a body and drove away,' Pine said. 'As far as we can tell, it was only the woman and her kid. We don't know anything about this third person.

'House belongs to an elderly couple named Martin and Elaine Wexler. Guy's a retired doctor. Must've done well 'cause he's vacationing somewhere in the South of France, from what we're told. We're trying to pin their location down.'

Darby shut off her flashlight. 'Why didn't you tell operations about the amount of damage in there? I could've had more people working here before I arrived.'

'I didn't make the call. I know who did – don't

34

worry, I'll tear him a new one. Sorry I couldn't talk when you called. It's been a madhouse here.'

Darby felt the heat of the night and her exhaustion move through her and press against the back of her skull. She didn't want to waste what energy she had left arguing.

'As you can see, I checked the woods.' Pine pointed to the mud caked on his shoes and trouser cuffs. 'No need to go back there. I followed the footprints – don't worry, I didn't disturb a thing – I followed them all the way to Blakely Road. That's where they ended. Whoever ran back there is long gone.'

Darby wondered if a vehicle had been parked on the dirt shoulder of the road. She made a mental note to check for tyre tracks.

'I take it you've been inside the house.'

'Oh yes,' Pine said. 'I won't be forgetting what I saw in there for a while.'

'Who else has been in there besides you?'

'Just the first responding officers, Quigley and Peters. That would be them standing over there in the corner. I kept them here in case you had any questions.'

'Did they search the entire house?'

'That's their job.'

She knew that but didn't like it. Imagined some key piece of evidence stuck to the bottom of a boot and then lost somewhere outside now, gone. 'Did they track mud up the deck steps?'

'Let's go ask them.'

'I'll be right there.' Darby clicked on her flashlight and turned back to the gate. She could hear Pine grunting as he waddled away.

She stepped into the woods and found two compost piles of dead grass clippings a few feet from the back fence. Mosquitoes whined against her ears and danced in the beam of her flashlight.

Moving up the incline, she thought about how much she hated these woods. Five years ago she had discovered a buried set of female remains – another victim of Daniel Boyle and . . . the other one, Boyle's mentor and killing partner, Traveler. A lot of their victims – the missing women, men and children, her childhood friend Melanie Cruz – had never been found, buried somewhere out here –

Darby stopped walking, and listened to the sound of a mobile phone ringing somewhere in the darkness ahead.

6

Darby ran up the incline, boots sinking deep into the wet ground, the beam of her flashlight zigzagging through the darkness. She reached the top quickly and without much effort.

The ground levelled off to a bumpy, uneven area of half-buried boulders and downed tree limbs and branches. The phone rang again, a soft, pleasant sound that reminded her of wind chimes. It came from somewhere straight ahead. She moved quickly, ducking underneath limbs, dried branches crunching and snapping underneath her boots.

A third ring, very close.

There, a small square of light glowing in the darkness about thirty or so feet ahead. She moved her flashlight to it. A BlackBerry, judging by its size and shape. She reached into her back pocket for an evidence bag.

Branches snapped in the darkness somewhere ahead of her. She swung her flashlight to the sound, the beam whisking past trees and another steep incline leading up, up.

A man dressed head to toe in black tossed something into the air. Before he ducked behind a tree she caught sight of the night-vision goggles strapped across his shaved pale head, a gloved hand clutching a sub-machine gun against a tactical vest holding grenades.

Darby dropped her flashlight and ran, knowing what was coming. *Whatever you do, don't turn around, don't turn –*

An explosion followed by a blinding light that lit up the woods. *Stun grenade*, she thought, ducking behind a tree.

The light died away. She stripped out of her bunny suit. She couldn't hide wearing white, couldn't run in the coveralls.

Voices shouting from the backyard, footsteps cracking branches close by, bodies whisking past leaves and branches. *How many people are in here?*

SIG in hand, Darby flicked the switch for the tactical light and swung around the tree. Through the gaps between the branches and tree limbs she caught sight of two men hauling a body up the incline. Two white males wearing suits. The body also wore a suit. White male, white shirt covered in blood, a blue latex-covered hand bumping across the ground as he was dragged away.

'*Freeze. Boston –*'

Automatic gunfire muted by a silencer tore into the bark above her head.

Darby dropped to her knees, hugging her body close to the tree trunk. Voices shouting *Get down* and

Take cover. She thought she heard Pine's voice in the mix. She swung around the other side of the tree and brought up her weapon.

Flashlights crisscrossed through the darkness and she could see thick clouds of grey and white drifting through the trees near the first incline. The man who had thrown the stun grenade, the one with the shaved head and night-vision goggles, had moved out of his hiding spot. He stood near the spot where she'd found the phone.

He threw another grenade into the air, in the direction of the backyard. Darby turned away from it and closed her eyes, waiting. Automatic gunfire erupted from somewhere above her.

When she heard the explosion, she opened her eyes and, using the trees for cover, started moving to the bald man.

He darted up what looked like a second incline and disappeared from her view.

Darby gave chase. For the past week she had run in this oppressive heat with a sixty-pound backpack full of sand strapped to her back. She wasn't weighed down now. Even in the mud, she ran fast and well.

The man had a good lead. There was no way she could close the gap. She debated about stopping to fire when he disappeared from her view.

A car door slammed shut. Tyres peeled away in a squeal of rubber. By the time she reached the top, all she found was a pair of dimming red tail lights coming from a car far down the dark road. In the distance she could hear the wail of multiple police sirens. Someone had radioed for back-up and the Belham dispatcher had sent out several units.

As impressed as she was by the quick response time, it wouldn't do any good. Blakely Road, she knew, connected to Route 135. From there the car could jump on to the main highway, Route 1, and disappear.

Worse, she couldn't offer up a description. She hadn't seen the car or a licence plate. As for the men, the only thing she could say with any certainty was that all three were white. No, make that four. The body was that of a white male.

Darby holstered her weapon and made her way back down the incline, her legs wobbly from adrenalin. Dozens of flashlights moved through the thick haze of grey and white smoke filling the woods. Everywhere she heard men coughing.

She cupped her hands over her mouth. '*Stand down. I repeat, stand down.*'

A group of patrolmen rushed to her with their guns raised, their eyes red and watery from the smoke. They tried to hold their arms steady as they coughed.

One of them saw the gold shield clipped to her belt clip and the laminated ID badge hanging around her neck. He motioned for the others to lower their weapons.

Darby addressed the group. 'Is Detective Pine back here?'

The tall one with the cleft chin nodded, wiping at his eyes. He could barely keep them open.

'Find him and tell him the shooters are gone,' Darby said. 'Tell him to meet me in front of the house – and tell him to get everyone the hell out of the woods until the smoke dissipates. Call for an ambulance and make sure they bring plenty of oxygen. Get going – wait, not you.' She grabbed the soft, flabby arm of a short patrolman with a pot belly. 'I need to borrow your flashlight.'

He handed it over and stumbled away, gagging.

It took her a few minutes to locate the spot where she'd first seen the man who had tossed the stun grenade. The area offered a lot of tree cover. A perfect place to hide – and watch. From this location she could see the backyard.

Her eyes started to water and her throat burned as she ran the beam of light across the ground. She found several footwear impressions – none of them useful – and a single aluminium-foil blister pack.

Ducking underneath the branches, she moved across the soft ground covered with pine needles and leaves. She threw an evidence cone next to the blister pack. Voices shouted to move out of the woods. One kept calling her name.

'*Coop. Coop, I'm fine. Meet me in the backyard.*'

She made her way back to the incline and saw that most of the flashlights had been shut off. The ones still on were moving away, retreating back to the house.

A patrolman was on his hands and knees, struggling to breathe. Darby helped him to his feet, then wrapped his arm around her shoulder. She grabbed the last evidence cone from her pocket and slowly retraced her footsteps back to the spot where she'd found the mobile phone. It was gone.

7

An hour later Darby walked to the corner of the backyard where Pine stood running water from a hose over his face. He had breathed in too much smoke. She could hear his laboured wheezing over the water splashing against the flagstone walkway. He didn't care about getting wet. His clothes were already soaked and covered in mud.

Coop was also in the backyard. He stood alongside Michael Banville, watching the photographer taking bracketed shots of the back gate. There was no reason for Coop to be out here supervising photography. Darby knew the real reason: he was pretending to be busy so he could keep an eye on her.

Both Coop and the photographer wore protective goggles and breathing masks. Grey and white clouds of smoke drifted through the woods and into the backyard. On her way out, she had found a grenade still hissing smoke. The grenades had a slow burn rate. It would be at least another hour before anyone could go back inside the woods.

By some miracle of God none of the officers had disturbed the bloody handprint during their mad rush into the woods. The same couldn't be said for the blood she'd found on the grass. The evidence markers had been trampled.

Only one patrolman had been seriously injured in the skirmish. A stun grenade had exploded near his head.

'Christ, this shit stings,' Pine said. 'What the hell is it?'

'Hexachloroethane. It's a chemical used in smoke grenades. Keep flushing out your eyes.'

'My lungs feel like they're on fire.'

'You should get to one of the ambulances for some oxygen.'

'In a minute.' Pine rubbed his eyes under the running water. 'Something exploded in front of me. There was this bright light and then I couldn't see.'

'That was a stun grenade. It causes momentary blindness.'

'How do you know so much about this shit?'

'SWAT training.'

Pine drank from the hose, wincing as he swallowed.

'The guy you saw, the one wearing those night-vision glasses?'

'Goggles,' Darby said.

'Whatever. You get a good look at him?'

'No. I just saw a flash before he ducked behind the tree. Black clothing and black gloves, a tactical vest holding grenades.'

'Any way you can trace them?'

'The stun grenades explode on impact. If we find

enough fragments, we might be able to locate a serial or model number. As for the smoke grenades, we can give the numbers to the manufacturer and see where they were sold. Maybe they were stolen from a munitions locker at a police station or an army base.'

'You don't sound too confident.'

'You can buy them on the black market. Go to any gun show in the South and you can have your pick. A lot of weekend-warrior types collect them. We'll run the numbers but most likely it's going to lead to a dead end. The guy with the night vision is too smart to leave us something to trace.'

'How do you know this guy is smart and not some sort of Rambo douche bag?'

'He came prepared.'

'For what? A shootout in the woods?'

'He came prepared for a fight. Artie, what time did the 911 call come through?'

'Ten twenty.'

'And how long before the first responding officers arrived?'

'Ten thirty-three. There was a unit in the area.'

'Did the officers search the woods?'

Pine shook his head under the running water. 'I was the only one who went back there.'

'What time was that?'

He thought about it for a moment.

'I'd say around quarter past eleven, give or take.'

'So we're talking almost an hour between the 911

call and the time you entered the woods,' Darby said. 'If those men had been back there watching the house, they would've had plenty of time to haul away the body.'

'But you saw it.'

'He had a lot of blood on his shirt. If this person got shot with one of the Magnum rounds, you're talking a massive amount of blood loss in a short amount of time. He could have bled out while running through the woods.'

'And somehow his buddies found him.'

'Which leads me to believe he placed a call before he passed out,' Darby said.

Pine dropped the hose. He shut off the tap and reached inside his pocket.

'You thinking these guys arrived the same time you did?' he asked, mopping his face with a handkerchief.

'They were in the woods when we were talking by the back gate. I think they were waiting for us to leave before they started to haul the body. If they'd started moving around, they would have made too much noise. We would have heard them.'

'When I went through the woods, I didn't see a body back there. There was *no one* back there.'

'Maybe the guy with the bloody shirt found a place to hide. I don't think the others were there when you were. The guy with the night vision? He was carrying what I'm sure is a compact HK MP6. It definitely was a sub-machine gun. And I know I saw a scope. If he had been back there when you were, he could've taken you down with a single shot to the head. He planned to come out of hiding, find the phone and leave. Nobody would've heard a thing.'

'You're saying all of this was for a goddamn phone?'

'It's gone, isn't it?'

Pine didn't answer. His eyes were red and puffy, his face pale.

'A phone is a key piece of evidence,' Darby said. 'You've got logs of incoming and outgoing calls, maybe even an address book full of contacts. Who knows what we would've found? Night-vision man certainly thought it was important enough for me not to get my hands on it. He came out of his hiding spot to treat me to a stun grenade. Then he covered the woods with HC smoke canisters and gunfire to keep everyone back.'

Pine looked at the evidence bag gripped in her hand. 'What did you find?'

'A blister pack for nicotine gum. The guy with the night vision is apparently concerned about his long-term health. You should be too. You're looking a little unsteady on your feet.'

'I haven't run like that since . . . well, it's been a long time.'

'Let me help you to the ambulance.'

'I can manage.' Pine opened the gate to a carnival of blinking red, white and blue lights.

'Artie, have the Feds come to see you?'

'About what?'

'About any ongoing case in Belham, surveillance, anything along those lines.'

'No.' Pine's mouth parted and his brow crinkled with thought. 'Wait, are you suggesting the Feds are involved with what happened here tonight?'

'I'm saying it's a possibility. The guys I saw hauling the body away? They wore suits. The guy with the night vision had a tactical vest with stun and smoke grenades, and he was carrying the kind of machine gun used by Hostage Rescue. He's not a weekend warrior. He knew exactly what he was doing.'

'That's one hell of an assumption.'

'Maybe. But he could easily have taken me down while I was back there – he had several opportunities before I reached the phone. And I think he deliberately shot at the tree above my head. He didn't want to kill me, just wanted to pin me down until he got to the phone. You see the muddy footprints on the deck?'

Pine nodded, dabbing his eyes with the handkerchief. 'I talked to the patrol guys. They didn't leave 'em.'

'They're also on the living-room carpet in front of the sliding glass door. I think someone ran across the backyard, tracked mud up the steps and then shot their way *inside* the house. I found two holes in the opposite wall. Who would want to shoot their way inside a house?'

'The person who killed and tortured that woman.'

'One person can't subdue two people and then ransack an entire house, especially one this size. We're talking two people at the very least – and they sure as hell wouldn't have shot their way in. They had to find a way to get inside quietly, without being detected. They needed time to subdue the mother and son, and they needed time to search the house. Shooting your way inside isn't quiet or subtle. It's more in line with a rescue attempt, don't you think?'

Pine thought it over, rubbing his tongue along his bottom teeth.

'All I'm saying is that I wouldn't put it past the Feds,' Darby said. 'We should look at every possible angle.'

'I'll dig around.'

So will I, Darby thought.

8

Darby used one of the clean towels she kept in the back of the crime scene vehicle to wipe the mud from her face, arms and hands. The muggy night air smelled of car exhaust and her clothes reeked of cordite.

Everywhere she looked she saw faces lit up by revolving emergency lights. Faces behind TV cameras, faces behind cameras exploding with bright flashes. Voices spoke behind the crackle of police radios and the rapid machine-gun click of camera shutters snapping. The sounds grated on her already scorched nerves. Too close. Too much commotion, too much goddamn noise and too many people crowding the streets. She wanted to send everyone away. She wanted a cold shower and a stiff drink. She wanted some time alone to quiet her mind before heading back inside the house.

That wasn't going to happen. It was time to make a careful study of the house.

Darby wiped the last of the mud from her boots. She threw the towel on the front floor of the Explorer and changed into a clean bunny suit. From the hatchback she grabbed the new Canon digital SLR camera, which created a digital negative – a raw file that couldn't be doctored in any way. She walked across the front lawn tucking her wet hair underneath her hood. Thunder rumbled in the distance. She hoped the Wonder Twins arrived before the rain. She'd have to send them directly into the woods. She couldn't wait.

She put on a pair of latex gloves, stepped inside the foyer and studied the walls. No bullet holes. She checked the dining room and kitchen. No bullet holes.

Coop looked up from his clipboard.

'I'll be upstairs,' she said.

He nodded and went back to making notes. He made no attempt to follow. They had worked together for so long he knew she preferred to go through a crime scene alone first so she could think. She couldn't do that with someone looking over her shoulder, taking notes and constantly asking questions.

Darby stood alone on the first-floor landing. Cool air rushed down on her from an overhead vent. Her damp clothes clung to her skin. She couldn't stop sweating.

Five doorways, each door opened, the lights turned on. Clothes had been tossed into the hall. Bathroom items were scattered across the blond oak hardwood flooring in front of her – a tube of hair gel, hairspray, tampons and pills.

Looking into the bathroom, she saw a medicine cabinet, its doors open, the shelves wiped clean.

Mouthwash, shampoo and pill bottles lined the bathtub. Each bottle had been emptied and searched. Two prescription bottles were floating inside the toilet.

They were looking for something small. A key maybe.

Across the hall was a small, carpeted room used as a home office. Shades drawn, desk overturned and closet shelves emptied. Every inch had been methodically searched.

Had the house been broken into before the mother and son arrived? Then, frustrated at failing to find whatever it was they needed, had they started to torture the mother for information?

Fingers pulled back, broken.

Tell me where it is.

Fingers cut off one by one.

Tell me where it is.

Did she tell? Did she know anything? Darby moved to the two rooms at the end of the hall.

The first, long and airy, contained only a sewing machine and a chair. Shades covered the windows.

The mattress in the second room had been pulled from the bed, cut with a knife and searched. No shades covering the windows; she could see members of the Photography Unit still taking pictures of the back gate. Clothes on the floor, the kind a male teenager would wear – Abercrombie & Fitch T-shirts and jeans, athletic shorts, sneakers and flip-flops. She found an empty red duffel bag with a shoulder strap, the kind used for travelling, lying underneath an over-turned nightstand.

Darby took pictures, then moved down the hall and stepped into the master bedroom, surprised to find it neat and orderly. A big-screen plasma TV hung on the wall across from a king-sized sleigh bed. The twin cherry-stained chests-of-drawers hadn't been overturned or searched; the drawers were still intact. Like all the rooms with windows facing the street, the shades had been drawn.

The only item in here that had been disturbed was a suitcase sitting on top of a leather footstool. Clothes inside, a few tossed against a leather club chair set up in the corner.

Had the search been interrupted? Had someone been standing here when the gunshots went off?

Darby found a small piece of blue latex caught on a zipper's metal teeth. In her mind's eye she saw the dead man from the woods, latex gloves covering his hands.

Did you touch this suitcase?

She pictured him standing here, his gloved fingers searching through each pocket when the first gunshot rang out. She saw him reaching under his suit jacket for his sidearm and then rushing for the stairs, heading downstairs into the kitchen and seeing . . . what? *What did you see?*

Darby pinched the bridge of her nose and closed her eyes, trying to focus on the faceless man who had touched this suitcase. Snapshots of what had happened in the woods – stun grenades exploding with light; the man with the night-vision goggles; two men hauling a body up the incline to the waiting car. The dead man wore a suit and latex gloves. White shirt covered in blood. Someone had shot him.

You were inside the house, weren't you? And I know you didn't come here alone. You had to have brought at least one other person to help you search a house this size. Was this person shot and dragged away?

Did you help subdue the woman and her son? Did you tie them up and go back to searching the rooms while your partner tortured her? Or did you help? Were you standing in the kitchen when you heard the gunshots and exploding glass? I think you were, my man. If you had been upstairs when you heard the gunshots, you would've had time to draw your weapon. You would have come downstairs firing. I would have found evidence of gunshots.

I think you were caught by surprise. I think you were in the kitchen when someone shot you in the chest. I think you didn't have time to pull your weapon.

Darby opened her eyes, wondering what had happened to the dead man's partner. Was there another body lying somewhere in the woods? Or had the man with the night vision and his crew already carried away a second body?

She felt confident that the night-vision man and his two suited partners hadn't been inside the woods at the time of the shooting. If they had been there, watching, they would have been long gone by the time the first responding officers arrived.

A trail of blood ran across the living-room carpet, down the porch steps and across the grass. A bloody handprint was smeared on the gate. She pictured the man running through the dark woods. Was he trying to find the incline leading up to the street? Did he have a car parked somewhere on the road?

She hadn't found any vehicles parked along the shoulder.

And the men from the woods, someone had to have summoned them. She thought about the phone lying on the ground and pictured the man in the white shirt bleeding from his chest as he made the call. Did he drop the phone as he searched for a place to hide and wait? Why hadn't he reached the road? Had he passed out from blood loss along the way?

Darby wondered if he had dropped anything else inside the woods.

Why didn't your partner or partners inside the house help you? What happened?

Darby heard car doors slamming shut. She pulled back the shade and saw the lab's second crime scene vehicle parked against the kerb. Two men, a Mutt and Jeff combo if ever there was one, paced the pavement near the bonnet. Randy Scott, thin and impeccably neat with black hair greying around the temples, stood a foot taller than his stocky partner, Mark Alves. She had hired the duo from the San Francisco Crime

Laboratory, where they had gained a reputation for uncovering crucial, overlooked evidence on a number of high-profile cases. If something else had been dropped in the woods, they would find it.

Someone knocked on the bedroom door. She turned and saw Coop.

'The Wonder Twins have arrived,' she said.

'I know. Randy called to let me know he was here.'

'I'll go speak to them.'

'I'll do it. You need to go to St Joseph's Hospital in Belham. I just got off the phone with operations. A Belham patrolman called looking for you. The kid says he wants to speak to a Belham cop named Thomas McCormick. Isn't that –'

'Yes,' Darby said, blood beating in her eardrums. 'That's my father.'

9

Darby stood with Pine and a Belham patrolman around the corner from the nurses' station, next to a trolley holding discarded cafeteria trays. The odours of sour milk and steamed vegetables were a welcome relief from Pine's cigar stench.

The patrolman's name was Richard Rodman. His thick grey hair, carefully combed and parted, did not match his youthful face. Darby thought he looked like a budding politician stuffed inside a cop's blue uniform. He held a white-paper mailer spotted with blood from the teenager's bloody T-shirt. The emergency room physician had cut the shirt off the teenager and then had the good sense to transfer it to a paper bag. Plastic bags broke down DNA. Not all doctors knew this.

'I was sitting on a chair outside his room when he opened the door and asked if I knew a Belham cop named Thomas McCormick,' Rodman said. 'I said no, I didn't, and the kid said everyone called McCormick Big Red. Kid said he needed to talk to McCormick but wouldn't tell me why.'

Rodman looked at Darby. 'I remembered seeing you on TV last year when you caught that whack-job, what's his name, the guy who shot women in the head, put Virgin Mary statues in their pockets and dumped them in the river.'

'Walter Smith,' Darby said.

Rodman snapped his fingers. 'That's the guy. What happened to him?'

'He's in a mental institution. He'll be spending the rest of his life there.'

'God bless us all. The news story I saw did this profile on you and I remembered something about you growing up in Belham and your old man being a cop. So I went to the nurses' station, used a computer to do a Google search, then called operations and here we are.'

'Did you tell the boy that Thomas McCormick is dead?'

'No. I figured it might be better if you tell him. You know, use that as your way in.'

'Has anyone come to see him?'

Rodman shook his head. 'No phone calls either.'

'I think it's better if I see him alone.'

'I'm fine with that. The less, the better, I say. The kid's really shook up.'

Darby turned to Pine.

'I think it's a good idea,' Pine said.

Darby pushed herself off the wall and grabbed the small digital tape recorder from her back pocket. 'Where is he?'

'Straight down the hall,' Rodman said.

Darby opened the door. The teenager had turned

off the lights in his room. In the dim light coming from the window next to his bed, she could see that someone had worked him over good. The left side of his face was swollen, the eye nearly shut.

He sat up in bed, a blanket covering his legs. His bandaged arm, perched in a sling, rested against his bare chest, tanned from the sun. Tall and lean, he had barely any muscle tone.

'Hello, John. My name is Darby McCormick. I understand you wanted to see my father.'

'Where is he?'

His voice was raw. And young.

'May I come in?'

He considered the question for a moment. His blond hair was cut short, his forehead damp with sweat. All-American good-looks. The ER doctor had used butterfly sutures on the split skin.

Finally, he nodded.

She shut the door and sat on the end of the bed. The skin along his wrists and eyes was red. Patches of missing hair above the ears. She could see that he had been crying.

'Where's your father?' he asked again.

'He's dead.'

The boy swallowed. His eyes went wide, as if a door had just been slammed shut in his face.

'What happened to him?'

'My father was a patrolman and pulled over a car,' Darby said. 'The person behind the wheel was a schizophrenic recently released from prison. My father approached the vehicle and for some reason this person shot him.'

'And he died?'

'My father managed to radio for help, but by the time he was rushed to the hospital he had lost too much blood. He was already brain dead. My mother made the decision to pull him off life support, and he died.'

'When?'

'Before you were born,' Darby said. 'How old are you?'

'I'll be thirteen next March.'

Twelve, Darby thought. *Someone had tied a twelve-year-old boy down to a kitchen chair seated across from his mother.*

'What happened to your arm?'

'I strained a muscle or something, and the doctor gave me this sling,' John said. 'Can I ask you a question?'

'You can ask me anything you want.'

'The person who shot your father, did they catch him?'

'Yes, they did. He's in jail.'

The boy looked at the gun clipped to her belt. 'Are you a cop?'

'I'm a special investigator for the Criminal Services Unit. I help victims of violent crimes. Can you tell me about the people who taped you down to the kitchen chair?'

'How'd you –' His lips clamped shut.

'The skin along your wrists and your cheeks,' Darby said. 'Those are marks left from duct tape.'

He turned his head to the window. He blinked several times, his eyes growing wet.

Darby placed a hand on his knee. The boy shuddered.

'I'm here to help. You can trust me.'

He didn't answer. From outside the room came a steady *beep-beep-beep* from some piece of machinery and the murmured voices of Pine and the patrolman. The talking stopped. Darby wondered if they were standing near the door, trying to listen.

'But how do I know?'

'Know what?'

'That I can trust you,' he said.

'You asked for my father.'

'And you said he's dead.'

'I'm his daughter.'

'So you say.'

Darby reached into her pocket. She removed the creased photo from her wallet and placed it on his lap.

'This is a picture of my father,' she said.

He picked up the photo of her father dressed in his patrolman's uniform. A gap-toothed six-year-old girl with emerald-green eyes and long auburn pigtails sat on his lap.

'Is this you?'

Darby nodded. 'Do you recognize him?'

'I've never met your father.' He handed the picture

back to her. 'For all I know this photo is a fake.'

'See this laminated card hanging around my neck? The picture matches the one on my licence. Here, look.'

He did.

'I'm Thomas McCormick's daughter.' She said the words softly; she didn't want this to be a confrontation. 'You can trust me. But if you want me to help, you have to be honest with me.'

He said nothing.

'What's your father's name?'

'I don't know,' John said. 'I never met him.'

'Do you have a stepfather?'

'My mom never got married.'

'Do you have any other siblings?'

'No.'

'What about aunts, uncles or cousins?'

'My mom . . . It was just me and her.'

His lips clamped shut again, then his eyes. His chest heaved in the air and he started to tremble.

'It's okay.' Darby took his hand. 'It's okay.'

'My mom . . .' He cleared his throat and tried again. 'She said that if something happened to her, if I ever got into trouble or was scared, I had to call Thomas McCormick. She said he's the only police officer to trust. She told me not to talk to anyone else, under any circumstances.'

He started bawling.

'My mom's dead and I don't know what to do. I don't know what to do.'

Darby grabbed a box of tissues from the nightstand. John Hallcox did not take the tissues but he took her hand and held it while he sobbed.

Drops of rain flecked the window. She wondered if the Wonder Twins had found anything inside the woods. It was easier to look out of the window and think about Randy and Mark searching the muddy ground for evidence, to think about the ransacked house with all of its blood and broken glass, than it was to watch the twelve-year-old boy's face.

A memory came to her: squeezing her father's big and callused hand. It was the size of a baseball mitt. He lay in a hospital bed similar to this one, hooked up to tubes and monitors, and she had dug her fingernails into his skin, drawing blood, knowing he would wake up before the doctor removed him from life support.

'I'm sorry, John. I'm truly sorry for what you're going through.'

At last the awful crying ended. He grabbed several tissues and wiped his face.

She placed the digital recorder on the bed. 'When you're ready to talk, and with your permission, I'd like to tape this conversation. That way I can listen to you and not take notes. Is that okay?'

John nodded.

'I'll help you through this. Sometimes I may have to interrupt you with a question or I may ask you to clarify something. I need to make sure I have all the facts straight in my head. If you don't understand something, ask, okay?'

He cleared his throat. 'Okay.'

The boy clearly didn't know where to start.

Gently, she said, 'Tell me about the people who came inside your house.'

'There were two of them. Two men. I was on the sofa watching TV when I heard the door open. I thought it was my mom coming home so I didn't get up.'

'You were home alone?'

'Yes.'

'And where was your mom?'

'She said she had to go to a couple of job interviews and do some errands and wouldn't be back until late. She told me to stay inside the house until she got home.'

'Why? Was your mom worried about something?'

'She was always worried. No matter where we lived, she was always telling me to make sure the apartment was locked up. She'd always make sure the windows were locked before she went to bed. Every day when I came home from school, she'd call to ask if everything was okay. I thought . . . My mom didn't make a lot of money and we never lived in the best neighbourhoods. When we were in Los Angeles, our apartment got broken into and she freaked out. Two weeks later we were living in Asbury Park. That's in New Jersey.'

'Did you move around a lot?'

'Yeah.'

'Do you know why?'

'I think it has something to do with her parents,' John said. 'They were murdered before I was born. She never got into specifics or anything. The only thing she told me was that the people who did it were never caught. I think she was scared they might come for her or something.' He swallowed and then took in a sharp breath. 'And they did. They found us and killed her.'

'You said "they". There was more than one person?'

'You mean inside my house?'

'We'll get to that. I want to know about the people who murdered your grandparents.'

'I don't know names or anything. My mom just said people came into her parents' house one night and shot them to death while they were sleeping. My mom said she wasn't there – I don't know where she was. She told me these people were never caught.'

'What are the names of your grandparents?'

'I don't know. My mom never talked about them. I

don't even know where they lived. I asked her – I was, you know, curious about what had happened – but she wouldn't go into any details. I think that's what made her paranoid about using computers.'

'What do you mean?'

'She never went on the internet to order anything. She couldn't, anyway, 'cause she didn't have a credit card – she always paid cash for everything. She thought people could spy on you if you were on the internet.'

'Was she worried these men who murdered your grandparents would somehow find her?'

'I guess. I mean, that's what I thought.'

'Do you know how old your mother was when her parents died?'

'No.'

'Where did she go to live?'

'I don't know. I'm sorry.'

'You don't have to apologize, John. You're doing great. Let's talk about why you came to Belham. You said something about a job opportunity. What kind of jobs?'

'She didn't tell me specifics. My mom . . . She's fun and everything, takes me places, but there are certain things she's real private about. At least with me.'

'Like what happened to her parents.'

'Right. She told me they were murdered before I was born. She was always afraid of something happening. And she's not, you know, gushy with her emotions. She keeps them bottled up. When you talk to her about what's bothering her, she won't tell you.'

John was talking about her in the present tense, as if she were going to come through this door at any moment, sit down on the bed and hold him, tell him everything's going to be fine.

'Tell me about your mother's friends,' Darby said.

'I never met them. For all I know, she didn't have any.'

'How long have you been living in Belham?'

'Just a couple of days,' he said. 'We were only going to stay for, like, a week, or something.'

'Do you know the names of the people who owned the house?'

'No.'

'Okay, let's go back to when you were on the sofa. You said you heard the door open.'

'It was the door at the end of the kitchen hall, the one that lead out to the garage. I know that because it makes this swishing sound against the floor when it opens.'

'Did your mom leave one of the garage doors open?'

He thought about it for a moment.

'I . . . I remember when my mom left, she told me to lock the door – the door at the end of the kitchen hall. But I don't remember hearing the garage door shut. I'm not sure. It's all confusing. It's like I have all these snapshots flashing through my head all at once. It's hard to keep track.'

'That's normal.'

'So when it opened later, I thought it was my mother. And I was half-asleep on the sofa. I remember it was dark – I could see the backyard through the sliding glass door in the living room. That's when I saw him, the man with the gun. He was standing at the end of the sofa telling me to stay quiet.'

'Describe him to me. Tell me everything you noticed, even if you don't think it's important.'

'He wasn't wearing a ski mask or anything, which I thought was kind of odd. The other guy wasn't either. I mean, that's what you do when you rob a house, right?'

'Right.' Darby felt excitement bumping in her chest. *Two* men had entered the house and the boy had seen their faces. He could give descriptions to a sketch artist. A long shot, maybe, but if the pictures ran on TV someone might recognize them.

'He was a white guy,' John said. 'And he was wearing this warm-up suit – the kind the Celtics wear. Had a Celtics hat too. A baseball cap. He was old. He kind of looked like someone's grandfather but his face was, like, weird.'

'Weird how?'

'He didn't have any wrinkles. His skin was, like, all smoothed back. It reminded me of Mrs Milstein – she was our neighbour when we were living in Toronto. She got a facelift and her skin was real tight and kind of shiny. My mom said Mrs Milstein had gotten a facelift. This Celtics guy had the same kind of face, and his hands ... they weren't right. They looked like they belonged on someone else. They were all wrinkled and hairy, and I saw these big veins sticking out on them. They reminded me of the hands I saw on the really old guys at nursing homes.'

'When did you get a close-up look at this man's hands?'

'When he was ...' He swallowed again. 'He made me get up from the sofa and sit on one of the kitchen chairs. That's when I saw the other guy. He was standing in the kitchen. He pointed a nine-millimetre at me while the Celtics guy taped me down to the chair.'

'You recognized his gun?'

'I watch a lot of cop shows. *CSI, Law and Order* — stuff like that. The cops always carry nines. And when they interview the victims, they always ask for details.' His voice sounded so terribly frail. 'So when I ... When all of this was happening, there was, like, this voice in the back of my head telling me to pay attention to everything. The little details are what catch these guys.'

'You're doing a great job, John. This is really helpful. Tell me about the man standing in the kitchen.'

'He was wearing a suit – not a warm-up suit, I mean the kind a banker or lawyer would wear. He wasn't wearing a tie, though. He was a white guy and kind of ... not fat but he had a gut on him. I remember he kept checking his watch.'

'Was he wearing gloves?'

John nodded. 'Blue ones, the kind the forensics people wear on TV.'

'Do you remember what colour his shirt was?'

'White.'

The body she'd seen in the woods had had a white shirt and blue latex gloves.

'Did these men talk to you?'

'The Celtics guy did,' John said. 'He said he just wanted to take a look around the house and he couldn't do that while keeping an eye on me. 'Relax, champ, this will all be over before you know it,' is what he said. Then he put tape across my eyes and patted me on the shoulder. He didn't talk to me after that.'

'Do you remember hearing anything? Did you hear their names? What they said to each other?'

'I didn't hear their names. They swore a lot. They started searching through the kitchen, ripping open the drawers and throwing out plates. All I kept hearing were things smashing against the floor.'

'What were they looking for?'

'I don't know. I thought ... I was pretty sure I heard a phone ringing and then the smashing stopped. I know the garage door opened, I remember hearing it. That's when everything got real quiet. Then they grabbed my mother.'

He swallowed again, his shiny eyes growing wide with fear as his mind started replaying what had happened to his mother.

Darby moved him away from it. 'Why did you ask to speak to my father?'

He didn't answer. He looked down at the tissues balled in his fist, his eyes darting back and forth as if he had dropped the answers to the question.

She leaned closer. 'You can trust me, John.'

He reached for the tape recorder and shut it off.

11

Darby waited for the boy to speak, afraid that if she pressed him, he'd shut down.

Two minutes later he did. He wouldn't look at her.

'I promised my mother. I promised her I'd tell the truth only to Thomas McCormick.'

'The truth about what?'

'About my grandparents,' he said. 'About why they were killed.'

Don't push or you'll lose him.

She waited.

'I know who did it,' he said. 'I know their names.'

'Look at me, John.'

When he did, she said, 'You're not alone in this any more. Whatever it is that happened, I can help you. You can trust me.'

'Sean.'

'Is that the name of one of the men who murdered your grandparents?'

'No. That's my real name. Nobody is supposed to know. Only your father knows. My mother –'

He stopped talking, snapping his attention to the voices shouting outside his room. He looked frightened.

The door opened. The boy jumped, hitting the back of his head against the wall.

A searing anger lifted Darby off the bed. She got to her feet as the lights were turned on.

Pine and the patrolman crowded the doorway. They seemed out of breath. They were speaking to her but she didn't hear them, her attention locked on the man standing near the foot of the bed. He wore a crisp tan suit and a floral tie, his short black hair damp with the rain.

A Federal agent. The smug expression on his face gave it away, even before he flashed the tin.

'I'm Special Agent Phillips,' he said in a calm and somewhat effeminate voice. 'I'm going to have to ask you to leave the room, Dr McCormick. I'm officially taking over this investigation.'

Darby pushed the Fed away from the bed and got in his face. 'He's not going anywhere.'

'I beg to differ. His mother is a fugitive. They've crossed state lines, which makes this a Federal investigation. And you should know better than to question him without an adult present.'

'He's not a suspect, you idiot.'

Phillips looked at the boy. 'I'm taking you to the Albany field office in New York. We'll place you –'

'I'm going to give you a choice,' Darby said. 'You can walk out of here standing, or you can be thrown out of here.'

Pine stepped forward, clearing his throat. 'He's got a fugitive warrant, Darby.'

'I don't have time for this,' Phillips said, and pushed her to one side.

Mistake.

She grabbed his wrist, twisting his hand behind his back. She grabbed the back of his shirt collar, dragged him across the floor and shoved him face first against the wall.

The Fed yelped in pain. She didn't let go. She applied more pressure to his arm, wanting to snap it. Instead, she leaned in close to him and said, 'You don't listen too well, do you?'

She pulled him away from the wall, dragged him to the door and threw him into the corridor. He fell against the floor, gritting his teeth and sweat popping out on his forehead as he glared up at her.

'Keep your ass out of here,' she said.

What she saw in his eyes she had seen in too many men – an insecure boy trapped in a man's body. A guy like Phillips would lay in wait, nursing his wounded ego and pride. He'd take his embarrassment and then channel it into his only real talent: finding *the* most spectacular way to screw you over.

'Calm down,' Pine said behind her. 'Nobody here wants to hurt you.'

Darby turned and saw Patrolman Rodman reaching for his sidearm.

The boy was holding a gun – a small .38 revolver, aimed at Pine.

74

Where the hell did he get the gun?

'*Stay back,*' John – *Sean* – screamed. '*I'm not going with him.*'

Darby moved in front of Pine, raising her hands near her head. 'You're right, you're not going with him.'

'*You can't make me. YOU CAN'T MAKE ME.*'

'Look at me,' Darby said. '*Look at me.*'

He did, lips quivering. Tears spilled down his cheeks and the gun shook in his hand.

'You don't have to go with him, I promise.' Her heart was beating fast but she wasn't afraid. 'And I promised I'd help you, remember? You can trust me.'

He didn't answer. He scanned each of the faces staring at him.

Darby cocked her head over her shoulder and said, 'Everyone, out of the room.'

Pine hesitated.

'Do it,' Darby said. '*Now.*'

When everyone had left, she backed up slowly and shut the door.

The boy's frightened gaze shifted to the recorder lying on the tangled blanket.

'It's off,' Darby said. 'It's just you and me, Sean.'

He started sobbing but didn't lower the gun.

'You've been through a lot tonight,' Darby said. 'You're scared, you're angry and upset. I understand what you're going through. My father was murdered. Whatever this is about, I'll help you solve it.'

'You can't.'

'I can. I *will*. I gave you my word. Whatever this is about, you can trust me.'

He kept sobbing.

'Put the gun down on the bed,' Darby said. 'Just put it down and then you and I will talk. Just me and you, okay? I promise –'

He slammed the muzzle underneath his chin and pulled the trigger.

12

Jamie Russo popped the boot, then considered the two handguns lying on the passenger seat: her .44 Magnum and a Glock with an extended magazine. She went with the Magnum, slid it inside her shoulder holster and stepped out of the car. The right side of her face throbbed and she could still taste blood on the back of her throat.

A full moon hung in the sky above the rock walls of the old Belham Quarry. She had left the car headlights on and could see the edge of the cliff. She wasn't worried about being seen. No houses for miles and she doubted anyone came out this way any more, especially at this time of night.

She walked to the back of the car, her sneakers sinking in the soft, muddy earth.

The man she knew only as Ben lay on his back inside the boot. His clothes and swollen, cut face were smeared with blood and covered with shards of glass. His icy-blue eyes were open, squinting underneath a pale square of dim light.

Thank God, she thought, sighing with relief. Before leaving the house, she had quickly bound the gunshot wound on his thigh with duct tape to keep him from bleeding out. During the long, slow drive through the back streets, then navigating her way through the maze of winding trails that led to the quarry, she had choked on the possibility that he would die.

A sick fear mixed with excitement rushed through her veins as she gripped him by his Celtics jacket and hoisted him up into a sitting position. She wasn't worried about him hitting her again. She had duct-taped his hands behind his back and tied his ankles together before dragging him across the kitchen hall to the garage.

Thick strips of duct tape covered his mouth. She yanked the tape down across his lips, taking skin and hair.

Ben's eyes clamped shut. He gritted his teeth, hissing back a scream. She stared at him, taking in his features again: the dishevelled black hair matted against his sweaty, tanned face; his broken nose; big ears sticking out from the sides of his head; perfect white teeth.

Caps, she thought, and then stared at his neck. The first time she had seen him, that night in her home, he'd had what she called 'rooster neck', a wrinkled curtain of flesh dangling underneath his chin. It was gone now, and the skin along his face was smooth and tight, not a wrinkle anywhere. *He's had a facelift. And his eyes . . . I could've sworn they were brown.*

Ben opened his eyes. They were bloodshot and

rheumy. After he had hit her back at the house, a good solid right cross that had nearly knocked her off her feet, she had wrestled him to the kitchen floor and slammed his head twice against the broken shards of glass.

Ben rested the back of his head against the opened boot lid. Moths batted against the lid's single bulb.

'How long have you been following me?' he croaked.

Hearing his voice released the vice-like grip on her heart. For the first time in years, she felt as if she could breathe.

'You going to answer my question?'

'Today,' she said. 'This . . . morning.'

'Where?'

'Drugstore.'

'Drugstore . . . drugstore . . . The one in Wellesley Center?'

'Yes.'

'You've been watching me all day?'

She nodded. He'd left the drugstore and climbed into the passenger seat of a black BMW with tinted windows. She tailed the car on the highway as Ben and his partner drove to Charlestown. An hour later, when the BMW pulled into the narrow driveway of a small corner home, she watched, from the minivan's rear-view mirror, Ben and the driver step out of the car. The driver was a few inches taller than Ben, maybe six two, and had grey curly hair and a dark tan. He wore white shorts and a bright floral Hawaiian shirt that couldn't hide his enormous stomach.

She found a parking spot at the far end of the street and watched the house for the rest of the morning and afternoon. She left the minivan once to run across the street to the drugstore to buy a couple of energy bars, a bottle of water and a box of latex gloves.

At half past eight the BMW pulled out of the driveway. It stopped once, in front of some shitty tenement in Dorchester to pick up the white man in the suit, and then the three of them drove straight to the house in Belham.

'You followed me all day and not once did I see you,' Ben said. He shook his head. 'I must be getting soft in my old age. What's your name, hon?'

'Say . . . it.'

'If I knew your name, don't you think I'd tell you?'

He blinked several times, then squinted as he tried to focus on her face. Fine white scars from the multiple corrective surgeries covered her jaw line, cheek and forehead. The side effects from the steroids and seizure medication gave her face a puffy, bloated look that no amount of dieting or exercise could diminish.

'Five . . . ah . . . years,' she said. 'Five years . . . ago, you . . . ah . . . ah . . . came, ah . . .'

'What's with your voice? You retarded or something?'

'No.'

'Then what is it? Some sort of birth defect?'

Jamie couldn't get the words out. She knew what she wanted to say: *Five years ago, you came into my house and shot me in the head. You shot my two children while your two partners were downstairs torturing my husband.* Her problem was actual speech. The .32 slug that had entered through her lower jaw, shattering her cheekbone and severing the optic nerves of her left eye, had lodged itself in the front lobe – Broca's area, the neurologists had told her, the brain's central processing system for language and speech. While she could understand language just fine, could form and process complex sentences easily inside her head, the brain damage had saddled her with expressive aphasia, this maddening, incurable condition that limited her speech to no more than four words at a time, mostly nouns and verbs delivered in a slow, telegraphic manner. On a good day.

'Shot,' she said.

'Someone shot you in the face?'

'You . . . ah . . . did.'

Ben staring like he didn't recognize her. Like he didn't remember.

'You . . . ah . . . shot me . . . and . . . ah . . . my children. Carter and . . . ah . . . ah. . . Michael. Your. . . ah . . . two partners . . . ah . . . murdered . . . my . . . ah . . . husband. Dan . . . Dan Russo.'

'Can't say I know anyone by that name.'

'He . . . ah . . . ah . . . a contractor. Wellesley.'

'That his company name? Wellesley?'

A slight grin on Ben's face, having fun with this.

'Lived . . . ah . . . in . . . ah . . . Wellesley. You're . . . ah . . . two . . . ah . . . partners, they . . . ah . . . ah . . . killed him. Rope. Tied it and . . . ah . . . ah . . . neck. Strangled him. Waste disposal . . . my house. Wellesley. Five . . . ah . . . years . . . ah . . . five years . . . ago.'

'I think you've got me confused with someone else.'

No. No, she didn't.

This morning, after she had dropped off her prescription, she had turned around and seen, at the far end of the aisle, a man looking over shelves stocked with pain relievers. This man had the same thin, almost feminine lips as the man who had forced his way into her home. The organizer, the man she knew only as Ben.

No . . . No, it can't be him, she had thought. Why would Ben come back to Wellesley after all this time? Ben and his two partners, the ski-masked men who had murdered Dan in the kitchen, had disappeared from the face of the earth five years ago. Those men were never found and never would be.

And Ben, she remembered quite clearly, had had a blond crew cut threaded with grey. The man standing in the aisle wore a dark blue baseball cap over long black hair that curled around the ears. Ben had had pale skin. This man had a dark tan and was dressed like someone who spent his days lounging on a boat

– Sperry Top-Sider shoes, khaki shorts and a pair of aviator sunglasses hanging in the V of a white untucked Oxford shirt. He wore a thick gold wedding band and a gold Rolex Yacht-Master watch. Ben hadn't worn a wedding ring.

Jamie remembered watching as the man reached for something on the top shelf. On the wrist of his right hand and stretching across his palm was a thick rubbery white scar shaped like a mutant starfish.

Ben had had the exact same scar. She had seen it when he wrapped the duct tape across her mouth. She hadn't seen the two men who had entered the house. Later, she'd heard one of them call upstairs: 'Let's go, Ben.'

'Partners,' Jamie said, reaching inside her windbreaker for the Magnum. 'I want ... ah ... their names.'

Ben hawked a gob of bloody phlegm over the side of the car, then leaned back against the boot lid. Nothing lived behind those eyes. Just two glassy lifeless balls polished to a bright shine. Soulless.

'Partners,' she said. 'Names.'

He didn't answer.

She pressed the muzzle against his forehead, blood pumping through her limbs.

Ben didn't flinch.

'I ... I ... will ... ah ...

'Oh, I definitely think you'll kill me. You shot your way inside the house, shot me in the thigh – and you did one hell of a job taking down my friend. You're a regular Calamity Jane, blazing new frontiers.' His voice was surprisingly calm. 'Nobody learns to shoot like that unless they're a cop. You still on the force, sweetheart? I'm assuming you are, since you go around carrying that big gun you've got.'

She didn't answer. She had retired from her patrolman days after Carter was born. After Dan had died, she carried the Magnum with her everywhere. For protection.

'Why . . . ah . . . woman and . . . ah . . . boy . . . ah –'

'Are you asking me what I was doing inside the house?'

She nodded.

'That's confidential information,' he said. 'Sorry.'

'Man . . . ah . . . ah . . . who drove . . . ah . . . you, was . . . ah . . . he . . . ah –'

'Take a look at this from my point of view. I have something you need – the missing pieces of the puzzle, you could say. I give it to you and you blow my brains out and you, what, leave my body in the boot? Is that the plan?'

Jamie didn't answer. When she had indulged in this fantasy, she'd always imagined Ben begging for his life. She'd imagined him crying and screaming. Sometimes she'd imagined him pious and remorseful, reduced to a blubbering, child-like state where he confessed all of his sins. But now, in real life, out in the hot, dark woods buzzing with mosquitoes, Ben was acting as if having a gun pressed to his head was normal. As if he'd been in this exact situation before and knew how to play it.

'I'm gonna let you in on a secret,' Ben said. 'I'm a cop.'

13

'Cop,' Jamie repeated.

Ben grinned, flashing his bloody teeth. 'Glad to see that bullet I put in your head didn't impair your hearing.'

A sensation like slicing razor blades ran up her spine, reached the base of her skull and then made its way through the scarred meat of her brain. Brought her back to the place she had lived every day since the shootings – a space of perpetual darkness where the air felt like concrete blocks stacked against her skin, her bones threatening to crack with each breath.

'Badge,' she said.

'I'm more of the undercover variety, so I don't carry one. Bad for business.'

Her heart banged away inside her chest.

Ben licked his swollen, bloody lips. 'I don't expect you to take my word for it, so here's what I'm going to do. I'm going to give you a number to call, and this person will explain the facts of life to you. You got a phone?'

She had left it inside the minivan. Driving to Belham, she had called Michael to tell him she was still at the hospital and wouldn't be home until late; she asked him to give Carter a bath. She'd tossed the phone on the passenger seat and forgotten about it until now, her focus on tailing the BMW without being spotted.

'A simple yes or no will do,' Ben said.

'My . . . ah . . . husband.'

'Danny.' Ben saying it as if they had been the closest of friends.

'Why . . . you . . . ah . . . did you –'

'The person you're about to call will explain everything. Let me know when you're ready to start dialling. If you don't have a phone, you can borrow mine. It's in my right-front pocket.'

Jamie didn't move – was suddenly afraid to move. Something about the way Ben had shifted the tables on her, dictating what he wanted her to do in that calm voice of his, kept her feet planted.

'Tell . . . me.'

'The number is six one seven, two –'

'No,' she said. 'Husband. Why?'

'You've got to speak to my man. He can –'

'No. You . . . ah . . . ah . . . explain.'

'I understand you're pissed and want your questions answered right now. Don't begrudge you that in the least. I mean, you've prayed for this moment for a long time and want it to go your way.'

Ben closed his eyes for a moment, then took in a deep breath. In her mind's eye she could see the locked door at the end of the hall – the dead room. She had replaced the beige carpet and repainted the walls. It looked and smelled new, but each time she went in she thought she could still smell blood. She remembered Michael screaming behind the duct tape covering his mouth. Ben had covered their eyes with duct tape, but she had tipped over her chair and, while she was struggling on the floor, the tape had slid down; she saw Ben take out a gun and fire at Michael but there was only a dry click and Michael looked at her and her first thought – and it shamed her to admit this – her first thought had been to protect Carter, he was younger, more vulnerable. She remembered Ben putting on a pair of bifocals and studying the gun and then saying, 'Goddamn chamber's empty. Imagine that.'

She remembered everything. Every moment, every sound and scream.

'Here's our dilemma,' Ben said, opening his eyes. 'I can't think too well on account of the blood loss and the fact that you slammed my noggin against the floor. What I'm saying is I'm a little fuzzy on the details. You want your questions answered, then I suggest you start dialling now because I think I'm going to pass out.'

'Partners,' she said. 'Names.'

'You need to talk to my supervisor. I swear, with God as my witness, he'll tell you everything you need to know.'

Please, Mrs Russo, please don't scream or run.

Ben saying those words as he stood inside her

kitchen holding Carter. Her eighteen-month-old son's tiny fingers wrapped around the Colt's barrel, trying to put it in his mouth.

Just do what I say, Mrs Russo, and I swear, with God as my witness, we won't hurt you or the kids. We just want to have a little talk with Danny when he gets home, okay?

Jamie slammed Ben's face against the side of the boot. He fell sideways, fresh blood pouring from his nose.

'Christ, you mean business, don't you?' he said after he finished gagging.

'Names,' Jamie said.

'Make the phone call.'

No. It was a trap. What was the person he wanted her to call going to do? Trace the call? A cop could do that with a warrant. Did the phone have some sort of GPS unit in it that could locate him? Anyone could do that with the right software and equipment – as long as the phone was turned on. Was it turned on right now?

She reached into his pocket and removed the mobile. It was something called a Palm Treo. It was turned on; a tiny green light blinked, sending out a signal. She took out the battery and stuffed everything inside her jacket pocket.

A new expression on Ben's face now: anger.

'Make the call,' Ben said again. 'That's the only way this is going to work.'

Her eyes grew hot and tears spilled down her

cheeks. In her mind she saw Carter sitting in the bath-tub, saw the two hard, round, white scars the size of half dollars on his back left by the exit wounds.

Jamie placed the Magnum's muzzle against Ben's kneecap and fired.

Ben howled in pain, the sound tearing something free from inside her chest. Something that cooled her blood and made her limbs shake.

'*NAMES.*'

Ben couldn't answer. He was screaming, the tendons in his neck bulging underneath the skin like rope as he flopped around inside the boot.

She tucked the Magnum back inside the holster, then grabbed him by the jacket. Ben tried to fight her, struggling with his bound wrists and ankles, but he was too weak, in too much pain. She threw him on the ground.

'*N-N-N-NAMES.*'

His mouth quivered, spitting up blood. He didn't answer.

She looked at his knee, then slammed her foot down on the shredded pulp of skin and fractured bones.

Ben howled again, his face turning a deep, dark red – the same shade Dan's face had been when she found his head resting inside the kitchen sink.

Ben made a weird gurgling sound. As if he were drowning. She grabbed him underneath the arms, lifted him up and dragged him across the damp ground. His body jerked and he vomited blood.

She threw his legs over the edge of the cliff, then pulled him up into a sitting position. She pushed his head forward so he could see the oily slick of water shimmering in the moonlight far below.

'N-n-n-n-names,' she sputtered against his bloody ear. 'P-p-p-partner . . . n-n-names.'

Ben sucked in air. Vomited.

'Tell me. Tell or . . . ah . . . ah . . .'

He didn't answer.

She shook him. 'Off ledge . . . throw you . . . water . . .'

Ben wouldn't answer.

'Drown . . . in . . . ah . . . drown. Water. You'll drown.'

Ben refused to speak. She let go of him and reached for the Magnum, prepared to shoot his other knee, to shoot him into pieces until he spoke.

His body slumped against the ground. Ben didn't cough or move – oh, Jesus, oh, Jesus, no. She dropped to her knees and pressed her fingers against his slick, bloody neck.

There, a faint pulse.

'N-N-N-Names!'

Jamie shook him. He stared up at her, his head bobbing from side to side.

She slapped him across the face.

He groaned. His lips quivered.

'TELL . . . AH . . . TELL ME.'

Ben didn't answer but his lips kept moving. Blood trickled out of his ears. He was bleeding out. Dying. The answers she needed were caged somewhere inside his skull and she wouldn't know them unless Ben woke up. He *had* to wake up.

She pressed her mouth against his, the slick, bloody mess sliding against her lips, and screamed air into his lungs until she was dizzy. She pulled her mouth away, gagging, then pumped his chest with her fists the way she'd been taught – three sharp pumps. Ben didn't move or make a sound. She screamed air down into his lungs again. Ben lay still. Jamie pounded his chest with her fists and he didn't move and she kept hitting him and screaming for him to wake up even though she knew it was too late.

14

Jamie scrubbed the blood from her face and her scraped and swollen hands using napkins and a half-full bottle of water she'd found in a McDonald's bag tossed on the back floor of the Honda.

She checked her face in the side mirror. The left side was swollen but clean. She couldn't do anything about the blood on her clothes and sneakers until she got home.

You better pray to God you don't get pulled over.

She tossed the bloody napkins inside the boot. Ben stared up at her with a puzzled expression. *Why so sad, hon? Did you really think I was going to tell you what you needed to know? You were going to kill me anyway, so what was in it for me?*

Ben could have told her everything and she still would have killed him. She had known that the second she decided to follow him from the drugstore.

Jamie reached inside the boot, pinched his eye and came away with a bright blue contact lens. Ben's real eyes were brown, just as she remembered.

She searched his zippered pockets and found a Tiffany key ring and wallet. She wondered if one of the keys opened the house in Charlestown. Maybe the fat guy in the Hawaiian shirt lived there. Maybe he was the man who had killed her husband.

She stuffed Ben's things in her pockets. Slammed the boot lid shut, placed her hands on the bumper and started to push. The damp ground was muddy but sloped forward and after a moment the car started to pick up speed.

I'll let you in on a secret, Ben had told her. *I'm a cop.*

Bullshit. An undercover cop or Fed wouldn't have forced his way inside a house and shot two children in cold blood. A cop wouldn't have allowed two men to shove someone's hand inside a running waste-disposal unit and wrap a noose around their neck. A cop wouldn't have broken into a house and slit a woman's throat. Ben had made it up, a last-ditch attempt to spare his life.

The front tyres dripped over the edge. Jamie gave a final push and let go. She stood hunched forward with her hands on her knees, sweating and sucking in the muggy night air as the car disappeared from her view.

For a moment the only sounds she heard were the crickets chirping from the woods. Then a loud splash that sounded far away, as though it was happening in another place, at another time. Standing at the cliff's edge, she watched the car being swallowed inside a cyclone of silver moonlit bubbles. Growing up in Belham, she remembered the time some drunk had fallen over in the water. For days divers searched for the man's body. It was never found.

Her muscles tensed and her skin grew cold. What if the car didn't sink? What if the water was too shallow? In the evening's chaos she hadn't thought through that possibility.

All her worrying, it turned out, was for nothing. The car sank below the black water shivering with moonlight. The surface grew calm again.

She headed towards the path, hot and uncomfortable underneath the bloody windbreaker. She wished she could take it off but it covered the shoulder holster and Ben's Glock, which was wedged in the back of her jeans. The extended magazine kept digging into her lower back.

She had a long walk ahead of her. She had parked on Kale, a busy neighbourhood off Blakely full of other suburban homes with minivans much like her own. She knew she couldn't watch him from the neighbourhood – too risky, too exposed; plus Ben or his partner had started drawing the front shades of the house. Fortunately, she knew Belham and knew where to park.

Jamie hoped the teenager was okay.

She hadn't known he was inside, not at first. Standing in the hot, dark woods behind the house, she had debated about moving to the back fence for a closer view, then ruled it out. The homes were too close together. Someone might be watching from a window, see her and call the police. Safer to watch from inside the woods.

In addition to the Magnum, she'd brought the small pair of binoculars she kept in the back of the minivan. (Michael liked to use them; Dan had bought them for sporting events and those rare times he went hunting. She kept them in the glovebox.) From her vantage point she could see only part of the kitchen. She had an excellent view of the sliding glass door leading into the living room and for a long time watched Ben search every inch of the room, even going so far as to cut the chair and sofa cushions. Not once did she see the teenager tied down to the chair.

That changed later, when she heard a car pull into the driveway, and the mechanical chug as the motor hauled up the garage door.

Jamie remembered trying to find a new vantage point. The tree limbs kept obstructing her view. Walking through woods in the dark, in a hurry and without the aid of a flashlight, wasn't desirable. She kept tripping and bumping into things. It was slow, tedious work.

By the time she'd found a new spot, the blonde-haired woman in the blue T-shirt was taped down to a chair seated across from her son, their eyes covered with duct tape. The boy's mouth was taped shut but not the woman's; Jamie could see her screaming as the man with the suit started breaking her fingers. Ben stood behind him holding a barber's straight-edged razor.

Jamie reached for her phone, then remembered

she'd left it in the minivan. It didn't matter. Even if she had brought it, by the time she stammered through the 911 call the woman and boy would be dead. Ben had just cut off one of the woman's fingers.

Jamie's first thought – and it shamed her to admit this – was evidence. As a former cop, her fingerprints were stored on a database. She couldn't leave her prints or any other evidence for the police to find; she had to protect her children. She fumbled at her zippered pocket for the latex gloves.

What happened next came back to her in a series of flashes: running down the incline, slipping and falling. Getting up and tripping again. Finally finding the gate. Unzipping her jacket, grabbing the Magnum and sprinting across the lawn. Moving quietly up the back steps, not wanting to alert Ben and his partner, then discovering that the sliding glass door was locked. The woman screaming. Two shots and the glass shattering. Climbing inside. From the living room, firing two shots at the suited man, hitting him in the stomach. Swinging the Magnum to Ben and seeing the woman's cut throat. A shot to the thigh and Ben falling backwards, on top of the boy, tipping over the chair. Kicking Ben in the stomach and then grabbing the handcuffs from the suited man lying on the floor, bleeding out of his chest. Wrestling Ben on the floor and cuffing him. Then picking up the spent brass.

A quick search of the woman's pockets revealed

the set of keys for the Honda. With Ben cuffed and taped inside the boot, Jamie came back, picked up the straight-edged razor and cut through the boy's bindings. She left the strips of tape covering his eyes, placed the cordless phone she'd found on the floor in his hand and ran fast to the waiting car.

Jamie wished she could talk to the boy. Hold his hand and share her story, a fellow traveller who could help him navigate his way through this new landscape of grief.

Jamie drove well under the speed limit in case any cops were out on patrol. She turned on the radio and moved the dial to Boston's all-news radio station, WBZ.

She had to wait fifteen minutes to find out what had happened in Belham.

Police hadn't released the names of the woman or the boy. A reporter on the scene described 'an intense shootout in the woods behind the home that included stun and smoke grenades'. The reporter didn't have any details, as 'police have refused to comment'.

Jamie wondered if the fat man in the Hawaiian shirt was involved. He had parked the BMW at the end of the street. Had the police somehow found him? Maybe tried to corner his BMW? Had Mr Hawaii tried to escape through the woods?

The reporter had a breaking development. One of the victims, a male teenager who had been rushed to hospital, had apparently committed suicide. Nothing more was given, but the reporter urged listeners to stay tuned for further details.

Suicide. The boy had seemed around the same age as Michael, her thirteen-year-old. Jamie drove the rest of the way home numb all over.

Forty minutes later she pulled into her driveway. She didn't open the garage, not wanting to wake the kids. She ran to the back of the house and unlocked the cellar door. She heard the beep for the burglar alarm, entered the code, and then placed Ben's Glock and the things from her pocket on Dan's old desk – a slab of plywood the size of a door set across two metal filing cabinets. When he was alive, Dan would come down here to catch up on paperwork or to read through one of his woodworking magazines.

She picked up Ben's wallet. No credit cards, just a licence with the name Benjamin Masters. Local address too: Boston. *Has he been living here all this time?*

She picked up the Glock, turning it over in her hands.

Three safeties, three modes of fire: safe, automatic and semi-automatic. Laser-targeting sight mounted against the frame. She examined the barrel and found the model number. A Glock eighteen. She'd never heard of it. She ejected the extended magazine and read the words stamped into the metal tubing: RESTRICTED IN THE USA.

The rounds had a pitted nose. The hairs on the back of her neck stood up.

She knew about hollow-point rounds, how they expanded when they hit the victim's skin, the pressure from the rush of blood expanding the snub-nose tip and turning it into a spinning mushroom of razor-sharp lead claws that shred tissue and organs as it spiralled its way through the body. Hollow-point rounds were one-stop shots. Even with immediate medical attention, victims usually died from massive blood loss.

If Ben had shot me, she thought, placing the Glock back on the desk, *I wouldn't be alive right now.*

Standing inside the kitchen, she stuffed all of her clothing and the spent brass inside a rubbish bag. She tossed the bag inside the garage. She'd find a place to dump it later. She walked back down the hall to use the shower. Scrubbed clean, she grabbed a pair of cotton shorts and a T-shirt from the dryer and went upstairs to see the kids.

Michael's room first. She kissed him on the forehead. Michael, with his sandy-brown hair and lean swimmer's build, looked so much like his father it was painful.

Carter wasn't in his bedroom.

She found him sleeping in her bed.

Jamie crawled underneath the sheets and cuddled up next to her six-year-old. He smelled clean. Good. Michael had remembered to give him a bath.

She wrapped her arm around Carter's small waist and pulled him close. The blond stubble of his buzz cut tickled her chin.

She was too wired to sleep. She stared out of the window at the dark sky and rubbed her fingers across the thick lines of scars covering his stomach – permanent reminders of the scalpels that had cut him open to save his life. The ER doctors had managed to stem the bleeding and repair the damage to his stomach and lungs.

'Dead,' she whispered against Carter's ear. 'Killed him.'

Her son breathed softly beside her. He didn't suffer from nightmares any more, not like he had the first year, when he'd wake up screaming in the middle of the night. Sometimes he'd crawled into bed with her. Sometimes she'd woken to find him standing at her bedroom window, chewing the corner of his ratty blue blanket. She'd asked him what was wrong but the answer was always the same: *I'm watching for the bad men, Mom. Do you think they'll come back?*

Jamie hugged her son.

'I will . . . find . . . find . . . partners,' she whispered. 'Kill . . . them.' She said the words to Carter. To the cool air inside the locked house. To God. 'I will . . . kill them to . . . to . . . keep you and Michael safe.'

Day 2

15

The following morning, at half past eight, Darby sat in her office chair with her feet propped up on the corner of the desk. She stared out of the windows overlooking another grey sky while listening to Dr Aaron Goldstein, a Boston-based neurologist brought in to treat the boy, John/Sean Hallcox. The man spoke in a dry monotone, as though he were reciting from a medical textbook.

'The bullet entered underneath the boy's chin,' Dr Goldstein was saying. 'Instead of traversing the cranial cavity and leaving through an exit wound, the bullet ricocheted inside the skull, with massive tearing caused by the shock waves. This resulted in –'

'Doctor, I don't mean to be rude, but I was in the hospital room when John Hallcox shot himself. I know the bullet didn't pass through the skull. I want to know his condition.' She popped a couple of Advils in her mouth and washed them down with cold water fizzing with Alka-Seltzer.

'We performed a debridement,' Goldstein said. 'The procedure involves removing bone and bullet fragments from the brain. We removed a good majority of them, but I'm sorry to say there were some fragments that were so deeply imbedded near sensitive areas that I had to leave them behind. I'm more concerned about what we refer to as secondary effects.'

'Swelling and bleeding from ruptured blood vessels.'

'Yes.' A bright tone in the man's voice, surprised that she knew such things. 'With gunshot wounds to the head there's always a high risk of oedema and, in Mr Hallcox's case, infection. We're treating him with strong antibiotics, but these kinds of infections – the ones involving the brain – are extremely difficult to overcome. Fortunately, he hasn't experienced a seizure, but he's still in a coma.'

'Where does he fall on the Glasgow Coma Scale?'

'I can't give you an accurate GCS score at the moment. Because of the intubation and severe facial swelling, he can't talk and I can't test his eyes' responses.'

'Do you think there's a chance he'll be able to talk?'

'To you?'

'To anyone, Doctor.'

'There's always a possibility, but I'm inclined to say no. I doubt he'll survive – not from the gunshot wound but from the infection. Does he have any family in the area? My understanding is the mother died rather tragically.'

'She was murdered.'

'Well, if you find any family members, please let us know. Certain arrangements will need to be made. That's all I can tell you right now, Miss McCormick.'

'Would you call me if there's any change? I'd like . . . I want to know how he's doing.'

'Of course. What's the best way to reach you?'

They exchanged numbers. Darby thanked the doctor, swung her legs off the desk and dialled directory inquiries to ask for the number of the FBI's field office in Albany, New York.

She introduced herself to the woman who answered the phone and asked to speak to SAC Dylan Phillips.

'Let me connect you to his office,' the woman said.

Phillips wasn't in his office yet. Darby left a message with the man's secretary.

Pine had told her he was working on locating the owner of the house, Dr Martin Wexler and his wife, Elaine. Darby didn't want to wait. She turned to her computer. When she had the information she needed, she started working the phone.

An hour later she had tracked down one of Wexler's children – his eldest son, David, who lived in Wisconsin. He had the number for his parents' home in the South of France. The names Amy and John Hallcox didn't mean anything to him.

Darby called the number. A machine picked up, the voice in French. She left a detailed message along with her office and mobile numbers, and asked them to call regardless of the time.

Darby hung up and sat in the silence of her office, her thoughts drifting to John Hallcox – *Sean*, she reminded herself. The twelve-year-old was lying in a coma. Her father had lain in a coma for a month. His GCS score had been 1. He never opened his eyes, never made any verbal sounds or physical movements. He was brain dead.

She remembered gripping his hand in her own while the doctor explained to her mother what would happen to Big Red after his life-support machine was turned off. Darby remembered digging her fingernails into his callused palm and drawing blood. She remembered hoping – no, *believing* – the pain would wake up her father. Then the machine was turned off and they waited for his body to die. Darby propped her elbows on her desk and looked at her hands. They were bigger now, the callused skin on her palms and fingers stained with dried blood. Sean's blood. She had held him while screaming for help.

A soft knock on the door. She looked up and saw Police Commissioner Christina Chadzynski.

'May I come in?'

Darby nodded. Chadzynski took one of the chairs across from the desk, crossed her legs and folded her hands on her lap. This morning she was dressed in a stylish black suit. It was the only colour she seemed to wear. The woman was thin and trim – she was an avid runner – but no amount of exercise, sleep or makeup could hid the fatigue etched in the skin around her ice-blue eyes.

'It's quiet in here,' Chadzynski said.

'The entire lab is in Belham processing the house. Did you read my report?' Darby had filed it late the previous night before crashing on the office sofa.

'I read it first thing this morning,' Chadzynski said. 'It's all over the news, what happened in Belham, the hospital, all of it.'

'Did the news mention anything about the FBI trying to take over the investigation?'

'No, they didn't.' She seemed to be drawing out her words, measuring each one carefully before she spoke. 'Those men you saw in the woods – have you heard anything?'

'Nothing's come over the wire about any hospitals treating a white male for a gunshot wound, but Pine and his men are calling around just to be sure. He's on his way to Vermont to meet with the police to go through Amy Hallcox's apartment.'

'You mentioned the woman's parents were murdered but you didn't list any details.'

'Her son didn't give me any, and I can't find any homicides involving the name Hallcox.'

'Do you have any news on the boy's condition?'

'I just got off the phone with the neurologist,' Darby said, and told Chadzynski about her conversation with Dr Goldstein.

'How did the Hallcox boy get the gun?' Chadzynski asked. 'It wasn't mentioned in your report.'

'I didn't find out until this morning. He had a thigh holster. His baggy shorts covered it.'

'I can't believe no one noticed it.'

'He wasn't a suspect, so there was no reason for anyone to pat him down. When the EMTs brought him to the hospital, the kid refused to let anyone touch him. Threw a fit, the doctor told me. He was in shock, so they gave him some space to calm down. Based upon what the boy told me last night, I wouldn't be surprised if the mother gave the revolver to him.'

'What's this business about him requesting to speak to your father?'

'I don't know.' Darby rubbed her face, then ran her fingers through her hair. She couldn't remember a time when she had felt this tired. 'Right now your guess is as good as mine.'

'Did you get any sleep?'

'Maybe a couple of hours. Every time I shut my eyes, all I can see is that kid slamming the muzzle underneath his chin. If that Fed hadn't come into the room, Sean wouldn't be in a coma.'

'The boy was in shock, Darby. The commotion alone –'

'Sean was talking to me. I'd finally got him to a place where he trusted me – he told me his real name was Sean. He was going to tell me the truth about his grand-parents – why they were killed, the names of the people who did it. He was going to tell me everything and then that prick came in waving his badge and saying he was taking over the investigation and moving the kid. He scared the shit out of him.'

'That might very well be true. But, with all due respect, your professionalism can be called into question.'

Darby leaned back in her chair, waiting for the rest of it. Chadzynski might have a cop's blue blood running through her veins but she had the heart of a politician. She was quietly assembling people to help plan her campaign to run for governor. The real reason for her visit was damage control.

'I understand you assaulted him,' Chadzynski said.

'Is that what he called it?'

'I'm asking you.'

'We had a minor confrontation. I mentioned that in my report.'

'Yes, I know. I also know about your personal history with the FBI. Tell me what happened.'

'Did you read the part where Special Agent Phillips didn't stick around the hospital? That he bolted along with my tape recorder?'

'You're positive about that accusation?'

'I checked with everyone who was there. Except Phillips, of course. When I get through with him, he'll be shitting bones for a week.'

'Eloquently put, as always. I haven't spoken to Special Agent Phillips or anyone from the Albany field office. I need to know how to handle this, so tell me *exactly* what happened.'

Darby's phone rang. She looked at the caller-ID.

'Speak of the devil,' she said, and picked up the phone. 'Darby McCormick.'

'This is Dylan Phillips returning your call. How can I help you, Miss McCormick?'

Darby didn't answer.

The voice on the other end of the line was deep, husky. The Federal agent she met last night had had a slight lisp and a voice that wasn't as deep. It was lighter, almost effeminate.

'Miss McCormick?'

'I'm here. I take it you don't know who I am.'

'Should I?'

'We met last night at St Joseph's Hospital.'

'I think you have me confused with someone else. Last night I was at dinner with my daughter and her fiancé.'

'Are you looking for a fugitive named Amy Hallcox?'

'I don't recognize that name. What's this about?'

'I don't know yet, but someone impersonated you last night. I'll call you back when I have more details.'

'Please do.'

Darby hung up and turned to her computer. She logged on to the National Crime Information Center.

'*Shit.*'

Darby scooped her keys off her desk.

Chadzynski stood. 'What's wrong?'

'NCIC didn't have a listing for Amy Hallcox. There is no fugitive warrant.'

'Where are you going?'

'To the hospital,' Darby said, coming out from behind the desk. 'I need to pull last night's security tapes.'

16

Jamie woke up to bickering voices. Her bedroom door had been shut and Carter was no longer beside her.

'Stop bossing me around,' Carter said from behind the door.

'*Keep your voice down*,' Michael hissed. 'You'll wake up Mom.'

Too late, she thought, and looked at the alarm clock. It was going on eleven.

Shit. She had overslept and the kids had missed the bus for camp. She'd have to drive them. She whipped off the covers and got out of bed, her head groggy, pounding.

'I'll get dressed when I want to,' Carter said. 'You're not the boss of me, pancake balls.'

'Dumb-dumb, how many times do I have to tell you "pancake balls" doesn't make any sense?'

'Oh, yes, it does.'

Jamie opened the door. Her two boys were huddled at the end of the hall in front of the dead room – Carter barefoot and dressed in his Batman pyjamas, a black Batman mask covering his face; Michael wearing baggy shorts, sneakers and another one of Dan's old Bruce Springsteen concert T-shirts. They were too big for Michael's slender frame but he wore them anyway – to stay close to his father, she suspected, to try to keep him from fading.

'Jesus, Mom,' Michael said, coming closer. 'What happened to your face?'

'Fell. I . . . ah . . . tripped in . . . ah . . . ah . . . hospital. Garage. Hit . . . ah . . . bumper. Car bumper.'

Michael stared at her the way Dan used to, with that X-ray vision glare that told her he'd caught her in a lie.

She looked at Carter and said, 'Get . . . ah . . . dressed.'

'Okay, Mom.' He grinned at his older brother before ducking into his bedroom.

Jamie went into the master bathroom and started brushing her teeth. A moment later she saw Michael's reflection in the mirror. He stood in the doorway, his arms crossed over his chest.

'How'd the hospital tests go?'

'Fine,' she said around her toothbrush. 'You . . . ah . . . eat?'

He nodded. 'I fed Carter too.'

'Thanks.'

'You were gone a long time.'

She spit out toothpaste. 'Fine. Honest.'

'You didn't get home until after three in the morning.'

A mild irritation crept its way through her. Michael was always monitoring her comings and goings, clocking the time of her arrivals and departures.

Why are you getting angry at him, Jamie? You were gone all day, then you called and fed him that lie about having to stay late at the hospital to have another MRI and now here you are with the right side of your face swollen. He's worried about you. For Chrissakes, go easy on him.

'Mom, I've been doing some thinking, and I don't want to go to sports camp any more.'

'Why?'

'I'm too old for it. And I was thinking I could help you around the house for the rest of the summer. Mow the grass, do some cleaning. The garage could use it. The house hasn't been cleaned since . . . you know.'

Since your father was murdered.

It was a tempting offer, having both Michael and Carter close to her now. She might have indulged the idea if it wasn't for Ben. She needed to devote her time to finding his two partners. After she dropped off the kids, the plan was to head to Ben's Boston address. She wanted to see what was in his house, if anything.

'I'm not scared staying alone at the house – I was fine yesterday while you were at the hospital,' Michael said. 'I can watch Carter for you too. And we can spend some time together before school starts.'

Jamie rinsed out her mouth and shut off the water. She turned to him and said, 'You . . . ah . . . need . . . ah . . . need . . . to, ah . . . be with . . . ah . . . friends.'

'What friends? They avoid me. It's like I'm invisible.'

'Have . . . ah . . . you . . . talked . . . ah –'

'Mom, I just said they *avoid* me. They don't call me to hang out or do anything. Even their parents avoid me. Remember last week when we were at the grocery store and saw Tommy's mother? Remember what happened?'

Unfortunately, she did.

Standing in the cereal aisle with Michael and Carter, she saw Tommy Gerrad's mother, Lisa, turning her trolley into the aisle. Jamie waved hello and then, in her broken, fragmented speech, suggested that Tommy should come over and hang out with Michael, play on the Xbox or maybe even make a plan to see a Pawtucket Red Sox game. Both boys loved baseball.

Lisa Gerrad made up some excuse about how booked the summer was with camp and holidays. She checked her watch, said she had to get to an appointment and moved past them as if the shop had suddenly caught on fire.

'Think about the money you'll save,' Michael said. 'I know money's tight.'

Jamie sighed, not wanting to think about money right now, how Dan's meagre investments, and her disability and SSI payments, barely covered the monthly bills. She had used the payout from Dan's small life insurance policy to put a serious dent in the mortgage, but even after refinancing at a lower rate, she still had to pay Wellesley's property taxes, which just kept going up year after year.

'Thank . . . ah . . . you, but . . . ah . . . ah . . . you . . . ah . . . need to . . . ah . . . go. To camp.'

Michael didn't speak, but the fight hadn't left his eyes.

She didn't have time to argue. She brushed past him and went downstairs to gather Ben's things, reminding herself to dump the bag of bloody clothing in the back of the minivan.

The kids didn't talk during the twenty-minute drive to Babson College. Carter played a game on his Nintendo DS. Michael sat in the front seat, earbud headphones connected to the iPod resting on his stomach, and stared out of the window as if he were on the way to his funeral.

Jamie pulled up to the main building, a massive brick structure with white pillars in the front. Kids ranging from as young as five to as old as sixteen bounded up the steps and ran around the lush, green campus shaded with trees.

'Take . . . ah . . . bus . . . ah . . . ah . . . home, okay?'

'Okay, Mom.' Carter kissed her on the cheek.

'I . . . ah . . . may . . . ah . . . home late.'

Carter grabbed his backpack and opened the door. Michael didn't move. He was looking out of the front window at Tommy Gerrad, who was standing with a group of other thirteen-year-olds near the steps. They were all whispering to each other, staring at the minivan.

Jamie debated about whether to say something to Tommy. She had known him since pre-school. Spoiled and sometimes bratty, but all and all a good kid.

'Mom, why do you hate me so much?'

She spun around on her seat, her stomach clenching. She tried to speak but couldn't get the words out.

'Okay, maybe hate was the wrong word,' he said. 'But you don't like me. You feel *something*. Is it because I look like Dad?'

Yes, Michael was a spitting image of his father, and, if that wasn't painful enough, Michael, just like his father, always asked complicated emotional questions in this nonchalant way, as if they were speaking about mathematical equations instead of feelings. Like Dan, Michael kept his true emotions bottled and locked away on some shelf to gather dust.

'I know I remind you of him,' Michael said. 'What he did to us.'

I still don't know what your father did to us, Jamie wanted to say.

'Forget it,' he said, and opened the door. 'You'll just go on pretending.'

'Pre . . . ah . . . ah . . . Pretending?'

'That you wished I was dead.'

A cold, sick sweat broke out across her skin. 'I . . . I . . . ah . . . don't . . . ah . . . ah . . .'

'Ever since he died, it's like you can't stand being around me – and don't say you don't because you and I both know it's true. I'm more like Dad, and Carter's more like you. If I was dead, you would have moved on.'

To what? Jamie wanted to say. *To where?*

'I know you wouldn't have kept the house,' he said. 'I know you wanted to leave here but didn't because of me. I had to beg you to stay.'

'Not . . . ah . . . not true.'

'About the house or that you wished I was dead?'

She started to speak, stammering the words as usual.

Michael, either sick of waiting or not wanting to hear what she had to say, opened the door. She tried to grab his arm but he had already stepped out of the car.

'Michael, don't . . . ah . . . wait –'

He shut the door and walked away. She stared after him, blinking back tears.

She *didn't* hate him and she *didn't* wish he was dead. Jesus! How could he have said such appalling things? Yes, after Dan's murder, she had wanted to pack up and move. Michael had put up a fight, but even if he had wanted to move, it wouldn't have mattered. The house couldn't be sold. She had called a number of real estate agents. They were interested until they recognized the address.

But you don't like me. You feel something . . . *it's like you can't stand being around me – and don't say you don't because you and I both know it's true . . .*

Michael had never been a touchy-feely kid, not even

as a baby. He had rejected her breast, preferring the bottle. He screamed after he finished eating, wanting to get away from her. Michael didn't cry when Dan fed him. They had a special connection, Michael and Dan, the two sharing a bond and a secret language spoken mainly through gestures, nods and grunts. And now Dan was gone, leaving Michael marooned in some strange wilderness without a guide or compass.

Jamie needed to be busy. She took Ben's mobile phone from her pocket, wanting to reconnect the battery and take a closer look at what was stored on it. Maybe there would be something –

A knock on her window startled her.

She whipped her head around and saw a tall, lanky man with short white hair and thick-framed glasses. Her 68-year-old parish priest, Father James Humphrey.

She rolled down the window. 'What . . . ah . . . why . . . ah . . . you here?'

'I help out with the sports programme.' His soft voice still carried traces of his Irish brogue. His grandparents had come over on the boat, and all the Humphrey children – nine brothers scattered across the north-east – had kept the accent alive.

He seemed to be waiting for her to say something – or maybe he didn't know where to start. She hadn't seen him or gone to church since Dan's murder.

'I . . . ah . . . can't talk . . . ah . . . now. Got . . . ah . . . busy day.'

'What happened to your face?'

'Accident,' she said. 'Fell.'

'Against a man's fist?'

Her face flushed.

'My brother Colm, God rest his soul, was a boxer. I recognize a shiner when I see one.' Humphrey's kind and gentle eyes were free of judgement. 'What happened, love? Who hit you?'

'Accident,' she said again. 'I have . . . ah . . . go. Appointment.'

He nodded and shifted his gaze to Carter's car seat. 'Are you still seeing the therapist?'

'Yes.' Humphrey had given her the name of a therapist who specialized in helping victims of trauma. The woman, Dr Wakefield, agreed to work pro bono. Jamie had visited the woman for a month and then stopped going.

Humphrey looked back at her.

He knows, she thought. *He knows I've lied to him, I can see it written all over his face.*

'Have to . . . ah . . . go. Goodbye . . . ah . . . Father Jim.' Jamie put the minivan in gear and drove away.

17

Darby placed last night's security tapes on the passenger seat of her car. There had been no need for a warrant. Hospital officials were glad to cooperate.

On her way out, she had checked on Sean's condition. The neurologist, Dr Goldstein, had gone back to Boston, so she spoke to one of the ICU nurses, a heavy older woman with silver hair.

'He's brain dead,' the nurse said, with great sympathy. Then she touched the small, plain gold cross on the chain resting against her white shirt and added, 'When you find a family member, I suggest you tell them to make funeral arrangements.'

Darby pulled out of the car park's south exit, away from the crowd of reporters huddled around the main doors hoping to find a doctor or nurse willing to talk about Sean's condition.

Driving through the streets on the way back to the city, she kept checking her rear-view mirror for the brown van with the dented front bumper.

Ten minutes later, at a busy downtown intersection, she spotted it six cars behind her. She had first noticed it on her way out of Boston. The van never got too close. It didn't need to. Her car, a forest-green

1974 Ford Falcon GT Coupe, stood out in the busy traffic and was easy to follow.

Darby glanced at the dashboard clock. Quarter to twelve. The woman's autopsy was scheduled today at three. Forty minutes to get back to Boston. That gave her a little over two hours to examine the body for evidence. Plenty of time to go to the Belham house and drive back to the city.

Walton Street was blocked off with news vans. She took the next left, on to Boynton, and drove slowly with her attention locked on her rear-view mirror. The van didn't follow. It whisked straight past Boynton.

She pulled on to Marshall and parked in the driveway. Belham PD had brought in more sawhorses to corral the swelling number of reporters.

The patrolman guarding the front door had a sunburned face. After she showed him her ID, he put down his coffee cup and wrote her name on a clipboard.

'Have any Feds been inside?' Darby asked.

'No, ma'am.'

'Any Feds asked to go in? Have you seen any around the house?'

'No one's asked to go in. As for your question about them poking around, I can't say that I've seen anyone. I've been here since six.'

'Can I see your clipboard?'

'Sure.'

She scanned the list of names. Boston Lab personnel and Belham detectives. She handed the clipboard back, thanked him and entered the house.

Lab techs stood in the foyer dusting surfaces for prints. Bagged evidence lined the stairs. She moved around them and made her way to the master bedroom. Fingerprint powder covered the walls.

Her kit was right where she had left it when Coop summoned her to the hospital: next to the leather club chair. She removed her camera and made her way back downstairs.

Techs dressed in bunny suits soaked through with sweat were busy collecting evidence from the chairs. Coop had tagged them – a reminder to personnel that the chairs were to be transported to the lab. Walking through the kitchen of drying blood, she was glad to see everyone using the new digital SLR cameras to document everything.

She found Coop in the living room. He had set up a fuming tent around the leather cushions.

He pulled the mask down and said, 'Lots of smooth glove prints. We –'

'You still keep those binoculars in your kit?'

'I do.' He tapped it with his foot. 'What do you need them for?'

'I'm going to do some sightseeing. I'll be back in a few.'

'Come see me when you're done.'

Darby jogged through the woods. When she

reached the top of the second incline, she stopped running and examined the trees. Here was a tall, dead pine, the upper trunk split by lightning.

Coop's binoculars had a leather strap. She fitted it around her neck, then placed the binoculars against the small of her back. She did the same thing with the camera.

She jumped, grabbing the overhead limb with both hands and pulling her feet up, the leather straps pressed against her throat. Wrapping her legs around the limb, she hoisted herself up and straddled the limb. After a moment of wrangling with the straps, she stood and made her way to the trunk.

Climbing, she tested the weight of each limb. An occasional car whooshed by on the Blakely Road and in the distance she could hear branches snapping, Mark Alves's deep voice shouting something to Randy Scott. She couldn't make out what they were saying. She stopped climbing when she had a clear view of the neighbourhood.

Binoculars in hand, she searched the areas where the van would be able to see her car. She was surprised to find it parked on the corner of Walton and Cranmore, far away from the house and far from the news vans with their satellite feeds.

The van had Massachusetts plates. She scooped the pen from her shirt pocket and wrote the number on her forearm. Then she removed her phone from the belt clip and dialled the main number for Belham police.

'This is Darby McCormick from Boston's Criminal Investigative Unit. I'm working with Detective Sergeant Artie Pine on the homicide on Marshall Street. I need you to send a couple of squad cars to Walton Street to apprehend the driver of a brown van. Tell them to drive up Cranmore and park their vehicles so they block access to Walton – I'll explain why when they get there. I also need them to run a plate for me.'

She gave the operator the plate and her mobile number, then switched to the camera and took several pictures of the van. The camera lens wasn't powerful enough to focus on the front plate.

The door opened. The man who stepped out had a round, shaved head. She wondered if this was the same man she'd seen last night wearing the tactical vest and night-vision goggles.

The man buttoned his light grey suit jacket and started running. Darby snapped pictures, catching sight of the slight bulge from the handgun he wore on his belt.

Baldy shoved his way past the throng of reporters and cameramen, then grabbed the elbow of a TV cameraman dressed in jeans, sneakers and a white shirt. Sunglasses covered his eyes and he wore headphones over a baseball cap.

More pictures and then she quickly zoomed in on his face and managed to get a good, clear shot of Baldy speaking into the cameraman's ear. The two pushed through the crowd and were off and running.

Darby kept taking pictures as the van backed on to Cranmore. A screech of rubber and someone slammed on their car horn. Watching the van's tyres spinning with smoke, she wondered if Baldy had a police radio or a scanner in his car. Maybe someone had called to tip him off.

18

The East Boston address listed on Ben Masters's licence belonged to an abandoned automotive garage called Delaney's. The sign, with its faded red lettering on wood bleached from the sun, sat above a front door boarded up with plywood sheets. All the windows had also been boarded up and sprayed with graffiti. Two big padlocks secured the chains wrapped around the chain-linked gate for the car park. Weeds grew out of cracked asphalt.

Did the garage hold some sort of significance or value for Ben? Or had he simply chosen this site because it was abandoned? It was maddening to wonder.

She turned around and drove up a street of triple-decker houses. She would need to buy a pair of bolt cutters on the way home, and find a hammer and a crowbar. She could come back with them tonight.

The Charlestown house sitting on the corner of Old Rutherford Avenue and Ashmont Street was painted a robin's-egg blue. Jamie did three drive-bys to check the windows. They were all dark. No vehicle was parked in the driveway.

Idling at the stop sign, she looked across the street to the white mail box spotted with rust. Gold decals for the number '16' were taped to it. She didn't see a name.

She pulled to the side and double-parked against the cars filling every empty spot along the narrow one-way street. She hit the button for the hazard lights, left the minivan running and stepped out tugging the brim of the Red Sox baseball cap to push it further down her forehead. Sunglasses covered her eyes and Dan's old Red Sox windbreaker covered the shoulder holster and Glock. She had swapped it for the Magnum. If something went down inside the house, she didn't want to leave the police anything that could connect her to Belham.

A quick glance to make sure no one was watching and then she opened the mail box. It was stuffed with letters and catalogues. *Thank God.* She pulled out a handful of envelopes and quickly rifled through them. All bills, every one addressed to the same person: Mary J. Reynolds. Another glance to make sure she was alone and then she shoved them back into the mail box and turned her attention to the aluminium screen door.

Beyond it, an old wooden door that looked as if it had been installed a century ago. The wood around the oval glass built into the centre had warped and cracked from water. Two deadbolts. They looked new.

Pressing her face up against the screen, she saw a

dark foyer and a hall of dingy white walls and scratched hardwood flooring. At the far end, a kitchen with cardboard boxes stacked on the worktops. Some of the cupboards had been left open. The shelves were empty.

Jamie rang the doorbell and ran back to her minivan. She pretended to be talking on Ben's mobile while watching the house out of the corner of her eye.

The front door didn't open.

She had Ben's keys in her pocket. She could try unlocking the door now. No, not yet. She had to be sure no one was home. She had to be sure. She drove away to look for a place to park.

The last time she had stepped foot inside Charlestown was years and years ago as a newbie cadet fresh out of the Boston Police Academy. Back then, during the early eighties, the Irish gangs had ruled every inch of these streets. Now, with all the mob leaders dead or behind bars, a wave of gentrification had swept through the town, stripping the old neighbourhood establishments to make room for upmarket restaurants, coffee shops and antique shops more in line with the tastes of the new upper-middle-class residents who had gobbled up the overpriced houses and condos. This new Charlestown reminded her of a slightly less ritzy version of Beacon Hill – old brick buildings with no back gardens, just window boxes and the occasional tree planted on the cracked pavement. No garages, maybe just the odd driveway big enough for a single car. Just like Beacon Hill, every Charlestown resident who owned a vehicle had to squeeze it into a sticker spot along the street.

Half an hour later, she found a tiny car park attached to a brick building belonging to an accounting firm – and within walking distance of the house. She squeezed the minivan into the last spot and left it running for the air-conditioning.

She placed the battery in Ben's phone, turned it on and dialled directory inquiries.

'City and state,' the operator said.

'Charlestown. Mass . . . ah . . . ah . . .'

'Massachusetts?'

'Yes.'

'Name?'

'Mary . . . ah . . . ah . . . Reynolds. Ashmont . . . ah . . . Street.'

Jamie heard the *click-click-click* of a keyboard on the other end of the line as she grabbed the pad of paper and pen that were in the glovebox.

The operator connected her free of charge. Jamie pictured Ben's name and number being displayed on the house phone's caller-ID. If the man in the Hawaiian shirt or anyone else was inside, she hoped he'd see Ben's name and pick up.

On the eighth ring, when no answering machine picked up, she hung up. No one was home.

Raindrops plopped against the windscreen. The

sky had grown darker. It was going to start pouring any minute. Good. People stayed inside when it rained. Jamie got out of the car and started walking.

Ben's Palm Treo had a tiny but fully functional keyboard and a 2 × 2 colour screen with a numeric touch keypad. She touched a button and up came a screen with icons for voicemail, contacts and a call log. A gold bell blinked in the top-left-hand corner of the screen. She touched it with her fingernail. Ben had three missed calls and two new voicemails.

She accessed the voicemail, then hung up when the mechanical voice asked for a PIN number. She didn't need a PIN number to access the contacts.

Three contacts: Judas, Alan and Pontius. No full names or addresses, just different phone numbers.

Judas and Pontius. Her years of Catholic school delivered the obvious glosses: Judas Iscariot, one of Jesus' disciples, had betrayed God's one and only son; Pontius Pilot, the Roman governor, had condemned Jesus to death.

Were the two names some sort of code? Again she recalled Ben's comment about being some sort of undercover cop.

She checked the call log. Eight calls, all from Judas. She wondered if Judas was Mr Hawaiian Shirt, the man who had driven Ben and the suited man to Belham in the BMW. She suspected he hadn't been caught by the police. The news hadn't reported anything. She had checked the TV and radio.

She removed the battery. No way to track the mobile signal now.

A heavy rain broke out, drilling the streets and parked cars. She started running.

When she reached Ashmont, she looked at the building directly across the street from the Reynolds home. Most windows were dark but she spotted several glowing with light. She didn't see any shadows moving behind the glass.

Now a final glance around the street. All clear. She fished Ben's fancy Tiffany key ring from her pocket as she moved up the front steps and opened the aluminium door.

She tried the first key. It didn't unlock either deadbolt. She tried the next one and the next as the rain slapped her head and shoulders, water dripping over the brim of her hat.

Come on. One of these keys has to —

The first deadbolt clicked back. She tried the same key in the second one and heard it unlock.

The key didn't work on the doorknob, but the one next to it did.

Jamie unzipped her jacket and stepped inside the tiny foyer. The hot air trapped between the closed windows reminded her of her grandmother's house: a small, neat home with air smelling of steamed Brussels sprouts, air that no matter what the time of year smelled of sickness and death.

No one came running. From her pocket she

removed a facecloth and quickly wiped down the areas she had touched with her bare hands. Then she put on a pair of latex gloves, eased the door shut and locked it. Time to make a quick survey of the house.

Jamie removed the Glock, comforted by the feel of it in her hand, and moved up the worn burgundy runner to the first floor.

Hands down, the Reynolds woman had the world's ugliest bathroom. Pink ceramic tiles ran halfway up the walls and covered the floor; there was a shower stall of cracked grout black from mould; the rusted vanity had a mirror covered with water spots.

The empty bedroom down the hall had bare white walls with scratches and nail holes that hadn't been patched. Cobwebs in the corners. Dull-blue carpeting worn thin, burn marks from dropped cigarettes. She checked the tiny closet. Empty.

Six quick steps across the hall and she stepped into a second bedroom. Same white walls, same shitty carpet. No closet. She headed downstairs.

The kitchen had been decorated back in the late sixties or early seventies by someone who was clearly colour blind. The chocolate-brown wallpaper, faded in spots from the sun, clashed oh-so-beautifully with the mustard-coloured cupboards and the orange-and-black chequered linoleum floor. The rips and tears in the wallpaper had been mended with glue, and the squares of scuffed linoleum that had started to bubble and peel had been nailed or tacked down.

Attached to the kitchen was a small, square-shaped living room full of boxes sitting on emerald-green carpeting – some open, some still taped shut. A brown three-seater sofa and a matching loveseat and chair had been pushed into the corner of the room.

The storm had not let up; the sound of the rain drilling against the windows and roof echoed throughout the room. She found the phone, a small black cordless model with a digital answering machine, sitting on top of three stacked boxes leaning against a dark yellow wall between two windows.

The ANSWER button was turned off. She pressed the PLAY button. A mechanical voice said 'no new messages'. She kept her finger on the button. *Beep* and then a voice exploded from the speaker: 'Kevin, Carla Dempsey from down the way.' Extra-thick Boston accent, the deep and husky voice cured from a lifetime's addiction to Marlboros that probably started right after the woman popped from the womb. 'I saw you packin' up and everything and swung by to give you my condolences about your ma but the door was locked. That woman was a sweetheart, God rest her soul. Take care.'

A slight pause and then the machine added, 'Tuesday, two thirty-three p.m.'

Beep.

No more messages. She walked back into the kitchen.

Marking pens, rolls of packing tape and bubble-wrap sat on a circular maple table. The worktops and cupboards were bare. The mahogany-stained door in the back of the kitchen opened to a dark stairwell leading to the basement. It took her a moment to find the light switch.

The cellar was cool and damp and smelled of mildew and something else . . . something rotten. The basement was also surprisingly large, lit by a single bulb hanging above the washer and dryer. The flooring around the stairs was concrete but the back half, the part past the stairs, was dirt. A shovel rested against a handful of small cardboard liquor boxes stacked on the floor in front of the dusty pieces of an old oak bedroom set.

Facing her was an unbelievably tall antique armoire with a red lacquered finish and gold-leaf accents. The clawed feet had sunk into the dirt and the armoire leaned slightly to the left. The top part of the armoire, carved into wings, nearly touched the ceiling. Behind the armoire, Jamie found a half-unearthed grave full of bones.

19

Jamie's eyes shifted away from the grave to a cardboard liquor box. Her scalp tightened and a prickling sensation shot its way across her damp skin as she stared at a collection of human bones stained brown from their long time buried in the soil. Several of the longer bones had been snapped in half so they'd fit inside the box.

Among the bones were two human skulls. One with long hair was wrapped inside a plastic bag.

The upstairs door opened. Heavy footsteps thumped across the floorboards directly above her head. The door shut and another pair of footsteps followed.

Two people. Two people were inside the house and one of them was walking across the kitchen – the basement door was open, the light on.

She couldn't hide behind the armoire. There was a foot-long space between the floor and the bottom of the armoire. When they came downstairs – and they would, they would – they'd see her sneakers and the cuffs of her jeans. Find a place to hide, then take them by surprise. But where?

She swung her attention to the opposite corner. An

ancient black oil tank and hot-water heater sat in the shadows. It would have been a perfect hiding spot, had the two tanks not been sitting six inches away from the wall. No way to get behind them. No space behind the washer or dryer. She looked at the furniture stacked next to the armoire.

A chest-of-drawers, long and wide, sitting flush against the floor. Hide behind there, lie flat and wait.

Standing behind the chest, she grabbed one edge, hoping to God the drawers weren't weighted down with stuff. The chest lifted with ease off the floor and without a sound. Carefully she dragged it a few inches across the dirt. There. Now it would conceal her.

'Ben, you down there?'

The male voice sounded like a marble-mouthed Kermit the Frog. This voice, Jamie was sure, didn't belong to the man who had called to Ben from the bottom of her stairs.

Jamie lay on her back with her knees bent, the backs of her sneakers pressed up against her rump. The Glock, gripped in both hands, rested between her knees. She stared at the cobwebs strung between the copper pipes and wooden floorboards, listening to the heavy footsteps descending the stairs. Now they were moving across the basement. They stopped somewhere near the armoire.

Craning her head, she looked through the two-inch gap between the wall and the corner of the chest and saw a pair of white high-top basketball sneakers and a bright floral shirt hanging over jeans. Curly grey hair. Ben's driver.

The second person came downstairs. Jamie listened to the approaching footsteps. They stopped on the other side of the chest.

'You've got to be shitting me, Pete. You think my basement's bugged? That I got, what, cameras installed down here?'

Jamie heard something placed on the top of the chest. *Click* and a high-pitched whine filled the room, then disappeared.

'Your house was bugged once before.' A light, airy voice with a slight lisp – the kind of man who fought with his fingernails. 'You always play it safe. When you don't, mistakes get made and that's when you get caught. You should know that better than anyone.'

'Something wrong with your wrist? You keep rubbing it.'

'I sprained it playing tennis.'

The footsteps moved away from the chest, stopped.

'Who's in the box?'

The man with the effeminate lisp – Peter. She couldn't see him or Ben's driver. He had moved away.

'Linda Burke and some other broad whose name I forget,' Ben's driver said.

'I'm surprised your mother didn't smell anything.'

'We buried them deep and covered them with lime.'

'Burke . . . I remember the mother. Dianne. She

moved out of town, what, a year or so after her daughter disappeared?'

'Something like that.'

'Whatever happened to her?'

'We buried her next to her daughter.'

'Lovely.'

'How about we skip the trip down memory lane and get down to business?'

'Have you talked to Jack?' Peter asked.

'No. I decided to lay low, wait for you guys to call me. Where is he?'

'Watching the house. Tell me what you saw last night.'

'I wasn't anywhere near the house. I was parked up the road, on Claremont. When Kendra's Honda pulled on to Walton, I called Ben and gave him a heads-up. Then I sat in the car and waited for the call. Next thing I know there's a squad car pulling on to the street. What did Tony have to say?'

'Not much. When he called, he said someone shot their way inside the house. Got hit twice in the chest and was bleeding out. He thought the shooter was a woman.'

Jamie blinked the sweat from her eyes and flipped the switch on the Glock to semi-automatic fire.

No, not yet. Wait. Listen.

'I wouldn't put too much stock in it,' Peter said. 'The guy was delirious from blood loss. He called again to tell me he was in the woods. By the time Jack and his team arrived, Tony was dead.'

'He didn't say anything about Ben?'

'No. Has he called you?'

'Not yet. You?'

'Neither Jack nor I have heard from him. We need to find his body.'

'Ben's alive.'

'What makes you say that?'

'There's a puddle near the front door, and the basement light is on. I turned it off when I left this morning. I gave him a set of keys to the house. He was going to hang here for a day or two before heading back to Phoenix or San Diego or wherever he's living now.'

'He should have called one of us by now.'

'Maybe he lost his mobile. All the numbers are programmed in there.'

'There's a GPS unit in his phone. The phone keeps turning on and off at odd intervals. The signal doesn't stay on long enough for us to track him.'

She had been right about Ben's mobile. It had a GPS unit and they were trying to track it.

'Maybe it's broken,' Ben's driver said. 'Or maybe Ben's playing it safe. He's old school. He never trusted mobile phones, thinks the signals are too easy to pick up. I agree with him. You can buy the equipment you need at a RadioShack.'

'Those mobile phones are encrypted. There's no way anyone can randomly listen.'

'You need me to take care of Tony's body or did Jack take care of it?'

'Jack took care of it. When was the last time you spoke to Tony?'

'After I dropped him off at the house,' Ben's driver said.

'When you saw the police, did you call him?'

'What do you think?'

'How many times did you call?'

'I don't know, Peter, I wasn't keeping track. And what were you thinking, busting into the kid's hospital room like that?'

'If the Sheppard boy ended up talking to that McCormick woman –'

'Who?'

'Darby McCormick,' Peter said. 'Thomas McCormick's daughter.'

'What was she doing there?'

'She's the head investigator for Boston PD's Criminal Services Unit – and she's the one who heard Tony's phone ringing in the woods. Her training is in forensics. Not a good development, Kevin.'

Ben's driver, Kevin, didn't speak.

A long silence followed.

'It couldn't be helped,' Peter said. 'I had to do *something*.'

'So you say.'

'She doesn't know who I am. And there's no way she'll find out either. My actions last night proved to be beneficial. The McCormick woman taped the conversation with Sean. I confiscated the recorder. Sean didn't tell her anything. She thinks his name is John Hallcox. There was no mention of Kendra. Personally, I don't think the boy *knew* anything.'

'Where he'd get the gun?'

'I don't know yet. Why did Kendra come back here? Do you know?'

'Nope. I want to listen to the tape. Ben will too.'

'You should have followed her.'

'We didn't have much lead time. Jack had to get his gear and –'

'Then you should have waited. You never were good at operation planning. Or patience.'

'It was Ben's call, and Tony went along with it.'

'I'll remind you, *again*, that *you* work for *us*. What happened last night in Belham, what happened here in Charlestown and in this basement – this *glorious* blight is because of two people. You and that serial killing psycho.'

'Glorious blight,' Kevin repeated. 'Are you a K-Y cowboy, or did they teach you to talk that way at Yale?'

'All that time standing on the side of the fence has really warped your brain.'

'What are you going to do about Big Red's daughter?'

'We'll figure something out.'

'Yeah, and you'll have Ben and me clean it up. You Ivy League pricks don't like getting your hands sticky.'

Someone – Peter, Jamie suspected – started jingling change and keys.

'Whatever you're going to do, don't take too long to decide,' Kevin said. 'I'm planning on going to the Caribbean next week after I put my mother's house up for sale.'

'I'll tell you when you can leave.'

'Yes, sir. Is there anything else, sir, or may I leave now? I'd like to go to the Tap.'

'The what?'

'The Warren Tap. It's a bar. Not the kind you'd hang out in, mind you, but back in the day, if Ben had a problem, he'd leave a message there for me. Don't worry, it's in code. All that secret shit you guys like.'

Footsteps moved across the floor.

'Here, take this,' Kevin said.

'What's this for?'

'It's a shovel. You use it to dig up things. There's one more in that hole. Get to work and I'll help you with the other one when I get back. You can use those gloves there on the workbench so you don't ruin your manicure.'

'I don't think so.'

'Your boss offered your burial removal services,' Kevin said. 'Welcome to my side of the fence, champ.'

20

The front door slammed shut. Jamie listened to the man breathing somewhere near the armoire as she replayed fragments of the conversation. The man named Peter had tried to visit the boy named Sean and ended up speaking to this McCormick woman from the Boston PD. How had he gained access to the room? Had he posed as a cop? *Was* he a cop?

Enough thinking. Time to act.

She was about to sit up when she remembered the keys and phone tucked inside her jacket pocket. If she sat up too fast or moved too quickly, the keys would make noise. If the man heard anything, it might give him enough time to reach for his gun – or swing his shovel.

He started digging. She lifted her head, looked through the gap: she saw tanned hands gripping a shovel, and white shirt cuffs with gold cufflinks sticking out from a blue suit jacket. She couldn't see his face.

Too close, she thought, panic fluttering against the walls of her heart. *The moment I stand up he'll see me.*

I'll be back in a few minutes, Kevin had said.

Jamie placed one hand on her right pocket, feeling the keys and phone beneath the nylon fabric. Hugging her body close to the back of the chest, she slowly moved up to a sitting position. A pins-and-needles sensation worked its way through her legs.

Peter kept digging.

Do it now and do it fast. If he reaches for the gun or tries to run, drop him.

She got to her feet fast, blood rushing to her head, making her dizzy.

'Freeze.'

The man jumped, dropping the shovel. He was taller than she expected – his lisp and soft, effeminate voice had conjured up an image of a short man with flabby arms. The middle-aged man standing in front of her had a lean build. He wore a dark blue suit without a tie. The jacket was unbuttoned and she could see a shoulder holster.

Using her hip, she pushed the chest to one side.

'Floor,' she said, stepping over the grave. 'Get . . . ah . . .'

Don't stutter your way through this: just say one word at a time.

'Flo . . . Floor. Now.'

His brown eyes blinked, then narrowed. 'I know you.'

'*Floor.*'

'Okay, okay. Just take it easy . . . it's Julia, right?" He hiked up his trousers before kneeling. Then he clasped his hands behind his head. 'I remember reading about you in the papers.'

She slammed him down against the floor, pressed

the Glock against the back of his head. He breathed in dirt and started coughing.

'Don't . . . ah . . . ah . . . move.'

He turned his head to the side and said, 'You have my word.'

She pulled back his suit jacket and reached for the shoulder holster.

'Since you were hiding down here, I think it's safe to assume you heard my conversation with Mr Reynolds.'

She tossed the nine into the grave.

'And I'm assuming you're the one who shot up the Belham house last night.'

She ran a hand across his belt. No handcuffs. She needed something that she could use to tie him up. She looked at the workbench. Paint cans and tools covered in dust.

You need to find something to tie him up and gag him – and you better do it quick before Kevin comes back.

'What happened to your husband and children, I didn't have anything to do with that. You have to believe me. That . . . that was all Kevin and Ben. You know Ben, don't you? He was at the house last night. Did you speak to him? What did he tell you?'

There was nothing here with which she could tie him up, nothing at all.

'I can tell you everything you need to know, but I need to sit up. I have asthma and I'm finding it hard to breathe. I need my inhaler. I'm going to sit up, reach inside my pocket for it, and then we can talk, okay?'

He spoke calmly. She didn't like it. Was he going to try to stall her until Kevin came back? Did he think she was that stupid?

'If you want me to talk, I need to use my inhaler first,' he said. 'If I don't, I'm going to pass out.'

You've wasted too much time. Kevin will be back here any minute and then what are you going to do? Shoot your way out of the house? If you die, Kevin will bury your body someplace where it'll never be found. The kids will be left wondering what happened to you as they're shipped off to foster homes. Cut your losses and get out of here.

She stood.

'Ben's . . . ah . . . partners. Two men . . . ah . . . at . . . ah . . . my house.'

'Let me get my inhaler.' Breathing hard, wheezing. 'I'm going to reach into my pocket –'

'Names . . . ah . . . first.'

'Just give me a second, okay?' Slowly he reached inside his jacket pocket.

She shot him in the chest.

The exit wound sprayed the back wall with blood. He put out his hands and said, 'Wait, please,' and she pressed the trigger and held it down, the Glock's semi-automatic action kicking in, spitting spent shells into the air.

Jamie wrapped the jacket's nylon hood around her head, tying it off underneath her chin. Ears ringing, she ran up the stairs to the front door and looked out of the oval window. No one outside. She tucked the

Glock inside her shoulder holster, zipped up her jacket and opened the door. No one coming. Her gloved hands inside her pocket, she jogged across the street, which was still pounding with summer rain.

21

Darby sat in the back of the hot taxi as it fought its way through the heavy traffic on Mass. Avenue. She had Artie on the phone. The pounding rain and car horns made it difficult to hear.

She pressed her palm against her other ear to try to block out the noise. 'Say that again.'

'I said I'm on my way back from Vermont. I just finished going through Amy Hallcox's place. Can you hear me?'

'I can hear you.'

'Someone tossed it. It's a small house and she doesn't have a lot of stuff – there's barely any furniture in there. Got in touch with the landlord and the guy said she's been living there for about a year, pays on time, no problems. She had about two months to go on the lease but I get the feeling she might've been planning to move again. She's got a bunch of empty boxes stored in one of the rooms. As for why it was tossed and what they were looking for, right now your guess is as good as mine.'

'Anybody see anything?'

'No. The house is real isolated – the closest neighbour is a mile away, so these guys took their time. We asked around but nobody knows the Hallcox woman or her kid. Based upon what you told me last night, I'm figuring he knows something.

'I got your message about the kid's condition and the hospital tapes,' Pine said. 'What did you find?'

'I dropped them off at the Photography Unit before I went to the ME's office. I'm headed back to the lab right now. I have someone running down the plate number for the van. I haven't heard anything yet.'

'What about evidence on the woman's body – did you find anything?'

'Some fibres and hairs stuck to the duct tape and clothes. She didn't have anything in her pockets. I'll get to work on the clothes today.'

'Amy Hallcox's missing Honda is bothering me.'

'That's been nagging at me too. I'm thinking the shooter took it.'

'You said the kid didn't mention anything about hearing a shooter.'

'He didn't have a chance to tell me. Artie, someone shot their way inside that house. And we know, based upon what the boy *did* tell me, that there were two men inside – the guy in the Celtics gear and the guy in the suit. I'm thinking the shooter took down the suit first, then dragged the second guy to the Honda. The drag marks lead down the kitchen hall and stop inside the garage. And there's only one set of the bloody footprints on the garage floor.'

'Why drag away a dead body?'

'How do we know the Celtics guy was dead? Maybe the shooter wanted him alive.'

'Then why not take this person *before* he entered the house?'

'I don't know yet. But we do know that someone ran up the back deck stairs and tracked mud into the living room. Those footprints lead up the steps but not down. I'm thinking the shooter was watching from the woods.'

'So now we're talking about an entirely separate person – a third party that wasn't part of what went down in the house or that Rambo group we met in the woods?'

'Yes. And I also think the shooter cut the kid loose.'

'Why? What's the reason?'

'I don't know. If that son of a bitch hadn't –'

'I saw the guy's badge and ID. They were the real deal. So was the paperwork.'

'I'm not blaming you, Artie, I'm just pissed off. He played us and cost the Hallcox kid his life. I just wish I knew what the hell he wanted with him.'

'Have you seen any sign of Phillips or whoever he is?'

'No. '

'What about the others?'

'Not yet.'

'What about the prints taken from the house? Any luck there?'

'The lab techs got back about an hour ago. They've just started working.'

The taxi came to a sudden stop against the pavement.

'I've got to go,' Darby said. 'I'll call you as soon as I know something.'

She ran through the rain clutching a clear plastic bag. It held brown-paper bags of evidence to keep them from getting wet. She was soaked by the time she reached the front doors of One Schroeder Plaza. She had to go through the maddening check-in process before she could reach the lab.

She logged in the evidence, then went to her office to check messages. She had one. Nicholas Garcia, the homicide detective liaison to CSU, asked her to call him back. She had asked him to run the brown van's plates.

Garcia answered on the first ring and got right to it.

'They're phantom plates,' he said. 'They don't exist.'

'So how did they get the plates?'

'Probably through a contact at the DMV. It's not as impossible as it sounds. You pay someone on the inside to get the plate and then they erase any way to trace them.'

'Can you look into it for me?'

'I wouldn't pass up such an exciting opportunity.' Garcia chuckled. 'Don't pin your hopes on finding anything. I've been down this road before.'

Darby was walking down the corridor to talk to Coop when her mobile rang. Ted Castonguay, the head of the photography unit, had finished reviewing the tapes and digital pictures and wanted to speak with her inside his office.

She found the former college wrestler seated at a desk in a quiet but cluttered corner. His shoulder and back muscles looked like rocks moving underneath cloth as he worked the mouse.

She grabbed a chair and wheeled it over to him, looking at the flat-screen monitor holding a black-and-white video still of the hospital's elevator. The time-stamp recorded on the videotape read 'August 15, 2009. 1.03 a.m.'.

Castonguay knew she was harried and frantic. He didn't waste time with pleasantries.

'This is the time you entered the hospital,' he said, clicking the mouse.

The security video started. The camera was pointed down at the white corridor. She could see part of the nurses' station.

The elevator doors opened and she saw herself and Pine walk out and move down the corridor until they disappeared. A moment later they reappeared with Patrolman White, and the three huddled around the corner from the nurses' station and began talking.

Click and the video started fast-forwarding.

'Eighteen minutes elapsed from the time you stepped off the elevator to the time you went to talk to the Hallcox boy,' Castonguay said. 'The Fed appears just under twenty-two minutes later.'

Twenty-two minutes. *He must have followed me from*

Belham. She watched the images fast-forwarding across the monitor and thought about the TV cameraman she'd seen watching the house this morning. If he had been there last night, mixed among the other reporters, he would have seen her getting inside Pine's Lincoln Town Car.

Castonguay started playing the video at its normal speed. She looked at the digital timestamp on the bottom-right-hand corner: 1.23 a.m.

'Here's where it gets interesting,' Castonguay said. 'Watch the elevator.'

She did. When it opened, the video started to fill with static. She couldn't see the person who got out of the elevator – she couldn't see anything.

The static grew stronger and then images disappeared.

The screen went dark.

'That's it,' Castonguay said, and swivelled around in his chair to face her. 'I checked the tapes for the other cameras. There's nothing else, just static and then they all go dark.'

'Any idea what caused it?'

'For all the cameras to shut down like that, you're talking some sort of HERF – a High Energy Radio Frequency weapon – or maybe a directed magnetic pulse. Could even be a microwave pulse. The two people talking to you in the video, they were standing in the corridor while you were talking to the vic. Did they say anything about being burned?'

'They didn't say anything to me.'

'I doubt it's microwave anyway. Those devices aren't easy to conceal. Let me ask you this, then: did they report feeling nauseous or dizzy? Any vision problems?'

'Not that I know of, but when I saw them standing in the doorway of the room, they were both struggling to catch their breath – like they had just finished running a marathon.'

'Breathing difficulties are one of the symptoms of close exposure to electromagnetic or HERF exposure.'

'My understanding is that to use a HERF weapon, you have to have a parabolic reflector and aim it at a target.'

'Yes, you're correct. And I should mention that to build one of *those* devices, you can find the materials you need in any electronics store. They're somewhat big and bulky. Not easy to conceal. I was thinking along the lines of the smaller devices I've seen over the past year – the ones the size of, say, a paperback book or a pack of cigarettes that use a high-energy radio frequency. These smaller devices act more like a grenade – they have a certain blast radius. The smaller the device, the smaller the blast radius. You hit a button, flood an area with HERF and cook the electronic circuits in the area. That's the only thing I can think of that would have caused this kind of damage so quickly. I'd be interested to see if the security cameras or any other nearby equipment was damaged last night.'

'I'll call and ask,' Darby said. 'These HERF grenades – can you build them?'

'Not to my knowledge. I know the army uses them. They're part of their non-lethal weapons tactics programme.'

'What about the CIA or the FBI?'

'I don't see why not.' Castonguay turned to the keyboard. 'Now I want you to look at the pictures you took.'

22

'I just need a moment to tinker with the file,' Castonguay said.

Darby went to her office to use the phone. She called St Joseph's and asked to be connected to the nurses' station on the fourth floor. A new rotation had started. After identifying herself to three different people she finally found one left over from the day shift.

When she came out of her office, Castonguay had a top-down picture of the cameraman loaded on the screen. The TV camera was mounted on his shoulder. Sunglasses covered his eyes and he wore headphones and a baseball cap. She could see blond hair covering the tip of an ear. The man posing as Special Agent Phillips had had black hair and darker skin.

'It looks like your HERF theory was correct,' Darby said, sitting down. 'I just got off the phone with one of the day nurses at the hospital. When she came in this morning, they were replacing the security cameras on her floor, and the computers and phones at the nurses' station were down. Some of the medical equipment in the rooms near the elevator had stopped working. They thought it was an electrical surge.'

Castonguay nodded, his attention focused on the monitor. He typed with one finger while the other hand worked the mouse, shifting the picture until the TV camera came into a sharper focus.

'What do you know about televisions cameras?' he asked.

'Not much. I try to avoid them whenever possible.'

'Lucky for you I know a lot about them. What we have here is called an ENG camera – an Electronic News Gathering video-recording camera. It looks like the real deal except for this.'

Using the mouse, he drew a circle around the handle mounted on top of the camera. Then he moved the chair away from his desk and said, 'Take a look.'

Darby stood up and moved closer to the screen. Next to the handle and mounted on top of the camera was a small device that resembled a black laser pointer. The end pointed at the house had a small but noticeably bright red light. She saw wires running from the end of the device that fed directly into the camera.

She turned her head to Castonguay. 'Is this a laser mike?'

'That's exactly what it is. You direct the laser to a surface that can vibrate – like glass. The laser picks up pressure waves caused by noises in the room.'

'I used one during a SWAT surveillance exercise.'

'And that's what your cameraman was doing. He was conducting surveillance on the house, trying to listen in on your conversations. The camera looks genuine – has a Sony camera head and a Betacam SP dock. It blended in perfectly with the other TV cameras.'

'How complicated is it to install a laser mike in a camera?'

'It's extremely complicated. I'm even willing to say it can't be done. This ENG camera was custom-built to conduct surveillance. Whoever you're dealing with has access to some very high-tech toys.'

He loaded another picture on to the monitor, a shot she had taken of the bald man opening the driver's door. The cameraman was running around to the back of the van.

Castonguay cropped the front windscreen, then went to work on enhancing it. A moment later she saw someone sitting in the passenger seat. She could see only his hands resting on dark-coloured trousers, a blue tie worn with a white shirt.

Sitting on the dashboard was a device that resembled a police scanner.

'I've tried enhancing the picture from different angles,' Castonguay said, 'but I can't get a lock on his face. But see this shadow here?' He pointed to the area between the two front seats. 'This may or may not be part of a leg and an arm. I'll need more time to enhance it.

'That's all I have. I'll have printouts of the pictures to show you in another hour or so. Just do me one favour. When you get your hands on this camera, you're to let me know immediately. I'm dying to play with it.'

'You got it.'

Three men were interested in Amy Hallcox and her son – the black-haired man who had posed as a Fed, the cameraman and the bald driver. Had they been the men she'd seen in the woods last night?

She thought back to the picture of what might be another person sitting in the back of the van. A fourth man. Were there more? How many people were following her?

Darby opened the door of the fingerprint suite. Coop, wearing safety glasses and blue latex gloves, was hunched over a lab bench examining a bullet. He had already tried dusting it for prints.

She saw the bullet's pitted nose and knew what it was: a hollow-point round. The same ammo had killed her father.

'It's a nine-millimetre Parabellum round,' Coop said. 'I found it in the kitchen, underneath an over-turned sideboard. Someone must have dropped it.'

'Any prints?'

He shook his head.

'We could fume it with cyanoacrylate,' she said. 'If the Super Glue finds a print, we can try using different luminescent stains, then enhance it in the VMD unit.' Vacuum Metal Deposition, she knew from experience, yielded better-looking latent prints.

'I'm going to try something else first.' Coop picked up the shell casing with a pair of tweezers and placed it on a circular metal dish that sat underneath a probe.

Darby looked over his shoulder. Her jaw dropped.

'Is that a scanning Kelvin probe?'

'It is,' he said. 'Jesus, I haven't seen you this excited since the last time U2 came through Boston.'

She placed the bag holding Amy Hallcox's finger-print card on the bench beside them, dimly aware that the usual humour was absent from his voice. Her attention was on the probe. She had read about it but had never seen a real-life demonstration of one.

'How did you get your hands on it?'

'This unit is courtesy of my new friends in London,' he said. 'Do me a favour and turn on that monitor.'

She did and then pulled out a chair and watched Coop adjust the controls of a small device resembling a futuristic microscope. Human sweat dried fairly quickly. What lingered was a mix of organic and inorganic compounds. Was Coop suggesting that these compounds and chemicals could be detected by this probe?

'What sort of developer are you going to use?'

'You don't need to use a chemical or a powder.'

'Then how are you going to find a latent print?'

'The beauty of this new technology, Darb, is that once you touch metal with your bare fingers, the inorganic salts from your skin corrode the shell casing – you "brand" your print on to the metal. You can't wipe it away.'

'What if a shell was fired? The heat would destroy the organic compounds left behind – amino acids, glucose, peptides and lactic acid.'

'Doesn't matter. The probe can retrieve prints from fired shells, even detonated bomb fragments, where temperatures can reach as high as five hundred degrees Celsius. The Kelvin probe uses voltage to examine the surfaces where a fingerprint may have been deposited.'

'So what you're suggesting is that no matter what, you can't wipe away a fingerprint.'

'Exactly.' He pressed a button on a small box attached to the probe. 'Watch the monitor.'

Darby saw a magnified image of the bullet on the screen. 'Looks like you've got something.'

Coop studied the faint, spidery lines of a partial latent fingerprint on the monitor.

'I'm going to have to create what's called a voltage map,' he said. 'It's a three-dimensional rendering of the latent print. It will take a couple of hours. How'd the autopsy go?'

'They're doing it right now.' Darby's attention had shifted back to the hollow point lying on the dish.

'Did you examine the body?'

She nodded, then said, 'Would a scanning electron microscope destroy or alter the fingerprint in any way?'

'No.'

'Then before you do the voltage map, I want to

borrow the bullet for a moment and take a closer look at the cartridge's headstamp. It doesn't look right.'

Coop, using tweezers, picked up the bullet for a closer look.

'I don't see anything unusual.'

She pointed to the round metal base. 'The spark plug looks smaller than normal, don't you think?'

He shrugged, then pushed his chair away from the table. 'Go for it.'

23

Darby picked up the dish holding the bullet and carried it across the room to the lab's brand-new scanning electron microscope. She loaded the cartridge into the chamber, shut the small door and then sat down, turning her attention to the console. Coop wheeled a chair next to hers.

The SEM's terminal screen showed a magnified black-and-white image of the bullet's headstamp. A thick white ring glowed in the middle, around the primer cap. Printed in the centre were two neat rows containing both letters and numbers:

GLK18
B4M6

'What the hell is that?' he asked. 'Some sort of stamp?'

'That's exactly what it is.' She printed off two copies of the image, then created a digital copy and sent the jpeg to her email. 'What we're looking at here is what's being hailed as the latest technological advance in ballistics identification – microstamping.'

'That technology hasn't made its way into mass production.'

Darby nodded. 'At the moment, the gun lobbyists have successfully prevented microstamping from seeing the light of day, but that may change soon. California is trying to push through a bill that would require microstamping to be implemented on all firearms over the next five years. If the bill gets passed, it'll be the first state in the nation to have this.

'Currently, we need to find the handgun and examine it to see if a particular bullet was fired through it. Microstamping eliminates that. It creates a ballistic fingerprint. A handgun's firing pin is engraved with a unique microscopic code that stamps the gun's make, model and serial number on the primer cap. The first row – in this case, GLK18 – is supposed to be the stamp for the handgun, the bottom row the code for the shop that sold it.'

'So I'm assuming there's going to be some sort of database that'll store these numbers and codes.'

Darby nodded. 'The database gives us not only the make and model of the handgun but where it was sold, who purchased it – everything.' She worked the small joystick mounted on the keyboard in an effort to examine the edges of the cartridge's headstamp. 'And the database will also provide us with information about other crime scenes where cartridges with the same stamp were found. The beauty of this new technology is that you can see the stamp only through a scanning electron microscope.'

'But since this technology isn't in mass production yet, there's no way we can trace it.'

'This bullet has to be a part of a batch of test ammo.'

'A prototype, in other words.'

'Exactly. Only a handful of companies are doing microstamping, so this prototype or whatever it is should be easy to narrow down.'

'The stamp on this first row here, GLK18,' Coop said. 'I'm guessing it's a Glock eighteen.'

'That would be my guess too.'

'I've never heard of a model eighteen.'

'That's because they're not sold here. It's a military-issue weapon commissioned by the Austrian Counter-Terrorism Unit, EKO Cobra. As far as I know, they're the only ones who use it. Take a look at the engraved letters around the headstamp.'

Coop put his arm around the back of her chair and leaned forward for a closer view. She could feel his arm touching her and was suddenly pierced by the thought of his moving away – not to another state but to another country.

'R . . . E . . . and what looks like an S,' he said.

She took a deep breath, trying to wash away the sinking feeling in her stomach. 'There's a company called Reynolds Engineering Systems that's one of the leading developers of microstamping. They're based in Washington, I think. Or Virginia.'

He turned to her. Their faces were inches apart.

'How do you know all of this stuff?'

'I do a lot of reading.' She turned to the keyboard to print off more copies.

'You need a hobby.'

'This *is* my hobby. Have you seen the Wonder Twins?'

'They're in Exam Room 2 working on the binoculars.'

'What binoculars?'

'Randy found a small pair of binoculars in the woods.'

Darby wondered if one of the men she had seen last night had accidently dropped them.

She stood up. 'I'll get on the horn and see what I can find out about this microstamp.'

'Wait.' Coop grabbed her wrist as she stood. 'When you were examining Amy Hallcox's body, did you see a tattoo?'

'She had one above her left breast. A small heart.'

'Did it have a black arrow through it?'

It did. 'How did you know that?'

'I need the fingerprint card for Amy Hallcox.'

'It's on the bench near the Kelvin probe.'

He walked across the room, grabbed the bag containing the Amy Hallcox fingerprint card and disappeared around the corner. Darby followed.

Coop stood at the last bench, his favourite spot, a small corner suite arranged around a grouping of windows that offered strong sunlight. Not today. The sky was black and heavy rain continued to pelt the windows.

He already had a fingerprint card set up on the bench. He slid Amy Hallcox's card from the bag and examined it with a fingerprint magnifier. By the time she stepped up next to him, he had pushed the magnifier to the side.

'It's a match,' he said, more to himself than to her.

'A match to what?'

He slid a fingerprint card yellowed by age across the bench. She looked at the name typed at the top: KENDRA L. SHEPPARD. White female. No age or other information was listed.

'Who's Kendra Sheppard?'

'She was . . . she was from Charlestown,' he said. 'Got busted a couple of times for prostitution. When you and I went inside the house and I saw her, I thought my mind was playing tricks on me. That I was imagining it.'

She remembered Coop standing in the dining room wiping his sweaty forehead, his face as white as a sheet.

'When you were outside talking to Pine, I took a closer look at Amy Hallcox's face,' he said. 'Kendra had a small mole on her cheek – I told her she looked like a blonde version of Cindy Crawford. And Kendra also had a scar underneath her bottom lip. She got that when she was eighteen. We came out of Jimmy DeCarlo's house and she fell down drunk on a piece of glass. I had to take her to the hospital for stitches.'

He grinned at the memory, then took a deep breath and said, 'Even then I still didn't believe it, so when I got back to the lab, I pulled Kendra's prints. I wanted to make sure before I said anything to you.'

'And there's no question?'

'None. Amy Hallcox is Kendra Sheppard.'

Coop crossed his arms over his chest, muscles rippling underneath the tight polo shirt, and focused on some private thought. 'All this time, I thought she was dead. Now I find her two decades later tied down to her chair with her throat cut and . . .' He shook his head as if trying to clear away the images. 'It's just weird, you know?'

Darby nodded and placed the fingerprint card back on the bench. 'Why did Kendra change her name?'

'I only knew her as Kendra,' he said. 'At one point in time, she was my girlfriend – my first serious girlfriend, I guess you could say.'

24

Darby leaned the small of her back against a lab bench and grabbed the edges.

'She wasn't a bad kid,' Coop said, his eyes on Kendra Sheppard's fingerprint card. 'Not the brightest bulb, especially when it came to the realities of living in Charlestown – she had no common sense or street smarts.'

Coop lived in Charlestown and knew everyone – not a hard thing to do when you lived in a place that was just one square mile. He and his three older sisters had grown up in the small historic neighbourhood, the site of one of the first battles of the American Revolution – Bunker Hill – and later, during the 1980s, a hotbed of Irish mafia activity. Coop was thirteen when his father had been killed in an unsolved hit-and-run – the same age Darby had been when her father was murdered. That common wound had cemented their friendship during the early days at the crime lab.

'Kendra had a good heart,' he said, 'and, Christ, she was wild. Loved to party, loved to booze it up and do blow. I was willing to overlook the coke because she was so goddamn attractive. But when I found out about her getting busted for prostitution, I couldn't handle it and broke up with her. Not a good time in my life.'

'Why did you think Kendra was dead?'

He blinked as if waking up from a dream. 'What's that?'

'You said, "All this time, I thought she was dead."'

'Her parents were murdered. They were shot to death while they were sleeping.'

That matched what Sean had told her.

'When did this happen?'

'April of '83,' Coop said. 'I remember it because I had just gotten my licence. I know Kendra wasn't home when they were murdered because the police were looking for her. I don't know where she was. By that time we weren't speaking. She didn't go to the wake or funeral, she just . . . vanished, so I assumed the worst.'

'She have any family in Charlestown?'

'An aunt and uncle. Heather and Mark Base. They don't live there any more. After the murder, they packed up and moved somewhere in the Midwest, I think.'

'Sean told me his grandparents were killed.'

'Sean?'

'That's John Hallcox's real name.' She hadn't had a chance to talk with Coop about her interview with the boy – or this morning's encounter with the brown van. After speaking to the Belham patrolmen who'd arrived on the scene, she'd driven back to Boston to work on Amy Hallcox's body before the autopsy.

'Sean told me his grandparents were murdered but said his mother wouldn't tell him how they died – or where they lived,' Darby said. 'He had just started talking about what had happened inside the house when he shut off the tape recorder and told me his real name was Sean. That's when the guy posing as a Fed came in with this shit about the mother being a fugitive and –'

'Wait, the guy wasn't an actual Fed?'

'No, but he sure as hell looked and acted the part – had the ID, badge. Pine said he saw the Federal warrant and it looked legit. I didn't find out he wasn't the real deal until this morning.'

'Jesus.' Coop propped up his elbows on the bench and massaged his forehead with the heels of his palms.

'I should have suspected something after he disappeared from the hospital,' she said. 'I thought he left to call an early-morning meeting for damage control – you know how the Feds are, protect their image at all costs.'

'So Amy Hallcox wasn't a fugitive.'

'No. I checked NCIC, it was all bullshit. This guy was after the kid.'

'Why?'

'I don't know yet.'

Coop looked at her. 'He must have known *some-*

thing. Why else would a twelve-year-old be carrying a gun?'

'I agree. I don't know who this guy is, but he's probably working with the guys I saw following me this morning.' She told him about the brown van and what Ted Castonguay had found in the pictures and the hospital videotape. 'What's going on with the fingerprints you lifted from the house?'

'They're running them through the database as we speak. As for evidence, we've just started processing it. What else did Sean tell you?'

'He said the people who killed his grandparents were never caught.'

'He's right.'

'Were there ever any suspects? Do you remember hearing anything?'

'Nothing jumps to mind.'

Darby grabbed the clipboard and pen lying on the bench, turned to a fresh sheet of paper and wrote down the names for the aunt and uncle. 'What were the names of Kendra's parents?'

'Sue and Donnie.'

'Does Kendra have any friends living in the area?'

'I wouldn't know.'

'Did she tell you why she was hooking?'

'No.'

'She never tried?'

'Sure she did. She tried a lot, as a matter of fact. She kept calling the house, came around a few times and tried cornering me at school. And I ignored her. I wasn't interested in hearing why.'

'I'm sure you heard some stories. Charlestown is small –'

'I didn't want to know why she did it. If someone started talking about it, I left the room. In fact, I made it a point of burying my head in the sand. I was seventeen when I found out my nineteen-year-old girlfriend was blowing guys around town in hotel rooms and cars.' He glared at her, eyes bright with anger. 'I didn't want to know specifics. I was embarrassed, okay?'

Why is he acting so defensive?

'Coop, I've just found out Amy Hallcox's real name is Kendra Sheppard.' She spoke the words calmly. 'And you're the person who told me. You told me her parents were murdered and that she disappeared. You told me you two dated, so I'm asking you questions, trying to get some background information on her.'

He was no longer looking at her. He was staring out of the window. The rain running down the glass cast shadows across the benches and walls.

A moment later he sighed and threw up his hands. 'What else did Sean tell you?'

'He said his mother was always afraid these people would find her. She seemed paranoid about it – she didn't have a computer and wouldn't hook up to the internet because she was afraid these people might track her down. I got the sense he believed the people who killed his grandparents are the same ones who killed his mother.'

'But they didn't kill him.'

'I think they were interrupted.' She explained her theory of a possible third party – the shooter who had entered through the sliding glass door and taken down the man in the suit.

'Sean told me the guy wearing the Celtics gear was an older white male who may or may not have had a facelift,' Darby said. 'At the moment that's all we know about the Celtics guy. We have no idea where he is or what might have happened to him. Do you have any ideas or theories?'

'About the Celtics guy? Based on that description, he could be any Boston yahoo.'

'I meant why these people were so interested in finding her.'

'Haven't the foggiest.' Coop stood up. 'Why did Sean Sheppard ask to speak to your father?'

'His mother said if he was ever in trouble to talk to him. She told him to speak only to him.'

'So you don't know the connection to your old man?'

'Not yet. Was Kendra arrested for prostitution in Charlestown?'

'As far as I know.'

'I'll go pull her record.'

'I'm going to get to work on that Nicorette wrapper you found and the shells the Wonder Twins recovered from the woods.'

'Okay. If you remember anything else, let me know.'

'Will do.'

'Thanks.'

Coop moved past her. She looked down at Kendra Sheppard's fingerprint card.

Darby had known him for so long, had spent so much time with him both on and off the job, that they had become in many ways like an old married couple, in tune with each other's moods and idiosyncrasies. She knew what was lurking behind Coop's anger.

He's afraid.

25

Darby opened the door to Exam Room 2. The Wonder Twins had placed a small pair of binoculars inside a fuming chamber.

Mark Alves, his Portuguese skin tanned the colour of mahogany, pointed to the binoculars and said, 'I don't think we're going to get any prints off them. Hopefully we'll have better luck with this stuff.'

He pointed to the items on the table: a bloody straight-edged razor and labelled strips of duct tape.

Randy Scott, a pencil tucked behind his ear, stood next to Darby, flipping through pages on his clipboard. He smelled of sunscreen. He never tanned and avoided the sun. His father and brother had died of melanoma, the same skin cancer that had killed Darby's mother.

While she waited, Darby looked at the well-worn binoculars. NIKON was stamped on the plastic chassis. The manufacturer had installed a thick black rubber armour to prevent damage in case they were dropped. The rubber had cracked because of age and exposure, and she saw scratches on the lenses and a mended crack along the side the owner had repaired with glue. The heads of two Phillips-head screws had been stripped.

'Okay, here it is,' Randy said. 'The bloody footprints on the driveway, walkway and front steps belong to the EMTs. We matched them to the boots they were wearing last night. The footprints you found in the garage match the ones on the deck and kitchen floor. And the size and shape matches the muddy footprint on the living room carpet.

'We lifted a really good footprint from the garage and kitchen floors. The sole and tread marks match a type of sneaker called the Gel Nimbus, made by Asics. They're a size nine. They're also a woman's sneaker.'

'A *woman's* sneaker,' Darby repeated, more to herself than to Randy.

'That's according to the national footwear database we use, and I triple-checked everything just to make sure. That being said, I'm not suggesting a woman was inside the house. It could be that a man accidently bought them. It *does* happen on occasion. Tell her, Mark.'

Mark didn't answer, just kept writing on his clipboard.

'Tell me what?' Darby asked.

Mark sighed. 'There was this one time I *accidentally* bought a pair of women's sneakers. I went to a basement sale and some of the sneakers were mixed up. They fit, they were comfortable, so I bought them.'

'You said you liked the cute yellow stripes,' Randy said. 'That's why you bought them.'

Darby laughed. Mark shot Randy the finger and returned to his notes.

'I checked our footwear . . . database,' Randy said, grinning. The lab's footwear database consisted of a collection of three-ring binders. 'I didn't find a match to any evidence from local cases.'

'What did you find in the woods?'

'This way,' he said, opening the door.

She followed him to a small conference room. Bagged evidence sat on the table. He had tacked pictures of the evidence to a wall. Across from it, on a whiteboard, he had drawn a topographical sketch of the woods, dividing sections into twenty-eight quadrants and marking the areas where he'd found evidence.

'These areas right here – Quadrants 1 through 7 – are directly behind the back fence,' Randy said. 'The gentleman you encountered with the night-vision goggles stood behind the tree in Quadrant 17 – the same place you found the blister pack. That area gave him a great tactical advantage. He could see the woods, and he had quick access to the second incline that led up to the road.

'The first stun grenade landed here, in Quadrant 10, where you found the phone. We recovered the spent shell casings from that area and from the top of the second incline, Quadrants 24 and 25. They're all Smith and Wesson forties. We dug the slugs from the tree trunk and sent them up to ballistics.

'He threw three smoke grenades, and, as you can see, they line the second row here near the top of the first incline, Quadrants 9 through 13.'

'He created a smoke screen.'

'That's exactly what he did. He kept everyone back in order to provide enough time for him to grab the phone and for his partners to haul away the body. All the items of evidence we recovered were in tight, concentrated areas. Except for this.' He pointed to the top-left-hand corner, Quadrant 22. 'This is where I found the binoculars. It's far away from the other footprints we found in the woods. The footprints I found in Quadrant 22 match the ones left on the deck steps and on the garage floor.'

'Do the sneaker prints match any of the others you found inside the woods?'

'No, they don't.'

Darby stared at the grid map, thinking about the person who had shot their way *inside* the house and cut Sean Sheppard lose. If this shooter was part of the group she'd seen in the woods, why were they standing so far away from the others?

'That's all I have,' Randy said. 'Do you want to examine the evidence yourself, or would you like me to work on it?'

'I want to see one of the Smith and Wesson for-ties.'

He handed her a bag. He had bagged each spent round individually and marked it with a number to correspond to its location on the grid map. *Christ, he's thorough.*

Using a pen, she examined the spark plug. It seemed to be the right size. No irregular borders or markings.

'I want to run each one of these through the mass spectrometer.' She told him about the microstamp.

Darby checked her watch. Quarter to four.

'Mark and I won't leave until we're finished,' Randy said. 'I know this is a top priority.'

'I was just checking the time. I need to make some phone calls.'

'Well, we'll be here if you need us.'

'Nice work, Randy.'

'Nothing to it.'

26

Darby sat in her office chair, typing on her keyboard. She had, courtesy of Police Commissioner Chadzynski, a computer with direct access to the Boston Police Department's Crime Justice Information System, the same network used by homicide detectives and patrolmen.

She found the case file numbers for the murders of Donnie and Sue Sheppard. No details were listed. She looked at the date. April 13, 1983. Homicides prior to 1985 hadn't been transferred to the database. The murder books and physical evidence were stored in one of the trailers out in Hyde Park. She picked up the phone. The desk sergeant who took the call promised to deliver the murder books and the associated evidence to the lab no later than noon tomorrow.

A Google searched revealed that RES did, in fact, stand for Reynolds Engineering Systems. The company was based in Wilmington, Virginia. According to its website, RES was one of the leading developers of microstamping technology.

She had to wait on the line for more than half an hour while her call was transferred to various department heads. Each time she had to reintroduce herself and explain the reason for her call. Each time, the person she talked to had to bump the call up to his or her superior. Finally, a vice-president came on the line, and after much discussion he put her in touch with the head of the division in charge of microstamping, a pleasant-sounding woman named Madeira James.

Darby went through the whole rigmarole of who she was and the reason for her call. James put her on hold. Ten minutes later she came back on the line.

'Sorry to keep you waiting, Miss McCormick, but I needed to gather some materials and also check in with some people. Everyone here is, well, more than a little alarmed at the possibility that one of our micro-stamped prototypes is connected to a homicide investigation.'

'I understand.'

'Those codes you found stamped on the bullet, could you please give them to me again?'

She did.

'Okay,' James said. 'That bottom row of numbers, B4M6?? Those codes correspond to a batch of test ammo we ran on . . . Here it is, January 16th of last year. According to my notes, the ammo was used for an in-house demonstration.'

'Do you mean a demonstration for company executives?'

'It's possible. The bigwigs like to check in once in a while to see how their money's being spent. The demo could have been given to a law enforcement agency. We're trying to get everyone on board with the new technology, to show them how it will change ballistics identification. Of course, the gun lobbyists are fighting it tooth and nail.'

'I need to know the names of the people who were at this demonstration.'

'I don't have that information here. It's on the other side of the building, under lock and key.'

'You can't access it?'

'Not right now – the vault, as we call it, is about to close for the day. I have to fill out a form to access the records, and I need to get it signed by several people, including the president. I know it sounds like a bureaucracy – and you would be right – but the main reason is we have to be wary of corporate spying. There are four competing companies who are developing some sort of microstamping technology. Only one company will be chosen. We're talking, potentially, hundreds of millions of dollars, so you can see why we need the extra security.'

'The first row, GLK18. Is that the code for a Glock eighteen?'

'That's what I have here in my notes.'

'What do you know about handguns, Miss James?'

'Not much, I'm afraid. I'm just involved in the technology part.'

'The Glock eighteen isn't available here in the States.'

'I see where you're heading. We routinely test different types of ammunition on various weapons – handguns, shotguns, sniper rifles, you name it. Some are illegal, such as semi-automatic weapons, and because we can't purchase them, they're donated to us through various law enforcement personnel. It's all legal.'

'What about the FBI? Have they donated weapons?'

'They have. They're staunch supporters of microstamping. They want to make sure the stamping works on ammo used in various weapons. I seem to recall their bringing a handgun called . . . a Bar . . .'

'Barak,' Darby said. The double-action pistol, she knew, had been originally developed to be used by the Israeli Defence Force and was now used by Israeli police. 'When can you get me that list of names?'

'I'll fill out the paperwork tonight and get to work on it first thing tomorrow morning. I can give you copies of the sign-in sheets, if you want. What's the best way to reach you?'

Darby gave the woman her phone numbers and email address. She thanked her and hung up, about to head to ballistics to see if a Glock eighteen had been used in any local or national homicides, when her phone rang.

'Darby McCormick.'

'Miss McCormick, my name is Charlie Skinner.' The man's voice sounded as if his throat were wrapped in barbed wire. 'I'm the superintendent for MCI-Cedar Junction. I need to talk to you about the man who murdered your father.'

27

Darby remained standing, her heart thudding inside her chest as she watched the raindrops running down her office window.

Her beeper vibrated against her hip.

'Miss McCormick? Are you there?'

'I'm here.' She checked her beeper. Operations had paged her.

'Is this a good time, or should I call back tomorrow?'

'No, Mr Skinner, I'd like to talk now.' She had a strange cramping sensation in her throat. 'Can I put you on hold for a moment?'

'Of course. Take your time.'

She put Skinner on hold and dialled Coop's office.

'Do me a favour,' she said after he picked up. 'Ops just paged me and I'm on the phone. Call ops, get the details and talk to the detective. I'll meet you in your office when I'm finished.'

She picked up Skinner's line.

'Thanks for holding, Mr Skinner.'

'Please call me Charlie. I'm probably old enough to be your grandfather. Miss McCormick, the reason for my call is that John Ezekiel has requested to speak to you.'

'About what?'

'He said he has some information regarding a woman named Amy Hallcox.'

Darby sat on the edge of her desk. 'What sort of information?'

'He wouldn't tell me. He's under no obligation to do so. Isn't Amy Hallcox the woman who was murdered in Belham?'

'Yes. How does he know her? Did he say?'

'No, he didn't. But I can tell you she went to visit him yesterday afternoon.'

The day she was murdered.

'She came in at three thirty and spoke to him for an hour,' Skinner said. 'That's the maximum time we allow. Ezekiel is in Ten Block – that's our maximum-security wing – and since he's been on good behaviour, we allowed the visit.'

'When was he moved from general pop?'

'Let's see . . .' She heard the *tap-tap-tap* of keys on the other end of the line. 'After Ezekiel was arrested, he got into a lot of fights with inmates. Nothing serious but he spent a lot of time in solitary. That changed five years ago when he murdered another inmate in the shower – he broke the man's neck. We had to move him to Ten Block. Ezekiel's been quite a problem, especially with the psychiatric nurses. He's schizophrenic and they have to inject him with medication. Right after we moved him, he glassed one of the male nurses.'

'Glassed?'

'Sorry, that's one of our local prison terms. A male nurse coined the phrase. Ezekiel unscrewed one of the light bulbs in his cell, crushed the glass and mixed it with his faeces. When the nurses came to give him his daily injection, he threw the mixture at them. They wiped their faces and ended up getting cut pretty badly from the glass. One of them had to have surgery on his eyes and has been partially blinded. Thanks to Mr Ezekiel, we had to install grates around all the lights in Ten Block Have you spoken to him before?'

'No. Did he specifically ask for me?' Her name hadn't been mentioned in the papers or the news regarding the Belham murder.

'He asked to speak to you – and only you,' Skinner said. 'He also told me that if you refused to come, he won't speak to another detective. Have you ever interviewed a prisoner before?'

'No, I haven't.'

'Then let me explain how this works. I can arrange a room where you can speak to Mr Ezekiel in privacy. Don't be surprised if he suddenly decides not to speak to you. He's under no legal obligation to share the knowledge of his meeting with Miss Hallcox, if that's what this is all about. He may, in fact, request a lawyer.'

'Has he asked for one?'

'Not yet, but that doesn't mean he can't – or won't

– change his mind. Murderers are, at their core, noth-ing but cowards. It's been my experience that when they're in the presence of the victim's family, they simply shut down. I'm not saying he will, but I am saying you should be prepared for the possibility. And you have the added burden of his schizophrenia. He's medicated, but I'm told that disease is tricky to treat. From what I've read here, he still suffers from delu-sions – thinks people are watching and listening.'

'Has anyone else visited him?'

'Not according to what I've got up on my compu-ter screen, but these records only go back fifteen years. That's about the time we switched over to using computers. Now we use them for everything. I'm an old-fashioned man, and I must admit I miss paper.'

'I'm assuming you kept all the old paper logs.'

'You assume correctly.'

'Can you pull them? I'd like to know who else has visited Ezekiel.'

'I can do that, but that may take a few days. You'll have to fill out paperwork. I can email it to you, or you can fill it out when you come in.'

'I'll do it when I come in. When can I see him?'

'We need to make some preparations, so how about tomorrow morning at ten?'

'Ten's fine.'

'This is going to sound odd, but I have to say it. Please adhere to the female dress code policy. You'll find the details on our website. Read it and have yourself a good laugh.'

Darby hung up, called ballistics and asked the person who answered to run a Glock eighteen through their database.

She walked down the hall feeling unsteady on her feet and strangely light-headed, as though she had just woken up from anaesthesia. Her mind recalled the single image she had of John Ezekiel – a black-and-white newspaper photograph of him staring down at his cuffed hands as the judge read the verdict of his life sentence. She remembered Ezekiel's high forehead and blond hair; the hard, knotted muscles in his forearms. Eyes that seemed too small for his large face. Darby remembered that the photograph had been bigger than the small article tucked away in the back pages of the *Boston Herald American*.

When she opened the door to the fingerprints unit, she saw Coop standing behind his desk.

'Homicide in Charlestown,' he said, tearing a sheet of paper from a pad. 'Lead detective is Stan Jennings. I couldn't get him on the phone, but ops told me what we need to know. The victim's lying in a dirt basement full of human remains.'

28

Darby sat behind the wheel of the crime scene vehicle waiting for the dozen or so Charlestown cops to clear the people crowding the streets. The afternoon's pounding rain had finally stopped and the predominately Irish residents packed the streets and pavements. They watched from their windows and stoops, rooftops and decks. Some drank beer, and she saw more than one person passing a bottle wrapped in a brown-paper bag. Almost everyone was smoking.

Homicides in Charlestown, she knew, always produced a carnival-like atmosphere. The die-hard townies who had prised themselves away from their TV sets and bar stools had come here not so much to see if they knew the victim (chances were they did) but rather to find out who in the neighbourhood was out talking to the police. Charlestown still operated by a strict code of silence similar to the Italian Mafia's *omertà*: your secrets and sins belonged to the town, and the town took care of its own. You didn't go to the police, you didn't talk to the police. This tribal value system had helped to confer upon Boston's smallest and oldest neighbourhood the distinction of having the highest unsolved homicide rate in the city and the state year after year.

'They're acting like the police are here to hand out free scratch cards,' Darby said.

Coop nodded, looking at the sea of faces passing by the windows. He had been unusually quiet during the ride. The moment he had entered the SUV, he had grown sullen and fidgety; he kept shifting his seat.

At first she had thought Coop might know the victim waiting for them in Charlestown. When he said he had no idea who lived there, she had told him about her conversation with Superintendent Skinner. Coop had answered in grunts and nods.

Clearly Kendra Sheppard was still on his mind, but Darby sensed it was more than that. He wasn't ready to talk about what was really bothering him yet, so she dropped it. Over the years she had learned one thing about him: he couldn't be pushed. Try it and he'd lock up and shut down. He'd talk to her when he was ready.

A patrolman tapped the Explorer's hood and waved her through.

Darby parked the crime scene vehicle in the middle of the street. There was nowhere else to park. Cruisers had blocked off the surrounding streets slick with rain. Stepping out of the car into the grey evening light, she spotted several TV cameras pointed in her direction and wondered if the cameraman she'd seen in Belham had followed her here and was lurking somewhere close by.

When she opened the hatchback, Coop grabbed one of the vacuum-sealed packages holding a disposable

Tyvek biohazard suit and headed for the house. The patrolman guarding the front door held it open for him.

'Coop, you forgot your mask and face shield,' Darby said.

He didn't answer – or maybe he hadn't heard her. He had already ducked inside the house. She stared after him, wondering why he was in such a rush.

Rummaging through the hatchback, she was relieved to find the new 3M respirator masks. In addition to its excellent particle filtration efficiency, this newer model had a cool-flow value that reduced heat and humidity build-up inside the mask. She grabbed two and an additional face shield. She tucked the bag for the biohazard suit under her arm and, kit in hand, lugged everything to the house.

Stepping inside was like stepping back through time, to the late sixties or early seventies – dark hardwood floors and shag carpeting, and in the kitchen one of the ugliest and most depressing wallpaper patterns she had ever seen.

She placed her kit on the kitchen floor. The young patrolman leaning against the worktop had a chubby face fresh with sunburn. His upper lip was shiny, greasy. She spotted the small jar of Vicks VapoRub on the table.

'Help yourself,' he said.

Darby held up her mask. 'I'm looking for Detective Jennings.'

'He's downstairs.' He jerked his thumb to the open door at the end of the tiny kitchen. 'Stairwell is narrow so be careful of the evidence cones on the steps.'

'Thanks.'

'No problem. Enjoy the show.'

Dressed in her biohazard suit, she carried the equipment down the steps, eyeing the clumps of dirt next to the evidence cones. Where had the dirt come from? When she reached the cellar floor, she found her answer: the floor in the back part of the basement was made of dirt, common in old homes.

Coop, dressed in his biohazard suit and wearing his thick blue gloves, stood in front of a giant armoire that looked as if it belonged in the palace of a Chinese emperor. She saw several footwear impressions in the dirt.

A short and painfully thin older man wearing bifocals and a frumpy blue suit took the handkerchief away from his mouth and came over to introduce himself.

'Stan Jennings.'

Darby shook his hand. The man's shirt collar was at least two sizes too big and the dark circles under his eyes matched his black hair.

Jennings told her about the 911 call that had come from the neighbour across the street, an older Italian woman who babysat her three-year-old grandson while her daughter was at work.

'This old gal smokes by the window on account

of her grandson's asthma,' he said, his tone loud and excited, like that of a man who'd just discovered he had inherited a windfall. 'She heard what she thought were gunshots. Next thing she sees is some guy dressed in a Red Sox windbreaker exiting the house. Guy was wearing a cap and had his head tilted down on account of the rain so she couldn't see his face.'

'Who owns the house?'

'Kevin Reynolds.' Jennings searched her eyes and a grin crept across his face. 'You don't know who he is, do you?'

'No. Should I?'

'Where you from?'

'I grew up in Belham.'

'Then you must know who Frank Sullivan is.'

'The head of the Irish mob?'

'That's who I'm talking about.'

She knew the name, of course – everyone who lived in and around Boston carried stories about the man that ranged somewhere between ruthless gangster to some sort of modern-day Robin Hood character who kept their streets safe by either murdering drug dealers or making them magically disappear.

But Sullivan and all the other big-time mafiosos – that period of time had occurred during her junior high school years back in the early eighties. She had no idea what Sullivan looked like, and what she knew about the man could fit inside a thimble. Son of a poor Irish immigrant couple who died shortly after arriving in Charlestown. Started out his career delivering cars to chop-shops and then later introduced Charlestown and South Boston to heroin while running guns to Ireland through Chelsea Pier. She remembered something about Sullivan dying in a botched raid involving two boats in Boston Harbor.

'Kevin Reynolds was Frank's right-hand man, his personal pit bull,' Jennings said. 'Kevin's mother kicked the bucket about two weeks ago – nothing suspicious, just passed away in her sleep. He's putting the house up for sale, which explains why he's digging up these bodies. Not a good selling point.'

'You have him in custody?'

'Not yet. He's probably split town. The son of a bitch is real crafty. I'm sure he's –'

'Excuse me for a moment,' Darby said, eyeing the spent shell casings.

She carefully navigated her way around the sets of footwear impressions zigzagging their way across the dirt, not wanting to disturb them, and arrived at the nearest casing. Crouching, she examined it.

'This is the same round we found in Belham two days ago,' Darby said, cocking her head in Jennings's direction. 'I'm sure you heard about it on the news: the home invasion involving a woman and her son.'

'Woman was murdered and her kid shot himself at the hospital.'

She nodded and stood up.

'Do you know a woman named Kendra Sheppard? She's from Charlestown.'

'Her family was murdered in '83,' Jennings said. 'Shot to death in their sleep by two different kinds of ammo. I helped work the case. Kendra disappeared before the funeral. I helped work that case too. Nobody knew what happened to her. I wouldn't be surprised if she was one of the bodies buried down here.'

'She's not. The murdered woman we found in the house was going by the name of Amy Hallcox. We checked her prints against Kendra Sheppard's. They match.'

Jennings's eyebrows arched. 'How long has she been living in Belham?'

'She was living in Vermont. According to her son, she came here for some job interviews. Did you know she was arrested for prostitution in Charlestown?'

'I remember something about that.'

'Any idea why? She was nineteen.'

'Sullivan wasn't into prostitution, if that's where you're heading. His big thing was extortion. The cocaine and heroin came later.'

'Why were her parents murdered, do you know?'

'I'm sure Sullivan was behind it. When he was alive, you couldn't piss on these streets without his permission. Either Sullivan killed the Sheppard family or he commissioned someone to do it. Do I have proof? No. But you can bet Sullivan was somehow behind it.'

Out of the corner of her eye she saw Coop moving the beam of his flashlight inside a cardboard box splattered with blood.

'When Sullivan moved into Charlestown,' Jennings said, 'half the people here were murdered or disappeared without a trace. And that doesn't include the victims who lived in and around Boston. The guy was as evil as Hitler and just as thorough. Ran Charlestown like it was a goddamn concentration camp. By the time he died, this place was like Auschwitz, a ghost town.'

She turned her attention to the body sprawled against the dirt floor. She could see only the navy-blue trouser legs and shoes; the rest was hidden behind Jennings.

'For that to happen,' Jennings said, 'you've got to have some very important people on your payroll – people on the inside who can manipulate things, people in the know. People –'

'Hold that thought.'

Darby had stepped aside to get a clear look at the body. White male dressed in a suit jacket. The majority of gunshots had hit him in the chest. Two shots had hit the man's right leg. One had hit the femoral artery and he had bled out.

That shot hadn't killed the man who had used the name of Special Agent Phillips. The single shot to the side of the forehead had done the job.

29

Darby put on her thick blue gloves and crouched next to the body. She found a leather billfold tucked in his front pocket.

Jennings's scuffed black shoes stepped beside her. She opened the billfold: FBI badge and Federal ID for Special Agent Dylan Phillips. Pine was right: the credentials looked like the real deal. She started checking the other pockets.

'You know this guy?' Jennings asked.

'I met him yesterday at St Joe's Hospital. He posed as a Fed, had this ID and badge with him, even a Federal warrant.'

'What was he doing there?'

'He wanted to take Kendra Sheppard's son into protective custody.' She pulled a black wallet out of the back trouser pocket. Connecticut driver's licence and assorted credit cards issued to Paul Highsmith. The licence photo matched the one in the ID for Special Agent Phillips. *How many names does this guy have?*

'This guy's name isn't Phillips or Highsmith,' Jennings said. 'His real name is Peter Alan. When I knew him, he was a Federal agent for the Boston office.'

Darby stood. Coop had moved off to examine the furniture stacked in the corner.

'I knew Alan back in the day, ran into him more than once here in Charlestown,' Jennings said. 'He used to run informants. Placed a lot of 'em inside witness protection so we couldn't get at them – guys like Billy O'Donnell. They called him Billy Three Fingers. Guy was an expert safe cracker. He, ah, encroached on Sullivan's turf and when Sullivan broke Billy's right hand, Billy started picking locks with his left. After Billy entered WITSEC, I couldn't gain access to him. Feds wouldn't let me speak to him.'

'And why is that?'

Jennings popped a stick of gum into his mouth. 'Do you know how Sullivan bought the farm?'

'All I remember is Sullivan died during a raid on the harbour. I was in high school when it happened, what, '81?'

'July of '83.'

The same year Kendra Sheppard's parents were murdered – the same year my father was murdered.

'Let me give you a quick history lesson to bring you up to speed,' Jennings said. 'Sullivan operated out of Charlestown from the late sixties. By the time he died, you're talking about a good twenty-year stretch when he either murdered people or made them disappear, including a lot of young women like the ones buried in this basement. Sullivan liked 'em real young. The ones who got involved with him ended up dead or vanishing into thin air. Don't ask me for an exact number, because I started to lose count. Suffice to say I've got files of missing women who at one time or another were in Sullivan's orbit.

'Now when the guy was alive, he was untouchable, which is odd when you stop to consider that you had the Boston Feds gunning for him, Boston PD, the state police. The son of a bitch was always one step ahead. I remember this one case where we planted bugs in his car. Real technical operation, took four hours to install them. The next day a whole bunch of us are tailing Sullivan. He pulls up next to my car, rolls down the window and says, "Hey, Stan, those bugs you planted in my car, do you want them now or do you want me to swing by your office later?"'

'So Sullivan had bought off cops,' Darby said.

'Oh, I'm sure he had cops and guys from the state police on his payroll, but I'll do you one better. I think Sullivan was an informant for the Feds. Now ask me how I can possibly say that.'

'How can you possibly say that?'

'Thank you for asking. See, the Italians in the North End, they went down like flies, one right after another. Sullivan, though, kept running his business – thrived, in fact. Not once was he arrested.'

'What about Reynolds?'

'Nope. It was like the two of them were untouchable.'

'Who set up the sting on Boston Harbor?'

'That would be the good people at the FBI's Boston field office. Special Agent Alan was working with one of my informants, the aforementioned safe cracker Billy O'Donnell. Billy got busted and was facing a permanent vacation at one of our fine supermax prisons, so he did some wheeling and dealing with Alan, told him he had some very significant information on Mr Francis Sullivan. Alan agreed to the deal, and Billy told him that Sullivan was bringing in a major score of heroin by boat. Alan told his superiors and set up a sting on Boston Harbor, where the transaction was supposed to take place.

'One of the undercover guys,' Jennings said, 'a Fed named Jack King, was in communication with the command post when Sullivan for some reason stepped aboard and started shooting. King got shot, and by the time the cavalry arrived, both boats were engulfed in flames. No survivors. Sullivan and the two guys from his crew, the undercover Feds on the boat – everyone was burnt to a crisp. Divers came in the next morning to pull out their bodies. No survivors.'

'Were you there?'

'Oh, no, this was strictly a Feds-only party. No ATF, no state or local police. Boston Feds had a major hard-on for Sullivan. Once the Italians were out of the way, they came under some serious pressure to deliver Sullivan next. It wouldn't look good if the Boston cops or staties delivered Sullivan's head on a silver platter, no, *they* had to do it, so *they* locked us out. They threw our informants into WITSEC so we couldn't get access to them. In other words, we were left in the dark.'

'Was Reynolds involved?'

'In the sting? Probably. Sullivan never went anywhere without Reynolds in tow. The Feds tried to prove it – Boston PD tried too, after the fact, but Kevin had a rock-solid alibi. He's a crafty prick.'

Darby took off a glove and rubbed her sweaty forehead. She couldn't see how all the pieces fit together: Kendra Sheppard using an alias; the Feds; the bodies buried in the basement of a home owned by the mother of Kevin Reynolds, a former henchman for the now-deceased ringleader of Boston's Irish mafia. *And don't forget your father. Big Red is somehow involved in all of this – your father and the man who murdered him.*

Jennings grinned, kneading the gum between his nicotine-stained front teeth. 'I haven't told you the best part.'

'Well, don't keep me in suspense. Tell me.'

'You're going to love this. I mean, you really are going to love it. Special Agent Alan here?' Jennings tapped the dead man's shoe with his. 'He was one of the undercover agents planted on the boat. He's supposed to be dead.'

30

'Forgive me for asking the obvious question,' Darby said, 'but you're positive Special Agent Alan was on the boat?'

'I am, but you don't have to take my word for it,' Jennings said. 'Read the FBI transcripts. That is, if the FBI will let you. It took me, oh, I don't know, three months of visiting their office every morning before they finally produced the transcripts of what happened that night.'

'Did you ask to listen to the audio?' Darby knew the Feds recorded the communications between the boat and the command post.'

'As a matter of fact, they did,' Jennings said. 'Sadly, they wouldn't allow me to listen to the tapes, citing that they were part of an ongoing Federal investigation.'

Darby grinned. 'You don't trust the *Feds*?'

Jennings laughed. 'I know, I know. I should place more faith in our government officials. But I'm a stubborn old man, Miss McCormick. I've seen too many things here in Charlestown – things that would make the hair on the back of your pretty neck stand on end. I'll tell them to you sometime, but right now I want to know how a Federal agent has somehow resurrected himself from the dead only to wind up being shot to death inside Kevin Reynolds's basement – which is full of human remains, no less. If you have any ideas or theories, I'd love to hear them.'

For the next twenty minutes she led Jennings through her brushes with the unidentified men in the woods, the driver of the brown van and the camera-man with his laser mike.

'Now *that* is an interesting development,' Jennings said after she finished. Then he glanced down at the body. 'And *this* man is Peter Alan. I'll bet my salary for the entire year on it. But don't take my word for it. His prints will be stored in the database.'

Darby nodded. All federal and state employees – all law enforcement personnel – had their fingerprints stored inside the national fingerprint database, IAFIS. 'I'll print him here,' she said. 'I'll call someone from the lab to get the fingerprint card so we can get a head start.'

Footsteps moved to the top of the basement steps.

'Hey, Stan,' the patrolman from the kitchen said.

'Yeah, what's up?'

'Is there something wrong with your phone?'

'I don't think so. Why?'

'Tim's been trying to call you and said he keeps get-ting your voicemail. He's got a lead on Reynolds.'

'Coop called you earlier but couldn't get you on the phone,' Darby said. 'I tried calling you from the road and kept getting your voicemail.'

Jennings took out his phone and examined it. 'That's odd.'

'What?' Darby asked.

'It's dead. I thought the battery was charged when I left the house. I'll have to grab a spare.' He turned to the stairs and shouted, 'Get Tim on the phone; I'll be right up.'

Jennings reached into his pocket, came back with a business card and handed it to Darby.

'These gentlemen you mentioned seeing in Belham today: if you see them again I want to know. I might be able to help you identify them.'

'How will I get in touch with you?'

'Talk to Jake – that's the patrolman upstairs in the kitchen. He'll be able to track me down.'

'Before you go, post someone at the front door. If these men I mentioned are lurking around, I don't want them to gain access to the house. I'd also like to call Detective Pine from Belham and bring him into this, as the two cases are related.'

'As long as everyone shares, I don't have a problem.'

'You won't have a problem.'

'Good. Keep me in the loop.'

'Will do.'

Jennings ran up the basement steps. Darby turned her attention to the cardboard box packed with bones.

Two skulls stained brown from their time buried in

the soil. Judging by the smooth cheekbones and shape of the foreheads, both skulls belonged to Caucasian females.

'Darby.'

She turned to see Coop standing just a few feet away.

'While you were talking with Jennings, I tried calling the ME's office,' he said. 'I kept getting static.'

She took out her phone. It turned on fine but the screen kept flickering.

'All of our phones aren't working?' Coop said. 'That doesn't make any sense.'

She thought back to what she'd seen earlier on the hospital video. The man posing as Special Agent Phillips – Peter Alan, according to Jennings – had brought with him some sort of high-energy radio frequency device that fried the circuitry inside the hospital's security cameras, computers and phones. Was there some sort of HERF device down here?

Darby looked around the basement. A small black plastic device sat on the top of a chest-of-drawers. The unit was the size of a pack of cigarettes and had a tiny glowing green light. No buttons, only a switch. She turned it and the green light disappeared.

She checked her phone. The screen had stopped flickering.

'Try your phone.'

He did. 'It seems to be working. No interference. That device, is that the HERF thing Teddy C. told you about?'

'I don't think so. If it was, our phones would be dead. My guess is it's some sort of jamming device.'

'Then why is Jennings's phone dead?'

'Don't know.' She crouched again and searched the rest of the man's pockets.

Inside the suit jacket she found another black device – this one flat, maybe half the size of a paperback book. It had a thick rubber antenna and a blue LED with a frequency number. *I think I found your HERF device, Ted.*

The device didn't seem to be turned on – if it had been, their phones wouldn't be working at all.

Darby looked at the spent rounds scattered across the floor.

'There're nineteen of them,' Coop said.

A normal nine held sixteen. An extended mag could accommodate the number of spent shells lying on the basement floor. Given the tight pattern of shots on the body, she guessed the Glock eighteen had been set to semi-automatic fire.

Coop had moved to the dusty four-drawer oak chest lying at an angle next to the Asian armoire. He sidled up to an old mattress and dismantled bed frame leaning against the wall and turned on his flashlight.

'Take a look at this,' he said, and shined the beam of light behind the chest.

31

Darby saw several footwear impressions in the dirt – some good enough to cast. Each one was the sole of a sneaker, judging by its shape and tread pattern.

'The tread pattern is different,' Coop said, 'but it's the same size as the one you found in Belham.'

'I agree.'

'Kind of an odd place to be standing, don't you think?'

'Not if you're hiding.'

'Exactly. If you wanted to pop your Federal friend, why not do it when he's coming down the steps?'

'Good question.'

'I also took a look at the grave behind that armoire and found another human skull.'

'Why were you in such a rush to get down here?'

'Anything involving Kevin Reynolds makes me nervous.'

'You didn't mention anything about him when we were in the car.'

'I didn't know he was involved until we pulled up to the street,' he said. 'When I saw the house, that's when I knew.'

'Jennings gave you the address. You didn't recognize it?'

'Darby, I don't know *everyone* who lives here.'

'Do you know Reynolds?'

'Sure do. He introduced the town to herpes.'

'How well do you know him?'

'I don't. He's sort of a neighbourhood fixture – people still cross the street when they see him. At least the people who grew up here still do.'

'You've been awfully quiet.'

'I've heard Jennings's rap before.' Coop shut off the flashlight. 'I'll go get a fingerprint card. I'll call Mark and Randy, get one of them to come down here so they can take it back to the lab.'

'Tell me more about Reynolds first.'

'He worked for Sullivan from the time he was seventeen. Kevin was a bouncer at this local bar called McGee's. Place is a real shithole. You only went there if you were looking to score bad coke or get stabbed. Mr Sullivan saw Kevin in action a few times and offered him a job as a bodyguard and chauffeur.'

'Mr Sullivan?'

'Sorry, old habit. You saw Sullivan on the street, or if he came up and said hello, that's what you called him. Frank was big on respect. If you didn't show it to him or Reynolds or any of his flunkies, you'd better have a good dental plan, 'cause you'd be crawling home with two black eyes and at least one missing tooth.'

'Are you speaking from personal experience?'

'I never had any run-ins with either of them. I kept my distance. Not that it was easy. When I was growing up, Frank and his boys owned every inch of these streets. You did what you were told.'

Coop moved to the grave. 'I'm surprised Kevin's mom didn't smell these bodies. I wonder if they poured lime on them.'

'Do you know who they are?'

'Why are you asking me?'

'You grew up here.'

'Your point?'

'I'm sure you heard rumours about missing women.'

'Sullivan and his crew had a merry-go-round of young ladies. If you had the IQ of a Tic Tac, he moved you to the front of the line. Too bad the guy isn't still alive. You'd find him real interesting.'

'Why's that?'

'He was a serial killer. We're talking numbers that surpass those of Ted Bundy.'

'I don't recall anything about Sullivan ever being arrested.'

'He never was. The guy was untouchable. You can attain that status if you have inside help.'

'Anyone we know?'

He shook his head.

'Do you know the names of any of Sullivan's female victims?'

'No.'

'You must know something. The guy lived in Charlestown, I'm sure you –'

'Darby, I'm not a walking history book when it comes to all the shitheads who've lived here.'

'What's bothering you?'

'Sullivan is a sore spot for me. The people who lived here when I was growing up – my parents included – viewed him as this Robin Hood character who, okay, while not a nice guy, was actually good for the city because he kept drugs out of here. Which was bullshit. Sullivan started selling heroin in Southie, making big money, and he's walking around here telling people how he's going to kill anyone he catches selling it. The man was a genius at playing both sides of the fence.'

It's more than that, she thought.

'The other thing is, you know how I feel about Charlestown. How it's stuck with this townie reputation, that everyone living here is collecting welfare while planning to rob a bank or armoured car. Do we still have our fair share of yahoos and junkies? Absolutely. But name a place that doesn't. Of course, the press would lead you to believe that that's all we have living here. Charlestown's different now. We've got a better class of people. The gentrification wave cleaned up most of the shit, but the press won't report that. And when the news gets out that bones were found in Kevin Reynolds's house, it's going to resurrect all that Irish gangster bullshit again. It's like a skid mark you can't wash from your underwear.'

'Thanks for the visual,' she said.

'You're welcome. Now can we get to work?'

Darby didn't answer. Coop was keeping something from her; she could feel it in her gut. 'What is it about Kendra Sheppard that's really bothering you?'

He rolled his eyes.

'You're not being honest with me, Coop.'

'I'm sorry you feel that way.'

'You didn't talk in the car, you didn't –'

'You didn't say much of anything either.'

'What's going on?'

'Darby, I told you everything I know. Why are you turning this into a goddamn inquisition?'

Because you never were a good liar, Coop. I can see it in your eyes. And the more I keep pressing you, the more defensive you get.

'I'm going to go upstairs, get the fingerprint card and call the ME's office,' he said, emphasizing each word. 'You're more than welcome to escort me, since I'm getting the feeling you don't trust me.'

'I never said I didn't trust you.'

'Then can I get off the witness stand and do some work? Or do you want to waste more time grilling me?'

'Call ops and have them page Castonguay,' Darby said. 'I want him here taking the pictures. Tell him I think I found his HERF device.'

32

Jamie sat alone in the living room waiting for the TV commercial to end. She could hear Carter playing with his Spiderman figures upstairs in the bathtub. Michael was still in his room. When the kids came home from camp, Michael had marched straight upstairs and slammed his bedroom door shut. She went to talk to him. He had locked the door. He refused to talk to her and refused to come out for dinner.

She asked Carter what was bothering Michael and Carter just shrugged.

The answering machine provided a clue. She had forgotten to check it when she first returned home.

'Good afternoon, Miss Russo, this is Tara French, the director of the Babson sports camp here in Wellesley.' The woman's polite voice carried a good amount of caution, as if she didn't quite know how to broach a difficult topic. 'Please give me a call at your earliest convenience. I'd like to speak to you about –'

Michael, Jamie had thought, deleting the message. Something had happened at camp today. She'd give Michael some time to cool down, then get his version of whatever had happened and speak to the camp director first thing tomorrow morning.

The second message was from Father Humphrey: 'Jamie, please call me. I'm . . . I'm worried about you.'

The TV commercial ended. The newsreader for the New England Cable News channel, an ageing man with wiry grey hair and bright white teeth she suspected were dentures, started talking in a serious voice about the lead story, 'a grisly homicide and shocking discovery in Charlestown at the childhood home of Kevin Reynolds, a former close associate of Boston's notorious Irish mobster Francis Sullivan'.

Frank Sullivan. Jamie knew the name, of course, but she couldn't recall anything specific about the man's legacy beyond suspected murder, extortion and people who suddenly vanished into thin air. She had graduated from the police academy in February of '92 – nearly a decade after Sullivan's death. The Irish mob – and the Italian Mafia, for that matter – had been dismantled by the time she had started her first Boston patrols. A year later she had transferred to Wellesley, a town whose greatest threat was the occasional burglary. She met Dan during that year, got married and quit working when she was pregnant with Carter.

The horse-toothed newsreader disappeared as the screen switched to an Asian reporter who was broadcasting live from Charlestown. Jamie could see blinking blue and white police lights on the windows and wet pavement behind the reporter.

The reporter gave a brief rundown of what had happened early this afternoon: 'Charlestown resident Andrea Fucilla, who lives in an apartment building across the street from the childhood home of Kevin Reynolds, heard gunshots and called the police.'

The screen cut to an elderly woman with olive skin and a crooked nose holding up a pair of thick glasses. She stood under an umbrella but her stringy brown hair was damp from the rain. She spoke in broken English.

'I was on the phone talking to my daughter when I hear popping sounds like firecrackers. But didn't think it was firecrackers so I call police.'

'How did you know the gunshots came from the Reynolds home?' the reporter asked.

'I sit by open window smoking my cigarette and hear *pop-pop-pop*, *pop-pop-pop*. That's what I tell police. That and what I saw.'

'What did you see, Miss Fucilla?'

Jamie felt a sickening dread crawling across her skin.

'I saw a man come walking out of house,' the elderly witness said. 'I didn't get a good look at his face. His head was tilted down because of the rain. He wore Red Sox windbreaker and baseball hat.'

I saw a man come walking out of house. A man.

Jamie sighed deeply, the tension dissolving inside her chest.

The screen had switched back to the reporter.

'Police confirmed that a male victim was found shot to death inside the house but won't release the name or any further details regarding the human remains discovered inside the basement.

'Mary Sullivan, mother of Kevin Reynolds, died last month. Local residents have spotted Kevin Reynolds in Charlestown during the past few weeks and told us he was getting ready to put his mother's home up for sale.'

Now a split screen of the reporter and the newsreader.

The newsreader said, 'Is Kevin Reynolds a suspect?'

'Police have refused to comment but cited him as a person of interest,' the reporter replied. 'They are asking any resident who sees Kevin Reynolds to call.'

The screen switched again to show a photograph of Kevin Reynolds. The picture had been taken some time ago, Jamie thought. Reynolds had a pie-shaped face and pug nose, but his curly hair was brown, not grey. And his clothing was straight out of the eighties: rose-tinted sunglasses and a thick gold chain draped over a white Champion T-shirt worn so tight it showcased his budding man boobs.

A toll-free number flashed across the bottom of the screen. The reporter promised to bring viewers more details as the story developed.

Jamie felt certain Reynolds was one of the men who had murdered her husband. She knew she had to move on him quickly. First, she had to find a way to bring him out of hiding.

She got up from the sofa, wiping her damp palms on her shorts and nursing the idea she'd been mulling over since leaving Charlestown this afternoon. She was about to shut off the TV – she needed to get Carter out of the bathtub – when the newsreader launched into a story outlining Kevin Reynolds's history with Frank Sullivan.

On the TV screen, a black-and-white mug shot of Frank Sullivan's first arrest at twenty-two. He had thick and wavy blond hair and wore a trench coat. He held a Boston Police arrest card a few inches below his freshly shaved chin.

He had a scar on his right wrist – and it was of the same size and shape as the one Ben Masters had had.

She blinked, figuring her mind was playing a trick on her. The scar was still there. Same size, same shape.

She shifted her attention to Frank Sullivan's big ears sticking out from the sides of his head.

Ben had had the same ears.

Now pictures of a younger-looking Sullivan flashed across the TV screen. She was dimly aware of the horse-toothed newsreader saying something about how Sullivan, an only child born in East Boston to a single mother, had started off his career stealing cars before graduating to armed robbery. He was arrested for holding up a bank in Chelsea and served two years in a Cambridge prison.

Next, a surveillance photograph of a much older Francis Sullivan taken, according to the newsreader, the month before he died during a botched FBI raid on Boston Harbor. Sullivan bald on top, the hair on the sides of his head completely grey. Big ears and a wrinkled curtain of flesh dangling underneath his chin.

Ben had had the same rooster neck when she'd seen him inside her house. He'd had the exact same scar and —

Francis Sullivan is dead, a voice whispered.

Ben has the same ears — and that scar on his wrist, it's the <u>exact</u> same size and pattern.

It's a coincidence, Jamie.

No, it's not.

She tuned out the voice as she grabbed the remote control, frantically searching for the pause button. There. She pressed it, freezing the picture, and then dropped the remote and ran for the basement.

33

Jamie opened a drawer in Dan's desk and took out Ben Masters's passport and licence. She clutched the items as she ran back upstairs to the living room.

She opened the passport and held the photograph up against the TV screen, next to the picture of an older Frank Sullivan.

Ben had smaller nostrils but his nose was the same long, angular shape as Frank Sullivan's. Both faces were oblong. Same high forehead. And both men had square jaws and cleft chins.

Differences: Ben's rooster neck was gone. The skin on his face was tight and smooth, not a wrinkle anywhere. He had a full head of black hair.

Dyed, she thought. *He must have had the hair transplanted, or maybe it's a wig or a —*

Do you realize what you're saying? that inner voice asked.

Yes, she did.

Frank Sullivan was Ben Masters. There was no question in her mind.

She had encountered a handful of men in Wellesley – successful big-time executives who had undergone minimally invasive nips and tucks that, after a week of healing, left them looking relaxed and refreshed, as though they had taken a long vacation. These middle-aged men were struggling to maintain their youth. Nothing terrified a man more than losing his sex appeal to younger women, who, when you got right down to it, weren't paying attention to them anyway.

To complete his transformation to Ben Masters, Frank Sullivan had undergone a complete craniofacial reconstruction. He'd got himself a new head of hair but hadn't tucked his ears or done anything to hide the dimple on his chin. Maybe no one would recognize Frank Sullivan passing by in the street, but if you put these two photographs side by side anyone could see the similarities.

Do you still think this is goddamn coincidence? she asked that nagging inner voice.

It didn't answer.

Fact: Frank Sullivan is Ben Masters.

Fact: Ben Masters is Frank Sullivan.

Fact: Frank Sullivan and Ben Masters are the same person.

Jamie grabbed the remote and pressed PLAY.

She had to wade through five more minutes of commentary and then came the segment of Frank Sullivan's death during an FBI raid in the summer of 1983. Two of Frank's associates had died, along with four FBI undercover agents who'd been placed on the boat – Jack King, Peter Alan, Steve White and Anthony Frissora.

The men's four pictures came on the TV. Jamie hit PAUSE.

Peter Alan . . . He bore a close resemblance to the man she'd shot in the basement – and Kevin Reynolds had called him Peter. She couldn't be entirely sure, though. And Anthony Frissora, why did he seem so familiar?

The man I shot at the Belham house . . . I swear that's Anthony Frissora.

That inner voice perked up again: *So now you're saying that, in addition to killing one dead man who went by the name of Francis Sullivan, you're saying that you killed two more dead men – two dead Federal agents by the names of Peter Alan and Anthony Frissora.*

There was no doubt in her mind that Ben Masters was Frank Sullivan, but Peter Alan and Anthony Frissora . . . the pictures on the TV screen were at least twenty years old, but their faces . . . their faces *did* bear a close resemblance to the two men she'd shot.

She filed the thought away and hit PLAY.

Frank Sullivan's badly charred body, the newsreader said, was buried next to his mother's in a Charlestown cemetery.

Jamie wondered who was really buried in the cemetery, wondered how Frank Sullivan had managed to fake his death, and wondered how he had managed to get both the FBI and the Boston police to buy off on it. Her thoughts turned to the man she'd shot in the basement – the man she knew only as Peter.

I can tell you everything you need to know, he'd told her.

He'd worn a gun in a shoulder holster underneath his suit jacket. And she remembered him saying how he had tried to visit the boy named Sean at the hospital and encountered a problem with some woman from the Boston PD.

Was the man named Peter a cop? Clearly he was tied in to Kevin Reynolds and Ben Masters.

Frank Sullivan was now Ben Masters. Kevin Reynolds had worked for Sullivan. Reynolds had said he was expecting a call from Ben.

Has to be Ben Masters, she thought.

If the man named Peter was, in fact, some sort of law enforcement officer, had he helped Sullivan fake his death?

You're forgetting that this Peter guy was working with other people – the man you shot inside the house, the ones who removed the body from the woods, the ones watching the house. One man couldn't pull off faking someone's death, but if he had a whole group of law enforcement people working together to pull it off . . .

Frank Sullivan died in the summer of 1983. He resurrected himself as Benjamin Masters. Five years ago he broke into her house and killed her husband.

Why had Sullivan/Ben come out of hiding?

What happened to your husband and children, the man named Peter had told her, *I didn't have anything to do with that. You have to believe me. That . . . that was all Kevin and Ben.*

She watched the news for another twenty minutes. There was no mention of a missing man named Ben Masters, but she was sure there would be plenty of discussion about it between Kevin Reynolds and his people.

Carter called out for her.

'Mom! Mom, I'm getting cold!'

She shut off the TV and stood, trembling all over. She shoved the passport and licence into her pocket as she moved to the bottom of the stairs.

'Get . . . ah . . . towel. Dry . . . ah . . . dry . . . off. Be . . . ah . . . ah . . . up . . . ah . . . in . . . ah . . . minute.'

'Okay.'

Back in the basement, she took out Ben's mobile phone and slipped in the battery. She turned it on knowing she had to do this quickly, knowing that the signal was being monitored by this group of men. She knew one of these men was named Jack. She remembered Peter saying something about a man named Jack watching the Belham house.

The phone's screen had a message saying Ben had missed another eleven calls. She touched the message and the screen changed to the call log. Pontius had called. No calls from the man named Alan.

She found the box marked 'Messaging'. She touched it. A new screen now appeared upon which she could compose a message. She started typing 'Pontius' when the phone automatically filled in the name.

She composed the message she'd been playing with for the past few hours:

MEET ME AT WATERMAN PARK IN BELHAM AT 5 A.M. COME ALONE. WE'VE BEEN SET UP. DON'T TALK TO ANYONE. GET RID OF PHONE SO THEY DON'T TRACK YOU. WILL EXPLAIN WHEN YOU GET THERE, THEN HAVE ARRANGED SAFE WAY FOR YOU TO LEAVE. CASH, NEW ID, PASSPORT & DRIVER TO TAKE US. BE CAREFUL. MAKE SURE THEY DON'T FOLLOW.

Throughout the afternoon she had debated the 'come alone' part; it reeked of a set-up. She wondered whether it would alert Reynolds. If he didn't come alone, her plan wouldn't work.

This is too risky, that inner voice said.

Maybe, but this was the only way to bring Reynolds to her. She didn't think he'd pass up an opportunity to speak to Ben Masters/Frank Sullivan. Reynolds, with his repeated phones calls, was clearly in a state of panic about what the police had found in his basement. And now here came Ben to the rescue. She felt confident Reynolds would follow the instructions in the message. When someone threw you a life preserver, you didn't say wait, excuse me, but I need you to answer some additional questions before I grab hold. You clutched it and thanked the sweet Lord above for your tremendous good fortune.

What if something happens to you? Michael and Carter have already lost one parent. Don't take away another.

Jamie saw the photograph Dan had taped to the wall – the photograph of Carter, still a baby, sitting on Michael's lap on a beach at Cape Cod, their last vacation together as a family. Her two boys smiled at her from the picture, looking healthy, happy. No scars on their bodies. No memories of their father being tortured to death in the kitchen. No dead room.

You can figure out another way. You don't have to –

She hit SEND. The message lingered on the screen for a moment and then disappeared into cyberspace or wherever these things went. Jamie removed the battery, threw everything back inside the drawer and went upstairs to tend to her children.

34

Darby, who had just stripped out of her coveralls, paced the threadbare carpet in the empty bedroom at the top of the stairs waiting for Dr Howard Edgar to come back on the line. The state's new forensic anthropologist had moved into his Quincy home less than a week ago and was now rummaging around the strange rooms still packed with boxes searching for a pen and paper.

She had borrowed a mobile phone from a patrolman and had gone upstairs to get away from the noise. Jennings had gathered his troops inside the kitchen and she could hear him speaking.

'The lead we had on Kevin Reynolds? It turned out to be his cousin, which isn't surprising, since the two of them look so much alike. We need to find him. Some of you grew up here. I did too, so I know what you're thinking – the neighbourhood won't talk to us. Code of silence and all that bullshit. Tell them the remains we found might belong to local girls. That's your way in. Use that to get them to talk. Work your contacts. Call any retired flatfoot you know who walked these streets during the Sullivan regime. Any name you get will help us get closer to identifying these remains.'

White lights danced across the old bedroom walls. Darby looked out of the grimy bedroom window at the faces gathered below her.

The locals had pretty much packed it in for the night but the media seemed to have doubled in size. Reporters, cameramen and photographers stood shoulder to shoulder behind the sawhorses, every one of them anxiously staring at the front door. Word had leaked about the remains.

Edgar's nasal voice came back on the line. 'I'm sorry to have kept you waiting, Dr McCormick. What's the address?'

She gave it to him. 'Do you know how to get to Charlestown?'

'No, but it doesn't matter. My wife purchased a portable GPS unit for my car, so even a directionally challenged person like myself will have no trouble finding the address. Now tell me what you found.'

'Three sets of remains, one in a state of advanced decomposition. The other two are fully skeletonized. They appear female. You can forget using dental records to ID the remains. Their teeth were pulled out before they were buried. And the person or persons who did it also cut off their hands and feet. It's a classic mob burial before the days of DNA.

'I sifted through the dirt and didn't find any metacarpal or carpal bones. When you examine the tibia, you'll see grooves that I think are consistent with a circular saw.'

'Hopefully we can ID them through some other means,' Edgar said. 'I'd hate to use mitochondrial DNA testing. It's very time consuming, in addition to being expensive.'

Edgar was worried about the city's bean counters. Not a good sign.

'There may be more remains buried down here,' she said. 'I dug up only a small part of the dirt cellar. A good part of it is laid in concrete, so I'd like you to bring in your sonar equipment. You'll also need some additional bodies to help move the furniture. The space is rather small, so I'd suggest no more than three or four people.'

'Dr Carter left me a list of graduate students. I don't have the list handy, so I'll have to stop by my office first. I apologize: I'm not usually this disorganized.'

'There's no rush. You'll be here for a while – probably a good part of the night.' *And so will I*, Darby added privately. She had called in additional forensic teams to help process the house.

'Dr McCormick, unless there's some urgency, I'd prefer to examine the remains *in situ*.'

'I thought you might. I did a little digging around the bones to see if I could find any clothing or jewellery that might help us, but, other than that, everything is undisturbed.'

'Thank you,' Edgar said. 'I'll be there as soon as I can.'

Darby snapped her phone shut, wishing she could go home and take a long shower. Her damp clothes clung to her skin and she felt as grimy as this bedroom's window. She glanced at her watch. Half past ten.

Flashbulbs started popping from the street. She could hear the rapid machine-gun *click-click-click* of dozens of cameras snapping pictures, like this was a goddamn paparazzi event, as the two male attendants from the medical examiner's office, wearing masks and coveralls, walked down the front steps carrying a black body bag holding Peter Alan. Cameras were held in the air to capture and record the footage. Cameramen stood on the roofs of news vans and cars, on the pavement and front stoops, along with some of the neighbours. Across the street, on the corner, a woman wearing a pink tank top and matching short-shorts stood barefoot on the front stairs of a home talking to a burly, bald man.

That's the driver of the brown van. He's wearing the same light grey suit and brown trousers.

Without taking her eyes off him, Darby opened her phone and hit the programmed number for Coop's mobile.

'Where are you?' she asked when he answered.

'I'm in the basement.'

'Go upstairs to the living room and look out of the window facing the street. I'll explain when you get there.'

Baldy stood close to the woman, speaking near her ear. The woman's arms were crossed over her chest and she stared down at her bare feet.

Darby glanced around the street. No sign of a brown van. *It's probably parked on one of the side streets.*

'Okay,' Coop said, 'I'm here.'

'Look across the street to your right. See the woman with the tight pink shorts? Has the word "trouble" stitched across her ass?'

'I see her.'

'The guy standing to her right, the one that's built like a beer keg? I saw him this morning in Belham – he was the one driving the van,' Darby said. 'I want you to keep an eye on him while I talk to Jennings.'

35

Darby clipped the phone to her belt as she moved out of the bedroom. She took the steps quickly and made her way through the officers packed inside the kitchen.

Jennings stood in the archway between the kitchen and the living room. She stepped up beside him, catching sight of Coop watching the street through one of the windows, then turned to the crowd. Jennings was still talking when she cut him off.

'Excuse me, Detective. Gentlemen, I need your attention here, and I need it now . . . Thank you. I have to speak quickly, so listen up. There'll be no follow-up questions.'

She had organized her thoughts and spoke quickly but clearly.

'Jackson Cooper is in the living room watching an older white male standing across the street. This man is bald, about six feet, and built like a beer keg. He's wearing a light grey sports jacket and brown dress trousers. He's also armed. This is a person of interest both for this investigation and for the one that's currently under way in Belham. He's working with one or more people who may be posing as Federal agents. They may be driving a brown van with a Mass. licence plate.'

She gave them the plate number. 'Even if the van isn't here, I'm sure he didn't come alone. I want you to form groups and create a perimeter by going to the following street corners.'

She knew Charlestown well and rattled off the street names. Then she turned to Coop and said, 'Is the subject still across the street?'

'He is,' Coop said.

'Okay, good,' she said, turning back to the men. 'Get a visual before you leave. Under no circumstances are you to use your radios. I believe these people are monitoring police frequencies.'

She pointed to a man standing directly in front of her and said, 'Give me your mobile phone number.'

He did. She quickly programmed it into her phone.

'What's your name?' Darby asked.

'Gavin.'

'If I need assistance or if there's a problem, I'll contact Gavin. I'll let Detective Jennings take over from here.'

'And what are you going to do?' a patrolman in the back asked.

'I'm going to introduce myself,' Darby said, 'welcome him to the neighbourhood.'

Soft laughter.

She opened the back door to an alley of rubbish bins and black bags She ran across the alley, then hooked a left and sprinted across Thatcher Street, the gun holster knocking against her hip. Now a right on to Grover. In less than a minute she'd reach Grafton. Take a right there, run across it and then make her way back up to the top of Old Rutherford Street, where Baldy was standing. Maybe three minutes of running total.

All those mornings spent running in her SWAT gear had paid off. She felt light and fast on her feet and made good time.

She banged a right on to Grafton, surprised to see Baldy trotting across the pavement in his leather wingtips.

Why hadn't Coop called her?

Darby slowed to a walk, beads of sweat running down her forehead and into her eyes. Her heart pounded, but she wasn't winded.

Baldy stepped underneath a street light and she could see a mobile phone pressed against his ear. He had a good five inches on her – he was six foot two, she guessed – and he was twice as wide. She also got a good look at his pockmarked face. No question this was the same man she'd seen earlier today.

Baldy's eyes cut to her. She was removing her side-arm when he abruptly turned and ducked down an alley between two apartment buildings.

Shit. Darby started running.

A moment later she reached the corner leading into the alley, heard footsteps echoing. She turned into it and saw his shadow sprinting past rubbish bins. She gave chase, slowing when she reached the next corner. She turned, saw him running into the street, and followed.

Baldy wasn't in good shape but for such a big man he ran fast and well. And he had a solid lead.

Darby was closing the gap when she heard a car door shut. Tyres peeled away in a screech of rubber. By the time she reached the street, she caught a flash of a dark car before it disappeared.

36

Jamie placed the electric clippers on top of the newspapers with which she'd covered the bathroom vanity. She'd shave her hair down after she saw Michael. He had come out of his room earlier to use the bathroom. She hoped he hadn't locked his bedroom door again.

He hadn't.

She slid the door open and saw him lying on his side, fast asleep.

The right side of his face was swollen.

Michael didn't stir when she pulled back the sheets and climbed into his bed. She wrapped an arm around his waist.

This is the only way I can touch my child: by sneaking into his bed while he's asleep. This is the only way I can feel close to him.

Her eyes stung. Blinking back tears, she kissed his cheek and then lay close next to him, wide awake. Underneath his T-shirt she could feel the thick, rubbery scar on his chest from where the doctors had operated on him to save his life.

I'm so sorry for everything you've gone through, Michael — for everything you're still going through. If there were a way I could fix it, I would. I swear to God I would.

Michael stirred awake. His head popped up, his voice groggy, thick with sleep. He expected to see Carter – sometimes his younger brother crawled into bed. When Michael saw her, he looked alarmed.

'What's wrong? Are you sick?'

'I'm . . . ah . . . okay.'

His glare was as cold and unforgiving as an X-ray.

'What's that . . . You smell like the way the air does after fireworks have gone off.'

He smells the cordite, she thought. No amount of scrubbing with soap and water could remove the gunpowder odour. She had tried using the recipe given to her by her firearms instructor – scrubbing hands with lemons. Apparently, it hadn't worked.

'Your . . . your, ah . . . face, what . . . ah . . . ah . . .'

'Don't worry about it.' His head slumped back against the pillow.

'Fight?'

He didn't answer. He had turned back towards the window.

'Direct . . . ah . . . camp director . . . ah . . . she . . . called.'

He sighed. 'I got in a fight with Tommy Gerrad today.'

'Why?'

'It doesn't matter. I had to go to Miss French's office. While I was there, I told her I didn't want to be there any more, so I guess you're stuck with me.'

Jamie kissed the back of his head and hugged him. She felt his body stiffen.

He didn't push her away, though. He didn't remove her arm.

'Sorry,' she said, and hugged him again. 'Sorry for . . . way Tommy . . . ah . . . ah . . . how he . . . hurt you.'

Michael didn't answer.

'Love,' she said. 'Love . . . ah . . . you.'

'You went to him first.'

Jamie froze.

'You thought you could save only one of us,' he said, 'and you chose Carter.'

'*No,*' she said, clutching him. 'I –'

'I was there, remember? I saw you.' His voice, barely above a whisper, was stripped of emotion. 'You went to him first.'

He was right. She had gone to Carter first. After she managed to free herself from the chair, after she had called 911, she had used the kitchen knife to cut the tape binding his eighteen-month-old brother to the chair and started doing CPR on Carter while Michael, still tied to the chair, bled out. Her focus was on saving Carter first: he was so small, had been shot twice and was losing blood fast. By the time the EMTs arrived, Michael had passed out. Michael remembered what had happened, and this knowledge had lain between them for years, lengthening the already considerable distance between them. But this was the first time he had ever spoken the words out loud and it pierced her.

Jamie's breath came out sharp and fast. The words

she needed to speak were stuck somewhere on the broken road between her brain and tongue. She kissed Michael's neck, feeling her son's body shudder again, and then, unable to hold it any longer, started to cry. She kissed the top of his head, tears streaming down her face, and said, 'Sorry, Michael. Sorry.' She whispered the word over and over again, wishing she could travel far away from this bedroom – this house. Pack up and move them some place where their memories would be stripped clean, their scars erased. Where they'd wake up and greet each day without dread, without worry.

37

Darby dialled Patrolman Gavin and told him to get on the horn and pull everyone back. The person of interest had escaped. She hung up and went looking for Coop.

She didn't have to look far. She found him talking to the attractive woman in the tight pink shorts with the word 'trouble' stitched across her ass. Her name was Michelle Baxter. She had attended school with Coop, from kindergarten all the way through Charlestown High School.

Baxter reeked of beer and cigarettes. She wore bright red lipstick and had gone heavy on the makeup and eyeliner. She smiled and flirted with Coop, acting as if everyone around her had come out of their homes to attend a late-night block party.

'Where do you live, Michelle?' Darby asked.

'Right here.' Baxter waved a hand to the apartment building behind her. 'You want a beer or something?'

'Thank you, but no. We're on duty. Can we talk upstairs?'

'Sure, why not?' Baxter stubbed out her cigarette and walked up the steps.

Coop turned to Darby and said, 'Let me talk to her alone first. You know the deal about Charlestown –

nobody will talk to the cops. I live here, so I might be able to get her to open up.'

'The only thing that woman wants to do with you, Coop, is to find a way to get you into her bed. Besides, she invited both of us up. I think she'll talk to me.'

The dank stairwell smelled of stale cigarettes and cat urine. Someone was playing the Stones' 'Gimme Shelter'. Baxter swayed as she climbed the stairs.

'Here,' Coop said, grabbing her arm. 'Let me help you.'

'Christ, you're beautiful.' She kissed his cheek, leaving a lipstick mark. Giggling, she turned to Darby. 'Isn't he sexy?'

'The sexiest,' Darby replied.

The woman's fifth floor apartment had scratched hardwood floors and mismatched Salvation Army furniture. The kitchen table and worktops were covered with papers, magazines, packets of Ramen noodles and generic soda cans.

Baxter wanted to smoke, so she led them out to a balcony. Blue and white lights flashed from down the street. The whole neighbourhood was awake, and Darby saw more than one face crowding a window, watching the street.

Coop slid the sliding glass door shut, then stood against the back wall with his arms crossed over his chest. Baxter sat in a plastic lawn chair, propped the heels of her bare feet up on the railing and lit a cigarette.

Darby leaned the small of her back against the

243

railing, gripping it with both hands as Michelle Baxter tilted back her head and blew a long stream of smoke into the muggy air. Grey clouds wafted through the thongs and lacy bras hanging on the clothesline above Baxter's head.

'The man you were talking to earlier, the guy dressed in the grey suit jacket,' Darby said. 'You told us he was a cop.'

'That's right,' Baxter said, brushing the fringes of her chemically treated blonde hair away from her boozy, bloodshot eyes. 'Flashed a badge and everything.'

'By everything, do you mean you also saw his picture ID?'

'No, just the badge.'

'What was his name?'

'Don't know. He didn't introduce himself. Some people just don't have any goddamn manners, you know?' Baxter smiled but her eyes were dead. 'You from around here?'

'I grew up in Belham.'

'That's not Charlestown.'

'I know.'

'It's different here.'

'How so?'

'Just . . . different.' Baxter took a long drag from her cigarette. 'I read about you in the papers, when you caught that sicko who was hacking up women in his basement. You're some sort of doctor. Can you prescribe medication and shit?'

'I'm not that type of doctor.'

'That's too bad. So what kind of doctor are you?'

'I have a doctorate in criminal behaviour.'

'Explains why you're with him.' Baxter pointed to Coop.

Darby smiled.

'I keep seeing the two of you around town,' Baxter says. 'You guys dating, or is it one of those friends-with-benefits things?'

Coop spoke up. 'Darby has much higher standards.'

'It's true, I do,' Darby replied. 'Michelle, this cop you were talking to, when he flashed his badge, what did it look like?'

'Like how a badge looks. Like the one you got clipped to your belt.'

'Describe it to me.'

'You know, *gold*. Metal. Had "Boston Po-lice" written on it.'

'What did he want to talk to you about?'

'He wanted to know who I'd seen coming and going from Kevin Reynolds's house.'

Darby waited. When the woman didn't speak, she said, 'And what did you tell him?'

'I told him that I didn't see anything,' Baxter said, 'and that's the truth.'

'Why did he talk to you, though?'

'I don't understand.'

'Why did he single you out?'

Baxter shrugged. Her eyes became veiled, and she retreated back inside a place she had probably spent most of her life – a place behind heavily fortified walls and locked doors where no one could reach her.

'Darby,' Coop said, 'why don't you give us a moment?'

'She don't got to go,' Baxter said. 'Ain't nothing I'm going to say to you that I wouldn't say in front of her. Just because you live here, Coops, doesn't change the fact you're a cop.' She rolled her head to him with that dead expression in her eyes. 'Makes things nice and easy for you now, don't it?'

Darby said, 'What's that supposed to mean?'

'I'm just busting Coop's balls, is all,' Baxter said. She checked her watch. 'Can we wrap this party up? I'm bushed. I've been on my feet all night.'

'I didn't know Wal-Mart stayed opened so late,' Coop said.

'Don't start in on me, Coops, okay?'

'Did you quit or did you get fired again?'

'I had to give it up,' Baxter said. 'All the people working there *no hablo inglés*. Since I don't speak Spanish, I opted for early retirement.'

'So you're, what, back to stripping?'

'Go home, Coops. I'm too tired and too old for another intervention speech. Better yet, why don't you use it on yourself?'

'Good seeing you, Michelle. Take care.' He looked at Darby and nudged his head to the door.

'Michelle,' Darby said, 'the man you were speaking to wasn't a cop.'

'Then why would he be carrying a badge?'

'He's pretending to be a cop.'

'I don't know what to tell you. I saw a badge.'

'Then why did you speak to him? I thought you people lived and died by that whole code of silence thing?'

Baxter laughed softly. 'You people.'

'Why did you speak to him?'

'Didn't have much of a choice. This guy can be very persuasive.'

Can be, Darby thought. 'How do you know him?'

'Look, it doesn't matter. Telling you ain't going to change anything.'

'Then go ahead and tell me.'

Baxter took a long drag from her cigarette and stared into space, as if the life she had envisioned for herself was waiting for her somewhere on the other side of these flat roofs and dirty windows, a place light-years away from these historic streets where Paul Revere and other American Revolutionaries had successfully fought off wave after wave of invading British troops.

Coop stepped up next to Darby and said, 'This is a waste of time. Let's go.'

'My mother, God rest her soul, had a coke problem – a real bad one,' Baxter said. 'Towards the end, she started hocking pretty much everything we owned, which wasn't much to begin with, and when Mr Sullivan –'

'Michelle,' Coop said, 'you don't need to go down this road.'

'Why don't you grab yourself a beer or something?' Baxter said, flicking her cigarette into the air. 'Better yet, go to my bathroom medicine cabinet and feel free to use the stuff I take for my periods. That should take care of your PMS or whatever's crawled up your ass.'

38

Darby watched Baxter pull a bottle of Budweiser from the cooler set up next to her chair. Her attention – her concern – lay with Coop. For some reason the expression on his face triggered a memory of her mother – Sheila pacing the emergency waiting room while Big Red was being cut open on the operating table; her mother, a nurse, already knowing that the window of hope had slammed shut, that her husband of twenty-two years had lost too much blood and was brain dead.

'Now I always knew my mom liked coke,' Baxter said, tossing the beer cap on to the balcony floor. 'I caught her snorting it a couple of times with one of her boyfriends, but I had no idea how serious her problem was until Mr Sullivan told me. Mr Sullivan is Frank Sullivan, by the way. Everyone in town called him Mr Sullivan, even the old timers. The man was big on respect, as I'm sure Coops told you. Coops, you remember that time –'

'Let's skip the trip down memory lane, okay?' Coop said. 'Do you know the name of the cop or not?'

'Maybe Darby here would like to know what it was like growing up here in Chuck-town with Mr

Sullivan,' Baxter said. 'I'm getting the feeling you haven't told her about your own, you know, personal experiences.'

'Let's go, Darby. This is a waste of time.'

'So here's Mr Sullivan coming up to me one day after school saying my mother's been rushed to the hospital,' Baxter said. 'Overdose, he says. Naturally, I'm upset. My mom and me, we didn't get along too well, especially after my old man split, but I was only thirteen and the woman, despite all her faults, she was my whole world, you know?

'Mr Sullivan puts his arm around me while I'm standing there bawling, and the whole time he's telling me not to worry. He going to take care of the problem, get this shit all straightened out, he says. I get in his car and he takes me to the mall to buy some new clothes, makeup, perfume – whatever I want, he says. No girl my age, he says, should look the way I do.

'On the way home, Mr Sullivan tells me about all the money my mom owes for her coke problem – a figure that doesn't include what she's gonna owe the hospital since she don't got no health insurance. So he takes me back to his house, tells me to go upstairs and get cleaned up 'cause we're going over to the hospital so the three of us can sit down and have a nice little chat about how to fix the problem. I'm still crying and having this ... this out-of-body experience I guess you could call it when Mr Sullivan decides to get into the shower with me. He tells me to be strong. I've got to be strong for my mother.'

Baxter took a long drag from her cigarette. 'I always wonder what would have happened if I hadn't decided to try and fight him. Maybe then he wouldn't have used the gun.'

Coop pinched his forehead between his fingers. Baxter drank her beer. Darby stood stock still.

'The girls I met were real nice,' Baxter said. 'They were around my age. They showed me how to get these guys off real quick.'

'What girls?' Darby said. 'What are you talking about?'

'Mr Sullivan threw these private parties at these ritzy Boston hotels. He rented out the suites twice a month. Me and the girls he brought there had full use of the bar. Top-shelf stuff. And there was plenty of coke, H, whatever we wanted. I snorted a little H to take the edge off some of the rougher ones.'

'How many times did this happen?'

'I stopped counting after the first month or two.'

'Did you report this?'

'You mean to the police?'

'Yeah.'

Baxter laughed. 'Who do you think I was blowing at the hotel?'

Coop said, 'I think we've heard enough.'

'I didn't learn about the videotapes until later,' Baxter said. 'Mr Sullivan had set up video cameras in case some of these cops, I don't know, didn't cooperate with him or something. I think he ended up selling the tapes to some porno guys in China or Japan. They're into that real kinky shit over there. Hey, Coops, didn't you see one of the tapes at Jimmy DeCarlo's bachelor party?'

Coop didn't answer. The sweat on his face had nothing to do with the heat.

'What happened?' Baxter asked. 'To that tape, I mean?'

'I don't know,' he said, strangled by the words.

'Oh. I thought you might have destroyed it. Doesn't matter, it's probably already on some internet site.'

Darby said, 'Did you tell your mother what Sullivan did to you?'

'She already knew,' Baxter replied. 'Mr Sullivan showed her the Polaroids at the hospital, the ones where he had a gun pressed to my head. The ones of me sucking him off – those *really* upset her.'

'Your mother told you this?'

'She didn't have to. Mr Sullivan brought me with him to the hospital. I was there when he showed her the pictures. I think he wanted me there to drive his point home.'

'Did your mother go to the police?'

'Are you for real? She told me to keep my mouth shut and do my time or else I might wind up like some of Mr Sullivan's other lady friends. Since I'm sitting here talking to you, guess what decision I made?'

Darby felt her head spinning, not knowing what was worse: the way the woman spoke in the emotion-less tone of a lobotomy patient as she recounted the horrific details of her repeated rapes at the hands of cops and a former gangster; or how the horror had been sanctioned by her own mother.

'Michelle,' Darby said, 'do you know the names of any missing women who dated Sullivan?'

'Nothing's coming to mind. Ask Coop. He dated a couple of Mr Sullivan's young lady friends.'

'No,' he said, his voice raw. 'I didn't.'

'That's right, I forgot. You didn't date them, you just screwed them. You and the other boys at the hotel parties.'

Coop pushed himself away from the railing. 'I *never* took part in any of that shit, Michelle, and you know it.'

'Hey, I'm not judging you for dipping your wick. That's for priests, right?'

'Fuck this – and fuck you, Michelle,' he said. 'I'm out of here.'

Coop opened the sliding glass door, then slammed it back against the frame. Darby watched him go, wanting to follow, wanting to know what the hell had just happened.

39

Baxter picked up her pack of Marlboros and said, 'I think I embarrassed him.'

Darby, despite her shock and confusion, felt an undercurrent of anger at the woman. 'I'd say you went out of your way to provoke him.'

'Me and Coops got sort of a history together.'

'What kind of a history? Did you two date?'

'I wish. He's got much higher standards, unfortunately, and he's got his pick of the litter 'cause he's so goddamn pretty. Every woman I know wants to get in the sack with him. I'm sure you've thought about it, am I right?'

'What's the deal between you two?'

'That's for him to tell you. And I think it's time I called it a night.'

'Sit down. I have some more questions about these cops you met at the hotel parties.'

'I don't know any of their names, if that's what you're asking. For some strange reason, they didn't tell me.'

'Would you recognize their faces?'

'They wore Halloween masks. You can do all sorts of things when you wear a mask.'

'Did you overhear any names? Did any of the other women mention anything to you?'

'No and no. All I saw were their cocks. You got mugshots of pricks, I might be able to help you out.'

'The man who was speaking to you earlier –'

'He's a cop,' Baxter said, lighting another cigarette. 'Don't ask me for his name again because he's never had one.'

'What do you mean?'

'I mean there are people who float in and out of here like ghosts. Ask Coop. He'll tell you the same thing.'

'Was this cop one of the men you met at the hotel?'

'It wouldn't surprise me.'

'What about the girls at the hotel, did you know them?'

Baxter leaned her head back and stared up at the dark sky as she smoked. 'Most of them are dead or in jail.'

'Did you know any of them?'

'Some of them were from Charlestown. Mr Sullivan liked local girls. Town pride and all.'

'Was one of these girls Kendra Sheppard?'

'I don't know anyone by that name.'

'You sure? She grew up here. As a matter of fact, her parents were murdered about three blocks away. I'm sure you remember it. Her parents were shot to death while they were sleeping. Then Kendra mysteriously vanished.'

'Lots of people died here. Or disappeared.'

'Michelle, why did you tell me that story about you and your mother?'

'Thought you might appreciate a history lesson, Doc.'

'I think it's more than that,' Darby said.

Doors slammed shut in the distance. Baxter acted as if she'd heard a gunshot. She jumped to her feet and, clutching the railing with both hands, stared wide-eyed down the dark street at a group of people armed with buckets, shovels and sifting equipment standing around a van. Darby could make out the pudgy outline of Dr Edgar patting down his tufts of wild Albert Einstein hair.

'Who are those people?' Baxter asked.

'They're anthropology students.'

Baxter seemed confused.

'They're here to dig up the bones in the basement,' Darby said. 'We found three sets of remains. All women.'

Baxter didn't say anything. She watched the group of men filing into the house.

'It going to be hard to identify these women,' Darby said. 'Someone removed their teeth along with their hands and feet. If you know something that could help us –'

'Sorry, but I can't help you.'

'Can't or won't?'

'You can't find ghosts.'

'I'm not following.'

'I mean there are still some people who float through this town that don't have any names. They just come and go. Like ghosts.'

'Like the man you were speaking to earlier?'

Baxter kept her eyes on the house. 'You seem like a good person, but the thing is *nobody* here's gonna talk to you. They do and they're going to disappear or have an accident. That badge clipped to your belt? You might as well be smeared in dogshit.'

Darby leaned her elbows on the railing, next to Baxter, and said, 'Kendra Sheppard was living in Vermont with her son.'

No reaction.

'Kendra was living under another name – Amy Hallcox,' Darby said. 'She and her son came to Belham a few days ago.'

'How old is her son?'

'Twelve. A man pretending to be a Federal agent came into his hospital room, and Sean – that's Kendra's son – Sean was terrified at the thought of going away with this man and do you know what he did?'

Baxter didn't answer.

'Sean tried to commit suicide,' Darby said. 'Shot himself in the head. It seems he was carrying a gun with him for protection. Before he tried to kill himself, he told me that his mother was afraid of these people finding her. And they did. In Belham. Want to know what happened to Kendra?'

'Not really.'

'Someone tied her down to a chair and slit her throat.'

Baxter looked down at the railing and picked at a paint chip with a long fingernail decorated with fake diamonds, moons and stars.

'Do you know why anyone would do something like that?' Darby asked.

'No.'

'Did you know Kendra Sheppard had changed her name and run away?'

'No.'

'You willing to say that under oath?'

'Sure, why not? You can swear me in right now if you want. There's a Bible underneath one of the kitchen chair legs. I need something to keep the table from wobbling.'

'If you're scared, I can put you into protective custody.'

'With the Feds?' Baxter laughed. 'Thanks, but no. I'll take my chances here in the real world.'

Darby tried another way in. 'Michelle, what you went through . . . I can't tell you how sorry I am.' She hoped her true feelings came across in her voice. 'You didn't deserve that. Nobody does.'

'Wasn't looking for your pity. I just wanted to explain the lay of the land here.'

'I can give you the name of some counsellors who can work with you on a pro bono basis.'

'Talking isn't going to change what happened. It

don't erase what you carry around inside your head.'

'It can help.'

'Thanks, but I think I'll stick with Ambien and Percocet. They work wonders.'

Darby placed her business card on the railing. 'Tomorrow, when you're sober, give me a call and we'll talk.'

Baxter pushed herself off the railing and stubbed out her cigarette on the card. 'Feel free to help yourself to some beers on your way out.'

40

Darby closed the door to Baxter's apartment and stood alone in the dark hallway, feeling dizzy, wobbly on her feet. Not from the woman's story. Baxter's repeated victimization and humiliation by a sexual predator and possible serial killer ... that story and all of its variants had been around since the dawn of time. Darby had a collection of them dating back to her early days at the crime lab, when she'd be called to the hospital to administer yet another rape kit to a female victim – always young, always vulnerable. Hearing these stories and witnessing first-hand how each of these women had been abused and assaulted had inoculated her against the myriad ways in which men inflicted pain, fear and degradation (and then later, out in the field, death). See it often enough, listen to the same stories over and over again, and a normal, healthy mind has no choice but to protect itself. Much like the person nailing boards across the windows of his home to protect the vulnerable areas from yet another unpredictable hurricane, you had to batten down the hatches or risk permanent damage.

But every castle, no matter how well fortified,

always has vulnerable areas. It doesn't matter how many hurricanes it has endured or survived, each storm is different, unique in its own way. What had penetrated Darby, had made her legs feel boneless as she walked down the steps to the front door, was the way Baxter had spoken in a lifeless – no, *soulless* – tone about her personal horrors. It was as if God himself had whispered her fate against her ear. Sorry, but you don't have a choice here, you're just going to have to accept it.

And that was exactly what had happened. Baxter couldn't turn to the police. And her mother, the single person on the planet entrusted with the responsibility for protecting her, had told her daughter to keep her mouth shut and do her time. *Jesus.*

Darby opened the front door and spotted Coop pacing across the street. He was on his mobile. He saw her coming, said something to the person on the other end of the line and hung up.

He stepped out from the thinning crowds and met her in the middle of the street. In all her years of knowing him, she had never seen him this angry. Or hurt.

'Let's get one thing clear right here, right now,' he said, struggling to keep his voice calm. 'That crack Tipsy McStagger made about me going to those hotel parties and dipping my wick, as she so eloquently put it, is bullshit – complete and utter bullshit. I swear on the life of my mother.'

Darby nodded. She didn't speak.

'What, you don't believe me?'

'Of course I believe you,' she said. 'I'm still just trying to process what happened.'

'Go ahead and say it. I can see it in your eyes.'

'Did you see a videotape in which Baxter was being raped?'

Coop gritted his teeth, his face turning a deeper shade of red.

'Have I done things I'm not proud of?' he said after a moment. 'You bet. But you're talking about something that happened more than twenty years ago. I was nineteen and standing inside a room with a bunch of guys who'd done some serious hard time. If I'd gone for that tape, I'd be rolling up to crime scenes in a goddamn wheelchair.'

'Great group of friends you have there.'

'Look, I'm sorry about what happened to Michelle. It's a goddamn tragedy –'

'No, Coop, it's a crime.'

He held up his hands in surrender. 'No argument there. But you'll have to forgive me if I'm not acting, I don't know, all broken up at the moment. A lot of people around here, myself included, have gone out of their way to help Michelle out – I've got a list a mile long of people who went to bat for her, called in favours and got her a legit job, a place with health benefits, and every time she blew it off and ran right back to the pole. If you like, I can take you to someone who picked up the tab for her rehab. Twice.'

'What's the deal between you two?'

'There *is* no deal.'

'There's something going on. You kept trying to get me out of the apartment.'

'I wasn't interested in hearing her story again. At some point you've got to stop playing the victim card. You've got to make a decision to get on with your life, take responsibility and stop wallowing in all your shit.'

'Are you speaking from personal experience?'

'I'm done here.' He turned around and started walking away.

She grabbed his arm. 'I asked you to watch that man. Why didn't you call me when he left?'

'I tried, but all I kept getting was static.'

'Give me your phone.'

'What for?'

'Just give it to me.'

'I've had enough of –'

She ripped the phone from his belt clip, opened it and checked the log of outgoing calls.

Coop hadn't called her.

'Why are you lying to me?'

He looked away, across the street to the apartment building.

'That cop Baxter was talking to,' Darby said. 'You know who he is, don't you?'

He didn't answer.

'Baxter told me this guy is a ghost,' Darby said. 'She said you'd tell me the same thing. How do you know him?'

'Just drop it, okay?'

'I'm not going to drop it. If you know something – Coop, if you're *deliberately* keeping something that's interfering with this case, you need –'

'I want to be removed from this case and your unit. I want out of CSU.'

Darby opened her mouth but couldn't speak. She had heard Coop clearly – his words were echoing inside her head.

'I'll head to the station to start the paperwork,' he said.

'What reason are you going to put down on the transfer form?'

'Conflict of interest.'

'About what? Kendra Sheppard? Or do you know the names of the women we found in the basement?'

'I don't know their names.'

'But you have an idea, don't you?'

'I don't.'

You're lying. She could see it in his eyes.

'Why were you in such a rush to get inside Kevin Reynolds's house?'

He didn't answer.

'Why don't you trust me?'

'It's not a matter of trust,' he said.

'Then what is it?'

'The paperwork will be on your desk when you get back.'

'I'm not going to sign it.'

'Your choice,' he said and walked away.

Darby was still staring after him when her phone rang. She unclipped the phone from the holster and looked at the screen. Randy Scott was calling.

'The fingerprint Coop lifted from the hollow-point round rang the cherries on the database,' Randy said. 'IAFIS says the print belongs to a man named Francis Sullivan from Charlestown, Massachusetts.'

'That's not possible. Frank Sullivan is –'

'Dead, yes, I know. It says here he died in July of '83.'

'Then there's got to be some sort of mistake.'

'IAFIS says it's a 92 per cent match. I don't think there's a mistake.'

Darby looked down the street at Coop and saw him talking to Artie Pine. 'What about the prints from the house, have any come back?'

'I checked. Nothing yet.'

'I might need your help here, both you and Mark.'

'That's fine. We've almost finished processing the evidence.'

She hung up and shoved the phone into her pocket. She wanted one more run at Coop. He knew something, and she didn't understand why –

The house exploded. Splintered wood, debris and bodies flew through the air with a terrifying force and speed. The crime scene vehicle, the Ford Explorer, blew up next, and Darby felt a pair of invisible hands pick her up off the ground and hurl her backwards through the air. She clawed at the air and then slammed against a parked car, her head slamming against a window, shattering it as she blacked out.

Day 3

41

Jamie sat behind the wheel of the minivan, its windows rolled up and the air-conditioning left on low to keep her from sweating underneath clothing more suited to an early-autumn morning – jeans, her beaten and battered Timberland work boots, and one of Dan's baggy sweatshirts. It hid her breasts and the Magnum's shoulder strap nicely, the cotton a bit more breathable and much more comfortable than the windbreaker she'd worn inside Mary Sullivan's basement.

Jamie had also helped herself to Michael's knock-off Ray-Ban Wayfarer sunglasses and one of his favourite baseball caps – a ridiculously bright yellow one with the phrase LADIES MAN stitched next to a patch of a barely awake Homer Simpson dressed only in a saggy pair of tighty-whities. She wore the brim pulled low to hide the surgical scars on her forehead. She had used the clippers to shave her hair down to a crew cut. From a distance, especially in this ashy predawn light, she could easily pass for a man.

She leaned forward in her seat and for the second time this past hour checked her reflection in the minivan's rear-view mirror. Up close she looked like a lanky man — one with slightly effeminate features, sure, but the visible scarring along her jaw line, coupled with the fresh bandage slapped across the raw skin on the side of her face, would balance that out.

A skinny guy who got his ass kicked, she thought. Perfect. She needed to look the part of the driver Ben Masters had hired to take Kevin Reynolds to safety.

Jamie checked the minivan's dashboard clock: 4.45 a.m. Fifteen minutes until show time.

She grabbed the bottle of Gatorade. A fine white residue had settled across the bottom. She had taken six of her Xanax pills, crushed them with a spoon and poured the fine powder into the bright red water. One pill mellowed her out; an elephant like Reynolds would need at least three or four. Six, she figured, should probably put him to sleep. After he went nighty-night, she would tie him up, cover him with a tarp and then drive ten minutes up the road to a secluded spot on the other side of these woods.

If Reynolds didn't cooperate, she'd have to take him down here.

She wasn't particularly concerned about being spotted or heard. Unless someone had an avid interest in studying or weeds, there was no reason to come to Waterman Park. Her father, back when he was alive, had told her how the recession of the eighties had hit Belham hard, and the first thing on the chopping block was funding for the city's Department of Public Works. Waterman Park's fountain, jungle gyms, swings and slides had all been removed. All that remained was a long, wide field of tall burnt grass and bald patches of sun-baked dirt. And the bridge.

The bridge was the main reason she had selected this spot. One way in and one way out. You could walk across the bridge but you couldn't walk through the woods – not unless you wanted to fight your way through the thick brush. No way for Reynolds to sneak up on her.

Leaning back in her seat, her thoughts drifted back to Michael.

You thought you could save only one of us, he had told her, *and you chose Carter.*

Michael was right. She *had* chosen Carter. Wilfully, maybe even deliberately. And, while she could tick off a list of logical reasons why she went to him first – Carter was the youngest, her baby – she couldn't escape the truth that had lived inside her every waking thought since the day Michael was born. Michael was difficult. He had been a colicky and fussy baby who had grown into a stubborn young boy who took a peculiar delight and satisfaction in fighting her at every turn. She recalled one particularly nasty fight inside the grocery store when Michael was six. She had refused to buy him a sugary cereal he'd seen on a TV commercial and he responded by knocking the boxes off the shelf and stomping on them. She carried him out of the shop kicking and screaming.

By the time she reached the car she had lost her

cool, yelling at him until her throat was raw, and when he smirked at her with grim satisfaction she had wanted to hit him. She later confided to Dan that Michael was an emotional vampire, a creature that fed off her anger. Dan told her that she was being too harsh. Dan could say those things because Michael didn't act that way with him, just her.

Carter was the polar opposite. Carter was easy. Carter smiled and enjoyed people. Sure, he could be fussy and yes, he had his moments like any other normal kid. But even at almost seven Carter was remarkably empathetic. He felt bad when he did something wrong and apologized. Michael never did. Like Dan, Michael lived inside his skin, didn't show emotion or let anyone get too close to him.

Not true. Michael had allowed Dan to get close to him.

By turning to Carter that night, had she severed whatever thin thread she and Michael shared as mother and son? She wondered how Michael would react if he knew that the man who had shot him was dead, floating inside the boot of a car submerged beneath the waters of Belham Quarry. The scars on Michael's chest and back would heal, but what about his mental scars? Would knowing how Ben had suffered help Michael heal?

Killing Ben Masters had certainly helped her.

Jamie looked around the empty park. The last time she had been here was on that hot July afternoon she had buried her father. Dan was with her. She had come to Waterman Park, a favourite spot of their childhood, and told Dan stories about the long summers they had spent at the park with her parents. Back then, you could climb monkey-bars or wait your turn to use the swings or go down one of the four slides. Then you'd cool off in the concrete wading pool in the centre of the field, and sometimes around noon the high school gym teacher, Mr Quincy, would pull up in his Winnebago and sell sodas, shaved ice, hot dogs, hamburgers and snotties – French fries drenched in Velveeta cheese. An ice cream truck always rolled in twice a day. During the long winter months, the city turned the pool into a skating rink.

That afternoon with Dan, not one car or person had entered the park. The city's joggers, bikers and dog walkers took advantage of trails on the north side of the woods – a good eight miles away from where her minivan was now parked. She was the sole person here.

Make that two. A compact car was slowly making its way across the bridge.

42

Jamie slid her right hand underneath a copy of the *Globe* that was spread across her lap and gripped the Glock resting against her stomach. She had plenty of ammo left.

She let her mouth hang open as if she'd fallen asleep while waiting. From behind her sunglasses she watched the dark-coloured car come to a full stop at the end of the bridge. The driver didn't turn. The car just sat there, idling.

If it's Reynolds, she thought, *he's probably checking out the place to make sure he's alone.*

She glanced down at her lap. The papers hid the handgun and silencer perfectly. No way would Reynolds see it.

The car was making its way across the curving road of broken asphalt.

That odd mixture of dread and adrenalin was shooting through her veins. She felt jumpy and anxious but not afraid. She was definitely *not* afraid. No matter what Reynolds threw at her, she'd find a way to handle it.

Provided he comes here alone, Jamie. It all hinges on that single fact.

The car, a navy-blue Ford Taurus with a sagging back bumper, pulled up against the kerb near the entrance of the car park. The windows were rolled down and she could make out the face of the driver.

Kevin Reynolds perched his arm across the front seat and looked in her direction. Nobody else inside the car; he had come alone.

Reynolds took a drag from his cigarette and kept staring.

Was he waiting for her to come to him?

She had planned for that possibility. Michael's backpack, stuffed with his dirty laundry to give the appearance of money, sat on the passenger seat. If she carried the backpack the right way, she could hide the Glock behind it. Granted, it might get a little dicey – she wanted Reynolds *outside* his car, not in it. It would be much easier to take him down outside. She'd have more manoeuvrability if he decided to go for the gun.

Let him, she thought, feeling the tyre iron hidden beneath the left sleeve of her sweatshirt. One hit to the artery behind the ear and the blood would rush away from his brain and shut down his central nervous system. He'd go down fast.

And there was always the jaw. A good, swift crack would disrupt the fluid in his ear. He'd lose his balance and his knees would buckle. Win-win either way. *And let's not forget about the kneecaps.*

Reynolds flicked his cigarette out of the window.

He didn't get out of the car, just sat behind the wheel smoking and staring out of the front window.

He smells a set-up, Jamie.

No, he doesn't. If he did, he would be driving away.

Get out of here. Go home to the kids and —

Reynolds opened the door.

Mouth dry and heart beating faster, faster, she watched Reynolds step into the ashy light. He grabbed a pack of cigarettes from the front pocket of a short-sleeved black silk shirt. He wore it Tony Soprano-style – untucked to accommodate his ample gut. She couldn't tell if he was packing.

He lit another cigarette and looked towards the woods behind the minivan.

Come on, quit stalling. Come on over and introduce yourself.

Here he was.

Reynolds's high-topped sneakers crunched across the gravel. He paused in front of the minivan, smoking as he studied the person asleep behind the wheel.

Jamie didn't move or turn her head. She watched him through her sunglasses, watched him staring. Her finger slid across the trigger as she waited for him to come and knock on the driver's door. That would be the best play. Have him open the door and when he reached inside to wake up the driver she'd press the Glock against his stomach.

Reynolds walked back to the Taurus.

Opened the door.

Climbed behind the wheel.

Started the car and pulled into the car park.

Jamie's breathing was steady and shallow as he pulled up in front of the minivan. She could hear the low rumble of his car engine over the air-conditioning, and she could see him staring at her.

Reynolds hit the gas, tyres spinning as he shot backwards out of the car park.

Jamie threw the door open. The papers spread across her lap blew away in the hot breeze and the tyre iron tucked underneath her sweatshirt sleeve slipped past her hand and hit the ground. She had the Glock up, ready to fire, but Reynolds was too far away, speeding towards the bridge, scattering crows from the trees.

43

Darby's eyes fluttered open. She saw a steel bed railing and, beyond it, a wooden chair with maroon cushions bleached by sweat. She was lying in a hospital.

A clock hung on the wall at the foot of her bed. Half past six. Judging by the dim light filtering in through the blinds, she assumed it had to be morning.

She wondered how long she had been out.

She could wiggle her toes and hands. Good. She touched her face and felt thick bandages wrapped around the right side of her head. She didn't feel any pain.

She remembered what had happened – another good sign. That wasn't always the case with severe concussion or head trauma. Sometimes your short-term memory blacked out. She remembered seeing Coop talking to Pine when the house exploded. Splintered wood and debris –

Coop. Coop was standing near the house when it exploded.

Slowly she lifted her head. A bolt of pain that felt like a hot poker slammed into the centre of her brain. Her head dropped back against the pillow and she sucked in air through her gritted teeth to stem the vomit creeping up her throat.

A machine started beeping. A nurse came in and injected something into her IV line.

Darby was starting to drift away when she saw Artie Pine standing beside the bed. His torn shirt and thick, pale forearms were covered with soot and dried blood.

'You're going to be okay, McCormick, you're just a little banged up. Thank God you inherited your old man's thick Irish noggin.'

She wanted to ask him about Coop but couldn't focus.

Coop's okay, she told herself as she drifted off to sleep. *Pine was standing next to Coop, so Coop's okay. Banged up but okay.*

The next time she opened her eyes, bright sunlight flooded the room. Squinting, she looked at the wall clock: 9.13 a.m.

She lifted her head again. No nausea but a new kind of pain, one that felt like nails were pressing against every square inch of her skull. Her stomach hitched and she lay back against the pillow.

The male doctor who came in to examine her looked as if he had just graduated from puberty. MASS. GENERAL HOSPITAL was stitched above the breast pocket of his white jacket. He shone a light in her eyes and started asking her questions.

'What's your name?'

'Darby McCormick.'

'And where do you live, Miss McCormick?'

'Temple Street in Boston.' Her voice felt raw and hoarse. 'The month is August and I know the name of the president. Both my short- and long-term memory are fine.'

The doctor smiled. 'They warned me you'd be a pain in the ass.'

'They?'

'Your friends waiting in the hall.' He clicked off the pen light. 'You've suffered a Grade Three concussion, but you're not exhibiting the more dangerous symptoms – memory loss or vision impairment. The CT scan shows no brain trauma. Your face sustained several lacerations from glass. When you take off the bandages, you're going to see jigsaws of sutures. They'll heal in about three to four weeks. You shouldn't have any scarring.'

'I suffer from SIS.'

'What's that?'

'Shitty Irish Skin,' Darby said. 'I'll definitely have some scarring.'

The young doctor chuckled. 'Well, we can correct that down the road, so don't worry. Are you feeling up for visitors?'

'Absolutely. When can I leave?'

'Probably this afternoon,' he said. 'We shot you up with small doses of Demerol for pain management and to help you sleep. Do you feel nauseous?'

'Oh, yes.' Demerol never agreed with her stomach.

'That should dissipate in a few hours,' he said.

'You'll need someone to take you home. And you'll need to –'

'Stay off my feet, relax, don't push myself, etcetera, etcetera.'

The doctor gave her instructions on how to clean the wounds and promised to write her a prescription for Percocet. After he left, Darby used the hospital phone to call MCI-Cedar Junction, got Superintendent Skinner on the phone and explained where she was and what had happened. Skinner said he could arrange the meeting with Ezekiel for any time during the day; all he needed was an hour's notice. She promised to call him as soon as she left the hospital.

The door opened. She expected to see Coop. Instead, she saw Artie Pine. He pulled up a chair next to her bed.

'You were passed out when I found you,' he said. 'By the time I helped you to the ambulance you were talking, although I'll be goddamned if I could understand what you were saying.'

'What happened to Coop?'

'Who?'

'Jackson Cooper. The forensic guy who looks like David Beckham. You were talking to him when the house exploded.'

'Oh, him. The one with the muscles. Took a hell of a spill but he's fine. The commissioner is here. She's on the phone at the moment. She wants to – in fact, here she is.'

Darby tried to sit up.

'Lay back,' Pine said. 'I'll elevate your bed for you.'

Chadzynski, dressed in one of her utilitarian black power suits, stood at the foot of the bed. Darby's attention was on the man wearing a frumpy tan suit. He had cauliflower ears and a large, ugly nose that had been broken too many times. He leaned on the wall next to the door and looked at her with a humourless, dour expression – a man, she suspected, who preferred working with numbers and statistics to working with people.

'This is Lieutenant Warner,' Chadzynski said. 'When I heard about what had happened, I had him posted outside your room.'

Warner nodded hello.

'Detective Pine told me about the explosion,' Chadzynski said.

'*Explosions*,' Darby said. 'There were two. First the house and then the crime scene vehicle. The way the house went up, I thought it might have been a gas explosion. No flames, it just blew apart. Then the Explorer went next and I knew it was a bomb – two bombs.'

Chadzynski's normally emotionless face pinched with anger. Or was it fear?

'How many?' Darby asked.

'It's too early to say.'

'Edgar was in the house with his grad students.'

'Yes, I know. They're among the missing.'

'What about Stan Jennings? He's the lead detective from Charlestown.'

Chadzynski looked at Pine.

'I don't know about Jennings,' he said. 'I was on my way to the house when I ran into your forensic partner. I was asking him for an update when the house blew.'

Chadzynski said, 'Detective Pine, would you give us a moment?'

'Sure.' He looked at Darby and said, 'Doc says you can't drive home.'

'I live across the street.'

'No matter, I'll take you.' He patted her hand. 'I'll be waiting outside.'

Chadzynski spoke. 'Thank you for your generous offer, Detective Pine, but I'll take care of the transportation arrangements for Miss McCormick. And I'm sure you're anxious to get back to Belham, cleaned up and back to work.'

Pine looked as if a door had been slammed shut in his face. Darby watched him walk all the way to the door.

44

Darby reached for the plastic cup of water sitting on the nightstand.

Chadzynski folded her hands behind her back. Warner glanced out of the small window installed in the door, then turned to the commissioner and nodded.

'Lieutenant Warner does a sweep of my office and car two to three times a week to look for listening devices,' Chadzynski said. 'He performed one this morning and found listening devices installed in the panel of my car door.'

'The listening devices are sophisticated,' Warner said in a gravelly voice. 'They turned on and off by remote to save battery power, and have a three-mile listening radius.'

'Mr Warner has some people he trusts going through my office,' Chadzynski said. 'After they've finished, they're going to inspect your office, then the entire lab.'

People he trusts, Darby thought.

She licked her dry lips, looked at Warner and said, 'Who are you?'

Chadzynski answered the question. 'Mr Warner is the head of Anti-Corruption.'

The cops who worked in Anti-Corruption reported directly to the police commissioner. Only Chadzynski knew their identities.

'The news is playing actual footage of the explosion,' Chadzynski said. 'Some TV camera must have been recording. In any event, I had the bomb squad commander examine the footage and they believe the explosions were caused by an IED.'

An improvised explosives device, Darby thought. That made sense – two separate explosions, two separate charges.

'What kind, do we know?'

'The bomb squad says it's too early to say until they've sifted through the debris – they're at the site as we speak,' Chadzynski said. 'However, given the way the house and crime scene vehicle went up, they're in agreement that the IED contained either a plastic explosive, like C-4, or dynamite.'

'I don't think they were timed charges. I think someone was watching the house and detonated them.'

'Maybe it's this mystery man you met in Belham – the one with the brown van.'

'How did you find out?' Darby hadn't filed her report – she hadn't even had time to write it.

'I had Jackson Cooper in my office first thing this morning,' Chadzynski said. 'He brought me up to date. It's his opinion that the area around the house was pretty well sealed off.'

'It was.'

'He also told me a patrolman was placed at the front door. That you asked him and Detective Jennings not to allow any Federal agents inside the house.'

Darby nodded, knowing where Chadzynski was heading, why Lieutenant Warner and his Anti-Corruption squad were now on board.

'I think it's reasonable to assume that the IEDs weren't inside the house when you arrived – or on the crime scene vehicle,' Chadzynski said. 'To gain access to the house, someone either posed as a Boston police officer or was, in fact, an actual officer.'

'I agree,' Darby said. 'Is that why you asked Pine to leave the room?'

'I have no reason to suspect him of anything. It's simply a precautionary measure, but I want to restrict this investigation to people I can trust – you, and Lieutenant Warner. We now have to deal with this additional element, this victim found in the basement of Kevin Reynolds's former home, a Federal agent named Peter Alan who died during Frank Sullivan's boat raid.'

'Jennings said he believed the man was Peter Alan. We won't know until we run his prints.'

'The fingerprints came back this morning. It's Peter Alan. Mr Cooper told me.

'Four Federal agents died along with Frank Sullivan – Peter Alan, Jack King, Tony Frissora and Steven

White. If Alan is alive, I think we should go on the theory that the others are too.'

Darby nodded.

Chadzynski said, 'Mr Cooper also informed me that the man who murdered your father requested a meeting with you but he was vague on the details.'

'I was scheduled to speak with John Ezekiel this morning at ten about Amy Hallcox. Her real name is Kendra Sheppard. She visited him the day she was murdered.'

'Yes, I know. Mr Cooper told me. As for Ezekiel, I'll have Lieutenant Warner speak to him.'

'Ezekiel said he'd speak only to me.'

'Why?'

'I won't know until I talk to him.'

'Have you spoken to him before?'

'No,' Darby said. 'Never.'

Chadzynski digested this silently.

'Mr Cooper has asked to be removed from the CSU.'

'Yes,' Darby said, 'I know.'

'His request surprised me, as I'm sure it did you. I know how much you value him, both personally and professionally.'

Darby waited.

'He cited the reason as conflict of interest, but he wouldn't tell me specifics,' Chadzynski said. 'Do you have any ideas?'

'At one point in time he knew Kendra Sheppard on a personal level. They're both from Charlestown.'

'Mr Cooper neglected to mention that fact to me.'

'It must have slipped his mind.'

'I can tell by the tone of your voice you honestly don't believe that.'

No, she didn't. 'Commissioner, I'd like you to put some people on Michelle Baxter.'

'Who?'

'She lives in Charlestown, in an apartment building right down the street from the Reynolds house. She's the woman who was speaking to the driver of the brown van I saw yesterday in Belham – the mystery man, as you called him.'

'This is the first I'm hearing of this woman.'

So Coop hadn't told her.

'Is Mr Cooper deliberately withholding information that could help this case?'

'He identified Kendra Sheppard,' Darby said. 'He –'

'Please answer my question.'

Darby drank some water. Coop knew *something*; she could feel it in her gut. He was under no legal obligation to speak, but if Chadzynski found out he had willingly withheld information that could be helpful, he could kiss his Boston career goodbye. A disciplinary meeting would be held. Given his untarnished work record, he'd most likely be asked to tender his resignation instead of being fired – if he was lucky.

But if his deliberate withholding of information wound up contributing to the injury or death of someone, Coop would never work in law enforcement again, not to mention possible prosecution.

'Darby?'

'Yes. I think he's withholding something.'

'Then I suggest you speak to him. Today.'

'I will, after I talk to Ezekiel.'

'Are you feeling well enough to go to the prison?'

Darby nodded.

'Mr Warner will drive you,' Chadzynski said. 'I'd like him to take your vehicle. While you're inside the prison, he can check for listening devices.'

Darby described her car and told Warner about the garage down the street. She found her keys on top of the nightstand and handed them to him.

Chadzynski stepped away from the bed and was about to open the door when she turned around, her gaze level. 'You may want to remind Mr Cooper what he's putting on the line. I hope, for his sake, he's not deliberately withholding vital information.'

I do too, Darby thought, reaching for the phone.

45

Jamie sat in a lawn chair under a bright morning sun fishing a cigarette from the pack of Marlboros she'd purchased on her way back from Belham. She had started smoking at eighteen, then quit when she and Dan had decided to try to start a family.

Halfway through her second cigarette, she realized how much she missed smoking, how the nicotine cleared her head and calmed her nerves.

The kids were outside with her. Michael relaxed in a hammock set up in the shade between two elms, a book propped open on his stomach. He held it with one hand while the other dangled over the hammock's edge, gripping a humming red lightsaber. Carter, dressed in a brown Jedi robe, the hood covering his head, ran across the grass (which desperately needed cutting), alternating between awkward somersaults and jumps. He dropped his lightsaber and stretched out his arms, wiggling his fingers at his older brother.

'You're not paying attention!' Carter yelled.

Michael turned to him. 'What?'

'I'm using the Force on you.'

'What Force Power?'

'Lightning. It's shooting from my fingers.'

'Cart, you can't use that.'

'Yes, I can.'

'No, dumb-dumb, you can't. How many times did I tell you only the Dark Side can use Force Lightning? You're Luke Skywalker, remember? He's one of the good guys. They can't use that.'

'I'm a special Jedi Master. We know all the secrets.' Carter kept wiggling his fingers, making crackling sounds with his mouth, spittle flying everywhere.

'Whatever,' Michael said, turning his attention back to his book. 'I'm blocking it with my lightsaber like Mace Windu in Episode Three.'

Jamie watched them, smiling. Despite yesterday's ugly confrontation with Michael, she was glad to have both boys home. This morning's encounter with Kevin Reynolds had spooked her.

She had checked Ben's phone before coming into the backyard. Reynolds hadn't called or sent a text message.

She felt confident that Reynolds hadn't recognized her. Yes, he had stood in front of the minivan, staring at her through the windscreen, but she had worn sunglasses and pulled the lid of the baseball cap low across her forehead. Add that to the fact it was still dark out and there was absolutely no way in hell he could have recognized her.

Driving home, she had had a moment of panic, wondering if Reynolds had memorized the front licence plate. Had he left the park to have one of his cronies run the plate? The panic evaporated when she remembered there was no plate in the front. The plastic holder for the plate had broken a few months ago, and she had stuffed the plate into the back of the minivan in case she ever got pulled over by a cop.

Maybe he recognized your minivan.

Not possible. When Ben and his crew had been at her house five years ago, they would have seen a brand-new navy-blue Honda Pilot in the garage. Shortly after Dan's death, she had traded in the Pilot for a used minivan, not wanting to be saddled with the hefty car payments.

Still, Reynolds had left. *Something* had spooked him.

A sinking feeling bloomed in the pit of her stomach. *So close,* she thought. *He was so goddamn close . . . I should have got out of the car and shot him.*

Was Reynolds still lurking somewhere close to Charlestown? Or had he left the state?

You're not going to find him, Jamie. It's time to pack up and leave.

No. She wasn't going to leave *now*. For the last five years she had lived each moment with a held breath, her every waking thought consumed with the possibility that the men who killed Dan and the man she knew only as Ben would come back to the house and finish the job. By some miracle of God, she had found Ben, and now Ben Masters was dead. And she now knew Kevin Reynolds was the second man. She *had* to find him. She couldn't stop now, not when she was this close.

Did you suddenly forget the part when he tore out of the car park? He's gone, Jamie. You can't get close to him. You tried luring him in pretending to be Ben Masters. It was a good plan – it really was – but it didn't work out. Pack up what you need, take the kids and leave.

Ben's phone had only *three* contacts: Pontius, aka Kevin Reynolds; Alan; and this person named Judas. Why so few contacts? Maybe it was new and he hadn't got round to programming in the numbers. Or maybe he simply used the phone for emergencies, wanting only the numbers he needed on hand. She thought back to her moment in Mary Reynolds's basement, remembering Kevin Reynolds saying something about how Ben didn't trust mobile phones.

Jamie thought about Judas. He had three phone numbers. Call the numbers – not from Ben's phone but from a payphone. Call and see –

Do you honestly believe Reynolds hasn't been in touch with this Judas person? After what happened this morning at the park?

You don't know that Reynolds and Judas know each other.

You're right, I don't. And neither do you. For all you know Reynolds did, in fact, recognize you and is now speaking to Judas.

That's why I have to find out who he is. I have to –

What you have to do, Jamie, is keep your children safe. <u>That</u> is your priority. Or do you want to relive what happened in the dead room?

Her mind started filling with images. She tried to turn away from them, and then she saw herself removing her hands from the duct tape – by some miracle of God she hadn't died, hadn't passed out – ripping the tape off one ankle and standing, and there was no time to do the other one because Michael and Carter were bound to the chairs crying, bleeding out, and they needed an ambulance or they would die. She ran with the chair dragging behind her into the hall, down the stairs and into the kitchen, where she saw Dan hunched over the sink, what was left of his right hand – a shredded stump of raw muscle, torn skin and jagged bone – dripping blood into a growing puddle on the floor. She saw his head lying crookedly inside the blood-spattered sink, his skin a dark purple from the noose wrapped around his neck, the other end of the rope fed into the waste-disposal unit. She took a knife from the butcher block, cut the bindings on the other ankle and grabbed the phone as blood clogged her throat, and she kept crouching and staggering while the 911 dispatcher kept saying, 'I can't understand you, I can't understand you.' She saw herself standing in the room thick with gun smoke and Carter not moving and he was so small and he couldn't lose much blood and he'd lost so much, oh God Jesus, she descended on him first and cut through his bindings as Michael turned and coughed up blood and in between sobbing said he was scared and she screamed at him to hold on, hang on, baby, help is on the way – and she realized she was saying this to Carter, not Michael, and she was giving her baby mouth-to-mouth and watching his tiny chest rising and between each breath she was screaming to the phone lying on the floor next to him, screaming to the dispatcher to hurry up, Jesus, please hurry, please hurry, and then Carter opened his eyes and he was coughing up blood but he was breathing and his eyes were wide and scared and bright with tears as he coughed up more blood and started crying, '*Mamma? Mamma?*'

Jamie dropped her cigarette as she got to her feet, almost tripping over the lawn chair.

'*M-M-Michael,* come . . . ah . . . here.'

He waltzed across the lawn in his bare feet. Carter went back to practising his lightsaber skills.

Michael stood in front of her, arms crossed over his chest. 'What did I do wrong now?'

'How . . . you . . . ah . . . feel . . . ah . . . ah . . . moving?'

'You mean move out of the house?'

She nodded.

'Where are we going?'

'Where would . . . you . . . like . . . ah . . . go?'

Something lit up inside him. She could see it in his eyes, the way his body relaxed.

Michael sat on the end of the lawn chair and looked at her, startled, as if he couldn't believe his opinions and needs were actually being considered for once.

'Are you serious?'

She nodded.

'I've always wanted to live someplace warm,' Michael said after a moment. 'Dad told me once that you guys spent some time in San Diego.'

She smiled at the memory – a two-week holiday they'd taken in their early twenties. Boozy afternoons spent in Solana Beach and long walks through Del Mar and Coronado. Sunshine and beaches and making love in the hotel rooms, their bodies brown and warm and smelling of suntan oil.

'Dad said you came close to living there.'

She nodded again. They had talked about it, but their hearts lay in New England.

'Let's . . . ah . . . ah . . . pack . . . up. Go.'

'When?'

'To . . . ah . . . today.'

Surprise bloomed on his face – and some apprehension too. 'What's the rush?'

'No . . . ah . . . rush. Been thinking about . . . about . . . ah . . . you said. Unhappy here. No need to . . . ah . . . ah . . . stay any more.'

'What about the house?'

'Real estate agent,' she said. It might take a while until the house was sold, especially in this shitty economic climate, but they could make do on the savings until she got a job.

She leaned forward in her chair, smiling, and took his hand into her own. 'Fresh . . . start. Deserve it. You.'

'Do you think Carter would like it?'

'I . . . ah . . . think he . . . ah . . . be happy . . . ah . . . any place with . . . ah . . . you.'

'Okay.'

'You . . . You . . . ah . . . happy?'

'I am. It's just so, you know, sudden. And what's with the smoking?'

'Bad . . . ah . . . habit.'

'You shouldn't do it. There's a reason why they're called cancer sticks.'

'Can . . . ah . . . you . . . help . . . ah . . . pack?'

'Sure. Sure, I can. What's with the ultra-short haircut? You look like a guy.'

'It's . . . ah . . . so . . . ah . . . hot I . . . I . . . wanted . . . ah . . . shorter.'

'You can see your scars.'

'We . . . ah . . . need . . . ah . . . get . . . boxes.'

'You're going in for another operation, aren't you? That's why you practically shaved your head.' He looked so scared, vulnerable.

She cupped his face in her hands. 'No . . . ah . . . operation.'

'You're not lying to me?'

'No.' She kissed him on the top of his head. 'I love you.'

'I love you too.'

Walking back inside the house, Jamie imagined Kevin Reynolds somewhere close by, watching, and ran for her car keys.

46

Walpole's MCI-Cedar Junction, one of the state's two 'supermax' high-security prisons for adult male offenders, had a strict dress code for female visitors. No tank, halter or tube tops. No sleeveless shirts. No jogging suits or gym clothing. No clothing made of Spandex. No sheer or see-through material. Trousers had to be free of holes and rips and couldn't contain any open pockets like those found on cargo trousers. Skirts and shorts measuring less than four inches from the kneecap were deemed too revealing and not allowed – no clothing of any type that exposed a woman's midriff or back was allowed, no exceptions.

Darby placed her tactical belt, keys, wallet, badge and phone in a small plastic dish. After checking her sidearm, she raised her hands. A female guard, a heavy-set black woman, waved a metal-detecting wand over her body.

A young male guard somewhere in his late twenties, Darby guessed, wearing a short-sleeved shirt stood next to a metal door. He stared at the raw cuts and crisscrossed rows of stitches on the right side of her swollen face. Lieutenant Warner had driven her to her condo and stayed in the car while she went upstairs to shower. She dressed quickly, grabbing things from her closet. She realized she had forgotten a belt and pulled the canvas tactical belt from her chest-of-drawers. Not wanting to waste any more time, she had decided to forgo the lengthy process of trying to bandage her face.

'You wearing an underwired bra?' the female guard asked.

'No,' Darby said. 'And you'll be happy to know I remembered not to wear my crotchless underwear this morning.'

The woman let loose a dry chuckle. The male guard didn't crack a smile, too busy working hard on his *mess with me and you will pay* expression. The way his biceps bulged like rocks underneath his tanned skin made her think of Coop. She had tried calling him from the road, calling his mobile and his direct number at the lab, but kept getting his voicemail.

'Well,' the woman said, placing the wand on the table, 'I'm glad to see you took the time to read the dress code. Most people don't even bother. The women visitors, they are the *worst*. They strut on in here wearing short-shorts or some low-cut skirt without any panties, then get all belligerent when we tell 'em, ah, sorry, *ma'am*, but you can't come in here with your junk all exposed. Need to put on something just a *little* bit more formal.'

The woman slapped on a pair of latex gloves and

said, 'Please raise your hands again for me, Dr McCormick, I've got to search your pockets.'

Darby wanted to keep the conversation going, needing some distance from the thoughts scrabbling through her pounding head (Christ, did it hurt). 'My personal favourite was the one about no bathing suits.'

'We had to add that one, oh, I'd say about three years ago. This woman who worked at a strip club? She decided to visit her boyfriend right after her shift, came waltzing in here in five-inch stilettos and her ta-tas practically hanging out of her bikini top. The stories I could tell you.

'You all set, Dr McCormick. Your sidearm and your wallet will be waiting for you with me behind this desk when you come out.'

'Thank you.' Darby picked up the scuffed leather pad sitting on top of the X-ray machine. 'Can I take this in with me? I may need to take notes.'

'Let me see it.'

The woman searched through the computer-printed sheets the superintendant had given her on John Ezekiel. Then she examined the leather compartments and folds. She uncapped Darby's pen, a black plastic Pilot roller-ball with a metal tip.

'You got any other pens on you?'

'Just that one,' Darby said.

'Okay, you can take it in. But make sure you come back with it. I don't want to have to do a strip search on that man in there. Don't want to end my day on that note, you hear?'

Darby nodded, glancing at a colour video screen showing a private conference room of bright white tiles. In the centre, a gun-metal grey table and chair bolted to the floor. The other chair was not.

'We'll be looking in and watching, but we can't hear a thing,' the woman said. 'When they bring Mr Ezekiel in, they'll shackle him to the chair bolted to the floor, so you don't have to worry about any surprises – unless he suddenly turns into the Incredible Hulk.' She laughed at her joke. 'When you done speaking to him, just turn to the camera and wave. Or you can come up to the door and give it a good, hard knock. Billy Biceps over there will let you in and out.'

The woman grabbed her chest mike. 'We all set, Patrick. Bring him on in.'

The young male guard moved to the steel door.

Darby watched the second hand crawling on the wall clock.

Almost two minutes later a buzzer sounded. Locks clicked back.

The male guard opened the door.

Darby felt her heart climb high in her chest, the feeling similar to the one she'd experienced when abseiling down a ripcord from a chopper during a SWAT exercise. Legs steady, she moved past the guard and entered the conference room.

John Ezekiel no longer bore any resemblance to the mental snapshot she carried. His thick blond hair had that odd yellow tint she'd seen in heavy smokers. His muscles had wasted away and his pale skin seemed almost translucent underneath the hum of the overhead fluorescent lighting.

'Good morning, Dr McCormick.'

She had imagined a deeper voice. Ezekiel's voice, light and airy, reminded her of the pleasant and eager front desk clerk at a hotel.

The buzzer went off again. The electronic locks slammed home and Darby felt the sound echo inside her chest.

She approached the table.

'How do you know I'm a doctor?'

'I've been keeping tabs on you ever since I read about you in the newspapers,' he said. 'You're in the papers a lot. And on TV. You're a special investigator for Boston's Criminal Services Unit. Your specialty is forensics and deviant behaviour of the criminal variety. In other words, people like me.'

Darby pulled out a chair and sat. Ezekiel stared at her from the other side of the table. He had the dull, lifeless eyes of a marble bust.

Must be the medication, Darby thought. Ezekiel suffered from schizoaffective disorder – the depressive type, the most difficult to treat. According to the notes, his current medications consisted of the antipsychotic drug Clozaril and lithium, a mood stabilizer.

'I was told you wanted to speak to me about Amy Hallcox.'

'You mean Kendra Sheppard,' he said.

'Who's that?'

'You know who she is.' Ezekiel leaned forward in his chair, chains rattling. His eyes never moved from her face. 'Lying is not a good way to build trust. I can't tell you the truth if I don't trust you, do you understand?'

'I do.'

'Then don't lie to me again. If you do, the conversation's over.'

'Understood. Why did you want to speak to me about Kendra Sheppard?'

'Have you checked the room for listening devices?'

'No.'

He seemed puzzled. 'Why not?'

'It would be illegal for the prison to eavesdrop on our conversation.'

'The cameras are watching us.'

'They are, but I can assure you nobody is listening.'

'Assured by *whom*? The guards posted outside the door?'

'I don't have any equipment to sweep the room for bugs, Mr Ezekiel. What do you suggest we do?'

'Sit next to me. I'll whisper against your ear.'

'I don't think so.'

'I'm not going to hurt you, if that's what you're wondering. I can't. Look.' He tried to hold up his cuffed wrists. He couldn't, of course. She knew they were shackled to the chain around his waist, and he was shackled to the chair.

'It's for your protection', he said. 'And mine.'

'Even so, the prison won't allow it.'

'Ask them. Please.'

'No.'

'Then I'm sorry, I can't speak to you.'

Darby stood. 'Goodbye, Mr Ezekiel.'

'Be careful out on the streets.'

She knocked on the door.

'And promise me you'll stay clear of the FBI,' Ezekiel said. 'I don't trust those sons of bitches.'

47

Darby stepped into the adjoining room and stood under the harsh bright fluorescent lights debating about whether to feed into the schizophrenic man's paranoid delusions.

Ezekiel knew Amy Hallcox's real name. Kendra had come to see him, they had spoken, and now she was dead. Her son had tried to kill himself after a man pretending to be a Federal agent went inside his hospital room threatening to take the boy away into protective custody. And this man *was*, in fact, a Federal agent named Peter Alan who had supposedly died two decades ago and was now lying in the morgue.

Both guards were staring at her. She told them about Ezekiel's request.

The male guard, Billy Biceps, shook his head.

'No way in hell can we allow *that*,' the female guard said. 'That man in there's a known biter. He sinks his teeth in your ear, he'll rip it clean off your head.'

'Has he done that before?' Darby asked.

'Twice. Last time he tried to swallow the ear. He didn't, but he had mangled it so goddamn bad the surgeons couldn't reattach it. You want to walk around with a missing ear?'

'It might complement the scars on my face.'

'I thought doctors were supposed to be smart.'

'I'll talk to Superintendent Skinner,' Darby said. 'Where's your phone?'

Skinner wouldn't allow it. Darby kept pressing, stating her reasons, while watching Ezekiel on the video monitor. He was struggling to look underneath the table for listening devices.

She was thinking about what Skinner had told her about Ezekiel 'glassing' one of the psychiatric nurses when Skinner said, 'Fine, go ahead and do it your way. But if Ezekiel hurts you in a bad way, the prison isn't going to be held liable.'

'I understand.'

'No, I want to hear you say it.'

'I assume all liability.'

Back inside the private conference room, the doors locked, Darby picked up the chair, brought it around the table and placed it beside Ezekiel. Then she turned the chair around so it was facing away from the table. If he tried anything, she'd have some room to manoeuvre.

'You need to move closer,' he said.

She kicked her chair next to his.

'Thank you.' He smiled, flashing his crooked yellow teeth. 'You're a very brave woman, Dr McCormick. Very composed, in control of your emotions. I'm sure, if given the opportunity, you'd rip me apart with your bare hands.'

'You're right. I would.'

'I appreciate your honesty. Take a seat.'

She could smell the cigarette odour baked into his orange jumpsuit, the medicinal odour of the shampoo the prison used to delouse the inmates. He had nicotine-stained fingers and greasy brown fingernails. Those same fingers had been wrapped around the gun that had killed her father.

His eyes were no longer dull; they were bright and alive now, gleaming with satisfaction.

'You smell wonderful,' he said.

'I can't say the same for you.'

He let loose a low chuckle. 'What happened to your beautiful face?'

'Accident,' she said.

'It's amazing how much you look like him – your father, I mean. Tommy had the same dark red hair and those piercing green eyes. It's funny how genetics works, isn't it?'

'Did you know my father?'

'Very well. I admired him greatly. May I come closer?'

Darby nodded. The chains rattled as Ezekiel moved. She felt his whiskers brush up against her cheek.

His mouth was against her ear, and she could hear the slight wheeze from his lungs. His sour breath smelled like a rancid blast of hot air caught in a subway tunnel.

'Kendra introduced me to your father,' he whispered. 'I heard about what happened to her son, by the way. How is he?'

She moved next to his ear and whispered, 'He's brain dead. Who's his father?'

'Kendra said some guy knocked her up, and she decided to keep the baby. She wouldn't tell me the father's name. Did anyone have a chance to speak to the boy before he shot himself?'

'I did, for a little bit. He asked to speak to my father. He didn't know he was dead.'

'Kendra didn't know either, until she came to Belham.'

'I find that hard to believe.'

'Kendra left Charlestown before your father was murdered. I had no idea where she went – I wasn't supposed to know, and I never bothered to try to track her down. I didn't want to put her in danger. Nobody heard from her either. I asked her old friends. That's why Kendra survived as long as she did. She didn't call anyone back home, afraid that someone's phone may have been tapped and they'd find her. And there was no internet back then.'

'How did she find out?'

'She came to Belham, went to the house where you used to live and spoke to the new owners. They're from Belham originally and knew about your family. By the way, I was sorry to hear about your mother's passing.'

Ezekiel speaking with an exaggerated sorrow, as if he actually knew her.

'After Kendra found out about your father,' he whispered, 'she did a little research, found out my new residence and set up a visit. Needless to say, she was quite upset and wanted to know what had happened. She loved your father very much. Big Red was a remarkable man. One of a kind, you could say. I regret what happened to him every single day.'

Darby swallowed, found herself making a fist. She stared at his bony neck, a part of her hoping he'd try something. She'd snap his neck before the guards entered the room. *I won't kill him. I'll snap his neck just the right way so he'll end up a quadriplegic, spending the rest of his life in diapers and feeding tubes.*

'I know what you're thinking,' he whispered.

'What am I thinking, Mr Ezekiel?'

'You want to know why Kendra came all the way down from Vermont when she could have picked up a payphone, called the Belham Police Department and asked for your father. Someone there would have told her what had happened.'

'Why didn't she?'

'Police stations record everything now – phone calls, they have security cameras monitoring you the second you step inside. She didn't want to risk the possibility of someone recognizing her. Kendra didn't trust the police, but she did trust your father. The last thing he told her before she left was that if there was ever a problem to never, under any circumstances, call or come by the station. The phone lines were tapped, and he'd found out someone had bugged his office. Big Red told her to go by his house, and that's what she did.'

'Why was Kendra looking for my father?'

'What do you know about Francis Sullivan, the head of the Irish mob?'

That name again, Darby thought. 'I know he's dead.'

'I knew Mr Sullivan – that's what you called him, even if you worked for him. I'm embarrassed to say I went back to the trade that sent me away to prison the first time – selling drugs. I had a network of contacts. Mr Sullivan wanted to take advantage of that, and I needed the money. What do you know about Kendra?'

'I know she was arrested for prostitution.'

'Kendra had a drug problem. Coke. She worked the streets for a while before Mr Sullivan brought her to these hotel parties where she serviced a number of men. Including cops.'

Michelle Baxter had told her the same thing.

'Mr Sullivan,' he whispered, 'liked rough sex.'

Darby recalled what Baxter had told her about Sullivan holding a gun to her head.

'Kendra didn't mind it, so he kept her around. He had a thing for young girls, but that wasn't what got him off. I didn't believe the stories until . . . I walked in on him once. He was with a young woman – a teenager. I don't know her name, she wasn't from the neighbourhood, but I could tell she was very, very young. I didn't see the braces until . . . afterwards.'

He swallowed. She heard a hitch in his voice.

'Mr Sullivan had this poor girl on all fours. They were on the bed. Mr Sullivan was behind her, pumping away, holding her by the hair so he could slit her throat.'

In her mind's eye Darby saw Kendra Sheppard bound to the kitchen chair, her head nearly decapitated.

'I wanted to stop it, but the girl was already bleeding out,' he whispered. 'Mr Sullivan saw me – I was standing in the doorway, frozen. He was covered in blood, like he'd bathed in it. He got off the bed very calmly – I swear he did, I'm not imagining it. He didn't come after me. He pointed to the girl with the straight-edged razor, this poor young girl who was running into the walls and choking on her own blood, and he looked at me and said, 'Go ahead and give her a whirl, Zeke. She's still got some life in her.' That's when I got the hell out of there.'

Darby had to clear her throat. 'Where did this happen?'

'Kevin Reynolds's house in Charlestown. He lived there with his mother, Mary Jane. There's a bedroom to the right of the stairs. Mr Sullivan took all his . . . victims there. Sometimes Kendra would find him napping in there. She told me that, even in the winter, you could smell the blood. It didn't matter how many times they cleaned up or replaced the rugs, that odour never went away, she said.'

'After you saw this, what did you do?'

'I went into hiding for a few days. I knew Mr Sullivan was looking for me – I was a witness, a liability. I went to Kendra. She was a friend. I told her what I'd seen, and that's when she introduced me to your father.'

'Why?'

'When you were at the hospital speaking to Kendra's son, did he confide in you?'

'He told me his real name was Sean.'

'What else?'

'He said he knew the real reason why his grandparents were murdered. We didn't get a chance to speak about it.'

'Why not?'

'We were interrupted.'

'By the FBI?'

Her breath caught. That information hadn't been reported in the news.

'Listen to me very carefully,' Ezekiel said. 'The men who killed Kendra Sheppard – at one time they were Federal agents from the Boston office. These men's assignment was to dismantle the Irish and Italian mobs. But their main job was to protect Mr Sullivan.'

Darby recalled what Jennings had told her about Sullivan's special status. 'Was he an informant?'

'Mr Sullivan was much, much more valuable.' Ezekiel swallowed, his breath coming out sharply, excitedly. 'He was a Federal agent. The FBI had planted a Federal agent at the head of the Irish mob. Sullivan's real name is Benjamin Masters.'

'Kendra told you this?'

'No,' Ezekiel said. 'Your father did.'

48

Darby felt as though her stomach were packed with ice. Drops of sweat slid across her ribs.

'I know only two names,' Ezekiel whispered. 'When they were alive, working as Feds, their names were Peter Alan and Jack King. But you won't find them. They died in a boat fire, along with Sullivan. I don't know what their names are now.'

She swallowed and said, 'Mr Ezekiel, can you –'

'I know what you're thinking. "This man is a goddamn schizophrenic, he's making this all up." I'm not. The first time I was arrested, some quack slapped that bullshit diagnosis on me and it's stuck with me ever since.' Ezekiel was speaking fast, too fast, in a garbled rush to get the words out over his mounting anger. 'Was I paranoid? Did I think people were always watching me? You bet your ass I did. In my line of business, you always have to be careful. You never know who's going to sell you out. Paranoia is what keeps you alive on the street. But I don't hear voices that aren't there, I don't think aliens are reading my brain waves or any of that crap. Doesn't matter how many times I tell them, they still come around and inject that shit into my ass three times a week. All it does is keep me in a permanent fog, makes me easier to control. I don't blame you for being sceptical. But whatever my present mental condition is, it doesn't change the fact that Kendra Sheppard visited me, does it?'

'You haven't told me why she visited you.'

'Kendra was working with your father, giving him information on Mr Sullivan and his crew. Kendra was the one who found out that Sullivan was an FBI agent and told your father. That stuff about his prior arrests and serving time in prison? All bullshit. Planted information for his cover. Kendra found out who Sullivan really was, and she also found out about the Boston Feds setting up local witnesses and informants. Some were killed; some just disappeared. And then there were the informants and witnesses who were promised witness protection as long as they cooperated. Guess what? They're dead.'

Darby thought about Michelle Baxter's comment about being placed into protective custody. *Thanks, but no. I'll take my chances here in the real world.*

'This one guy, Jimmy Lucas?' he whispered. 'He was supposed to go into the programme. The Feds picked him up, brought him somewhere and Kevin Reynolds strangled him to death. I overheard Reynolds talking about it. Kendra did too, only she was smart enough to tape it.'

'She was taping their conversations?'

'At the hotel, at Kevin Reynolds's house. Sullivan

found out what she was doing, and he went to her house to kill her and her family. Only Kendra wasn't there. She was very smart – that's how she survived this long. She sensed Sullivan knew something was going on, so she split Dodge and went to see your father. She was helping your father, giving him tapes, helping him smuggle people out of Boston and Charlestown, from –'

'What people?'

'Witnesses. Some of the young women at the hotel parties. Kendra trusted a few of them – they helped her tape conversations, set up the listening devices and these pinhole cameras your father gave her. Kendra wanted to see Sullivan go down. She was helping your father build a case against him. It was brilliant when you stop to think about it. They had whole squads within the Boston police, the state police – officers, mind you, who were probably on Sullivan's payroll – and these groups were sharing information with the Feds, who naturally turned around and told Sullivan everything. And here was Kendra working with a *patrolman* from Belham.

'Your father knew what he was up against. Big Red heard the tapes, knew what these Boston Feds were doing, the names of the cops and state troopers Sullivan had on his payroll. Sullivan and his Federal friends, they were Charlestown's version of the Gestapo. Witnesses and informants could never come forward because they knew they'd be killed. Your father . . . he had to take matters into his own hands. He couldn't trust anyone on the Belham police force, but he couldn't leave these people blowing in the wind. He knew what he was up against, so he had to get them as far away from Charlestown as possible, get them new identities. We're talking dozens and dozens of lives that he saved.'

'Was my father working with anyone?'

'I don't know. Kendra said when she spoke to your father she was alone. I met him only a handful of times, always alone. Kendra brought me to him. I told him what I saw, and Big Red set me up in a safe house. A week later, your father was dead, and I was arrested. A month after that, Sullivan and his Federal buddies died in that raid on Boston Harbor, and that was the end of it.'

'Why were these men looking for her all this time?'

'Because the tapes she gave Big Red were only copies,' Ezekiel whispered. 'Kendra told me she'd kept the actual tapes – and she had notes on the Feds, times and places, that sort of thing. And she'd kept a list of the names of the people your father had smuggled out of the state. All this time, Kendra thought these Feds had died along with Sullivan. That changed about a year ago when she was living in . . . Wisconsin, I think. Working at a small insurance company, she told me. One day she left work, was driving home, when she realized she'd left something at the office, and when she pulled around to the front she saw Peter Alan heading inside the building. The other guy, a man named Jack King, was behind the wheel of a car parked right out front. She picked up Sean from school and started driving to look for a new place to live, just left all of her stuff behind.'

'What did she tell Sean?'

'Kendra said she told him *everything*. She had to, because after Wisconsin, they were always switching identities. That's why she decided to come forward, because of Sean. She didn't want anything to happen to him. After Wisconsin, they moved to New Jersey. Their apartment got broken into and she panicked and split for Vermont, changed her name again, this time to Amy Hallcox. She was a pro at changing identities. Always worked at places where social security numbers were easily available – places like insurance companies. She told me she was sick and tired of running, said it was time to come forward with what she knew before they killed her. She was the last one left.'

'The last of what?'

'The last of the people your father smuggled out of Charlestown. They're all dead. After she saw Alan, she did a little research. She took her list of names and found out that they had been murdered. All unsolved. This secret Gestapo unit of dead FBI agents – they had tracked them down and killed them.'

'How?'

'Your father must have had a list. They must have confiscated it. That, his tapes, evidence, whatever he had. They had a tough time finding Kendra because she kept switching her identities every time she moved.'

'Was the entire FBI involved or just the Boston office?'

'I don't know. Kendra told me about the Boston Feds who were involved, that's it.'

Darby thought about the ransacked house in Belham. Her home in Vermont had been searched.

'Kendra told me she'd kept the tapes, notes, all of it,' he whispered. 'I don't know where they are; she didn't tell me. I told her to let sleeping dogs lie. Besides, it wouldn't have changed anything. It's been twenty plus years since she left Charlestown. If she'd come forward with whatever she had, what would it have accomplished? The FBI would have maintained that the Federal agents who had died on those two boats were, in fact, dead. It would've just made her a target. And when they find out you've spoken to me – and they will – *you'll* be a target.'

'Is Kevin Reynolds a Federal agent?'

'Kendra had her suspicions,' he whispered, 'but she couldn't prove it.'

'Did she tell you who was on these tapes?'

'No, she didn't. We had only forty minutes to talk. I let her do all the talking. I just listened.'

'Does she know who killed my father?'

'No. I don't know either. I was in this motel when your father was murdered. I told this to my wonderful public-appointed lawyer, of course. The motel said they had no record of me staying there. No bills, nothing. It didn't matter. The Feds set me up. They stole my car, they found the gun I kept in my apartment – they planted enough evidence to leave no doubt that I'd done it. Without any evidence to support what I was saying, my lawyer thought he was listening to the paranoid ramblings of a schizophrenic.'

'My father wouldn't have left you alone in a hotel. He would have arranged for someone to watch you.'

'He said he had someone watching the hotel – someone he trusted. I don't know who he was, I never saw the guy.'

'I'll look into this.'

'*No,*' he hissed. 'I didn't call you to *help* me; I called to warn you about these so-called Federal agents. I have no idea if they're still working for the FBI, but, regardless, they're out there looking for these tapes. *Don't go looking for them.* You know what they did to your father; you saw what happened to Kendra. If you find these tapes, destroy them. Don't think you can expose these people. You can't trust anyone, especially people inside the Boston police department. Sullivan had plenty of *your* people on his payroll.'

'Tell me some names.'

'I don't remember their names, but I'm sure they're still out there. You start in on this, you'll wind up buried next to your father.'

I haven't started in on this, Darby wanted to say. *I'm already in it.*

49

Darby felt cold all over as she collected her things from the female guard. She was dimly aware of the woman speaking, making a joke to Billy Biceps about how everything must've gone well with Zeke 'cause the doc still had both her ears, ha-ha. Darby forced a smile, thanked the guards and stepped into a cool, bright corridor echoing with murmured conversations.

The rational part of her, which had been oddly quiet all this time, spoke up. *You actually believe everything Ezekiel has told you.*

A statement, not a question. Did she believe *everything*? She didn't want to believe any of it, but a good majority of the things he had told her – like Special Agent Alan, for example – were true. Some of the other things he had said clambered around the truth – too goddamn close to it. And if that wasn't bad enough, the man didn't fit the mould of someone suffering from a schizoaffective disorder. The delusion about the room being bugged should have dominated the entire conversation. His paranoid thoughts should have been rampant, but the man's speech had remained remarkably coherent. He had answered each of her questions, had easily moved from one topic to the next without confusion and – *and* – had shown a remarkable degree of empathy when speaking about her father.

And what about her father? At thirty-nine, her memories of Thomas 'Big Red' McCormick had started to blur and fade. As it was, she didn't have many memories to start with. She had barely seen him during her childhood, Big Red having to work a tremendous amount of overtime while Sheila attended night school for her nursing degree. A few random snapshots came to her – clutching her father's big leg on the subway as the crowded T-car rocked-and-rolled its way down the track; Big Red cracking peanut shells in his long, callused fingers at Fenway Park.

But, beyond her father's love of the Red Sox, Frank Sinatra records, good bourbon and cigars, she didn't have the first idea about what had made Big Red tick. He had been an unnaturally quiet man, more prone to listening than to talking. And he was always observing the world around him. In her memories he seemed constantly exhausted.

Kendra introduced me to your father . . . She loved your father very much.

I admired him greatly.

Big Red was a remarkable man. One of a kind, you could say. I regret what happened to him every single day.

Darby opened the main doors. The afternoon sky was a bright, hard blue and free of clouds, the air still unbearably hot and humid. She looked behind her, having the absurd feeling that Ezekiel had followed her outside.

Lieutenant Warner, sitting behind the wheel of her car, had parked in one of the spaces reserved for police. He had a good view of the entire car park and the prison's front doors. He saw her and pulled out of his spot.

She didn't want him behind the wheel, she didn't want him in her car. She wanted to drive alone, in silence, to process what had just happened.

Warner was on his mobile.

'Commissioner,' he said after she shut the door. He handed over his phone as he drove off, heading for the exit. 'Go ahead, it's safe to talk.'

Chadzynski wanted an update. It took Darby a moment to collect her thoughts. She spoke slowly, concentrating on her words. The commissioner listened without interruption.

Darby finished talking. A long silence followed. For a moment, she thought the connection had died.

'Commissioner?'

'I'm here. I was . . . I'm still trying to process what you've told me.' Another pause. 'You're suggesting that the head of the Irish mafia, a man responsible for the deaths of countless numbers of people as well as the disappearances of several young women, was a Federal agent.'

'I'm not suggesting anything. I'm just telling you what Ezekiel told me.'

'But just the *idea* of it . . . it's . . . Darby, Frank Sullivan was a vicious psychopath. He killed Boston cops, state troopers – he killed people from Boston and Charlestown and God only knows who else. I have stacks of files of unsolved homicides that are believed to be linked to Sullivan. I've always heard rumours about the FBI trying to place an undercover agent inside the Irish and Italian mafia, but if what Ezekiel said is true, it means the Federal government not only placed an undercover agent inside the Irish mob, they somehow made him the goddamn head of it. We're talking about a man who's a mass murderer. It means the Federal government is implicit in the murders and disappearances of, what, nearly a hundred people? Do you realize the magnitude of what you're suggesting?'

Unfortunately, she did. Not only had the Boston FBI – maybe even the entire Federal organization – sanctioned Sullivan's actions, they had also helped to cover them up.

Your father knew what he was up against, Ezekiel had told her. *Big Red heard the tapes, knew what these Boston Feds were doing, the names of the cops and state troopers Sullivan had on his payroll.*

'Do you believe Ezekiel?' Chadzynski asked.

'I do. Even if I wanted to dismiss it as some sort of paranoid schizophrenic story, Kendra Sheppard did, in fact, visit him. Ezekiel knew her real name. Knew where she was living, knew about her son – he knows too many details for it to be some sort of made-up story. And why ask to speak to me after all this time?'

I didn't call you to help me, Ezekiel had said. *I called to warn you about these so-called Federal agents.*

'The timeline bothers me,' Darby said. 'Kendra Sheppard's parents were murdered in April of 1983. She disappears, then my father is shot in May. Sullivan and these Federal agents – how many are these again?'

'Four,' Chadzynski said. 'Here they are, on the *Boston Globe*'s website. Peter Alan, Jack King, Anthony Frissora and Steve White. There's an interesting note in the article. They were all assigned to the Boston task force set up to dismantle both the Irish and Italian mafias. I'm starting to gather information from our files to see what we can find out.'

Sullivan and his Federal friends, they were Charlestown's version of the Gestapo.

'Ezekiel mentioned Jack King,' Darby said.

'Since we found Peter Alan's fingerprints on the database, it makes me wonder if the FBI didn't know what was occurring in their Boston office. If headquarters was involved with the cover-up, I'd assume they'd wipe the prints off the database. They could do it easily, since they own it.'

'We won't know anything for sure until we find those audiotapes and whatever else Kendra Sheppard had.'

'And Mr Ezekiel didn't give you any indication as to where this evidence might be?'

'No. For all I know these . . . this group of dead Federal agents might already have it.'

'We'll have to go on the assumption that they don't. I don't know if Mr Warner told you, but he found a listening device mounted underneath your dash, right below the steering column. It's the same model as the one he recovered from my office. He also found a GPS tracking unit. Are you coming back to work this afternoon?'

'I'm heading back to the lab.'

'Good. Mr Warner is going to sweep your office and the lab.'

'I don't see how these people could gain access.'

'Most likely, they couldn't. But I can't dismiss the possibility that these men have inside help. We have to limit our circle of trust.'

Sullivan had plenty of _your_ *people on his payroll . . . I'm sure they're still out there.*

'I agree,' Darby said.

'Now I have two matters to discuss with you. The first involves Michelle Baxter. She's disappeared.'

Darby closed her eyes and pinched the bridge of her nose.

'After I left the hospital, I sent a detective to go speak with her,' Chadzynski said. 'The door was unlocked. No sign of a struggle, although the detective told me it was impossible to tell, given the apartment's state of disarray. The detective didn't find a handbag, suitcase or any other sort of luggage, so it's possible the Baxter woman decided to leave town.'

'Does this detective have a name?'

'It's someone from Anti-Corruption.'

Chadzynski didn't elaborate.

'Please don't take it personally, Darby. It's not a matter of trust, it's protocol. I have to safeguard their identities. Any information I receive will be forwarded to you through me or Mr Warner.'

'I understand.'

'What do you know about Detective Pine?'

'I know he used to be my father's partner. Then Artie passed the detective's exam and went to Boston to work homicide.'

'His territory was South Boston. Two officers from Anti-Corruption have just started sorting through Pine's old police reports, but suffice to say that a good majority of the homicides Pine investigated have at least one thread that leads back to Frank Sullivan. Before that, Detective Pine was involved with TPF during the forced busing –'

'Excuse me for interrupting, Commissioner, but what's TPF?'

'Tactical Patrol Force. The unit no longer exists. It was disbanded during the late seventies after repeated complaints of officers using excessive force. You're probably much too young to remember this, but back in '65 Massachusetts passed the Elimination of Racial Imbalance Law. The Boston school committee, comprised mostly of white Irish

Catholics, had successfully blocked the law through a decade of litigation. Then, in '74, a Federal court judge ordered the desegregation of Boston's public schools. We had riots all over the city – President Ford delivered a TV speech urging Boston to cooperate.'

Darby knew about the riots – had read about them during a high school history class.

'During the first few weeks of school, the TPF was asked to protect buses delivering African-Americans to Boston schools,' Chadzynski said. 'Crowds of white Irish men and women threw bricks, rocks, you name it, through bus windows, at the students and TPF officers. Add to that the number of African-American groups there protesting. Needless to say, tensions were high and several officers were a bit too liberal with their nightsticks. Arthur Pine allegedly kicked an African-American man to death. I say allegedly only because the witness who came forward claiming to have seen Pine do this suddenly disappeared.'

Ezekiel said Big Red had put him in a hotel. Alone.

He said he had someone watching the hotel – someone he trusted.

Had her father trusted Artie?

'I'm not saying Pine is involved with what's happening now,' Chadzynski said, 'but, given what I've uncovered, I want Anti-Corruption to take a closer look at him. Until he's been properly vetted, I don't want you feeding him any information about these cases.'

'And when Artie calls me, what do you want me to tell him?'

'Tell him the truth. Tell him Lieutenant Warner has taken over the investigation. If Detective Pine has any questions, he's to contact Mr Warner. He's the lead on this now. You're to funnel all information through him. When are you planning on speaking with Mr Cooper?'

'As soon as I get back to the lab.' Darby felt a cold place in her stomach. 'Do I need to bring Lieutenant Warner with me?'

'No. I'll have him question Mr Cooper at a later point here in my office. You're to call me after you've spoken with him, then file a report and give it to Mr Warner.'

'Understood.'

Chadzynski hung up. Darby handed the phone back to Warner. He slipped it inside his pocket without taking his eyes off the road. He didn't speak, just kept driving. She could see the tall buildings of downtown Boston looming in the distance. She stared at them and for some reason was reminded of a quote from one of her father's favourite baseball players, the great pitcher Satchel Paige: 'Don't look back. Something might be gaining on you.'

50

Jamie walked down the garage steps lugging her suit-case, a battered black monstrosity she had purchased shortly before her honeymoon. It had travelled with her to St Lucia and then later, throughout the States with Dan and the kids. She hoisted it into the back of the minivan and stared at it for some moments.

I'm really doing this, she thought. *I'm just going to jump in my car with the kids and drive west until we find San Diego.*

She had been fine at the bank. When she gave the teller the signed form to close her savings and chequing accounts, she had expected a moment of panic. Instead, she'd had a burst of clarity. The teller came back with an envelope holding a little over five grand in cash, and when she held it, she knew leaving was the only way she could protect her kids now. To do it right, she'd need to create new identities for them. She knew how to do it. Carter was too young to understand, but Michael would. First, she would have a long talk with him about Ben Masters. Not now. Later, once they got settled. She walked out of the back smiling at the thought of a fresh start, a brand-new slate for all of them.

That feeling changed when she went to the liquor store in Wellesley Hills.

The young-looking guy who worked behind the counter – tall and lanky with thick black hair and smooth tanned skin – had gone out of his way to find some larger boxes. He insisted on bringing them out to the car.

'Are you Jamie Russo?' he asked.

She stared at him, wondering how he had recognized her.

He blushed. 'You sort of look like her. That's why I was asking.'

She nodded. 'I'm . . . ah . . . ah . . . Jamie.'

'I sort of knew your husband. Dan would come in every other week or so and buy a bottle of Johnnie Walker. We'd talk about the Sox or whatever for a bit. Your husband was a real good guy, and I . . . I'm sorry about what happened to him and . . . everything else.'

Dan bought a bottle of booze once a week, she thought numbly as she drove home. *How long had you been doing that, Dan? I never saw you drinking during the week – then again, how could I, since you were spending all of your time in the basement. What were you doing down there? Why were you drinking so much? And how come I never saw a single empty Johnnie Walker bottle in the recycling bin? Did you hide them in the rubbish?*

Jamie felt a sudden rising tide of bitterness aimed at this liquor store clerk who owned some piece of her husband she didn't know – *would* never know. A part of her wanted to turn around, drive back to the liquor store and interrogate him. *Do you know why my husband was drinking so much? Did he seem upset? Did he tell you anything? How did he act? Tell me about every conversation you remember because I want to fill this goddamn hole I've been carrying inside my chest for the past five years.*

She didn't turn around, just kept driving, suddenly aware about how she would always be anchored to Wellesley. By leaving, she would never know why Dan was killed. Sure, she could take some satisfaction in knowing Ben Masters was dead, but Kevin Reynolds was still out there, Reynolds and this still unknown third man, Judas.

She kept checking her rear-view and side mirrors to see if anyone was tailing her. By leaving now, she realized that no matter where she went, this was how she would spend the rest of her life – always looking in her rear-view mirror, always looking over her shoulder.

Jamie slammed the hatchback shut, went inside the house and grabbed the keys from the kitchen drawer for the dead room.

Michael was helping Carter select which toys to pack. She had given each a single box; she wouldn't have any more room inside the minivan with the clothes and boxes of documents and other paper-work she didn't want to leave behind. She had expected some resistance to this whole sudden pack-up-and-leave plan, maybe even a change of heart. Michael went right to work without any argument. Carter kept asking if they were going to live at Disney World.

She opened the door to the dead room and closed it behind her. Bright sunlight flooded the room. The furniture was still here, washed of blood, and she had thrown out the old bedding. All that remained were the mattress and the dusty valance covering the box spring.

She grabbed the pictures from the walls and placed them inside the box, thinking about the minivan, how Kevin Reynolds had stood only a few feet from it this morning.

So close, she thought. *He was so goddamn close, if only I had stepped out of the minivan more quickly . . .*

She heard a car pull into her driveway. She went to the window and saw a black Honda.

Oh my Jesus, that looks like Kevin Reynolds's car.

Jamie dropped the box, about to call out for the kids, when she saw a man in black trousers and matching short-sleeved shirt stepping outside. Father Humphrey.

She didn't want to invite him inside the house, didn't feel like fielding questions about her sudden move. She ran back downstairs and hit the button to open a garage bay.

Father Humphrey rushed inside, face flushed.

'Good, I'm glad I caught you,' he said. 'I've been calling you all afternoon.'

'I . . . ah . . . stepped . . . ah –'

'It doesn't matter.' Humphrey brushed past her, knees cracking, and walked across the garage. He hit the button for the bay door.

'What . . . ah . . . ah . . .' She couldn't get the words out, watching Humphrey dart around the minivan to look through a window.

'Has anyone come by the house?' he asked. 'Anyone you haven't recognized?'

Every muscle in her body tensed.

Humphrey moved away from the window. 'How do you know a man named Kevin Reynolds?'

Jamie opened her mouth but couldn't speak. The dread she'd been carrying wrapped its tentacles around her throat.

'His sister lives in Wellesley, not far from here,' Humphrey said. 'You might've seen her in church. She's a good woman, but I can't say the same about Kevin. A mean bastard, that one.'

'How . . . ah . . . ah . . . how . . . how . . .'

'Just listen to me,' he said. 'Just listen and let me do the talking.'

Humphrey's wrinkled face and bloodshot eyes kept disappearing behind the hot, bright stars exploding across her vision.

'Kevin comes to me for confession every now and then. He came to confession about an hour ago.

Afterwards, I found him sitting inside the pew. He wanted to have a friendly chit-chat about the church, fundraisers and so forth. Then he worked his way into asking questions about you. He knows what happened here and asked if I knew you, if you still lived in the area.'

Get the kids, she thought. *Get them and leave.*

'Being the good Catholic you are,' he said, 'I'm sure I don't have to explain to you the seal on confession. How a priest cannot break it even under the threat of death. I'm a man of God, but I'm also a man – *wait, Jamie, come back!*'

She ran for the stairs.

Father Humphrey caught up with her inside the foyer. He grabbed her by the arm, pulled her back.

'*Calm down.*' He shook her. '*Calm down and listen!*'

She screamed and tried to push him away.

'I have people who can help you, Jamie. These people have helped women like yourself, victims of crime – they've helped entire families start new lives in places where men like Kevin Reynolds can never find you. I'm going to call these people. They'll be here in under an hour.'

'*L-l-l-l-leave.*'

'A man like Kevin Reynolds has the resources to find you. These people will make sure he can't. And you don't have to worry about money. They'll help you until you get established, okay? I'll help you pack until they arrive.'

She pushed him away and ran for the stairs.

Jamie opened her mouth to speak, to tell the kids to get downstairs right now, they were leaving. The words died in her throat as a clear plastic bag was wrapped over her head.

51

Darby stepped out of the elevator with Lieutenant Warner and saw two men dressed in suits and ties waiting outside the doors for the crime lab. They saw Warner and reached for the bulky plastic briefcases sitting on the floor near their legs. *Must be the men here to sweep the offices for bugs,* she thought.

Warner didn't introduce the men to her. She didn't care. She was sick of talking and now she had to talk to Coop.

The lab was eerily quiet, the offices she passed by empty. The staff had most likely been called out to Charlestown to help assist the bomb squad in the collection of evidence and to help search for bodies and remains.

Coop wasn't in his office. She checked the fingerprint database. IAFIS had come up with a match on one of the prints.

She opened the screen. It was the fingerprint from the blister pack of nicotine gum. The print had a 96.4 per cent match to a man named Jack King.

That was one of the names Ezekiel told me – one of the dead Feds.

Sure enough, it was. The information on the screen

said that Special Agent King had died on July 2, 1983 – the same day Sullivan had died. All the notes were listed.

Coop had been here this morning. Surely he had checked the database. Why hadn't he called her?

Darby didn't find him in any of the other exam rooms, but she found Randy and Mark in serology examining Kendra Sheppard's bloody clothing and the personal items she had removed from the body yesterday at the morgue – a black plastic watch, a sterling silver Claddagh ring and a plain, thin gold necklace.

Randy put down his clipboard, his gaze fixed on the raw stitches covering her face. Both he and Mark looked exhausted.

'We thought you could use a hand with the clothes,' Randy said, 'so Mark and I came in early.'

'Thanks,' Darby said. 'Thank you both. I really appreciate it. Have any of you seen Coop?'

Randy shook his head. Mark said, 'I know he was here this morning. I haven't seen him since.'

Darby wondered if Coop was working at the bomb site. She checked in with the lab's secretary.

'He took a personal day,' the secretary said.

'Did he say why?'

'Not to me he didn't. Maybe he left you a message.'

Darby went to her office. No message from Coop, but there was one from Madeira James.

'Miss McCormick, I'm calling to follow up on our

conversation yesterday regarding the microstamped bullet you found. The company president has the form I signed to release all information regarding the test ammo and the demonstration. He's currently reviewing it with legal. As soon as I know anything, I'll call or email.'

The message had come in this morning shortly before ten. It was now a quarter to four.

The second message was from Rob Litzow, the desk sergeant in charge of the evidence trailers. He had been unable to find the evidence and murder books associated with the Sheppard murder in April of 1983.

Darby called Litzow. 'What happened to the evidence?'

'Don't know. It could've been mislabelled or lost. This happens a lot with older stuff. We'll find it, I'm sure, but it'll take some time.'

She recalled what Ezekiel had said about Sullivan having inside help within the police departments. *You can't trust anyone, especially people inside the Boston police department. Sullivan had plenty of your people on his payroll.*

She turned to her computer and said, 'I need a list of people who've checked out the Sheppard case.'

'Nobody's asked for it for the last five years, I can tell you that.'

'What do you do with the old logs?'

'They're in storage.'

'Find them and fax them over to me. And while I

have you on the phone, I want you to pull everything you've got on the murder of Thomas McCormick.' She read out the evidence and case file numbers.

Darby hung up and checked her email. Nothing from Madeira James. Randy had emailed her a copy of the evidence report he had filled out on the items he recovered from the woods. She printed out a copy, then picked up the phone and dialled James's direct number at Reynolds Engineering Systems. She got the woman's voicemail. Darby left a message asking her to call with an update.

Next, she tried calling the owner of the Belham house, Dr Wexler, in France. No answer. She left another message.

Now Coop. He didn't answer his mobile. She tried his home number. No answer.

Why are you avoiding me, Coop?

Darby went to the printer. Her head throbbed separately from the wounds on her face. *Thump-thump*, like a heartbeat. She sat back in her chair and pressed the heels of her palms against her eyes. The Percocet the doctor had prescribed for her would take care of the pain. It would make her feel sluggish and stupid. She grabbed some Advil tablets from her desk drawer and dry-swallowed them as she picked up the evidence report.

No prints or blood were recovered from the smoke canisters. Randy had given the serial numbers to the bomb squad. Good move. They would know where to look to see if they had been stolen. Running down the serial numbers, though, had taken a back seat for the moment now that the entire bomb squad was busy in Charlestown.

Darby flipped through the sheets and read through Randy's notes. The Wonder Twins had done an exhaustive job processing the evidence.

Something about the binoculars bothered her. She thought about Randy's grid map and carried the evidence report with her to the conference room.

52

Darby stood in front of the whiteboard. The binoculars had been found in the upper-left-hand quadrant of the woods, a good distance away from the incline leading up to the road. Randy had recovered sneaker prints near the binoculars. These same prints matched the ones on the back deck steps, and so belonged to the person who had shot their way inside the house. This person had been far away from the others. It was possible this person was acting independently of the other men – had no connection to them. Okay, so why did the binoculars bother her?

She flipped back through the pages. Here. Smooth glove prints and a couple of smudged latent prints Mark had tried to enhance without any luck.

She read the specs on the binoculars. They were made by Nikon. Inexpensive. Not the sort of thing a tactical person would use. The bald guy with the tactical vest had had night-vision goggles. The Fed, Alan, had used some sort of HERF device to fry the circuitry inside the hospital's security cameras. The TV cameraman she'd seen watching the house had had a camera with a laser mike. High-tech equipment. These binoculars were small, meant to be folded and tucked into a back pocket. You used them to watch birds, maybe a sporting event or a concert. They weren't used for surveillance.

She turned the binoculars over in her mind's eye. Saw the cracked plastic and the screws, the screw had –

Darby left the conference room and checked the binoculars out of the evidence locker.

The screws had been stripped. Someone had taken apart the binoculars to fix them. Someone had touched the inside of the binoculars. Mark had only fumed the *outside*.

She carried the evidence bag back to serology. She told Mark about the binoculars.

'Shit,' he said. 'I never . . . It didn't even occur to me.'

He took them to the exam room across the hall.

Randy said, 'The fingerprints came back on the Belham house. No matches except for those belonging to Kendra Sheppard and her son. The ones that we couldn't identify I'm guessing belong to the people who own the house.'

'Wexler,' Darby said, wondering why neither the man nor his wife had returned her call.

She turned her attention to the bloody clothes spread out across the bench.

Kendra found out who Sullivan really was, Ezekiel had said, *and she also found out about the Boston Feds setting up local witnesses and informants . . . Kendra told me she'd kept the tapes, notes, all of it. I don't know where they are; she didn't tell me.*

Audio tapes and notes are bulky things. She couldn't have carried them with her all the time. That meant she must have locked them away somewhere safe. Where? A safety deposit box?

No, Darby thought. *You have to fill out a form for that, you need to show a licence. Whatever identity she was using would have to have been logged on the bank's computer system. Kendra didn't trust computers. She wouldn't have wanted to give these men a way to trace her.*

So where had she stored these tapes?

'The clothes are pretty much dreck,' Randy said. 'Lots of blood, yes, but most likely it's the vic's. We're using . . .'

Randy's voice trailed off in her mind. Darby was thinking about an airport locker. That was anonymous. Stuff your items in the locker and pay a fee – you could use cash. Problem: you couldn't use an airport locker indefinitely. The fee covered you for a day or two, depending on the airport. An airport was anonymous but not convenient. Kendra would have wanted to keep the evidence she had close to her – within arm's reach. She'd need access to it quickly in case she had to run. She had been running for a long time.

'. . . just what they're reporting on the radio and TV about the bomb site,' Randy was saying. 'Dr Edgar and his grads students are still unaccounted for, along with Jennings. Lots of injuries but no names given, lots of witnesses . . .'

Running, Darby thought. Kendra had been on the run for twenty plus years, changing identities for her and her son. Ezekiel had said something about Wisconsin. Kendra working at an insurance company, Kendra seeing Peter Alan heading inside the building and Jack King sitting behind the wheel of a car parked right out front.

She picked up Sean from school and started driving to look for a new place to live, Ezekiel had said, *just left all of her stuff behind.*

Darby said, 'Randy, I need you to get Kendra's handbag from the evidence locker.'

'I searched it and didn't –'

'Don't talk, just go get it.'

In her mind she saw Kendra spotting the dead FBI agents. *What did she do? She drove away to pick up her son from school.*

Drove to find a new place to live.

Left all of her stuff behind.

But not everything – not the most important thing, a cold, flat voice said. *Kendra wouldn't have left behind the evidence. She needed that. So after she picked up Sean, she drove – she didn't stop, she just kept driving because she already had the evidence with her. She figured out a way to have it with her at all times, within arm's reach in case she needed to run. She had the evidence with her at all times.*

Randy removed the handbag from the evidence bag and placed it on the bench. Darby's attention never left the blood-soaked clothes, afraid that if she

346

looked away she'd lose the connection to the voice speaking to her: *She had the evidence with her at all times. She had the evidence with her at all times.*

Darby reached for the box of latex gloves. She put them on and started with the handbag.

Black leather Liz Claiborne wallet holding nothing but cash and a Vermont driver's licence for Amy Hall-cox.

Three plastic-wrapped tampons.

Next, the box of Altoids. Nothing in there but mints.

She had the evidence with her at all times.

You couldn't carry a handbag with you at all times. Kendra would have used something that she could have with her at all times.

What was left? Watch and jewellery.

The watch had already been dusted for prints. Darby picked it up. Black polyurethane strap and a black faceplate surrounded by a stainless-steel mask with a brushed-steel finish. The second hand ticked along steadily. Silver numbers but no manufacturing stamp identifying the watchmaker.

She turned it over. The back of the watch looked normal, but not the left side. A small rectangular piece of plastic. She grabbed a pair of tweezers and pushed out a plastic tab belonging to a small USB flash drive.

'Holy shit,' Randy said. Then his surprise turned to embarrassment. 'I never would've thought . . . I examined that watch myself and not once did I notice that.'

'You weren't supposed to. It's concealed. I need to take this to my office. Oh, and before I go, I should tell you that there'll be some people inside here momentarily sweeping the office for listening devices.'

'What's going on?'

'Sorry, Randy, I can't tell you. Orders of the commissioner.'

'Say no more.'

Darby thought about the USB drive. Kendra Sheppard had gathered information during a time when such devices had yet to be invented. That meant only copies of the original documents and audio recordings were on the drive. Had she destroyed the originals? Or had she stored them someplace safe?

She found Warner inside her office along with the other two men.

'I need to speak to you privately for a moment,' she said.

Warner pointed to the door. The two men nodded and left.

Darby slid the tiny flash drive into the USB slot of her computer.

The door shut behind her and Warner said, 'What's up?'

'I found Kendra Sheppard's documents.' Darby pointed to the computer screen holding a list of MP3 audio files and PDF files.

Warner slid next to her and leaned on the desk. He took out a pair of bifocals. Darby stared at the list.

Christ, there're dozens of files here. 'Judging by the size of these files, I'd say they were scanned.'

'Can you print them out?'

She nodded, then grabbed the mouse and clicked on one of the PDF files.

A window opened asking her for a password.

She clicked on one of the audio files and got the same window.

'Shit.'

'What?' Warner asked. 'What's wrong?'

'They're password protected.'

'You don't happen to know the password, do you?'

'No. And don't ask me to start typing in random passwords either.'

'Why not?'

'Because I might wind up erasing the files. I'll call the computer lab.' She reached for the phone.

Warner blocked her. 'I've got to clear it with the commissioner. You got a guy in mind?'

'Jim Byram,' she said. 'He's the best at this stuff.'

'Okay. Once he's vetted, I'll have him get to work on it.'

'These files are probably just copies. Kendra either stored the originals someplace else or destroyed them.'

Warner nodded. 'You talk to Cooper yet?'

'He's not here.'

'Where *is* he?'

'I don't know.'

'Then go find him. Find him and talk some sense into him. Then call me on your way back here. I'll need your help sorting through these files.'

She pushed the chair back and stood up.

'One other thing,' Warner said. 'These people who were following you . . . if you *think* you see anything, I want you to call. Don't go all Rambo on me, okay? We need these guys alive.'

Darby nodded and left, thinking about where Coop was, how she was going to get him to open up and talk.

She checked in to ballistics. They had no record of a Glock eighteen ever having been used in the commission of a crime.

53

Jamie awoke to a gauzy haze of thoughts. She tried to open her eyes and a dim voice – one that sounded eerily familiar – groaned in protest: *No, stay here with me.*

She recognized the voice – had slept next to it for close to fifteen years.

Stay here with me, Dan said. *Stay here where it's safe.*

Safe?

Safe from what?

It came to her, slowly at first. Father Humphrey had come to her house to warn her about Kevin Reynolds. *He knows what happened here and asked if I knew you, if you still lived in the area.* Humphrey's words. And . . . and . . . what? She had run into the house to get the kids. And Humphrey grabbed her, telling her to calm down. She remembered pulling free. Remembered running to the foot of the stairs, about to scream to the kids to come down right now, when a plastic bag was wrapped around her head.

Father Humphrey did that, she thought. *The priest who baptized both my babies and ate dinner at my house and saw to my husband's funeral arrangements while the kids and I were recovering in the hospital – that man wrapped the plastic bag over my head.*

She remembered feeling the plastic sticking to her lips as she sucked in air. Remembered struggling to prise his rough, callused hands from her throat and remembered her face slamming against the wall and pain exploding inside her skull – pain, oddly, she couldn't feel at this moment – she couldn't feel anything and for some reason that scared her the most. She should –

Rough hands slid across her cheeks. Fingers pushed her eyelids open and she saw Father Humphrey's face and his sad, bloodshot eyes. She couldn't seem to focus on the rest of the room but she could make out shapes and colours behind the priest – an emerald-green comforter covering a bed; a pair of drawn lavender curtains covering her windows and a lamp sitting on an oak nightstand.

My bedroom. I'm in my bedroom and I seem to be sitting up. Why can't I move my hands and feet?

For some bizarre reason she didn't feel afraid. She didn't feel anything. *My head should be pounding – it should feel sore, at the very least – but I don't feel any pain. I just want to shut my eyes and go back to sleep.*

'Come now, darling,' Humphrey said, gently shaking her head. She could smell cigarette smoke and booze on his breath. 'Time to wake up.'

He let go of her face. Her chin dropped against her chest and her body slumped to the side but she didn't fall. A long line of drool dripped on to her tan shorts.

Father Humphrey had duct-taped her to one of

the kitchen chairs. She could see the strips wrapped around her shins. He had tied her hands behind her back – the kids, oh Jesus God, Jesus Mary and Joseph, what did he do to Michael and Carter? Were they in the bedroom?

It took a great amount of effort to raise her head. 'That's my girl,' he said.

Her head flopped to the side, against her shoulder. The bedroom door was open and she could see the hall. The doors to the boys' bedrooms were shut. The door to the dead room was open. Father Humphrey had kicked it open. She saw the lock and pieces of wood lying on the carpet.

What did he do to the kids? And why don't I feel scared? Why do I feel so goddamn calm?

Father Humphrey snapped his fingers. 'Over here, love.'

Jamie rolled her head back to him. He sat on the edge of her bed with his legs crossed. Blue hospital booties covered his polished black loafers. It was hard to concentrate now, hard to keep her eyes open. Her head kept swimming; this serene calmness or whatever it was wanted to drag her back down into the place where Dan was now, this sweet, black oblivion.

The kids, a voice screamed to her.

She opened her eyes and looked at Humphrey and his hospital booties.

No, not hospital booties, she thought. *They're . . . they're . . . what's their names, the ones who investigate crime scenes . . .*

forensic. Yes. Forensic techs wear those booties when entering a crime scene . . . so they don't leave footprints.

'I didn't believe it when Kevin told me he saw you this morning, waiting for him in your minivan,' Humphrey said. His latex-covered hand held a mobile against his ear – Ben Masters's phone, the Palm Treo. 'What were you going to do to him, Jamie?'

The room kept going in and out of focus.

Concentrate. You have . . . to concentrate. Find kids.

The kids weren't in the bedroom – at least she couldn't see them. She looked at the opened door next to the nightstand and saw the familiar short hall with the two walk-in closets and the small area she and Dan had used for storage. No sign of Michael or Carter in there but –

Her eyes flicked to a dusty bottle sitting on top of her nightstand. It took her a moment to focus on the label. Johnnie Walker Blue. Had Humphrey brought a bottle of booze with him? No. No, he must have found it in the house but where? She didn't remember seeing it.

Empty glass next to the bottle. A burnt spoon, syringe and candle.

Humphrey covered the phone with his hand. 'How you feeling, love?'

'I . . . ah . . . ah . . . can't . . . ah . . .'

'Can't concentrate?'

'Yes.'

'Feel any pain?'

'Ah . . . ah . . . No.'

'Good. Gave you a little shot of heroin to calm you down – feels wonderful, doesn't it? I've never indulged myself, mind you, but I thought –' He held up a hand, motioning for her to stay silent, and then spoke into the phone. 'I'm at the Russo house. Everything's all set. Take your time.'

Humphrey hung up and stared at the phone, a grin tugging at the corner of his mouth.

'Listed me as Judas,' he said, smirking. 'I suppose I shouldn't be surprised. Ben was blessed with a dark sense of humour. The man is an Irish Catholic to the core. Do you know him as Ben or Frank? Which is it?'

Jamie couldn't hold her head up any longer. She rested it back against her shoulder and stared down the hall to the dead room.

'Doesn't matter,' he said. 'We'll get to all that in due course.'

She heard the clink of glass as Humphrey poured himself a drink from the bottle of Johnnie Walker.

'Where . . . ah . . . ah . . . where . . .'

'Where did I get the bottle?'

'Y-y . . . ah . . . yes.'

'From Danny's private hiding spot in the basement,' Humphrey said. 'We had a lot of drinks and talks down there that last month, mainly when you weren't home. Sad that a man has to hide a bottle from his wife. Then again, I always had you pegged as a meddlesome cunt.'

355

Jamie blinked. The mattress in the dead room came into sharp focus for a moment. She blinked again, wanting to hold on to the image, the clarity so she could –

A hand reached out from underneath the bed.

'You've got a tough decision to make,' Humphrey said. 'I'm not going to sugarcoat it. Before we get into that, I want you to tell me how you came to acquire Ben's phone.'

Jamie blinked again and forced her eyes wide open. Michael's hand had pulled back the valance. He lay next to his brother underneath the bed, his other hand covering Carter's mouth.

Michael whispered something to his brother. Carter's eyes were shut but he was crying, shaking.

'Come, Jamie,' Humphrey said. 'There's no use hiding it.'

How did . . . Humphrey fail to find the kids?

He still thinks they're at camp. He's waiting for them to come home.

Michael started sliding out from underneath the bed.

'*N-N-NO!*'

'I want to be reasonable,' Humphrey said.

Michael stopped.

'*Go . . . ah . . . back. Stay.*'

'I'm not following you, Jamie.'

Michael slid underneath the bed, retreating behind the valance. She turned back to Humphrey. It seemed to take a long time.

'Go . . . ah . . . back. Go.'

'I can't go back,' Humphrey said. 'You started this, love. And I should tell you that the man who's on his way here doesn't share my virtues. Especially when it comes to matters involving patience.'

Humphrey was lying on her bed, his head propped up on her pillows. He rested the glass on his flat stomach. The shades had been drawn. She thought she heard rain.

'Are you listening to me? Please pay attention, because I don't want what happened to Danny to happen to you. I really don't.'

'Dan . . . ah . . . happened?'

'They shoved his hand down a waste-disposal. What do you *think* happened?'

'I . . . don't . . . ah . . . ah . . . know.'

He lifted his head off the pillow. 'Dan never told you?'

'N-N-No.'

'Well, ain't that a hoot.'

He took a sip of his drink and stared up at the ceiling.

'The short version is your husband was a stubborn son of a bitch. I'll give you the longer version once you tell me how you got your hands on Ben's phone – there's no use denying it.'

Jamie licked her swollen lips, felt another string of drool drip from her mouth and plop against her leg.

'Whenever you're ready,' Humphrey said. He smiled, patient and pleasant, waiting for her to answer. I've got all the time in the world, that smile said. Nothing in the world can touch me. Not even God Himself.

54

Coop's house was a thing of architectural beauty – a white-painted New England saltbox with black shutters and two chimneys built at the turn of the twentieth century for the mistress of a lumber baron. It was one of the few houses that came with a driveway and a lawn – the size of a postage stamp, but still it was grass.

The house stood on a corner, cut off from the more famous downtown historic homes four blocks down the street. Darby eased her car through the gap between the waist-high white picket fences and parked behind Coop's Mustang. The sun had disappeared, giving way to yet another thunderstorm.

Stepping out into the heavy rain, she noticed the pair of opened bulkhead doors leading into the cellar. She eased the aluminium doors shut, then ran up the steps and stood under a canvas awning over a small deck. A gauzy ivory curtain covered the windowpane in the back door, and she could see Coop's shadow moving inside the living room just down the hall as she rang the doorbell.

He ducked around the corner and disappeared.

'Who is it?'

'Darby.'

'I'm sort of in the middle of something right now. I'll call you later.'

'I need to talk to you now, Coop. Open up.'

A moment later she saw his shadow coming down the hall. Locks clicked back and the door opened.

Coop stood in front of her, barefoot, dressed in jeans and a tight-fitting olive-green tank streaked with dust, dirt and sweat. His eight-month-old niece, Olivia, lay sleeping against his chest.

'My sister's babysitter bagged this morning so she called me in tears and asked if I could watch her,' he said.

Coop eased the door part-way shut, taking a quick survey of the street. Part of his scraped face was swollen. Bandages spotted with blood covered his arms.

'Jackie's boss isn't real understanding when it comes to the difficulties of single working mothers,' he said. 'You'd think he'd have more sympathy since he's been divorced three times himself and has got two kids –'

'You always booze it up when you're babysitting?'

'I can't have a couple of drinks?'

'I'm getting a contact high standing here.'

'Gee, Mom, I'd like to attend the lecture you're about to give – it sounds real inspirational, honest, – but I've got some things to do. How about I call you later and –'

She pushed her way past him, moved down the

yellow-painted hall and stepped into his living room; saw the empty and taped-up boxes covering nearly every inch of the tan carpet and felt a sick, dull thud in her heart.

Low music played from a portable radio/CD player sitting on his brown leather sofa – Bono singing a live rendition of 'Wake Up Dead Man' from a U2 concert recorded at Slane Castle in County Meath, Ireland. She'd given him the bootleg CD last year as a Christmas gift.

Coop strolled into the living room with a hand placed against the back of his sleeping niece.

'When were you going to tell me? After you left?'

'After I finished packing,' he said.

'You're going to London.'

'It was too good to pass up.'

Darby swallowed, heart beating fast.

Coop picked up a highball glass sitting on top of an old steamer trunk.

'You want a drink?' he asked. 'There's a bottle of Middleton Irish whiskey in the kitchen.'

She didn't answer.

He eased himself into a matching leather armchair.

'Don't give me that look,' he said. 'It's nothing personal. I didn't tell you because I didn't want you to sway me.'

Her face felt hot. 'When are you leaving?'

'Tonight.'

Darby didn't seem to know what to do with her hands.

'I'm taking the red-eye,' he said.

'Why the sudden urgency?'

'They needed me on this upcoming project, that new fingerprint technology they're developing.'

'Bullshit.'

'I don't know how many times I can tell you this, but I have no idea who those young women are.'

'How do you know they're young?'

'Frank liked 'em young.'

'How do you know they were involved with Sullivan?'

'This is starting to sound like a cross-examination. Should I call my lawyer and ask him to stop by?'

'I don't know, Coop. Did you do something wrong?'

He shook his head, sighing. He took another gulp of his whiskey, then crossed his legs and leaned to his right side.

'You always pack with the lights out?'

'Olivia fell asleep,' he said.

'When I rang the doorbell, I saw you run from the living room.'

'I was going to get my niece. She fell asleep on the floor. I was going to put her down on my bed when you rang.'

'You never were a good liar, Coop.'

'Did you come all the way here to bust my balls?'

'No, I came here hoping to talk some sense into you. The commissioner has you in her target sights. She thinks you're hiding something. So do I.'

'Sorry, but I can't help you.'

'That's it?'

'That's it.'

'Well, then, maybe I should just say goodbye.'

'I was going to call you later, honest, take you out to dinner and tell you about the job.'

'And if you and I were in a restaurant together, I'd be less likely to cause a scene.'

'I'm sorry, Darb. I'm not good with goodbyes.'

'Nobody is.'

'You are,' he said. 'Nothing gets past that stubborn Irish armour of yours.'

Not true, Coop. You did, despite my best efforts.

'Join me for a drink now,' he said. 'Grab a glass in the kitchen. You know where they are.'

'I've got to get going.'

'The case, it's always the case.' Coop put his feet up on the coffee table and sank back in his chair. 'What's that saying? A tiger can't change its stripes.'

Darby took a deep breath, wanting to clear the hurt from her voice before she spoke, or at least shave off the sharp edges. She stepped to the front of the chair and leaned forward placing a hand on each armrest.

'I'm very happy for you, Coop.'

'Thanks.'

'I'm going to miss you.'

'Me too.' He took a long pull from his drink. 'You're . . .'

'What?'

'You've been . . . a great friend,' he said, the words wet in his throat. 'The best.'

Darby forced a smile. She leaned forward and kissed his cheek. Her right hand reached around his back.

'Before I go,' she said, pulling the handgun from the back of his waistband, 'would you mind telling me why you need to carry a Glock for babysitting?'

55

Darby sat on the leather sofa less than a foot away from Coop's armchair. She turned the Glock around in her hand.

'Nice job filing away the serial number,' she said. 'Did you do it yourself? Or did someone give you this throw-down piece?'

Coop didn't answer.

Her phone rang. She ignored the call and said, 'Michelle Baxter is missing.'

'She left town.'

'How do you know that?'

'Because this morning, after you and I talked, I hit an ATM and went back to her place. I gave her the cash and helped her pack.'

'Because you know the man she was talking to, don't you?'

He didn't answer.

'This afternoon, when I went back to the lab, I went to your office to find you,' she said. 'I also checked the fingerprint database. The print from the nicotine gum pack came back with an ID. His name is Jack King.'

'I know. All this time, I thought he was dead.'

'When did you figure out he wasn't?'

'When I saw him talking to Baxter across the street,' he said. 'He's . . . That guy is as evil as they come.'

'Is that why you didn't call me? Because you didn't want me to run into him?'

'Yep.'

'How do you know him?'

Coop took in a sharp intake of air through his nose and moved Olivia from his shoulder to his chest. The baby stirred, her tiny fingers curling into a fist.

'You remember this?' he asked.

'Remember what?'

'Being this young,' he said, rubbing the baby's soft, downy hair. 'It's the best part of life and you can't remember being this clean. Untarnished and perfect. At our age, all you can remember is the scars. The places where you screwed up.'

Darby wanted to speak – wanted to bring him back to the present and guide him, as gently as she could, with her questions. But she could feel Coop circling around whatever it was that was bothering him and waited.

'Like when I was twelve,' he said after a moment. 'I'm dead asleep on the sofa and I hear a car muffler backfire and I'm thinking it's my old man. He drove this real shitbox Buick every evening to the GE plant in Lynn to work the third shift as a machinist, and here I am opening the door thinking my old man's come home and I see this guy from the neighbourhood, Tommy Callahan, running up the steps of the church right across the street. He's clawing at the door, screaming. That's when Mr Sullivan starts shooting. *Pow-pow-pow,* like firecrackers going off. And I'm watching Tommy C. collapsing on the front steps of the church. I'm watching him, you know, *die.*'

Coop traced a finger over Olivia's curled fist. 'Mr Sullivan's standing above him, and Tommy C.'s got his hand up. He's crying and begging. Mr Sullivan sees me watching from the front door and he pops three rounds into Tommy's head. Then Mr Sullivan frowns, wiping blood from his shoe on Tommy C.'s jeans and he says, "Hey, Coops, what are you doing up at this hour? Don't you got school tomorrow?"'

Coop took a sip of his drink. 'Kevin Reynolds drags Tommy C.'s body to the back of a car as Mr Sullivan comes walking right over to the house smiling like he's here for a social visit. He's sitting next to me on the sofa at one in the morning and my mother's up, wanting to know what's going on, and Mr Sullivan says "Relax, Martha, I just want to take Coops outside to my car and talk to him man to man. We'll be right back." I look at my mother and she doesn't say a word. Next thing I know, I'm sitting in the back of the car and Mr Sullivan is saying, "You see anything tonight, Coops?" And I tell him, I say, "No, I didn't see anything, Mr Sullivan." And he says, "I didn't think so. 'Cause if you did, we'd have a problem. And even if you *did* see something and, oh, I don't know, got it in your head to go to the cops, word is going to get back to me, and I'd hate to see your mother or one of your sisters wind up like this."

'That's when he showed me the pictures, these Polaroids of some girl missing her hands and teeth.'

Darby had to clear her throat before she could speak. 'Was Jack King involved in this?'

'The pictures, what I saw on the steps, what Mr Sullivan said to me – I told my mother. All of it.' Coop swallowed. 'I'm scared shitless, crying, and she's on the phone with my old man and the next thing I know it's five in the morning and we're down at McKinney's Diner and my father is telling me about how Mr Sullivan is keeping Charlestown clean and safe – he's keeping out the riffraff, is what he says. "Guys like Tommy C.," my dad says, "a guy who's trying to peddle drugs in our town, a guy like that had it coming." Mr Sullivan – that's what my father calls him – Mr Sullivan, he says, is a good man and sometimes good men have to make hard decisions. Decisions the police won't understand. My father tells me to forget what I saw and to keep my mouth shut – my father makes it a point, in fact, to drill it into my head for the next week. Guess what I did?'

'You kept your mouth shut.'

'That's right. I gave my parents my word. They were good people. Hard workers. They had a lot of love in their hearts, but they weren't exactly the two brightest people. Like everyone else who lived here back then, they looked at Mr Sullivan as this . . . this Robin Hood kind of guy, I guess you could say. At the time crime here was at an all-time low. No drugs, no girls on the streets looking for crack cocaine in exchange for blow jobs. Back then we walked the streets at night 'cause you knew you were safe.'

Coop took another sip of his drink and then held the glass near his face, staring at it. 'Thing is, what I saw? It's eating me up inside. I mean it's really tearing it up because, after all, I'm a God-fearing Irish Catholic and we're talking about my soul here. So I go to confession and tell the priest what I saw, everything that happened, the pictures, you name it. I'm telling him I want to go to the police 'cause it's the right thing to do. I ask him if he knows of a cop I can trust. You know what the son of a bitch said to me?'

'I'm guessing he told you not to go to the police.'

'That's right. Say three Hail Marys and two Our Fathers and all will be forgiven. And that's what I did, Darby. Thing is, though, the Big Guy in the sky had other plans for me. Next day I'm walking home from school trying to, you know, *reconcile* everything that's happened, and a car pulls up next to me and there's this huge dude who looks like Frankenstein minus the neck bolts flashing me his badge.'

'Jack King.'

Coop nodded. 'He told me to get my ass in the back seat. Being the good boy I am, guess what I did?'

'I think you got your ass in the back seat.'

'You're pretty good at this.'

'I've known you a long time,' she said, keeping her voice low, hoping it would bring Coop's down a notch and remove that jittery hitch in it. 'I know you're –'

'You don't know me, Darby.' He drained the rest of his glass and placed it back on the steam trunk. 'You *think* you know me because we've spent so much time together. But unless you've got an ability to read minds, see thoughts from moment to moment any time you want, you can never really *know* another person. That's why I don't see the point in getting married. You could go to bed every night with your wife, give her the ole high-hard one and your heart is swelling with love for her – I'm talking about that once-in-a-lifetime love you see in movies, the kind people rarely experience in their lives. The type where it hurts to breathe, right? And for all you know your significant other is fantasizing you're George Clooney or the pool boy or whoever while you're on top of her. And the thing is, no matter how much you love the hell out of someone, you can never really *know* that person. Not in the way you know and trust yourself.'

'I think I've earned your trust over the years.'

'You have,' Coop said. 'You definitely have. That's why I'm going to tell you the best part of the story, the part where Special Agent King takes me into Kevin Reynolds's basement.'

56

Darby shifted in her seat. The jumpy, nervous hitch she had heard in Coop's voice had disappeared. Now his tone was stripped of emotion, like Michelle Baxter's, and for some reason it triggered the memory of looking through the tiny window built into the ICU hospital door and seeing the flat-line on her father's heart monitor after her mother decided to pull him off life support.

'Special Agent King pulls up in front of Reynolds's house and tells me to get out of the car,' Coop said. 'I'm panicking, thinking, oh shit, this guy knows about what I saw and he's here to bust Reynolds and Sullivan. King doesn't ring the doorbell or knock, just opens the door, grabs me by the arm and drags me across the kitchen and into the basement. That was the first sign I had that something was seriously wrong.'

Coop stared at his hand as he rubbed the back of Olivia's head. 'I'm standing in the basement with King behind me and there's Mr Sullivan sitting in a kitchen chair cracking peanut shells in his hands and shooting me this look that says I'm in serious trouble. 'Course I already know that since he's got this young girl tied to a chair with duct tape and there's a big hole in the dirt floor right behind her.'

Darby looked at the front door, wanting to run for it and get as far away as she could from whatever Coop was about to tell her.

'You want to hear the rest of it, Darby?'

No, I don't.

'I don't have to tell you,' he said in a low voice. His eyes were too big and his mouth was quivering. 'There's still time to close Pandora's box. You can walk out of here with your conscience free and clear.'

'Maybe you should talk to a lawyer.'

'I'm not talking to a lawyer, Darby, I'm talking to you. You want to know the rest of it or not?'

'Tell me.'

'This girl, her hands, arms and clothes are caked in dirt because Mr Sullivan made her dig her grave in the basement with her bare hands. She's got duct tape over her mouth. She's shaking and crying, I'm crying because now the Fed's pressing a gun against the side of my head – I can feel the muzzle digging into my skin as Mr Sullivan tells me about how I've got this *real* important decision to make. Life changing, he says. One of us, he tells us, is going into that hole.'

Darby's skin grew cold. Coop stared up at the ceiling, at the fast-moving shadows made by the rainwater running down the living-room windows.

'Mr Sullivan turns to me and says, "Who do you think should be put in there, Coops? This young lady right here, who decided to go to the Feds and tell them about my hotel parties, or you? Word on the street is you're thinking about going to the cops when you promised me *and* your old man you were going to keep your mouth shut, keep our business right here in the neighbourhood? "

'That's when I realized my parish priest must've told Mr Sullivan about my confession. I didn't tell anyone. Not my friends, not my parents or my sisters. I was afraid of it getting back to Mr Sullivan and here I was stupid enough to believe I could trust Father Humphrey with the whole seal of confession thing.'

Darby gripped the edge of the cushion. 'This girl in the basement, did she know Kendra Sheppard or Michelle Baxter?'

'I'm sure she did, but I never got a chance to talk to her. I'm bawling, telling Mr Sullivan I didn't tell anyone, and he just stares at me cracking peanut shells like he's at a ball game. He keeps asking me the same question. Who do I think should go into that hole? Either I make a decision, he says, or he's going to make the decision for me. Guess what decision I made, Darby?'

Her stomach hitched. Bile rose in her throat. She had to swallow several times before she could speak.

'What was her name?'

'Don't know,' Coop said, his eyes growing wet. 'I'm ashamed to say I didn't bother to ask. It was probably better that way, since Mr Sullivan made me put a plastic bag over her head.'

Darby felt her midsection disappear.

'Of course, being the wonderful Robin Hood figure he was, Mr Sullivan yanked off the tape from her mouth so I could talk to her. You know, in case I wanted to say sorry before I suffocated her to death.'

Coop's dry, hoarse voice cracked over the words.

'She tried talking to me, I know she did, but I don't remember a word because the entire time I was holding that plastic shopping bag over her head I was thinking about my mother, how it would destroy her and my sisters if I was the one who ended up in that hole. If I was the one who disappeared. That was Mr Sullivan's specialty. I had heard stories, but now I was seeing it up close and in person.'

Tears spilled down his cheeks and his face crumbled. 'She didn't even put up a fight, Darby. It was like . . . like she had *resigned* herself to it.'

Darby couldn't move and all the while a voice inside her kept wishing that she could hit some magic rewind button on time, go back to her office and forget about coming here.

Coop wiped his eyes. 'After it was over, he made me put her body in the grave. I was burying her and not really feeling anything, I was in shock. But I was thinking about how I was going to hell. Mr Sullivan, he was all happy, kept telling me how proud he was. After she was buried he stuffed a wad of cash in my pocket. Two hundred bucks. That's how much her life was worth. He told me I was working for him now, and my new job was to keep an eye out on the streets, report back to him if I heard or saw anything in the neighbourhood.

'First, though, he said, I had to pay the piper. And if I didn't, he was going to pick up the phone and call one of his boys on the force, tell him about what had just happened here and give 'em this plastic bag with my prints all over it. And this Fed was going to back him up, say how I'd been working for Mr Sullivan and he'd seen me going into the house with this girl and heard screaming. And once I was in jail, Mr Sullivan said he was going to pay my mother a special visit.'

His name isn't Frank Sullivan, Coop. His real name is Ben Masters and he was a Federal agent who'd been planted inside the mob and I don't think he died and I don't know how he, King, Alan and the other two Federal agents placed on that boat managed to fake his death. All I know is that as every minute passes, this thing just keeps getting deeper and deeper, and I keep wondering when – or if – I'm going to reach the bottom.

Ezekiel kept whispering to her:

I didn't call you to help me; I called to warn you about these so-called Federal agents. I have no idea if they're still working for the FBI . . . You know what they did to your father; you saw what happened to Kendra . . . Don't think you can expose these people. You can't trust anyone.

Coop moved his niece so her tiny head rested underneath his chin. 'Mr Sullivan took me upstairs to what I guessed was Kevin's mother's or sister's room

– the sun is shining through these real lacy curtains, and there were all these religious pictures of Jesus and Mary and the pope hanging on the walls. And there was Father Humphrey sitting on the edge of the bed with his collar off and a glass of whiskey in his hand. The door locked behind me – they conveniently locked on the *outside* so I couldn't get out – and Father Humphrey kept smiling at me as he patted the spot next to him on the bed. Want to know what he did?'

'No,' she said, strangling on the word.

'Good, 'cause I don't want to rehash the gory details. And I'd hate to see you blush.'

'Coop –'

'I found the plastic bag, by the way. That's why I was in such a rush to get inside the house. I found the bag inside that box full of bones.'

'What did you do with it?'

'I threw it away.'

Darby stared at the carpet. She felt numb all over.

'I'd appreciate it if you left out that little detail when speaking to the commissioner,' he said. 'I don't want her to come looking for me. I already have them watching me.'

'Who? Who's watching you?'

'Why, the League of Extraordinary Dead Federal Agents. They're roaming around Charlestown.'

'Do you know their names?'

'No, but I know their faces. They're probably watching the house right now.'

'That woman you . . . met in the basement.'

'I don't know her name. And I'm proud to say that, being the stand-up guy I am, I never bothered to find out. Feel free to use your psych degree to draw your own conclusions. Just don't share them with me.'

'Ezekiel told me Kendra Sheppard was working with my father to help bring down Sullivan.'

'And look how well that turned out.'

'Did you know?'

'I knew Sullivan had a thing for her, kept her close. I found out about it after the prostitution bust.'

'And the other remains in the basement?'

'No idea. I've got a favour to ask.'

'What?'

'Take a long vacation until this blows over. Fake a heart attack. Buy a plane ticket and go somewhere, just do *something*. You need to get as far away from this as you can.'

'It's a little too late for that.'

Coop stood up and placed his sleeping niece on the sofa.

'You remember how my old man died?'

'Hit-and-run,' she said. Someone had run him over after he stumbled out of a bar in Lynn.

'What I didn't tell you was the phone call I got after we buried him. That Federal agent who'd brought me to Reynolds's house, *Special* Agent King? He called me at home and told me to keep my mouth shut or I'd be burying my mother next to my old man. That's why

Jackie and I decided to stick around in Charlestown. We wanted to keep an eye on my mother. Thank God she moved to Florida at the beginning of the year.'

'Kendra Sheppard taped conversations with these –'

'Don't tell me, I don't want to know. I don't need anything else floating around my head, and whatever it is, it's not going to make a shit's worth of difference now anyway. You can't take these guys down. They're like vampires. They came here, what, twenty something years ago, and turned Charlestown into *Salem's Lot*. Now they're back, and if you think you can kill them, you're wrong. You put one down and there'll be another one to take his place. They're –'

Darby heard the screech of car tyres.

Coop scooped up the Glock and ran for the front door.

57

Darby jumped to her feet, hand reaching for her side-arm. Coop, leaning against the wall near the foot of the stairs, peered through a window overlooking the front street.

His body relaxed. He let out a long sigh.

'It's Jackie.' He tucked the nine in the back waist-band of his jeans, covered it with his tank and threw back the deadbolt.

He ran to the sofa and picked up his niece. 'Stay here.'

Darby stood wobbly on her feet and watched as Coop ran barefoot through the rain pounding the streets and parked cars. He opened the back door of the car and placed the baby in the child seat.

Jackie rolled down the window. Darby could tell that the woman had been crying.

She looked around the street as Coop talked to his sister. Lots of parked cars. She couldn't see anyone behind the windows.

Coop ran back inside the house. He didn't shut the door and Jackie didn't drive away. The woman's face was pale, frightened.

'She wants me to go with her,' he said, picking up

his sneakers. Water dripped down his face. 'She thinks she's seen some guys watching her house.'

'I'll call some people, have them guard her until –'

'Until what? Don't tell me you think this is going to blow over.'

'The commissioner's head of Anti-Corruption has taken over the case, this guy named Warner. He can –'

'No police. I don't want them involved – I don't want anyone involved. Guys like King don't work in a vacuum, Darby. They always have help.'

'Warner knows I came over here to speak to you.'

'Tell him you couldn't find me.'

'He'll come looking for you.'

'Let him come looking. Better yet, buy me some time. Tell him I called you and promised to speak to you later, say, around eight. I'll already be at the airport.'

'And what if they go looking for you there?'

'Then I'll figure out a way to handle it.'

'Stay here, Coop. We can figure out a way –'

'I'm not staying here. I can't. I need to do this. I can't risk having anything happen to Jackie or my mother.'

'Your mother's in Florida.'

'Not for long,' he said. He straightened, gripped her lightly by the shoulders. 'Please let me do this my way, okay?'

'What can I do to help?'

'Lock up my place before you go.'

'I will as long as you keep your mobile phone on and promise to pick up when I call.'

'I promise. Make sure you do the same. I'll call you later, after I get Jackie squared away.'

Coop stepped into the rain. She wanted to go to him but her feet felt nailed to the floor.

He turned and rushed back to her. Grabbed her gently by the face and then leaned forward and kissed her hard on the lips. She kissed him back, just as hard, not wanting to let go.

He let her go. He swallowed back tears.

'I'd stay here if it would make a difference, I swear to God I would, Darby. But these guys are slick. They never go to jail. They always have inside help. How the hell do you think they managed to slip a bomb inside the house and on the Explorer?'

'I've got to see this through, Coop. I can't walk away.'

He closed his eyes for a moment, then swallowed. 'Take care of yourself, Darb. Be careful.'

'You too.'

Darby watched him get inside the passenger seat.

Get out, she wanted to say. *Come back.*

The Honda tore down the street and disappeared. She shut the door and turned back to the empty house, water dripping down her face and back.

Bono had stopped singing. Her eyes roamed across the boxes, the pictures still hanging on the walls, the dishes still piled in the kitchen sink. She stood there and took in the room, wanting to preserve it in her mind, wanting to try to hold some piece of him, knowing, right then, that this was it. Coop was leaving. He wasn't coming back.

Darby locked the front door and checked all the downstairs windows. She took the stairs to the first floor, reminding herself to go into the basement and double-check the hatch doors to make sure they were locked.

She was heading back downstairs when her phone rang.

'You're a genius,' Randy Scott said. 'Mark fumed the inside of the binoculars and found a print – a damn good one. It rang the cherries in the database, but here's where it gets weird. The print belongs to another dead person, only this guy's named Daniel Russo from Wellesley.'

'What happened?'

'He died in some sort of home invasion five years ago. The database doesn't give all the details. I have a case number but I don't have access to our computer system – I don't have the authorization. I know you do.'

'Is Warner still there?'

'No, he's gone. They're all gone, as a matter of fact.'

He's probably still with the computer guy, she thought. 'I'm on my way back to the lab. I'll see you in a few.'

Darby hung up and dialled Warner's number.

'Warner.'

'It's Darby. I've –'

'Your computer guy still hasn't broken through the password protection. The commissioner is here, and she wants to know if you spoke to –'

'Listen to me for a moment.' Darby moved across the living room, heading for the basement door to lock down the bulkhead. 'I've come across some information regarding the binoculars we found in the woods. A fingerprint. It –'

A shadow moved in the corner of her eye. She turned to the dark hall and caught sight of the butt end of a shotgun as it slammed against the side of her head.

58

'It was one of those wrong place, wrong time kind of things,' Father Humphrey said.

Jamie's eyes fluttered open. He was still lying on her bed, still holding the glass against his stomach and staring up at the ceiling. The bottle of Johnnie Walker, she noticed, was almost empty. *How long have I been out?*

'Danny was doing this home extension for a . . . mutual friend, I guess you could say. This gentleman was looking to fix up a house rather quickly, turn it around and put it back on the market – he's an absolute genius when it comes to property, this man. He's made a fortune. I knew Danny was struggling to get his business off the ground so I gave him Danny's name.

'And your husband jumped at the opportunity, Jamie. I mean he jumped through *hoops* when he found out this gentleman was willing to pay cash to get the job done fast. No receipts, nothing to report to the IRS. You should have seen the look in Danny's eyes. It was like I handed him a winning lottery ticket.'

Humphrey grinned, proud of his magnanimous gesture, and took a long sip of his drink.

Jamie managed to lift her head. It took some effort

but not as much as before. That warm, blissful feeling from what seemed like hours ago had started to trickle away. Pain had started to seep through the cracks. She could feel a dull throb from where her head had hit the wall, the scratching and soreness around her throat from the priest's fingers.

'The gentleman who hired your husband was very impressed by the quality of your husband's work. Danny had a gift, no question – and by God, what a work ethic! He cleaned up the work site at the end of each day no matter how late it was, no matter how tired he felt, just in case this gentleman I mentioned decided to swing by and take a look around. Danny knew this was a big job for him and he wanted to impress. He probably should have just headed home instead of turning around to go back and clean up.'

She forced her head back, then let it roll to the side so she could see the hall.

'So your husband goes back to the house to clean up and he finds this man's wallet sitting on this half-finished kitchen worktop. Danny calls the man and leaves a message on his mobile. Your husband wants to impress, wants to show what a good guy he is, and you know what he did?'

Jamie didn't answer. She swallowed, tasting blood.

Michael pulled back the valance. She saw Carter. He was scared but no longer crying. He turned and whispered something to his brother.

'Your husband,' Humphrey said, 'remembers that

his client spends most of his time on his boat at the Marblehead Yacht Club. It seems the two of them had several conversations about boats, Danny being some sort of yachtsman-in-training. So instead of pocketing the wallet and going home, your husband, the kind and generous soul that he is, gets back in his car and drives an hour north to deliver the wallet to the marina, finds the boat and guess who he sees sitting on the deck or whatever it's called drinking beers along with his client?'

She wanted to hold Carter. Wanted to hold him and Michael in her hands and press their cheeks up against her and tell them how sorry she was for letting them down. Again. Wanted to scream the words so her boys could hear them, hear her hurt. Her guilt.

'Danny hands over the wallet,' Humphrey said, 'and his client tells him to stay for a beer. Only Danny refuses because he recognizes the man sitting on the deck – Francis Sullivan. Only Francis isn't going by that name any more, being dead and all. And, truth be told, he doesn't even look like Francis Sullivan, not with all the surgery he's had, and – wait, I forgot. You already know this part, don't you?'

Jamie watched as Michael slid his foot out from underneath the bed.

'*No*,' she said.

'Danny didn't tell you?' Humphrey said. 'I thought he would have shared this with you since you were a cop.'

Michael was inching out from underneath the bed.

'Cops,' Jamie said. 'Call . . . ah . . . cops.'

Humphrey propped his head up from the pillow. 'You called the cops?'

'No,' she said. 'Dan . . . ah . . . didn't . . . tell. Me.'

'Danny recognized Francis,' Humphrey said. 'Danny told me. I don't know what transpired at the marina, mind you, since Danny didn't give me the exact details when he came to confession. But I could tell your husband was having this . . . crisis of conscience, I guess you could call it, at having the cursed luck of actually *recognizing* Francis Sullivan. Danny did a little research on the internet, found out that Francis had died tragically at sea and felt that he should come forward with what he'd seen – he wasn't exactly sure if the man he saw was Frank Sullivan but he looked goddamn close. I couldn't let that happen.'

Michael had slid out from underneath the bed. Carter held up the valance, a finger pressed up against his lips, telling her to be quiet.

'I'm a man of God,' Humphrey said. 'I don't want you to be tortured to death. The man who's coming here, he's . . . he'll do things to you until you tell him the truth. Tell me what you did to Francis and I'll give you a hot shot now, have you ride a nice warm wave right up to the Lord Himself.'

Get him out of the house. It's the only way to keep the kids safe.

'Take . . . ah . . . you.'

Humphrey sat up and cupped a hand over his ear. 'What's that, love?'

'Take you ... to ... ah ... see, ah, him. Sullivan.'

'Where is he?'

'Show ... ah ... you.'

Downstairs a door opened and slammed shut.

'Too late now,' Humphrey said, sighing. 'You had your chance.'

59

Darby drifted back to consciousness, heading towards a hot, roaring pain that covered what felt like every square inch of her head, jaw and face. She thought she smelled fried seafood and it triggered a hazy childhood memory (*or is this a dream?* she wondered) of a summer sunset at Maine's Kennebunk Beach and her father sitting next to her on a blanket, paper plates of fried clams between them, the white, waxy paper fluttering in the soft, warm breeze blowing up from the water, where her mother walked along the shore collecting sea glass and shells that she'd later put in a glass vase inside the kitchen. Darby couldn't remember how old she'd been or what she and her father had talked about (although, given the season, it probably had something to do with baseball), and as her eyes fluttered open she had the sense that her father had, at least during that moment in time, been truly happy.

The room was semi-dark. Hot. Her head hung forward and she saw her lap. She was bound to a chair – hands tied behind her back, thick strands of rope wrapped around her thighs and ankles. Her head was no longer throbbing; it was screaming like a fire alarm, triggering her panic.

The pain can be managed, she told herself. *The pain can be managed.*

She took in a slow, deep breath, catching the faint smell of machine oil behind the fried seafood.

'How's your head?' a man asked.

Darby swallowed, tasting blood. She took another deep breath and held it as she slowly lifted her head.

To her left, large bay windows dripping with rain. They looked out to a street light, the sky dark beyond the glass. Dull yellow squares of light with shadows from the raindrops covered a pale-coloured wall in front of her and, just a few feet away, the scarred top of a wooden table littered with paper cups, green beer bottles and a box that had probably been used to carry the grease-spotted cartons of fried clams, scallops and shrimp set up in front of the man who had talked to Baxter.

The driver of the brown van – the man who'd worn the tactical vest and left the blister pack of nicotine gum – sat on the other side of the table. Special Agent Jack King, or whatever name he was going by now, wore a dark shirt, no tie. She could see a small gold cross hanging from a chain.

Darby opened her mouth, relieved to discover she could move her jaw. 'How many times did you hit me with the shotgun?'

'Just once,' King said. Beads of sweat dripped down his bald head. 'When you fell to the floor, I switched to these.'

He held up his hands. They were covered in black leather gloves. 'They're lined with lead powder.'

That explained how he had managed to knock loose her cheek implant. She could feel it sliding underneath the swollen, throbbing mess of torn skin. He had split her stitches.

'My apologies for hitting you so hard,' he said, picking up a plastic fork, 'but I was told you knew how to handle yourself – "she's James Bond with tits" was what I was told. So I worked you over a little extra just to make sure you'd cooperate long enough for me to tie you up and bring you to the boot.'

He speared his fork into a fried scallop, grinning as he dunked it into a container of tartar sauce. Darby took in another deep breath, her chest constricting against the rope, and held it for a count of three.

'Nice car, by the way,' King said. 'Goddamn shame to ruin a car like that, but it had to be done.'

Darby exhaled slowly through her nose. Deep, slow breathing; that was the key to managing the pain, to keeping it at bay and keeping her heart rate low and her muscles relaxed. *The pain can be managed*, she told herself, taking in another slow, deep breath through her nose. *I can manage the pain. The pain can be managed. I manage the pain.*

'You don't mind if I eat, do you?' King asked. 'I've got a long night ahead of me and I hate working on an empty stomach.'

'Go right on ahead, Special Agent King.'

He ate another fried shrimp. 'How'd you find out?'

'Sorry, but that information is confidential.'

King grinned as he chewed. Darby spotted her SIG lying next to her mobile phone on the table. She stared at the nine, which was less than two feet away. *If I could only cut through this rope I –*

She straightened and pressed her back against the chair, hot bolts of pain slamming through the centre of her skull and drilling their way down her spine. She gritted her teeth, hissing.

THE PAIN CAN BE MANAGED.

'You want some Percocet?' King asked, forking another shrimp.

I CAN MANAGE THE PAIN.

'I can give you some,' he said. 'Percocet, Oxy, whatever you need.'

'No.'

'How about a beer? I've got Rolling Rock and Becks.'

'Maybe later, after you've been arrested.'

'You're an original, McCormick, I'll give you that. Your old man would be proud of you.'

'How do you know him?' Darby wiggled her fingers. She could feel the damp fabric of her shirt, the back waistband of her trousers. The rope didn't have much give; she felt it biting into the skin of her wrists.

'I never met him personally; just heard stories,' King said.

'Were you the one who killed him?'

He seemed to be considering the question when a mobile phone chimed. Hers. She saw the light come to life on the cracked screen.

King picked it up. Not a phone call; a text message. He read the screen and stopped chewing.

She pinched her belt between her fingers and pulled. 'Anything good?'

'Someone named Madeira James sent you an email, wants you to call her immediately.'

'Great. Can I borrow my phone for a moment?'

King didn't answer but continued reading the message.

Darby moved the belt another quarter of an inch. The buckle got caught on a trouser loop.

He read the message for what seemed like a long time. He put the phone down and grabbed a bottle of Rolling Rock. His face had changed.

'Bad news?' she asked.

'Nothing we can't handle.' He wiped his mouth. 'Got a proposition for you.'

'I'm all ears.'

'Kendra Sheppard had audiotapes, pictures and notes on certain people. Hard copy, in other words. We haven't been able to locate it.'

'That's too bad.'

'We need these files, so you have to tell me where they are. You tell me where Kendra hid these audiotapes, notes and whatever else she had, and I might be willing to answer some of those nagging questions you've got about your old man.'

'You're the one who tortured her to death – what did she tell you?'

'I wasn't there, I was –'

'You were in the woods. You came there to retrieve your friend.'

'Bingo. Kendra didn't, ah, hand over the information that was requested. My interest – *your* interest – is these tapes and whatever else Kendra has. I need to know where they are.'

'Small problem,' she said.

'And what might that be?'

'Kendra was dead when I found her. I mean, really dead. Unlike you, she didn't manage to rise from the ashes. How did you manage to pull off such a great disappearing act?'

'What did Sean tell you?'

'He didn't tell me anything.'

'You talked to Ezekiel.'

'Who?'

He sighed. 'We know Kendra visited him. And we know you talked to him.'

'How do you know that?'

'A little birdie told me. Problem is, the schizo shithead did that whispering trick and we couldn't hear so good. The listening devices we planted in there, as good as they are, there's still a lot of interference. The conversation you had with him, we can have it enhanced, but that's going to take some time, so I decided to bring you here and jump to the chase.'

Darby pulled on the belt – not an easy thing to do with only two fingers.

'You can stop your fidgeting,' King said. 'Even if you pull some sort of Houdini act, you're not going anywhere. You'd be dead before you reached the front door.'

'Brought your friends with you?'

'Yes, the whole gang is here. Now, back to Ezekiel. What did you two talk about?'

'Ask him.'

'No can do. He hanged himself in his cell this afternoon.' King winked, then popped a fried clam into his mouth.

Darby pulled on the belt. 'I take it his suicide wasn't voluntary.'

'We hired someone on the inside. We've got people everywhere.'

'How many people are involved in your little club again?'

'Too many, if you want to know the truth.'

'You should have hired someone to remove your fingerprints from the database.'

The humour left King's face.

'That's probably why you're in such a hurry, right?' Darby gave another hard tug on the belt. 'Now that your prints and Special Agent Alan's prints rang the cherries on the *Federal*-owned database, I'm figuring the head of the Boston office is getting a call asking why the prints of not one but *two* dead Federal agents have suddenly appeared. Oh, and a body. I forgot we have Special Agent Alan's body in a freezer.'

'It doesn't have to be painful,' King said. 'I can make it quick.'

'Good to know.'

'How much longer are you going to keep up the Clint Eastwood tough-guy routine?'

'I don't know. How much time do we have?'

King stood. Darby let go of her belt as he came around the table. He stepped behind her and gripped the back of the chair.

60

Darby clamped down hard on her panic.

The pain, she told herself. *Whatever happens, the pain can be managed and I can manage the pain, I CAN MAN–*

King spun her around to a long, wide corridor of empty bays in various states of decay – an abandoned automotive garage, judging by the looks of it. King pushed her across the bumpy concrete floor. Some windows were boarded up. At the far end, to the left, she could make out what looked like a door. No one else was in here.

The chair stopped moving. She heard a door open behind her. King grabbed the back of her chair again and shoved her into another semi-dark room with a single window. The noisy wheels squeaked as they rolled across the floor. Darker in here but just as hot.

Her knees slammed against a wall. Her head rattled, the pain screaming again, and for a moment she thought her skull would explode from the sheer force of it.

King turned her around to face an empty wooden chair. It sat in the corner, covered by shadows. King took the chair – no, not King. Artie Pine.

'Talk some sense into her, Artie,' King said as he walked away, 'or we'll do it my way.'

Pine sat, the chair groaning beneath his enormous bulk. He had changed his clothes since she'd seen him at the hospital this morning. She couldn't see his face – too many shadows – but she caught the slight rise in his chest, heard the quiet wheeze coming from his mouth.

A door slammed shut somewhere outside the room. *The door is at the end of the corridor*, she thought, wondering if that was the only way in and out of the bay.

Safe from Pine's gaze, she gripped the belt again and started pulling.

'For whatever it's worth, I'm sorry,' Pine said in a quiet voice. 'I didn't want it to go down like this.'

She didn't speak. *Let him think I'm disoriented.*

'Who's . . . that?'

'It's Artie.'

Darby licked her lips, giving the belt another hard tug. It caught on another trouser loop.

'Artie, what . . . What are you doing here?'

'You heard King. I'm trying to talk some sense into you.' His voice was soft and kind. 'Darby, these guys have invested a lot of time and energy into finding these tapes. If you don't tell me where they are, then King is going to have a run at you. Trust me, you don't want that.'

'Are you on these tapes? Is that why you're working with them?'

'This isn't one of those shitty Bond movies where I reveal all the secrets before you die.'

The buckle finally slid underneath the trouser loop. One more to go.

'Tell me where Kendra's hiding the tapes,' he said, 'or I'll have to bring King back.'

'Did you pull the trigger, Artie? Or did you set my father up? Which is it?'

Pine cleared his throat. 'What did Ezekiel tell you?'

Buy some time.

'He told me that Kendra found out about the FBI, how they set up a Federal agent as the head of the Irish mafia – Ben Masters. Is it true?'

He sighed. 'We don't have time for this.'

'It's a simple yes or no question.'

'Yes. Yes, it's true. The Feds planted one of their own agents as the head of the Irish mafia.'

'A man who turned out to be a serial killer.'

'Congrats, you connected all the dots.'

The buckle caught on the last trouser loop.

'What about the Feds placing witnesses and informants inside witness protection and making them disappear?'

'They never went inside witness protection,' he said.

'They just disappeared.'

'Yes. Now –'

'You set up my father, didn't you?'

Pine didn't answer.

'Ezekiel told me my father had someone watching the hotel – someone he trusted,' she said. 'I'm assuming that person was you.'

'I need to know where Kendra kept the tapes and notes. I need that evidence. We can't afford to have it floating around out there. You can see why they're anxious to find it.'

'She didn't tell Ezekiel where she kept the actual tapes, photos and assorted notes on Frank Sullivan – I mean, Ben Masters.' The buckle was still caught on the last trouser loop. 'That's the God's honest truth. I'd cross my heart, hope to die and all of that, but my hands are . . . well, you know.'

Pine stood.

Keep stalling him.

'I know where the copies are.' She bucked against the restraints, giving the belt another hard tug. Her head didn't like the movements; bile shot up her throat. She kept tugging . . . tugging . . . there.

'I'm listening,' he said.

'Give me a moment, my head . . . it's hard to concentrate.' She stretched her fingers, the rope biting into her wrists. She felt the belt buckle. 'I feel like I'm going to throw up.'

Pine leaned sideways against the windowsill, his arms crossed over his chest. She grabbed the belt buckle and pulled the blade from its sheath.

'I don't know where she kept the actual tapes and files, but I know she carried copies.' Darby drew out the words, trying to buy herself some time. 'She kept copies of everything on a USB drive. Scanned documents. Audio files and pictures. I don't know where the originals are.'

'Did you see them? These scanned documents?'

'I did. We're talking dozens and dozens of items.'

The handle gripped between her fingers, she moved the blade around and started sawing through the rope binding her wrists.

'What was on them?' Pine asked, growing impatient.

'You promise you'll make it quick? I don't think I can stand any more pain.'

Pine sat back in his chair and wheeled closer, his jowls jiggling. She could smell the cigar smoke as he placed his hands on her knees. 'You have my word.'

'You've got to answer some questions for me first. I think I deserve that.'

He sighed. 'Make it quick.'

Darby felt the tension in a piece of rope snap in half. 'How did they find Kendra?'

'Wexler – Dr Wexler, the owner of the house. He called me, said Kendra had phoned him to ask if she could stay at his house for a couple of days.'

'Why did Wexler call you?'

'We … worked together. He performed certain emergency medical services for us when he lived in Charlestown. You can't go to a hospital with a bullet or knife wound.'

'How does Kendra know him?'

'Wexler was her doctor in Charlestown. She kept seeing him when he moved to Belham.'

'She just phoned him out of the blue?'

'Yes. It was a stroke of luck.'

For you, Darby thought, working the blade and also wondering just how many people this group of Feds had on their payroll.

Coop's words came back to her: *These guys are slick. They never go to jail. They always have inside help.*

'Kendra couldn't stay at a hotel,' Pine said. 'You can't pay cash any more, you need a credit card. Kendra needed a place to stay for a few days, and she didn't want to stay anywhere near Charlestown, so she decided to take a chance, tracked down Wexler and called him. He offered her the use of his house.'

'And then took a sudden vacation so you could call your friends and set her up.'

'Now it's your turn.'

His phone rang. He answered it but didn't talk.

She wiggled her right hand out from the rope, felt it slip across her fingers and drop to the floor. Shit. *It's dark in here so just hope Pine doesn't see it.* She went to work on her left hand, sawing quickly, the blade cutting and nicking the skin along her wrist, palm and fingers.

Pine hung up. 'We've got two minutes or else King is coming in.'

'The files are password protected.'

'They're audio tapes. You can't put passwords on cassette tapes.'

'They're audio *files*. You know what a flash drive is?'

'No.'

'It's a little hard drive. You slide it into the USB port of your computer. Kendra transferred the audio tapes into MP3 files, took her notes and scanned them, and put everything on to this little flash drive that fit nicely inside a watch.'

'I want the hard copies.'

'I don't know where they are. But the commissioner has the USB drive. Once the computer guys crack the password, she'll have everything.'

Pine's eyes narrowed. 'Are you screwing with me?'

'Call her. I'm sure she'd love to hear from you.'

He stood and took out his phone. Darby tried to pull her left hand free.

It was stuck.

Pine didn't call Chadzynski; he spoke with King. She could make out his voice echoing over the tiny speaker in the quiet room.

Pine's face remained curiously blank, like that of a man waiting for a bus. He stood only a few feet away. She couldn't stand; her ankles were still bound to the chair legs. If she could only get one foot free . . .

Both your hands are free and he's only holding his phone,

403

not a weapon; you're going to have to make a move now before he —

Pine hung up. Darby came around with the knife, the four-inch blade sticking out between her fingers, and lurched.

61

Darby sunk the blade deep into Pine's scrotum. He howled and she twisted the blade once before yanking it free.

His hands flew to his groin, and when he buckled she aimed for his throat. He turned too quickly and the blade hit his cheek, sliding across the bone. He staggered and tripped. His enormous bulk toppled against her, shooting the chair backwards.

She banged up against the wall but didn't drop the knife. She started sawing away at the rope around her right ankle.

Pine was rolling on the ground, screaming, hands still cupped over his groin and blood spurting between his fingers. The screams echoed through the small room and she was sure King and whoever else was in here had heard them and were now running this way.

Snap and a piece of rope cut away.

'*You bitch,*' he wailed. '*You goddamn bitch, you'll pay, you're going to PAY.*'

One, two, three cuts and her right foot was free.

Pine, panting and howling, face red from the excruciating pain, reached for the sidearm clipped to his belt. She got to her feet, and with the use of one leg moved to him, dragging the chair behind her.

She jumped on top of him. Slammed her knee deep into his groin and when he howled she hit his throat. He started gurgling and she hit his throat again. She broke his nose. Then she got behind him and snapped his neck, and his arms and legs stopped moving, as if they had suddenly given up.

She pulled the sidearm from his holster. A Glock. She found the knife on the floor, dropped the nine next to her and started cutting.

Snap on a piece of rope binding her left ankle.

A door slammed open outside.

Snap and another piece of rope gave way.

Footsteps – walking, not running.

Snap, snap, snap and she twisted her ankle free.

King appeared in the doorway, expecting to see Artie alive and her dead. Surprise bloomed on his face when he saw her lying sideways against the floor holding a nine.

She fired. One shot and half his head disappeared.

Darby scrambled to her feet. King's body jerked and twitched on the floor. Dead this time. Dead.

'Please.'

Pine's wheezing, cracking voice.

He stared up at her in horror. He lay still on the floor, bleeding out from his groin.

'I can't . . . I can't feel my . . . I can't move my arms or legs.'

'You're paralysed,' she said. 'I made you a quadriplegic. Think about me when they're changing your
diapers in prison.'

'*Please . . . please don't leave me like this, the pain . . .*'

His words trailed off as Darby stepped over King's
body and started to check the garage.

Clear.

She ran back to find the wooden table that held her
SIG and phone. She slid the gun inside her holster.
Picked up the phone and tucked it inside her pocket.

A shotgun rested at an angle against the wall – a Remington 870 police entry with a fourteen-inch barrel, magazine extender, mounted tactical light and side saddle
holding six low-recoil shells. Perfect. She tucked Pine's
nine in the back waistband of her trousers, switched to
the shotgun and carried it with her as she moved, her
eyes locked on the door at the far end of the bay.

She remembered that Madeira James from Reynolds Engineering Systems had sent a message. *Wants
you to call her immediately*, King had said before reading
the message. When he put the phone down, his face
had changed.

Bad news? she had asked.

Nothing we can't handle, he said.

She ducked into one of the empty rooms and took
out the phone. Turned it on and saw the woman's
message and an attachment. She opened it and
scanned the text quickly. Then she turned the phone
off and tucked it back inside her pocket.

Darby moved out of the room and crept towards the door, staring down the shotgun sight. A shot had gone off. If there were other people in here, they'd coming running. They'd come running anyway, when King and Pine didn't return. She wondered how many people were in here with her. She had plenty of ammo but no body armour, no helmet or smoke grenades. No hostage situation either. Play it safe. Be patient.

Plenty of room to the right side of the door. Hide there. Wait for it to swing open and then come out from behind it.

She waited.

Two minutes passed.

Four minutes.

Six.

Crouching low, she threw the door open and backed away.

No gunshots.

She turned with the shotgun, ready to fire, saw nothing but a short, narrow corridor covered in shadows.

She moved down the corridor and when it ended she again crouched low against the wall. Heard the slow, steady purr of a car engine.

She spun around the corner with the shotgun. Another corridor. Dim light at the far end. She moved silently across the floor breathing in the hot, musty air. She paused at the corner. Waited. Listened for movement underneath the steady rain drumming on the roof and what sounded like a car engine idling.

Darby turned another corner and looked down the ghost ring sights at the calm face of Boston Police Commissioner Christina Chadzynski.

62

Chadzynski sat in front of a small laptop set up on an old desk. In the light coming from the computer screen Darby could see the pair of headphones wrapped around the woman's ears. The woman had a pleasant, almost angelic look on her face.

Darby heard a door slam shut, followed by the sound of a car driving away.

The corridor was maybe twenty feet long. She moved down it and heard a phone ring. A small square of light came to life on the desk. Chadzynski took off her headphones, letting them rest on her neck, and reached for the phone, which lay next to a shotgun. Both hands were covered with latex gloves.

'Freeze,' Darby said, and switched on the tactical light.

Chadzynski's face lit up with surprise. Then it disappeared, swept back underneath her cool composure.

'Hands on your head,' Darby said. 'Nice and slow.'

Chadzynski took off the headphones and placed them on the desk. She didn't stand.

Darby stood in front of her. Chadzynski leaned back in the chair and crossed her legs. Dust floated in the light coming from the computer screen.

'Who else is here?'

'I don't know,' Chadzynski said. No nervous hitch in her voice. She was in complete control of her emotions. 'I arrived only a few minutes ago. You'd have to ask Mr King. Since I don't see him, I'm left to assume he's dead.'

'You assume correctly. Place your hands on your head.'

'I have a way out of this for you.'

'Shut up.'

'My car is right out front. We can leave together. If you play your cards right, you'll come out of this looking like a hero. I can help you towards that end. I recommend –'

Darby swung the butt stock and raked it across the side of the woman's head.

The force knocked the commissioner off her chair.

Darby fitted the shotgun's strap over her shoulder and switched to Pine's Glock. Then she took out her phone and pressed a few of its keys.

'There's no one here but the two of us now,' Chadzynski said from the floor. 'It will be my word against yours. And I can assure you I'll win. I suggest you take me up on my original offer. If you don't, you'll never hold up under the scrutiny. The evidence is already stacked against you.'

Darby placed the phone on the desk. 'What evidence?'

'Recognize the computer? It's yours.'

Darby glanced quickly at the laptop, a white Apple iMac. She owned one. On the screen, she saw the audio files from Kendra Sheppard's flash drive. 'You broke the password.'

'And we copied the files on to your home computer,' Chadzynski said. 'Paperwork has been filed to show you checked Kendra Sheppard's flash drive out of evidence – Anti-Corruption has it in their hands right now. Since the flash drive is now gone, Internal Affairs will have no choice but to assume you destroyed it. I can, however, make it all disappear with one phone call.'

'You've got all the angles figured out, don't you? Know how to make evidence disappear, have people plant bombs inside a house and on my crime scene –'

'Do you want to spend the rest of your life in jail? We have enough evidence to show you deliberately tampered with these cases. How you deliberately destroyed evidence to protect your father. The boxes of evidence and murder book pertaining to your father? The ones that are supposed to be in storage? They're currently in a safe location with paperwork that leads back to you. The way the story will go down is that you came across evidence that showed your father was working for Frank Sullivan. He'll be known as a corrupt cop – as will you. I don't think you want that.'

'I know about your trip to Reynolds Engineering Systems. You went there last year with Lieutenant

Warner. That round we found inside the Belham house, the rounds we found in Kevin Reynolds's basement? They came from a batch of test ammo that mysteriously disappeared on the day you and Warner were there. The company was kind enough to send me the list.'

Chadzynski scrambled up into a sitting position, eyes blinking. Her small hand with its perfectly manicured fingers and big, sparking diamonds trembled as she touched the side of her face. The butt stock had split the skin above her cheek.

The woman wobbled, stunned and confused. She placed a hand on the floor for balance.

'Did you steal the ammo and the Glock eighteen?' Darby asked. 'Or did you have your pet do it?'

Chadzynski gripped the edge of the desk and slowly got to her feet.

'I'm guessing you let Warner do it,' Darby said. 'You knew that kind of ammo would be next to impossible to trace because it doesn't exist on the market. He was inside the Belham house, wasn't he? He was there when they killed Kendra Sheppard.'

'I can assure you he wasn't.'

'Then why did he kill Special Agent Alan?'

'He didn't.'

'Then who did?'

'You already know.'

'Tell me anyway.'

'Russo,' Chadzynski said.

413

'He's dead.'

'Not the wife. The wife is still alive and, coincidentally, living in the same house. She confessed to killing Ben Masters and the Federal agent, Alan.'

Darby thought back to that moment inside the lab with Randy Scott and Mark Alves. The footprints recovered from the deck steps matched the footprints found in the woods near the binoculars – a woman's size nine sneaker. A *woman* had been watching from the woods.

'Where is she?'

'She's still living in Wellesley,' Chadzynski said.

'Where is she right *now*?'

Chadzynski wouldn't answer.

'Call and find out,' Darby said.

'No.'

'Hands on your head, Commissioner. You're under arrest.'

Chadzynski gripped the bottom lapels of her suit jacket and gave them a sharp tug, straightening out the fabric.

'This list you have from RES, it won't hold up in court. You know I'm right.'

'We'll have to wait and see.'

'There are forces at work, people you'll never be able to find,' Chadzynski said. 'Arrest me and you'll be signing your own warrant.'

'You're probably right about that. That's why I recorded our conversation.' Darby picked up her phone. 'Who killed my father?'

'Let me use the phone and I'll tell you.'

'No.'

'I know where all the missing pieces are buried. You *need* me.'

Chadzynski grinned, probably thinking about her Rolodex full of people who could pull the necessary levers, make this moment disappear as if it were nothing more than a bad dream. She already owned the Anti-Corruption Unit.

She had Warner or one of her other henchmen plant evidence and remove my father's murder book and evidence files from the storage unit – she's spent years doctoring evidence or making it disappear to suit her needs. She killed my father and she –

Darby squeezed the trigger.

The shot blew out the back of the police commissioner's head.

Darby ran back to the main bay to Pine. She checked his pulse, and was unsurprised to find him dead. He had bled out.

She wiped down the Glock with her shirt-tail and dropped it on the floor.

Standing back behind the desk with her laptop, Darby used her shirt to pick up the shotgun. She dropped it next to Chadzynski, thinking about Sean Sheppard lying in a coma, brain dead, like her father.

63

Darby got down on her knees, warm blooding spilling out across the floor and touching her skin. She searched Chadzynski's pockets. No flash drive but she found car keys.

She switched to the shotgun she was carrying and opened the door. The police commissioner's sleek black Mercedes sat a few feet away.

There were no other vehicles in the car park.

She turned on the gun's tactical light and ran through the rain to the front of the building. The door and windows were boarded. She looked for a number – there, a sign above the door. She shielded her eyes from the rain and read the faded letters: DELANEY'S AUTOMOTIVE GARAGE.

Sitting behind the wheel, the shotgun resting on the floor of the passenger seat, she started the car. The Mercedes had a GPS navigation system built into the console. Her location was displayed on the screen. Perfect.

She drove away from the building, then turned around so she could watch it.

The wipers thumping back and forth, she dialled Randy Scott's mobile number.

'Randy Scott.'

'Please tell me you're still at the lab.'

'I am.'

Sweet relief flooded her.

'Darby.' His voice was hesitant, nervous. 'I don't know if –'

'Don't talk, just listen. I need Dan Russo's address.'

'I don't have access to the homicide database.'

'I know, I'll give you my password. Go in my office –'

'I can't. They've sealed it off.'

'Who sealed it off?'

'The commissioner was here earlier and she . . . she told us that you tampered with evidence. She has half the Boston police department looking for you and Coop.'

'It's bullshit. I'll prove it to you. I have Chadzynski's confession recorded on my phone. I'll send it to you, then I'm going to lead you to her body. You and Mark. I want –'

'She's dead.'

'*Listen to me.* I need you two here to secure the scene. First, I want you to go to the fingerprint database and give me the address that's listed with Dan Russo's name. Will you do that?'

'Hold on.'

Darby pulled out of the gate. The garage sat at the far end of a dead-end road. She looked at the tenement-type buildings and thought she was in East

Boston or Chelsea. She suspected this was a neighbourhood used to gunshots. There was a good amount of distance between the garage and the buildings. With the rain, she doubted anyone had heard anything.

Randy finally came back on the line and gave her a Wellesley address. She plugged it into the GPS.

'I need you to write down an address,' she said.

'Go ahead.'

Darby gave it to him. 'I want you to come here with Mark and photograph and document every piece of evidence. Go in through the side door and you'll find a laptop computer on a desk; there are audio files on it. You're to confiscate that immediately. Under no circumstances are you to let anyone touch it. Put it into evidence and don't let it out of your sight. After you're done, call the police. Tell them everything I told you.'

'Got it.'

'Can your phone accept audio files?'

'As far as I know it can.'

'I'll send you the audio file of my conversation with the commissioner.'

She hung up and called directory inquiries. There was only one listing for Russo. It matched the address Randy had given her.

Darby drove, dividing her attention between the road and the phone. She sent a copy of her recorded conversation to Randy and Mark. She also sent a copy to Coop.

64

Jamie could no longer see clearly. Kevin Reynolds had wasted no time in hitting her after she'd refused to answer his questions about the whereabouts of his partner, Ben Masters. Reynolds had hit her face so many times her eyes had almost completely swollen shut. When she still refused to answer, he kicked her in the chest so hard her chair had toppled against the floor, where she screamed the word 'stay' the entire time.

Thank God for Michael. Michael had kept his cool. Michael was still hiding, protecting his brother instead of trying to be a hero.

Reynolds had kicked again and again – in the stomach, in the shins; he had slammed his foot down against her hand and broken several of her fingers. Finally her mind snapped from the excruciating pain and she admitted to killing Ben Masters. It shamed her, admitting this. Reynolds wanted details. Wanted to know how she had killed him and where she had buried him. She came close to saying it. She was delirious with pain and could no longer think clearly. And in the midst of all of this her mind clutched the brass ring, the only thing that was keeping her alive: the location of Ben's body. She had to convince Reynolds and Humphrey to take her out of the house so they could drive to the location of the body. Once the house was empty, the kids would be safe, and Michael could call the police.

Jamie lay sideways against the floor, struggling to breathe. She was pretty sure Reynolds had broken several of her ribs.

'Take . . . you,' she said.

Reynolds stood somewhere in front of her. She could hear his sneakers pacing the carpet near her head, and he was breathing hard – not from the physical exertion but from anger.

'Take,' she said again. 'Take . . . ah . . . ah . . . you.'

Humphrey said, 'She's speaking.'

Jamie cracked an eye open and saw Reynolds's blurry shape leaning close to her.

'What's that, hon?'

'Take . . . you . . . ah . . . there.'

'I want you to tell me where he is.'

'Take . . . take . . . you.'

Humphrey said, 'Let her take us there, Kevin. What's the harm?'

'I still don't believe her,' Reynolds said. 'I think she's got him stashed away somewhere. I'm smelling a trap. This cunt is real crafty, was going to ambush me this morning. Ain't that right, sweetheart?'

Reynolds leaned in closer. 'You were a cop. You know who Ben is, don't you? Your husband told you,

I *know* it. Ben's worth more to you alive than dead. You call one of your friends on the force and tell them what you saw in the basement?'

Jamie licked her lips. It took a great effort to speak. 'No.'

'You're more stubborn than your husband. But I'm aiming to fix that.'

Jamie thought she heard a car door slam shut.

Humphrey said, 'Clean-up crew is here.'

'Tell them to pull into the garage,' Reynolds said. 'I want to load her into the van.' Footsteps walked past her and then she felt Reynolds grip the back of her chair and pull her up into a sitting position.

Now she felt his breath, heavy with booze and cigarettes, against her ear. 'I'm going to get you to talk. I don't care how long it takes or what I have to do, one way or another, you're going to tell me every little detail.'

65

Darby took the corner too quickly. The tyres skidded across the wet pavement as she pulled on to a long suburban street full of big homes and nice lawns. Lots of space between the houses, lots of the windows dark. She drove out of the skid and heard the GPS's computerized voice giving her the directions. The house she was looking for would be on her left, less than half a mile up the road.

Tearing down the street, she saw a brown van parked in a driveway. Through an open garage door, she took in the quick movements of three men dressed in suits and carrying big plastic tackle-boxes and large brief-cases. Her attention was fixed on the man lighting a cigarette by the van's open door – the man who had checked her car for bugs, the head of Chadzynski's Anti-Corruption Unit, Lieutenant Warner.

Warner saw the Mercedes and looked puzzled but not afraid – puzzled as to why his boss, the police commissioner, had decided to come here.

Concerned now, he stared at the Mercedes's tinted windows as he jogged across the front lawn. Darby tucked the SIG underneath her thigh, pinning the gun to the seat. Then she hit the gas.

The car bumped over the pavement and then tore across the front lawn, spitting up grass and dirt.

Warner turned, the cigarette dropping from his mouth, and started to run.

Darby hit the back of his legs. He bounced up over the bonnet. His head slammed against the windscreen, showering the glass in a web of cracks, and she saw his cheap suit disappear above her as he tumbled across the roof.

Gripping the wheel with both hands, she slammed on the brakes and drove out of the skid to prevent a head-on collision with the car parked at the top of the driveway. She slammed into it sideways in a screech of crushing metal and exploding glass.

The Mercedes came to a jarring stop. Darby was thrown against her seatbelt. She unbuckled it, quickly threaded the shotgun strap over her head and threw open the door.

Warner was on the front lawn. She could see him trying to get to his feet. She brought up the SIG and hit him twice with a double tap.

She swung her weapon to the garage, to a man in a dark suit standing in a doorway at the top of the steps. He let go of the blue tackle box in his hands and reached underneath his suit jacket for his sidearm.

Two shots to the chest and he went down, collapsing back inside the house.

She was about to move into the minivan parked in the garage when she saw a second man aiming a Glock.

Darby ducked behind the minivan as he fired. The windows exploded, glass raining down on her, and he kept firing. She counted the shots as she inched her way along the back bumper. She waited until she heard him running.

The door slammed shut. Darby came up and fired two shots against the door.

Sweep the garage.

Clear.

She moved up the steps and checked the doorknob. Locked. She hit the button to close the garage door and then killed the lights.

Switching to the shotgun, she blew off the hinges. Then she blew out the doorknob. She kicked the door down and swung to one side.

Muzzle flashes came from inside the hall. She swung the shotgun around and fired. Someone screamed and she pressed the trigger. *Click*. She pumped more rounds into the shotgun, then came around and fired again and again as she moved inside the house.

66

The hall, about twenty feet long, led directly into a brightly lit kitchen of beige tiles and oak cupboards. One man lay dead on the floor and another one was crawling away, trying to hide behind the kitchen island. The shotgun blast had shredded most of one leg.

Darby fired another shot at his chest and swung her attention to her right, her weak spot – the half-closed wooden door. She kicked it open and ducked to the side, expecting gunfire. Silence. No movement. She swung around and saw a ceiling lamp hanging above a small room with a bench built into the wall.

She ducked into a small room. She couldn't use the shotgun in a hostage situation – no accuracy. She threaded the Remington's strap across her shoulder and switched back to the SIG. Six shots left in the clip and a fresh one jammed in her pocket.

The shotgun resting against her back, Darby turned and checked the hall. Clear.

She looked at the man lying on the floor, bleeding out. He didn't move. Had to make sure he was dead. She fired a round into his back. He didn't move. One of her shotgun rounds had hit a plastic toolbox similar to the one she used for her forensics kit. Through the broken plastic she saw cleaning supplies – towels, latex gloves and small bottles of bleach leaking on to the tiles.

She stepped over the dead man's body, her boots sliding across the bloody floor, and stuck close to the wall as she crept towards the kitchen, thankful that the house was lit up.

Past the kitchen, she saw a living room. Light on in there. TV in the far-right corner, a long sofa and chair. Across from the kitchen island, an entranceway, probably for the dining room. Both good hiding spots – unless they were concealed upstairs. She wished she had her tactical vest. Wished she could kill the lights and go through this strange house with night vision.

Warner was dead. Two of his partners were dead. How many others were in here?

Too quiet.

Where were they hiding?

Have to go in hot. Fire fast and make it count.

She kept moving, hands steady on the SIG.

No room for error.

Legs steady.

No room for error.

Movement.

A man spun around the corner of the living room. Darby hit him in the chest. She fired three more rounds as he stumbled. One round went too high and hit the TV screen, exploding the glass.

She caught a blur of movement to her left as another man dashed into the kitchen. No time to spin around and fire; she dropped to the floor. Rapid-fire went over her head – the type that came from an automatic weapon.

The shotgun slammed against her back. Spent shells dropped against the floor as she swung her leg around and, using all her weight, kicked her assailant behind his knee.

Kevin Reynolds was knocked off balance. He crashed backwards against one of the kitchen island's bar stools. She brought up the SIG, fired a round into his stomach and spun her weapon to the foyer. Clear.

Darby scrambled to her feet and stood back against the wall. She felt her mobile phone vibrating inside her pocket as Reynolds screamed, writhing around the floor in pain. His weapon, a Glock with an extended magazine, lay only a few feet from his face. He saw it. His hand crept across the floor.

'Don't,' she said.

He reached for it.

Darby shot his hand. Reynolds screamed and she slid into the top part of the foyer, aiming her weapon at the stairs. Clear. She swung around and checked the living room. Clear. She returned to the kitchen and kicked his weapon away. He grabbed her ankle with his good hand, and she kicked his head and broke his nose. He wailed, his legs thrashing, knocking over more stools and a small table with a vase. The sound of the crashing glass and his screaming covered her footsteps as she bolted across the kitchen expecting gunfire.

No shots, and now she was inside the living room checking all of her blind spots. She saw only the dead man. Back to the kitchen. Reynolds had propped himself up on his forearm. Blubbering, he tried to crawl across the floor, heading for the blasted door leading to the garage.

Darby kicked the back of his head. Eyes moving around the kitchen and foyer, she whipped the hand-cuffs off her belt. She dropped them on Reynolds's back, then grabbed both of his hands and cuffed him.

She yanked Reynolds by the back of his hair, wanting to snap his neck.

'How many others are in here?'

He wouldn't answer.

Darby stood up and fired a round into his ass.

Reynolds howled in pain, the sound masking her footsteps as she doubled back through the dining room. Darby turned the corner and aimed her weapon at the top of the stairs.

Dim light came from an opened door to the right. A bathroom across the top of the steps. To her left, covered in shadows, a closed door.

Reynolds kept screaming as she moved up the steps, watching for movement, for shadows. Her eyes darted from the room with the light to the hall hidden behind her, her weak spot. Check there first. She moved from the wall and leaned her weight against the steps, still paying close attention to the light. She reached the top, saw the closed bedroom door. Next to it, an opened bedroom covered in darkness. She wished she had a tactical light and a stun or a smoke grenade.

Too exposed out here. She dived into the bathroom.

Someone was crying – a woman. The sound was coming from the bedroom to her left, the one with the light.

Hostage.

Across the hall she saw a fourth door leading into a bedroom covered in shadows. A bed and toys on the floor. She moved against the bathroom wall, near the doorway, and glanced quickly to an opened door in the middle of the hall. A lock and broken wood lay on the floor, the room beyond it pitch black.

Someone could be in one of those bedrooms, she thought. If she went out into the hall to deal with the hostage, she'd be exposed. Someone could swing around the corner from one of those bedrooms and fire a shot into her back.

No one had fired when she'd dived into the bathroom.

The woman's scream was a strange, strangled sound, as if she was fighting hard to breathe.

Punctured lung, Darby thought, and swung around the doorway.

A badly beaten woman was tied to a chair propped up against the wall. Standing behind her was a man dressed in a black shirt and white collar – a Catholic priest. A .32 revolver was gripped in his hands.

The priest fired, the round splintering the wood above her head. She crouched against the floor as he moved the gun to the woman.

Darby returned fire. The shot hit his shoulder. The priest fell back against the door behind him, slamming it shut. She fired again and saw the priest stumble against the lamp on the nightstand as she pushed herself back into the bathroom.

No gunshots. She checked the bedroom to her right. No movement. She ran to the hostage, slammed the door shut and kicked the priest's revolver underneath the bed. Checked the master bathroom. Clear. The bedroom door had a push-button lock. She hit it with her fist.

The priest had lost his glasses during the fall. He lay on his back, squirming, his shaking hand pressed up against the gunshot wound to his left shoulder. Both shots had hit him high on the chest and he was bleeding out on to the carpet.

The woman's head hung forward, limp, her scalp marred with what appeared to be surgical scars. Blood trickled from her swollen lips. Blood covered her T-shirt and shorts. Blood on the chair, blood on the carpet and walls. A tooth on the rug.

Darby wiped the sweat dripping down her face.

She stepped up to the woman and with her eyes on the priest said, 'I'm a police officer. You're safe.'

She removed her mobile and dialled 911. 'I think you've punctured a lung so I'm going to have to leave you right here until the ambulance arrives. If I lay you on the floor, you won't be able to breathe.'

Darby gave the dispatcher the address and asked for emergency assistance over the woman's wheezing, painful sobs. In the distance she could hear police sirens.

Darby hung up and approached the priest. She saw, scattered across the floor near his legs, an empty bottle of scotch, a ratty leather briefcase and a syringe. Candle and burnt spoon.

'What's your name, Father?'

The priest gritted his teeth, hissing back the pain. 'I want a lawyer.'

The woman's head lifted.

'*Preeee*,' the woman wheezed. '*Hump . . . ah . . .prey.*'

Darby felt the skin of her face tighten against the bone. 'Father Humphrey. From Charlestown?'

He didn't answer the question. He choked on the pain, tears welling up his eyes.

'I asked you a question,' Darby said, and brought her foot down on his shoulder.

The priest howled. He gripped her ankle and tried to push it away. Darby twisted her foot.

'*Yes! Yes, I used to be in Charlestown, now STOP, FOR THE LOVE OF GOD, PLEASE STOP!!!*'

She kept twisting her foot, her entire body shaking. 'Do you remember a boy named Jackson Cooper? He lived in Charlestown.'

'*I don't know him.*'

'Yes, you do. You molested him. Repeatedly.'

'*I WANT A LAWYER!*'

Darby released her foot.

The priest curled into a foetal position and started sobbing.

She raised the gun. 'Look at me.'

His lips quivered. 'You can't,' he said, and started to cry. 'I'm a man of God.'

'Not my God,' Darby said, and shot him in the head.

67

The gunshot had startled the woman. Her head shot up and she started coughing up blood.

Darby moved next to her. 'You're safe. They're all dead.'

The woman trembled against her restraints. Blood trickled down her chin. She was trying to speak.

'Say that again?' Darby moved her ear close to the woman's lips.

'Kevin . . . ah . . . ah . . .'

'Reynolds?'

'Yes.'

'I cuffed him downstairs. He can't hurt you.'

'Babies,' she wheezed.

'What babies?'

'Sons . . . ah . . . Michael. Carter.'

'They're here? In the house?'

'Hiding. Michael . . . . ah . . . hid brother. Safe.'

'Where are they hiding?'

'Dead . . . ah . . . room.'

Dead room? She must have meant bedroom.

'Safe,' the woman said. 'Hiding underneath . . . ah . . . bed.'

'I'll go get them.' Darby opened the door.

'*Ma-Ma-Ma-Michael*!' Russo's scream was a wet, crackling wheeze. '*Come . . . ah . . . out.*'

Darby ran across the dark hallway.

'*Come. Ah . . . ah . . . safe. Okay.*'

Darby stepped up to the door with the broken lock. Almost pitch black in there; the light-blocking shades had been drawn. She searched the wall and found the light switch.

Dried blood screamed from the walls. Pools of it covered the carpets and valance.

'*Bed,*' Russo wheezed. '*Un . . . ah . . . Un . . . der . . . ah . . . neath.*'

Darby got down on her hands and knees and gripped the valance. Dust blew into her face as she leaned forward and looked underneath the bed.

Nobody was there.

68

Jamie forced an eye open. Everything was blurry. She could see light down at the end of the hall, in the dead room. One of her boys was scrambling out from underneath the bed – Carter. She could make out the Batman mask hanging around his neck.

They're safe. My babies are safe.

Jamie started to cry. 'Okay . . . Carter. Okay, ah . . . now.'

Carter's tiny feet thumped across the hall. The woman detective didn't bother to try to stop him.

Michael was fast. He scooped up his brother before he reached the doorway. Carter tried to fight. He kicked and screamed. Michael turned him around and gripped him fiercely against his chest so he couldn't turn and see the bedroom.

But Michael was staring, his wide-eyed gaze locked on Father Humphrey's corpse and what little remained of the priest's head.

Jamie drew in a deep breath, the feeling like razor blades slicing through her lungs, and tried to scream.

'Go, *Michael!*' she cried. '*La* . . . *ah* . . . *ah* . . . *Go!*'

He didn't leave. He whisked his attention from

Father Humphrey to her and kept gulping air. Carter kept wailing and the goddamn detective kept standing at the end of the hall not saying or doing a goddamn *thing*.

Jamie looked at the detective and tried to scream the words: '*Take. . . ah . . . them.*'

The woman didn't move, just stood there staring back at her with those piercing green eyes.

Jamie bucked against the rope, almost tipping over her chair.

'*TAKE . . .*'

Her lungs burned with a crackling sound.

'*TAKE . . . AWAY . . . BABIES.*'

Darby heard the policemen running through the downstairs rooms. Heard them shouting orders as doors slammed open and shut. She didn't move or speak. Stood in the hallway frozen, watching in horror as the woman tied to the chair had an imaginary conversation with her two children – two boys the woman believed had been hiding underneath the bed of a room covered in dried blood.

'*Take . . . ah . . . please,*' the woman begged in her fractured speech. '*Take.*'

A shadow moved across the wall near the stairwell. Darby saw a young male patrolman standing on the stairs aiming his handgun at her.

'*Freeze.*' He crept up another step.

Darby raised her hands slowly. Then she clasped

her hands behind her head and spoke in a loud, clear voice.

'My name is Darby McCormick. I'm a special investigator for Boston's Criminal Services Unit. My wallet and ID are in my back pocket.'

'*On the floor. On your stomach.*'

Slowly she dropped to her knees. 'I'm armed. Shotgun and a SIG tucked in my right pocket.'

Darby lay against the floor, hands clasped behind her head. The patrolman did what he was trained to do. He grabbed her wrists, yanked them around her back and cuffed her.

She rolled her head to the side. 'The woman in the master bedroom is tied to a chair,' Darby said. 'She has a punctured lung. Don't move her. When the ambulance techs come, make sure you tell them.'

Knee-high black tactical boots tucked inside dark blue trousers rushed up the steps. A pair stepped up next to her and three more rushed inside the bedroom.

'Don't untie her,' the young patrolman called out. 'She might have a punctured lung.'

Darby felt a muzzle pressed against the back of her head. Heard someone trying to unclip the strap for the shotgun. Hands patted her down and hands pulled everything from her pockets.

A pair of EMTs came up the stairs. Darby stared off into space, trying to make out the conversation of the men barking orders downstairs. She could barely hear them over the crackle of radios surrounding her. She kept hearing one say 'Jesus Christ' over and over again.

A chest mike crackled and Darby heard a dispatcher's voice in a sea of static relay her information.

'Looks like you're legit,' the young patrolman said. He undid her cuffs.

Darby stood in front of five men, their gaze bearing down on her. The tall one with the pie-shaped face said, 'You mind telling us just what the hell is going on?'

Darby collected her things. 'Who's the detective in charge?'

'Branham.'

'I'll speak to him when he gets here.'

'I asked you a question, missy.'

'Get the hell out of here. All of you. You're disrupting a crime scene.'

Darby brushed past pie-face and moved to the other rooms.

A baby boy's room, decorated like something out of a Pottery Barn catalogue. The name CARTER was stencilled on the blue painted wall above a white crib. A mobile was covered in a thick layer of dust. All the furniture was – the chest-of-drawers and matching changing table, the oak shelves holding diapers and bottles and tubes of lotion.

The room across the hall belonged to an older boy. Racecar-shaped bed, the sheets unmade. Star Wars action figures and space ships scattered along the floor and play table, everything covered in dust.

Nobody had been inside either of these rooms for years.

A note on the bed, written in pencil: *Michael, I'll be home soon. Needed to go to the hospital. No camp today. You can stay home with Carter. Stay inside until I come home, and make sure the doors are locked. Love you, Mom.*

Darby stepped back into the hall thinking of Sean Sheppard.

The ambulance tech, a pudgy man with curly blond hair, walked into the hall. He blinked in surprise to see Darby standing instead of cuffed. She showed the man her ID.

'Are the kids downstairs?' he asked.

'There are no kids.'

The man frowned. 'She said they went downstairs. Wanted me to go check them out and make sure they were okay.'

'The kids aren't here. They're dead.'

'I don't understand.'

'You're not supposed to,' Darby said and walked down the steps. The air was heavy with gun smoke.

Kevin Reynolds lay dead on the kitchen floor. An older patrolman with a pot-belly and ruddy cheeks hovered close to the body.

'Is Detective Branham here?' Darby asked.

'Not yet.'

'See that Glock lying on the floor? That weapon and

those spent shells are most likely going to be an exact match to a recent homicide in a home in Charlestown. When Detective Branham gets here, tell him I'll be out front. I want to talk to him about this man lying here.'

'Kevin Reynolds.'

'You know him?'

'We tried to pin this son of a bitch down for what we think he did here about five years ago to this woman named Jamie Russo. Some sort of home invasion. Broke into the house, tied up the family in the upstairs bedroom and shot the two boys to death. Mother survived.'

'What about the husband?'

'Stuck his hand in a waste-disposal unit and strangled him – don't ask me why, I don't know. Nobody does.'

Darby stared down at Reynolds thinking about the room upstairs, the room with the lock and the dried blood splattered across the floor and walls.

'How old were the kids when they died?'

'Youngest was a toddler . . . one or two, I forget.' Darby saw the room with the crib and mobile covered in dust. 'And the older one?'

'Don't know.'

She heard footsteps coming down the stairwell. She moved into the foyer and watched as the two EMTs carried the woman, strapped now to a gurney, IV lines in her arm and oxygen mask on her face.

Darby didn't realize the old-time cop had stepped up next to her until he spoke.

'Jesus H. Bloody Christ. That's her. That's Russo.'

Darby watched as the EMTs wheeled the woman across the front door's threshold and then navigated the gurney down the steps.

'What was his name?' she asked the cop.

'Who?'

'Russo's older son.'

'Don't remember.'

'She does,' Darby said.

69

Darby staggered outside into a muggy night air drizzling with rain. Flashing blue, red and white strobe lights lit up the entire neighbourhood. At least half a dozen Wellesley police cruisers blocked off the street, parked at the far ends to give enough room for the two ambulances – and now a fire truck. She could hear its high-pitched siren wailing in the distance, building.

The driveway, covered in shards of glass and a couple of empty shotgun shells, had been taped off. A light grey smoke drifted from the gaps in Chadzynski's crumpled bonnet – the reason the fire department had been summoned. Darby watched two patrolmen tape off the body, its limbs twisted and broken, lying on the grass. Warner, the head of Christina Chadzynski's Anti-Corruption Unit. *More like the woman's personal hit squad*, Darby thought, catching sight of the wet blood on the man's torn clothes.

She needed to find a quiet place to call Coop. She walked numbly across the damp grass and into a big garden with overgrown grass.

At the far end she spotted a hammock set up between two thick pine trees. That looked good. Her legs carried her there and then fluttered with fatigue and relief after she plunked herself down on the wet fabric. Her heart thumped dully inside her chest, as if it wanted to go to sleep.

Shadows moved across the grass, which was lit by the windows of the house – every light had been turned on. Darby's gaze drifted up to the windows of the room with the dried blood splattered against the walls and carpet. She thought of her mother sitting on the side of her father's hospital bed, Sheila holding Big Red's rough and callused hand on her lap and reciting lines from Dylan Thomas's 'Do not go gentle into that good night', a poem her mother knew by heart. Sheila had said 'bless me now with your fierce tears, I pray' as the doctor shut off the life support machine. When her mother reached the end of the poem, she started again, holding back tears and saying the words clearly as she waited for Big Red's body to die.

When the fire truck's siren shut off, the only sound now the thudding throb of its engine, she took out her phone and dialled Coop's number. One ring and he picked up.

'Christ, Darby, where the hell have you been? I've been calling you for the past hour.'

Hearing his voice released the tightness inside her chest. 'Are you okay?'

'I'm fine, but I've been worried sick about you. I got that voice clip you sent me. What's going on? Why didn't you call me back?'

'I met Father Humphrey.'

Coop didn't speak. She could hear chatter and noises on the other end of the line. *He's at the airport*, she thought, and her heart started racing.

'He's dead, Coop. So is Kevin Reynolds. You don't have to leave.'

'What happened?'

'I'll tell you in person. Where can I meet you?'

'I'm at the airport.'

'You don't have to leave,' she said again. 'You and your sister can come home.'

'I'm going to London.'

She felt short of breath.

Don't leave, she wanted to say. *I need you here. With me.*

'I've got to go, Darby. Final boarding call.'

She could hear the sadness in his voice. *No, that's not entirely true.* She also heard relief. In six hours he would be walking through a new airport halfway around the world, walking through a new country where nobody knew his secrets. Where he could start afresh, maybe even reinvent himself.

'Take another flight, Coop. I'll pay for it. I want to see you before you go. Spend some time and talk –'

'It won't change anything.'

'Just listen to me for a moment.' She knew what she wanted to say – words that rushed through her a lot these days every time she saw Coop – but couldn't put them together.

Start with what happened back at the house.

'This afternoon, when you were about to leave, you came back.'

'I shouldn't have done that,' he said.

'I'm glad you did. I . . .'

Why is this so goddamn hard?

'I just wanted to say . . . I . . .'

'I know', he said. 'I feel the same way, for whatever it's worth.'

'It's worth a lot.' *And I was too stupid or too scared or too selfish or all of the above and probably a hundred other things to act on it. But I don't want you to leave. I don't think I'll be able to live with that.*

'If you feel that way,' Darby said, 'then don't leave.'

'I have to. I've wanted to get away from here for a long time. There's no reason for me to stay.'

What about me? I'm not a good enough reason?

'I've really got to go,' he said.

Darby squeezed her eyes shut.

'Okay,' she said, choking on the word. 'Have a safe flight.'

'Bye, Darb.'

'Bye.'

A soft click and the airport noise disappeared. Coop was gone.

70

Jamie lay on a gurney in the back of the wailing ambulance. With the use of her good eye, she watched the EMT with the pudgy face and curly hair clip an IV bag above her head. She tried to speak to him but her words were lost inside the oxygen mask covering her mouth.

She didn't feel any physical pain. They had given her some sort of shot and the pain had disappeared but not the worry. No cruiser-load of dope could take that away. That and love.

The EMT moved away in a blur and disappeared. Michael took his spot. He knelt down next to her and a moment later she felt his cold hands clamp around hers. The anxiety vanished, her heart swelling with relief. And love. He could be a stubborn shit, yes, but she loved him, Christ, she did, and if she could have one wish right now it was that Michael might know what she carried inside her heart.

Michael's face crumpled. 'I'm so sorry, Mom.'

She wanted to take off the mask and speak to him but the EMTs had strapped her down so she couldn't move.

'You . . . ah . . . did right . . . ah . . . thing,' she said, knowing Michael couldn't hear her but still needing to say the words.

'I wanted to run downstairs to the phone but I was afraid to leave Carter alone. I didn't want anything to happen to him. If anything did, you'd hate me.'

'Proud,' she said. 'Proud . . . of . . . ah . . . you.'

Michael started sobbing. 'He was so scared, Mom. So scared. I put my hands over his ears when you started screaming. I turned his face so he wouldn't see anything. I had my hands over his ears and he could still hear you screaming and he was starting to cry and I wanted to run – we both did – but I kept whispering to him that he had to be quiet. He had to be quiet no matter how much he was scared 'cause that was the only way we could protect you.'

He buried his face in her lap and squeezed her hand. She could feel him shaking as he cried.

'I love you, Michael. Proud.'

She turned her head to the EMT, wanting to ask him why he was just sitting there, and then she saw Carter's face, shiny with tears, appear above his brother's shoulder. She wiggled her fingers, trying to wave hello.

Carter crawled on top of the gurney. The EMT, thank God, didn't stop him. Carter kissed her forehead, then curled his small body beside hers, the stubble of his crew cut pressing up against her cheek. His head and all its scars still smelled faintly of soap.

He placed an arm gently across her chest. He kissed her cheek.

Jamie closed her eyes. She could drift off to sleep now. Michael and Carter were safe. There was no need to worry any more. Michael and Carter were safe.

'Mommy?'

She opened her eyes and saw Carter's face hovering above hers.

'Michael and me are here,' Carter said. 'You can go to sleep and when you wake up we'll be here.'

She smiled behind the mask. Carter smiled too.

Her babies. Her two brave boys.

'We won't go anywhere, Mommy,' Carter said. 'We won't never ever leave you. You won't ever be alone. Promise.'

This is the only thing that matters, Jamie thought. *This is what you lived for, this feeling you had for your children. And nothing — not even God Himself — can come between it.*

Epilogue

Christina Chadzynski was buried on a bright summer morning in her hometown of West Roxbury. Boston police had cordoned off the surrounding streets to accommodate the swelling numbers of officers and politicians attending the funeral. The media were out in full force, their numbers swelling behind the police barricades, to film the spectacle

While the murder of a police commissioner was front-page news, the real reason for their presence was to hunt for information about how dead FBI agents had somehow risen from the ashes. Had the FBI known? Had they deliberately helped in the subterfuge? So far, Boston PD and the FBI had managed to prevent anything from leaking out.

Well, maybe not for long, Darby thought, and checked her watch.

She stood with hundreds of other mourners at the cemetery. Her lawyer, a man named Benjamin Jones who had successfully handled a lot of investigations for Boston police officers, had insisted that she come. He wanted her front and centre, to show everyone she had nothing to hide.

She didn't have anything to hide, but that hadn't

prevented her from being suspended, with pay, pending an internal investigation.

She recalled her SWAT instructor's warning: *Every bullet has a lawyer's name on it.*

From behind her dark sunglasses she looked at the predominantly male faces across from her, staring and watching. Her. She had got used to the stares. Some officers, she was sure, had found out what really happened. There was no such thing as a secret inside Boston PD. She was also sure that some of those officers were wondering if their voices or names were on Kendra Sheppard's flash drive.

Darby hadn't been allowed to listen to or see what was on the USB drive. It had been confiscated by the Boston brass, along with her phone containing her taped conversation with Chadzynski.

For the past week the commissioner's death had been front-page news. The national news outlets were more interested in the discovery of the body inside an abandoned East Boston auto garage – Special Agent Jack King, a man who, along with Frank Sullivan and three other Federal agents, had supposedly died in 1983.

There was still no official comment from the FBI. The Boston Police Department's PR machine, though, was already in motion.

The PR rep cited how the police commissioner's Criminal Services Unit discovered the bodies of two other 'dead' Federal agents – Peter Alan, who had been found shot to death inside the basement of a home owned by Kevin Reynolds; and Steven White, who had been killed at the Wellesley home of Jamie Russo, a previous victim of an unsolved home invasion that had claimed the lives of her husband and two children. While the PR rep would not cite actual specifics of the 'ongoing investigation', it was reported that Police Commissioner Chadzynski had been shot to death by a nine-millimetre handgun belonging to Arthur Pine, a Belham detective who had died at the garage along with former Federal agent Jack King.

The Boston press, through 'inside sources close to the investigation', reported that Chadzynski had been murdered to prevent the exposure of the four FBI agents who had allegedly died, along with Frank Sullivan, in July of 1983.

The PR rep wouldn't explain what the commissioner was doing at an abandoned automotive garage.

There was much speculation in the press as to whether or not Frank Sullivan was alive but no mention of his real name or the fact that he was a Federal agent.

Darby checked her watch, wondering about the fourth and final agent, Anthony Frissora. As far as she knew, he had not been found. She doubted he ever would be.

The preacher gave a heart-thumping eulogy about Chadzynski's 'dedicated years of service to justice' and 'her tireless crusade to keeping Boston's streets safe'. Darby tuned it out, looking at the massive flower arrangements scattered around the coffin, and thought about Jamie Russo.

She had tried speaking to the woman on two separate occasions. Each time Russo showed her the same piece of paper containing the same message: 'My lawyer has advised me not to speak with anyone. And I can't allow you to speak to either Michael or Carter. They're traumatized by what happened, as I'm sure you can understand. They're being treated here at the hospital. The doctors have generously allowed me to stay here with them until they're released.'

Darby knew the woman had a lawyer. Wellesley police had found a wallet belonging to Ben Masters and a mobile phone that didn't belong to Russo. Police had also found a .44 Magnum. Since Wellesley was outside of Boston's jurisdiction, the state lab had been used to process the evidence. Darby had heard, through Randy Scott, that the state's ballistics had confirmed that the Magnum had been used in the Belham home. Jamie Russo, watching through the woods with her husband's binoculars, had shot her way inside the house to save Sean Sheppard.

Finally the fulsome eulogy ended.

Everyone bowed their heads and prayed.

Darby felt her new phone, a BlackBerry, vibrate against her hip.

A message had come in from Coop. She read it and waited.

Darby watched the coffin being lowered into the ground. She thought back to her father's elegant casket being lowered into its final resting place, the grass around her leeched of colour, tears sliding down her cheeks. Her father was dressed in a black suit, the only one he owned, and she remembered wondering if the newly dead could still feel heat, wondered if her father was still suffering in that casket. She remembered wanting to ask her mother and then stopped when Sheila ushered her away from the grave.

Now her mother was dead, buried next to her father, and here she was, their daughter, standing at the grave of the woman who had played some role in her father's murder. Why? Because her lawyer told her to. Because it *looked* good. She was here keeping up appearances. Darby wondered what her father would think of her now, standing here.

Suddenly all around her came the sound of mobile phones ringing. The preacher was not pleased and gave the crowd a disgusted look to show he meant business. It didn't stop everyone from checking their mobile phones.

Darby tried watching each of their faces. She was especially pleased by the blank look on the mayor's face as he listened to the audio clip of her conversation with the police commissioner. Coop had worked tirelessly the past week, calling his old friends and contacts to find out the mobile phone numbers of every Boston bigwig. Darby gave him the numbers for the movers and shakers inside Boston PD, all of whom were in attendance. That was phase one.

Phase two was to send out messages to the media, saying they could listen to Christina Chadzynski's message free of charge on the massively popular internet site YouTube.

The mayor hung up and looked at her, eyes like daggers. Then he mumbled something into the ear of Chadzynski's grieving husband and turned to leave.

The mayor pushed his way through the crowd. Now the senator excused himself.

The crowd started to dissipate around her. The preacher looked confused.

Darby watched the spectacle. She wasn't aware that Randy Scott was standing next to her until he spoke.

'What's going on?'

'I don't know, but it doesn't look good,' Darby said. 'What are you doing here?'

'I thought you'd like to know they found Dr Wexler in France. They're working on extraditing him back to the States. He's talking with the Feds, trying to work out a plea deal.'

A deal, Darby thought, watching everyone scattering across the grass.

'The Feds are slowly worming their way into the investigation,' Randy said. 'Now that they have Wexler on team Fed, they've asked to look at those pictures you gave the Photography Unit. I hear Boston PD's going to play along. It's a trading game. You tell me this, I'll tell you that.'

Then they'll play a final round of damage control. I'll scratch your back and you'll scratch mine.

'I'm in contact with this guy at the state's forensic lab,' Randy said. 'We've been coordinating evidence for the past week. He tells me that he has it on good authority that Kevin Reynolds is a Federal agent.'

'What a surprise.'

'Well, I thought you'd want to know. As for the evidence the police commissioner said she planted – your father's murder book and the associated evidence – I haven't found anything yet. I probably won't. The brass is forming an independent committee – a special task force – to look into the matter, and into Chadzynski. They've also confiscated the evidence to make sure it isn't tampered with. In other words, they booted everyone at the lab off the case.'

'Wonderful.'

'One other thing . . . Sean Sheppard died this morning.'

Darby took in a deep breath.

'I'm sorry.'

She nodded. 'I forgot to thank you for everything.'

'Nothing to it.' He forced a grin. 'See you soon.'

'I don't think so.' She started walking.

'Where are you going?'

Darby didn't answer. She tossed her badge into the grave and looked out at the roads, wondering which one led home.